ROAD FROM THE WEST

*Vanessa,*
*Enjoy the journey!*
*Rosanne E. Lortz*

# Road from the West

BOOK I
*of*
THE CHRONICLES OF TANCRED

## ROSANNE E. LORTZ

MADISON STREET
PUBLISHING

ISBN-13 978-0-9836719-0-9
Publisher: Madison Street Publishing

Printed in the U.S.A.

3 5 7 9 10 8 6 4 2

To David

# Table of Contents

# Cities of Note

Rome

Amalfi

Salerno

Bari

Durazzo

Aegean Sea

Sicily

Mediterranean Sea

Black Sea

Constantinople

Nicaea

Dorylaeum

Iconium

Marash

Edessa

Mosul

Heraclea

Tarsus

Antioch

Aleppo

Cyprus

Damascus

Baghdad

Jerusalem

Cairo

# POPE URBAN'S LETTER OF INSTRUCTION TO THE FIRST CRUSADERS

### DECEMBER, A. D. 1095

*Urban, bishop, servant of the servants of God, to all the faithful, both princes and subjects, waiting in Flanders; greeting, apostolic grace, and blessing.*

*Your brotherhood, we believe, has long since learned from many accounts that a barbaric fury has deplorably afflicted and laid waste the churches of God in the regions of the Orient. More than this, blasphemous to say, it has even grasped in intolerable servitude its churches and the Holy City of Christ, glorified by His passion and resurrection. Grieving with pious concern at this calamity, we visited the regions of Gaul and devoted ourselves largely to urging the princes of the land and their subjects to free the churches of the East. We solemnly enjoined upon them at the council of Auvergne [the accomplishment of] such an undertaking, as a preparation for the remission of all their sins. And we have constituted our most beloved son, Adhemar, Bishop of Puy, leader of this expedition and undertaking in our stead, so that those who, perchance, may wish to undertake this journey should comply with his commands, as if they were our own, and submit fully to his loosings or bindings, as far as shall seem to belong to such an office. If, moreover, there are any of your people whom God has inspired to this vow, let them know that he [Adhemar] will set out with the aid of God on the day of the Assumption of the Blessed Mary, and that they can then attach themselves to his following.*

# Part I

# Bohemond

# Chapter I

The stars changed their courses the day that Tancred the marquis tossed aside his sword and strode off the field of battle. It was not from fear, for he walked slowly, his back an easy target for enemy spears and arrows. It was not from anger—he walked deliberately, his eyes as serene as the sapphire sea beyond the hill.

Tancred's uncle Bohemond had had high hopes that day. After a month of siege, the city of Amalfi was weakening. Today's assault had been perfectly timed; each of the Norman commanders knew which tower of the maritime power was theirs to take. But when Tancred walked away, his contingent of men became confused and retreated in disorder. The wavering defenders regained their will to fight and pushed back the Norman knights. And so it came about that Amalfi's walls still stood in defiance, a beacon of hope to the other Italian cities under the yoke of the Northmen.

After the rebuff, Bohemond found his tents and, with the help of one of his squires, stripped off his blood-spattered mail. A few stray flies buzzed around his moist skin, but he brushed them away with a tolerant flick of his fingers. Then sitting down on the edge of a wooden chest he bent over to unlace his greaves. "Bring me wine," he said to the squire in a cool, measured voice. If he was angry at the day's failure, the squire could barely tell. Bohemond pulled off his leather jerkin revealing the powerful chest of a fighting man in his prime, and ran a large hand through his cropped, yellow hair.

Bohemond's brother Roger was not so restrained. "God's wounds!" he bellowed, bursting into the quiet tent. "What's got into that boy?

He's sabotaged the entire assault. Amalfi would have been ours by sundown if it were not for Tancred! Curse him!"

"Have you spoken to him?" asked Bohemond. Even while seated, it was apparent that he was a head and a half taller than his tempestuous stepbrother. He was fairer too—but then, that was to be expected considering the appearance of their different mothers.

"I've summoned him here," roared Roger, sloshing out a goblet of wine from the pitcher. "And by God, I'll flay him alive when he comes."

He had no sooner spoken than the tent flap lifted to admit their nephew—not Tancred, but his younger brother William. He was red in the face and breathing heavily, having carried out his Uncle Roger's errand with much haste.

"Where is he?" demanded Roger, his hand instinctively fondling the heavy gold chain that lay across his collarbone.

"My brother," said William, gasping for air, "is at his prayers. He begs leave of my lords to attend you anon."

"At his prayers?" repeated Roger in disbelief. Even Bohemond, who had schooled himself to dissimulate emotion, raised an eyebrow at this strange news. Since when had Tancred been a religious man?

"Is he wounded?" asked Bohemond. That would explain the unexpected departure from battle and the sudden display of piety.

"He did not seem to be," declared William sheepishly. He had no special knowledge of what lay behind Tancred's actions, and the disapproval in his uncles' faces weighed heavily on him.

"Is he daft?" exclaimed Roger, finding his own explanation for Tancred's remarkable behavior.

"Nay, I am in my right mind at last," said a firm voice at the door of the tent. The three men stared as Tancred boldly entered and poured himself a flagon of wine. He was a tall, well-knit warrior, just entering the full strength of manhood. In height, he nearly approached his uncle Bohemond, and his ruddy complexion and golden hair proclaimed that he had issued from the same Northern stock. Unlike the others, he had completely discarded all pieces of his battle harness and stood before them in only a blue tunic. Across it flamed a checkered bend of red and white squares, the crest of his mother's house and one that his uncles shared.

Tancred drank his wine with great thirst and repaid their stares with interest. He had none of the hangdog look that one would expect from a man who had just flown the field of battle.

Astounded at his audacity, Roger sputtered inarticulately while William cringed with growing concern. "Come here, boy," said Bohemond, his voice soft like the padded paws of a panther.

Tancred drained his wine with one gulp and advanced to stand before the tribunal. His uncles would now sit in judgment upon him— Roger with angry bellows, and Bohemond with that coldly glittering eye that his nephews knew so well.

"You are right to be angry with me," said Tancred abruptly, before either of his uncles could begin. "I gave you no warning of what I meant to do—but, believe me, I did not know myself until the battle was joined."

"But what came over you?" demanded Roger. "It couldn't have been fear—I've stood side by side with you in a dozen skirmishes since you were fifteen years old. You've yelled as loud and struck as hard as any man. I still remember when you skewered that pig of a Greek at Bari for trying to cheat you in the marketplace. God! That was a bloodletting."

At this praise, Tancred's fair skin flushed red to the roots of his golden hair. He seemed embarrassed by Roger's reminiscence, ashamed of having killed a scoundrel who—God knows!—would have done the same to him if he had had the opportunity. Bohemond's curiosity grew. Why this display of bashfulness? His nephew was neither shy of approval nor afraid to kill, and Bohemond knew Tancred's mettle more intimately than most, for it was he who had forged it.

Twelve years ago, Bohemond had come home from campaigning in Greece, sick of a violent fever and holding only a slender grasp on life. His father, his stepmother, and his half-brothers stayed behind, hoping to carry the campaign to the very walls of Constantinople. With most of his kin still abroad, Bohemond's servants brought their sick lord to the one place where they knew he would be received, the estate of his sister Emma.

At home in southern Italy, Bohemond's sister welcomed him with open arms and devoted herself to the task of nursing him to health. It was a long recovery through a long, torrid summer. Each day Emma would order the servants to carry her brother into the orchard where the shaded breeze from the Mediterranean could give some comfort to his feverish limbs. Unable to lift a hand himself, he watched Tancred and William, her two young sons, play at soldiers with sticks and stones.

"Emma," he had said reproachfully, when she came to bathe his temples with cool water. "Your lads are half grown already. Why have you found no one to teach them the sword and lance and bow?"

"That is a man's province," Emma had said. She smiled grimly and left it at that. Bohemond knew without asking that the oversight lay at her husband's door.

The man she had married was not like her father, and not like her brothers in the least. Odo the *Good* Marquis, the people called him. Odo the *Weak* was a more fitting nickname, thought Bohemond wryly. Bohemond's father, Robert Guiscard, had arranged the match with too little an understanding of the man's feeble spirit. He had land and title, to be sure, but he had gained none of these through his own achievement, and he would lose most of them through his own apathy.

Odo was too immersed in his prayers, his penance, his pursuit of spiritual learning to see that his sons were properly equipped with the knowledge that the world demands. And so Bohemond had taken their education upon himself. Giving them two daggers—inherited from the corpses of Byzantine soldiers—he sent them at each other in the orchard, while he shouted instructions from his sickbed. Later, when he was well enough to walk with a cane, he hobbled out to the practice yard and taught them to cut and thrust at the wooden pels. William, the younger of the two, was a sensitive child prone to tears when beset by hard knocks. But Tancred, on the other hand, had the courage and ferocity of a lion's whelp. Even when Bohemond had recovered his full strength, young Tancred never scrupled to attack him—though the encounter always left the assailant face down in the dust with a split lip or a bloodied nose.

Bohemond could see that same determination in Tancred's face now, as he stood before them in the tent. Roger had not ceased plying Tancred with questions. "Was it heatstroke that addled you? It was a devil's furnace out there today."

Bohemond raised a hand to quiet his half-brother. "Cease your prattling," he said. He could be subtle when the occasion demanded, but when he could, he preferred to command. "Come, Tancred. Out with it! Why did you leave?"

Tancred frowned. "You will not believe me if I tell you."

"Try me," said Bohemond coldly.

"Well, then, here it is. We formed our lines as you bade us and advanced with the siege tower against the wall. The men of Amalfi tried to fire it. One of them leaned over the parapet to hurl a wad of flaming pitch. I gave the command and my archers let fly. The man had two arrows between his shoulders before a lad could say hey. And then he tumbled, head over feet from the wall, striking the ground and rolling a little until his broken body came to a stop. I would not have given him another thought, except that a few minutes later, the body moved. I stared at him, wondering if we should send another arrow to dispatch him entirely. As I watched, his bloody hand fumbled at his mangled breast till he pulled out a crucifix. Then putting that cross to his lips, he kissed it and moved no more."

"Get to the point!" interrupted Roger impatiently.

"I will soon enough!" said Tancred, showing a flash of temper. His uncle muttered reproachfully but resumed his silence while Tancred resumed his tale. "When I saw him perish—the last thought in his mind of the cross and of our Savior!—my stomach sickened within me. That man was baptized, even as I was. He had eaten the body of Christ, even as I have. How many have I killed just like him?"

"Too many to count," said Bohemond with a shrug. "It is the cost of war."

"Too high a cost!" said Tancred hotly. "Why do we attack the city of Amalfi? Come, tell me, uncles."

"Because I am lord of Apulia," said Roger, "and Amalfi has forgotten to whom she owes fealty!"

"No, you are so busy counting your money," replied Tancred, "that you have forgotten how to rule a kingdom. Amalfi would not have revolted if you had not taxed the lifeblood out of her. And now Christian men must die so you can stuff your purse!"

"What would you have, Tancred?" interrupted Bohemond sharply. "Shall we refuse to do battle for the possessions our father left us for fear of offending your conscience? Your grandfather established an empire in Italy, and now you refuse to honor his memory by striving to maintain it."

"My grandfather drove out the pagans," said Tancred, clenching his fists involuntarily. "He pulled down the mosques and made Italy Christian again. That is an honorable use for the sword! But this siege—faugh! It makes me sick to think of the men we've killed." He lifted his chin with resolution and fixed his eyes on Bohemond. "I am resolved never to shed Christian blood again."

"You're as crazy as your father Odo was!" said Roger with a sneer. "He joined a monastery in the end—is that what *you* mean to do?"

"Yes, do you mean to give up women as well as the sword?" said Bohemond dryly. "Does the camp drab you had in your tent last night afflict your conscience as greatly as the man with the crucifix?"

"I have not said that I shall become a monk," replied Tancred, biting his lip at his uncles' taunts. "You two suppose that this is some childish whim of mine, but I tell you, that is not so! I shall go to Rome and seek out Pope Urban. He will advise me what I should do. He's sorted out matters for *you* often enough."

"The pope is not in Rome," said Bohemond dismissively. "He's been gadding about France for over a year now, holding councils, preaching reform, trying to find anyone he can to get rid of the antipope. Yes, go to Rome—and when you find it as empty, and stinking, and quarrelsome as it always is, come back to us again. We shall be here at the walls of Amalfi until she submits or until we destroy her."

Tancred nodded curtly and strode out of the tent with determination. The great burden that he had felt earlier was lightened somewhat. He had said his piece, and there was no going back now. And yet, despite this assurance, the gibes of his uncles still nettled him. What was there for him besides a life of arms?

The sound of running feet came fast behind Tancred, but he decided to ignore them. A few seconds later, William grabbed hold of his shoulder and yanked him around. "Let me go with you to Rome!" he said earnestly. William's face had not yet lost the roundness of youth. Tancred suspected that he would never lose the wide-eyed innocence with which he viewed the world.

"No, William," said Tancred firmly. "This is my own journey to make."

"You will need company on the road," insisted William.

"I will need you *here*," replied Tancred. "Our troops are still promised to Uncle Roger for this siege. I will not fight, but someone must lead them in my absence."

William sighed and shook his head. "You heard what our uncle said—the pope is not even in Rome!"

"Bohemond thinks he is the only one with any knowledge!" said Tancred angrily. "I heard from a trader two weeks ago that the pope had finished his travels in France. He was on his way to St. Peter's even then."

William hung his head and kicked the ground in gentle frustration. When had he ever been able to prevail on Tancred, to change his mind after he had purposed to do a thing?

"Cheer up, William," Tancred said, clapping his brother upon the back. "I'll stop and stand for no man on the road and return to Amalfi within the fortnight."

"God be with you," said William, still dejected.

"And with your spirit," replied Tancred briskly, his mind already on the journey ahead.

# Chapter 2

It was sixty leagues north from Amalfi to Rome, and good to his word, Tancred did not tarry on the road. He had only his man-servant Ralph to keep him company, and their horses were well paced and used to travel. On the evening of the third day, just as the seven hills were beginning to shimmer on the horizon, they met a large cavalcade going south along the road. They were Franks, by the look of them, and the number of knightly pennants was too great to count.

"I suppose we must turn aside till they pass," said Tancred, grudging the time he would waste while yielding the road.

"Shall I find out who they are?" asked Ralph, rubbing his red nose with a gnarled hand. He was a wiry old soldier who had served Robert Guiscard, Tancred's grandfather, and later transferred his allegiance to the young marquis.

"Yes," said Tancred tetchily, "but waste no time about it."

The Franks had a magnificent number of men in their train— Tancred estimated it at three thousand or more. Their arms were bright and new, and they rode jauntily, as if bound for some great tournament. Above the leader waved an impressive banner, as big as an ox, embroidered with a blood-red cross. Ralph fell in with them and began to talk. He had a way of talking in which he said much, learned much, and revealed nothing. Tancred had employed him as a spy more than once.

When the last shiny coat of mail passed him by, Tancred turned his mount back onto the road to continue his journey. Spurring his horse, Ralph soon overtook him and gave his report as they rode.

"Their leader is called Hugh the Great. He is brother to the king of France. From what I heard, he seems a pompous fool, and his men respect him not at all."

"But why is he in Italy with such a large company of men?" asked Tancred. Did the Franks mean to interfere with the Normans at Amalfi or on the island of Sicily?

"They are on their way south to Bari," replied Ralph. "From there they plan to take ship to the empire of the Greeks."

"To Byzantium?" said Tancred in surprise. His grandfather had tried to conquer the Greeks once before. He did not think this pompous prince could do it with only three thousand lances.

"Yes, and from Byzantium, on to the Holy Land. Did you see the banner above their leader? That red cross is a gift from the pope himself. He blessed both the banner and the expedition, for they are going to free the Holy Sepulcher from the infidels."

Tancred grunted. The Normans had heard rumors of the large gatherings of troops in France. Bohemond had laughed when he heard they meant to liberate Jerusalem. "There are lands closer to home for the taking," he had said, "richer lands too than a strip of green in the desert." Tancred had given it little thought at the time. He had but newly attained his majority, and the pleasure of commanding his own men was as exhilarating as a beautiful woman's smile. Once Amalfi capitulated, he had intended to cross the strait to Sicily and finish out the fighting season there—but the crumpled Amalfian with the crucifix at his lips had forestalled these plans.

Tancred was not given to weeping, but the story he had told his uncles welled up in his mind like tears—and he had not even told them the half of his misgivings. For several weeks before his battlefield revelation, he had had ghastly dreams: coffins of burning fire, rivers of boiling blood, deserts of searing pain. He knew not what these dreams portended, but at the end of each nightmare a black-cowled man stood forward in awful solemnity, and raising a cadaverous hand, pointed silently at the dreamer. "All this misery has come about because of thee, sinner. And thinkest thou wilt escape the judgment of thy God?"

The man's words were stamped on Tancred's mind like a slave brand. He shuddered violently, cold in spite of the summer sun.

It was only by force of will that Tancred's mind emerged from these grim thoughts. Returning his tongue to the task at hand, he continued questioning Ralph. "Did these Franks say where the pope is now?"

Ralph, oblivious to his master's internal torments, smiled and winked. "In Rome, my lord, just as you said he'd be." Bohemond was no favorite with Ralph, and the old servant was pleased to see Tancred's journey vindicated. The young master had been right and his overbearing uncle wrong. Ralph preened his moustache with triumphant fingers.

Encouraged by the news of the pope's whereabouts, the travelers pressed on, and by the end of the day they reached the gates of the Eternal City. Tancred had visited Rome before, in the company of Bohemond, whenever his uncle had dutifully answered the uncountermandable summons of Pope Urban.

The blond giant had not always been on such easy terms with his brother Roger as he was now. After their father Robert Guiscard died, they had squabbled incessantly over the inheritance, coming to pitched battle several times until the pope had intervened to partition their patrimony. It took a matter that consequential to entice the Norman count to come to Rome. Used to the comforts of Salerno, Bari, and the other southern cities, Bohemond braved the seven hills only when he must, and Tancred had been a mere stripling on their last visit.

The city, although renowned as the spiritual mother of Europe, was as dirty and faded as a plowman's wife. The two sacks she had endured over the last century did nothing to beautify her exterior. The churches were crumbling and the walls were as gap toothed as an old soldier. For the last twenty-five years the city had been split into two factions, one supporting the antipope Guibert, the other supporting the true Vicar of Christ. For some time now, the antipope's supporters had carried the field, barring Pope Urban from the Church of St. Peter and even forcing him into exile from Rome.

But as Tancred and Ralph entered Rome, they quickly learned that the wind had changed. The pope's banner hung from the Castel Sant' Angelo and there was no hint of riot in the city. The travelers, who had braced themselves for a scene of tumult, looked about in surprise and continued on to St. Peter's.

After crossing the Tiber, they encountered a young officer at the gate of the Leonine Wall. He was a short, black-browed Italian, his body standing to attention while his mind stared off into the distance. It was well that the city was so peaceful, for this sentry kept watch as well as the apostles on the Mount of Olives. Tancred snapped his fingers to capture the officer's attention, and his reverie vanished like a puff of smoke.

"Welcome, travelers!" he said, flashing an ivory smile. He looked approvingly at Tancred's shield, the red and white checkered bend across a field of blue.

"A pretty welcome, indeed, to see Rome so peaceful!" replied Tancred. "How did Pope Urban regain the city?"

The Roman laughed, slapping a sun-bronzed hand against his knee. "*Santo cielo*, it was the Franks, those Crusaders! They followed Papa Urban over the Alps and knocked down the doors of the city. Guibert's fled—good riddance!—and we have our own father back again."

"And the Franks have all gone?"

"All gone," said the Roman officer. "The pope thanked them and sent them off to the Holy Land—they mean to travel south and embark at Bari."

Tancred caught Ralph's eye. So it was Hugh the Great who had liberated Rome before setting sail to liberate the Holy Sepulcher.

"Where is Pope Urban now?" asked Tancred.

"He's in his apartments at the Lateran Palace," said the officer. "Are you seeking an audience with him?"

Tancred nodded and gave the man his name and title.

"I'll send a boy with a message," said the officer, "though I warn you that he's up to his ears in complaints and petitions from city officials and foreign ambassadors. He's been gone in France for over a year, you know, and we've only just got him back again."

The pope was indeed as busy as the officer claimed, and it was only owing to good fortune—or perhaps to his family name—that Tancred secured an audience with him for the next day. They could wait on the pope at sunrise, though it was doubtful he would have more than a quarter of an hour to spare. Tancred sighed and agreed. A short visit was better than nothing. He trusted implicitly that the pope's words would be the end to his nightmares.

"They've made few repairs to the buildings," said Ralph as they wandered through the streets searching for suitable lodging. Here and there he pointed out the char marks from the fire he had helped kindle. "I was in your grandfather's service then," he said, waxing eloquent about days a decade past. "We had beaten the Byzantines at Durazzo and were pressing onward through Greece, when Alexios—that sly dog!—hired a gadfly to nip us in the buttocks. He knew that Guiscard had made an alliance with Pope Gregory. And in order to protect his own empire, he paid the Germans to invade Italy. What could we do? Guiscard's honor demanded that he abandon the campaign and hasten back to Rome. And so we pulled up the tent stakes, left Bohemond behind with a tiny holding force, and trekked to the west. We lost the best chance we ever had to fight our way to Constantinople."

"But if my grandfather came back to protect Rome from the Germans," said Tancred, "why did you set fire to the city?"

"He did not come to protect Rome so much as to protect Pope Gregory." Ralph glanced up suspiciously at the windows overlooking the narrow streets. "This place is a hotbed of intrigue and treachery. After our army hurried back, we found that the chief families of this place had formed a treacherous alliance with the German emperor. They had ousted Gregory from the city and put him in danger of his life. Your grandfather was enraged at their insolence. He besieged the city, broke down the walls, and punished them all with fire and sack. I see what you are thinking—a pity that so many churches and monuments were destroyed—but these conniving bastards needed a lesson.

And besides, how else was he to pay the men? We had left behind all of the booty we'd won in Greece, and the warriors needed something to show for the campaign."

Tancred grunted and turned a keen eye to the wooden signs suspended above the dirty street. Spotting a dark shingle with a white pig painted upon it, the two men entered the building and secured lodging at The White Boar with little trouble. "Are you Crusaders, then?" asked the innkeeper with curiosity as he served them some onions and pottage. He was a round, jolly man whose good nature lent the charm that the inn itself lacked.

"No, not at all," replied Tancred. "We come to see Pope Urban about a personal matter."

The innkeeper laughed. His face was flushed from the wine in which he shared copiously with his guests. "Then you will be Crusaders before the week is out!" He wagged a knowing finger in front of Tancred's frowning face. "Our pope is very persuasive. My son and his wife left just last week after hearing the Holy Father preach."

"No, that is not our intention," said Tancred emphatically. He was here to seek forgiveness and exorcise the black-cowled man from his dreams, not to start a journey that would take him halfway across the world.

"I think it is time we were off to bed," said Ralph, sensing that his young master had much on his mind and was in no mood for the host's ribbing.

"Yes, yes, get you to bed, gentlemen!" replied the host with a wink. "It's a long trip to Jerusalem and you must get your rest."

# Chapter 3

The morning air was crisp and cold as the sun peeked over the Quirinal Hill and flamed red on the Tiber. The clear horizon promised a scorching summer day, but at sunrise the air was still as chilly as the catacombs beneath the surface. Tancred and Ralph paid for their lodging and saddled their horses, eager to arrive on time for the precious appointment.

The Normans approached the basilica attached to the Lateran palace, the oldest church in the city of Rome. They dismounted in the street, and Tancred silently handed Ralph the reins of his horse. He would see the pope alone.

A doorkeeper in religious habit admitted Tancred into the outer court of the church and he passed through a spacious atrium surrounded by colonnades. Gazing about in some confusion, Tancred wondered if he ought to enter the church sanctuary or if there was another route to the adjoining papal apartments. A barefoot monk answered his unvoiced question. "His holiness awaits you," said the monk in somber tones and opened a small postern that led into the Lateran palace.

Pope Urban was thinner—and older—than Tancred remembered him, but he seemed to have lost none of his gentle manner or his perspicacity. He greeted Tancred by name and asked after his mother Emma.

"She is well, your holiness," said Tancred and kissed the pope's hand in greeting. His fingers were curiously long and slender, the hands of a frequent writer. On his left hand a large golden ring depicted the Apostle Peter casting his net into the waters. Tancred had seen the impression of that signet on letters his uncle received.

Pope Urban's shoulders stooped slightly as he bent over the brazier to warm himself. "Your house is well known in this city," he said with a smile, "though perhaps not loved by all. A grandson of Guiscard! He served my predecessors well."

Tancred blushed appreciatively. The pope sat down in a chair and fixed a questioning look upon his guest. The pleasantries were over and it was time for Tancred to reveal the purpose of his visit.

But at that instant, Tancred's tongue became thick and heavy in his mouth. The brash audacity with which he had flung his story at his uncles deserted him now, and he knew not what to say.

"You need my help in some way, young man?" Pope Urban said encouragingly. "A matter of spiritual import, or perhaps you are in some trouble?"

"Yes," said Tancred, and like a torrent the words began to come, the tale of the bloodcurdling nightmares, the black-cowled man, and the epiphany at Amalfi.

"And I cannot escape the certainty," said Tancred in conclusion, "that everything about my life before now has contradicted the commands of Our Lord. He said that when a man asks you for your tunic, you are to give him your cloak as well—but warfare demands that you seize not only these two garments, but also anything else that you can lay your hands upon. He said that after one cheek has been struck we ought to offer the other too—but the life of a soldier does not even allow you to spare your own relative's blood."

The pope frowned and tapped his fingers together thoughtfully. "I am no Daniel. I cannot interpret your dream for you, though it seems, by the imagery, to be a presage of some future event. But regarding the siege at Amalfi, your conscience does you credit," said the pope. "It is right to feel guilt over the shedding of Christian blood."

Tancred hung his head. The gut-stabbed merchant at Bari lay on his mind like a millstone. "I am resolved," said he, "never again to willingly slay a Christian. But what of the lives already lost? Sometimes I lie awake trying to figure how many men I have killed by my own hand. And then what of the men that were killed by my orders?"

Urban stood up and began to pace the room. "There is a way to do penance for these sins."

"Aye," said Tancred, a little bitterly. "There is the monastery. I must put on a hair shirt and become a bead man like my father."

Urban smiled and put a hand on the young knight's shoulder. "Yes, there is the monastery, but I do not think that the life of a Benedictine is for you. No, no, the grandson of Robert Guiscard would wither and die in the walls of the cloister! The truth is that men such as you are best fitted for a life of battle."

Tancred looked up in surprise. "Surely, I thought in my heart that I must give up the sword to seek my salvation!"

"There is a way to sin by the sword and there is a way to use it rightly," said Urban. He continued to pace the room with energy. "Have you heard of the great pilgrimage to the East that many are taking?"

"Yes," said Tancred. "I passed Hugh the Great and his company on my way to Rome and saw the cross you had given him. It seems a noble quest, to retake Jerusalem, but I do not see the urgency. The pagans have held that city for over four hundred years, and the popes have sent no army to reclaim it. Why have you called for this crusade now?"

Urban looked at Tancred thoughtfully. "You ask questions as your grandfather would have done, young man—short and shrewd." He tapped his fingertips together and smiled. "And in return I will give you a long and labored answer. A year ago I received a letter from the emperor of the Greeks. His empire is being overrun by the pagans. These fierce followers of Mahomet have fought their way to the very walls of Constantinople. Emperor Alexios begged me to aid him by sending an army of mercenaries to help reclaim his land.

"When I received his message, I turned it over in my mind. Here, I thought, is a grand opportunity for the Church of the West. For too long we have been separated from our Eastern brethren by misunderstanding, folly, and schism. This expedition holds the power to bring our two branches of the faith together as one, and not just Rome and Byzantium, but also the Armenian, the Syrian, and the Egyptian Christians.

"Added to this is the opportunity to retake Jerusalem. True, Emperor Alexios thinks only of his own lands in Asia, but after liberating those cities from the Turks, our host of knights would have the momentum to push on to the south. With the help of the grateful Greeks, we could carry the Crusade to the walls of Jerusalem.

"You say well that the infidels have held the Holy Land for over four hundred years, but in these last days they have become increasingly monstrous. They destroy the churches the apostles established or take them for the worship of their own idols. They bar the pilgrims from the holy places and torture them in the cruelest ways they can devise—tearing out their bowels, using them as target practice for their arrows, beheading them with their curved blades. Of the treatment of our women I will not even speak—such abominations are better left unsaid."

Urban shuddered and rose to his feet. "With these outrages and with Alexios' invitation, there is a need and there is an opportunity such as we have never seen before. This is why the Crusade must go forward *now*! All France is astir with this message. With Hugh the Great you encountered a mere fraction of the warriors on their way to the East. Here is a cause worth fighting for, is it not? What say you? Will you join the army of holy warriors and lay your sword on the neck of Christ's foes?"

Tancred swallowed hard, moved by Urban's impassioned words but convinced of his own unworthiness. "I am far from holy, father." The picture the pope had depicted of a suffering city in need appealed to him, but he hesitated to embark on such an adventure while bearing the heavy burden of guilt that weighed him down. His dreams were enemies enough to deal with for now.

"You will become holy through this journey," said Urban forcefully. "Do you think that a man who suffers the perils of the ocean, the deserts of Asia, and the swords of the Saracens will find his suit rejected in the Day of Judgment?"

The pope put a bony hand on the marquis' shoulder and looked him full in the face. "*This* is your penance, Tancred—to put off the sins of the secular life and to put on the armor of Christ, to forsake the way of fleshly warfare and to embark on this pilgrimage to the East. Jerusalem calls out for succor. Will you answer her? The Holy Sepulcher cries for a champion. Will you pick up the gage?"

Tancred's eyes widened and his ears began to tingle. Here was the path to escape perdition. Here was the road to remission of sins. Last night, he had dismissed the innkeeper's description of the pope's powers of persuasion as hollow banter. Now he felt the full force of Urban's words washing over him like the rising tide.

"Yes, a thousand times yes, father," Tancred said impetuously. He bounded forward to kneel in front of the pope, placing his sword at Urban's feet. "Let me swear fealty to you," he said, "for I shall never draw my sword again except in service to the Church. Let this Crusade be mine!"

"Are you certain you wish to take the cross?" asked Urban somberly, as if seeking to dispel some of the passion he had just evoked in the young man. He did not wish to lead an impulsive young man into rashly uttering an unbreakable vow. "There is no drawing back once you have sworn, under pain of excommunication."

"I am certain," said Tancred. He had been quick to oaths his entire life, but no one had ever accused him of being light with his word once the words were said. "There is no better way for me to obliterate my past and ensure my eternal future. The Church of Rome will be my liege, and I will follow her commands as faithfully as ever a knight obeyed his lord."

The marquis pressed the pope's hand with his own. "And besides this, I make you another promise. When the pagans' armies fall and Jerusalem's walls are breached, I shall be the *first* knight to enter the Holy City and reclaim her for Christendom."

"A bold promise," said Urban, but he did not disapprove of it. He received the young knight's homage gladly, and called a servant to bring a cross of red cloth. As they waited for the servant to return, Urban explained the mission in greater detail.

"Last week, the Feast of the Assumption of the Blessed Virgin, was the date I scheduled for the Crusaders to depart," said Urban. "But not all of the armies have followed my direction. Many of the poorer folk—stirred into a frenzy by a hermit named Peter—took to the road for Constantinople early in the spring of this year. It was not my intention to send unarmed peasants with wives and children on this quest, but once they heard of our noble goal, there was no stopping them. I know not how they have fared—I fear only evil can attend them with so few knights and men-at-arms in their company.

"The official Crusaders—those who received my blessing—have not contrived to take the road on the appointed day either. The Germans have left already, you saw some of the Franks departing under the command of Hugh the Great. I would that they could have gone under the command of Hugh's brother, the king of France, but until he sets his own house in order he is no fit leader to reclaim the House of God. The rest of the Franks are still marshaling their forces under Raymond of Toulouse. The Duke of Normandy has pledged to go, but he still lacks the funds to equip a force—unless he can persuade his brother to lend the money. A motley group of heroes, no? Thankfully, our Heavenly Father can be trusted to bring these disparate groups together and weld them into an army fit for His holy purposes."

"Who will lead us all?" asked Tancred. He wrinkled his nose at the thought of taking orders from French Hugh, though as brother to the king of France he undoubtedly ranked higher than the other leaders of the expedition. The Duke of Normandy was a name that inspired greater trust, but still Tancred was of no mind to be at the beck and call of a lord he did not know. "I have sworn fealty to you and to the Church, Father," said Tancred, "not to one of these foreign princes."

"And it is the Church who will lead you in this journey," said Urban reassuringly. "I cannot leave my see empty, prey to that imposter Guibert, but I have appointed a worthy proxy. Adhemar, the bishop of Le Puy, will keep order in the army. You will render him the obedience you would give to me."

A black-robed monk entered silently and, with the nimble fingers of a tailor, began to attach the blood-red cross to the right shoulder of Tancred's tunic. "You must tell your family of your pilgrimage," said Urban with satisfaction as he watched Tancred receive the badge of his undertaking. "There must be others of Robert Guiscard's offspring who would rejoice to take the cross."

"Perhaps," said Tancred with a shrug, but he doubted that his relatives would show much enthusiasm for the effort. Roger Borsa would spend no gold on an enterprise that promised no gain, and Bohemond would mock the mission mercilessly. Tancred's soul still stung from the contemptuous arrows the latter had let fly at Amalfi. He would be glad to take his troops two thousand miles away from the uncle that had trained him.

"I have a younger brother who might be glad to go with me," said Tancred, thinking warmly of William. He looked down at the red cross as the tailor finished his stitches and tied off the string. "But even if I go alone, I would not draw back. It is the will of God, and He will be my helper."

# Chapter 4

Tancred and Ralph returned to Amalfi within a fortnight, expecting to find either the siege as they had left it or the city in submission at last. But when they arrived they discovered that the city's walls had not been breached, the city's will had not been broken, and yet the Norman army had deserted its objective, disbanded, and disappeared.

"You there!" said Tancred to a man laboring in his fields near the road. "Where is Roger Borsa's army that was camped here?"

The brown peasant wiped his forehead with a thick forearm and leaned upon his sickle. "They've gone away again," he said.

"Why?" asked Tancred incredulously.

"Well," said the man slowly, scratching his head with a grubby finger, "It was on account of some great procession that came through here—Franks, by the look of them. They had a huge banner with a cross on it, and their leader seemed a mighty proud man with lilies on his shield and—"

"Yes, yes, you mean Hugh the Great," said Tancred, trying to hurry the man along.

"I don't rightly know what his name was," said the peasant with a shrug. "He said he was going to the Holy Land—going to save our mother Jerusalem from the infidels, said he. And these Normans, why, it was like fire to thatch! They dropped their tents quick as a cat can pounce and said they'd come along. There was a tall fellow in a red mantle—looking like you, lad, but older. When he heard about this expedition, well, he stripped off that fancy cloak and tore it into scraps with his own two hands! The soldiers began to pass them about, and we had several of them at our cottage, begging my Maria to sew red crosses on their shoulders."

Ralph whistled in amazement. "As I live and breathe—your uncle Bohemond has taken the cross!"

Tancred frowned. He would have cursed, but he checked himself. "For no good purpose, I'll wager." The newfound satisfaction in his quest was diminished and somehow tarnished with this news. This Crusade was for true pilgrims, not opportunists like Bohemond. What could be his uncle's motive in joining the expedition?

Tancred struck his horse sharply with his heels. "Come on, Ralph. They'll be bound for Bari—we'll catch them there."

"Have pity on these old bones," said Ralph with a laughing groan, as Tancred's horse took the road at a canter. He tossed the peasant a *denari*, urged his own horse on to follow his master, and braced himself to repeat a journey nearly as long as the one they had just completed.

When they arrived at Bari on the eastern coast of Italy, Tancred and Ralph found the city a-bustle with horses, ships, and enthusiastic Normans. Ralph, who went to reconnoiter at a nearby tavern, came out with the latest news. "That old peasant told no lies. Every Norman with a fighting spirit is ready to take the cross and sail for Constantinople. Your uncle Roger has elected to stay in Italy, but Bohemond is all on fire to leave. He's assembling supplies and troops and has hired a fleet of merchant men to carry him across the Adriatic."

"Is William here with my men?" demanded Tancred.

"That I haven't heard," replied Ralph, "though the fellow did say that Bohemond's sister had come to town. Your mother will know where William is."

Tancred's mother Emma had found rooms at the convent in Bari, and as soon as he learned of her whereabouts, Tancred hastened there to see her. Emma was a tall woman with fair hair that had just begun to silver. It hung down in two plaits on either side of her shoulders, reaching almost to her waist. Tancred remembered her clothing in his youth as being plain and somewhat austere, but after her religious husband's retreat into the cloister, her dresses had become more elaborate. The sleeves of her crimson tunic nearly grazed the floor, and her pointed shoes were richly embroidered with filaments of gold.

Entering his mother's chambers unannounced, Tancred knelt quietly beside her chair. Emma looked up from her needlework and smiled as if she had been expecting him. "My son," she said fondly, kissing Tancred upon the brow. She lifted his chin and fixed her eyes on his. "I have heard many tales of you since last we talked."

"I have taken the cross, Mother," said Tancred, gesturing at the blood-red emblem sewn onto his right shoulder.

"So has all the world," she said, a little sardonically. "When the fleet sails, I think there will be not one of my menfolk left in Italy. William has taken ship already, and you will be soon to follow."

William is gone?" asked Tancred in surprise.

"He left with the Franks just two days past. He could not wait, he said, for you to return or for our kinsmen to gather ships."

Tancred stared in disbelief. How strongly William must have been moved to take such a step without consulting his elder brother!

"I hear my uncle Bohemond also means to sail," said Tancred. He swallowed hard to keep from sneering as he said it.

"Yes, Bohemond will cross to Greece as soon as he can gather money and men." Emma looked at Tancred curiously. She was a perceptive woman with wisdom behind her gray eyes. "You are displeased with that, I think."

Tancred bit his tongue. "It is no matter to me."

Emma forbore from pressing that point and turned her conversation elsewhere. "It costs a great deal to outfit a company for this venture. Have you thought on that at all, my son?"

Tancred shrugged. "I have money, do I not?" The young marquis was accustomed to allowing others to manage his estate, and he had no accurate idea of how much ready money lay in his coffers.

Emma laughed. "If I sell off the upper meadows and the lower springs, mayhap you will have enough to furnish a hundred men with armor and horses. But you'll have no strongbox to take on the road with you. Whatever provisions you need, you'll have to gain with the strength of your arm. Whatever wages you pay, you'll have to garner from the booty of the conquered."

Emma ran a hand through her son's cropped yellow hair and continued with feigned nonchalance. "But perhaps there is a better way. Your uncle Bohemond is wealthier than we. If you enlist your men in his company, they will be provided for on the sea and in the desert."

Tancred opened his mouth to speak, but Emma's words proceeded hurriedly. "I knew how it would be when you returned, that your heart would be set on this Crusade like all the others. And so I have already spoken to my brother. He has agreed that he will equip your troop and that you may travel with him as his lieutenant."

"I'll thank you to make no such arrangements for me!" cried Tancred, rising to his feet in anger. He clenched his fists and growled beneath his breath.

"Lower your voice, sirrah!" said Emma sternly, afraid that the nuns would hear his outburst. She put her needlework aside and rose slowly from her chair. The full skirt of her crimson dress billowed out around her. "Since when do you despise my brother so much and disdain his company? Has he not taken you under his wing and taught you as his own son?"

"I am acutely aware of all he has *done*," said Tancred, "but I think that it is you, Mother, who are not aware of all that he *is*. Tell me—why has your brother taken the cross?"

She looked at him narrowly. "To liberate Jerusalem."

Tancred laughed hollowly. "No, not Bohemond. He does not give a fig for the Holy City. Power and land and riches and glory are his only thoughts. I know this because, as you say, I have sat long under his wing. I have watched him in peace and in war and have seen his power-hungry strivings. And in truth, until I talked to Pope Urban, I had no other thoughts myself. But now, it is different. I have sworn my fealty to the Apostolic See, and I go for no other purpose than the salvation of my soul and the liberation of the Holy Sepulcher. But to go on this Crusade with a man like Bohemond—why, it cheapens the whole expedition!"

Emma stood as silently as a stone pillar waiting for Tancred's ranting to cease. "You are very proud, my son, and you are very sure of your own heart. But I have lived longer than you in this world, and I know what you do not—that most men are ruled by contradictory passions, and the lion and the lamb can lie down with each other inside one soul. You think you know your own heart and you think you know the heart of your uncle,"—she laughed harshly like the call of the crow—"but time will show you your folly."

Emma seized Tancred's arm and drew him close to herself. It was almost an embrace, had it not been so rough. "Now, hear the words of your mother," she said, and her voice cracked sharply like a whip against the ground. "Whatever your objections may be, you *will* go on this journey with your uncle, or you will go without my blessing."

Tancred began to bluster, but she held up a hand to quiet him.

"I do not say you must take his coin. I do not say you must adopt his aims. But there are many perils on the road to Constantinople, and a raw youth like you must travel with a seasoned soldier. Bohemond was weaned on warfare and cut his eye teeth in Greece. He knows the cunning of the emperor you go to aid. He will help you on your journey, my son."

Tancred's brow folded in on itself. His choler had faded a little, and he was willing to concede the wisdom of his mother's suggestions.

He sighed. "I will do as you say."

"Swear it," said Emma.

"By the breasts that gave me suck," said Tancred solemnly, "I swear that I will journey under the command of Bohemond—for as long as he pursues his pilgrimage to Jerusalem. Does that satisfy you?"

"I am content," said Emma, releasing her hold on him. The intensity of her tone faded to briskness. "Now we must see about the money for your arms and your passage." She reached down to unbuckle the jeweled girdle that hung about her hips. "Here, take this to sell. If you men can give up your lives for the liberation of the Holy Sepulcher, I at least can give up some of my finery."

Tancred took the gold chain ornamented with cut emeralds and thanked his mother with a kiss. "If God grants me half your spirit in my old age, I shall think myself blessed. Do not fear for William—I shall find him as soon as I sail." He stroked her golden crown of hair and pressed her hand.

"Leave me be, leave me be," she said impatiently, pushing him away. "I must send letters to your bailiff to arrange the sale of the land. You've work enough of your own without dawdling here."

Tancred strode out of the convent cell, eager to find a goldsmith and to change his mother's girdle into bezants. Behind him, Emma's iron face melted a little and a few tears darkened the red fabric on her breast. "He'll not come home again, that's the way of it," she breathed. She tossed her pale gold braids over her shoulders fiercely. "And yet, I'd not have him sit in the cloister like his father for all the world."

# Chapter 5

Both Bohemond and Tancred spent the next three months mortgaging and selling their lands, recruiting followers to their standards, and arming their men. A horse and a simple suit of armor cost more than the yearly wages of a knight, and lords were expected to provide these things for their entourage. Tancred could have applied for money from either of his uncles, but instead he sold most of his land and pawned all of his jewels to outfit his men. In the end he accoutered nearly five hundred knights and men-at-arms, more than his mother had deemed possible, but only a fifth of the following that Bohemond had gathered.

Throughout this time, Bohemond never once alluded to the words that had been spoken in his tent outside Amalfi. Perhaps he assumed that Tancred's newfound scruples had dissipated like the August heat. Perhaps he had forgotten the whole matter himself.

Tancred adopted a compliant but reserved attitude toward his uncle, keeping the frustrations he had revealed to his mother under close lock and key inside his breast. If he must honor his promise and travel with Bohemond, it was prudent to make the best of it. As they conferred over ships and soldiers and cargo, the two Normans simulated the easy camaraderie that had characterized their former years. A close observer would have noticed a change, however, and marked the cold glitter in each man's eye when the other's back was turned.

When a Greek trading vessel put in at the end of the harvest, Tancred asked for news of William. Had his brother reached Constantinople under the banner of Hugh the Great? The trader, surprised to find the young Norman fluent in the Greek tongue, answered his questions affably. He knew nothing of William, but by Abraham's beard, he had a story to tell of Hugh!

The French prince had sent twenty-four knights ahead to the Greek port Durazzo, informing the emperor's agents of his coming and instructing them to prepare lavishly for his arrival. "But his arrival was not so dignified as he hoped!" said the trader with glee. "The flotilla that Hugh hired for the passage had no true sailors. They missed the signs of a storm brewing on the Ionian Sea, and many of them foundered with all their passengers! The mighty prince himself took a swim in our ocean and washed up ashore a few miles from Durazzo."

"Did all of his company come ashore as well?" asked Tancred, anxious for William's safety.

"That I could not tell you, master," said the trader.

As they were speaking, an olive-skinned journeyman from the Greek quarter of Bari came up and plucked the trader on the sleeve. He had curly, chestnut hair and deep-set eyes, and casting a black look at Tancred, he whispered briefly in the trader's ear. The trader, ready to hear anything from a fellow countryman, adopted a look of surprise then glanced at Tancred hostilely.

"What route does Hugh mean to take to Constantinople?" asked Tancred, determined to glean more information about his brother's whereabouts.

"I am sorry, sir," said the trader, his confiding nature changed suddenly into surliness, "but I've too much to do to stand around here answering your questions." He turned his back on Tancred and fiddled with some of the rigging on his ship.

The Greek journeyman smiled maliciously then walked off with his poison. Tancred's first impulse was to collar him and question him, but he thought better of it and bided his time. "What does that fellow have against me?" he asked Ralph later, pointing out the journeyman amidst a crowd in the market.

Ralph squinted, trying to identify the man among the sea of people. "Why, I believe he is brother to the Greek merchant Alexander that you killed here in Bari several seasons ago," replied Ralph. "It seems he has not forgotten the matter."

Tancred blushed hotly. "The fellow tried to give me false coin!"

"Aye, and a blade in the belly put a stop to that," said Ralph. "The brother's a goldsmith, though of ill reputation among his fellow tradesmen. I've heard tell that he's taken in Alexander's widow and children. Thankfully, the merchant had no sons, so the brother's the only one you'll have to face if it comes to a blood feud."

Tancred winced at the memory of the murder, his newfound conscience walking like a barefoot child over the broken shards of the past. His old self would have boasted about the incident; his new self writhed in constant torment for sins committed long ago.

Ralph looked at his master sympathetically. "Well, that's one more peccadillo this pilgrimage will cure. Any day now and your uncle will give the word to hoist anchor and embark."

It was a family affair preparing to set sail across the Adriatic. Besides Bohemond and Tancred, there came Bohemond's cousin Richard of Salerno. Richard was fifteen years Tancred's senior, but his inferior in arms and bearing. He had the same close-cropped blond hair that most of the southern Normans wore, but his similarity to Tancred extended only so far. He was of medium height and slight of build, although his friendliness with the wine cask presaged the portliness that would come with old age. A large, curved nose encumbered his smooth-skinned face, and his lips were thin and bloodless. Richard had often tried to curry favor with the young marquis, but Tancred had disliked him from childhood.

That dislike was intensified five summers ago when Richard had approached Emma asking for the hand of Tancred's sister. The man's overfamiliarity coupled with his coarse cruelty repulsed Tancred. He told his mother to forbid the match. "I've seen him break a horse for spite and toy with his dogs with a dagger," he said.

"*You've* killed dogs before," replied Emma.

"From necessity, not pleasure!" objected Tancred.

But Emma, a female version of her brother Bohemond, did not share Tancred's scruples. Richard was the count of Salerno, a prosperous Norman stronghold close to Amalfi, and he was rich to boot. The man was clever and endowed with a flattering tongue, and her daughter Altrude had no objection to the union. Once these two strong-willed women had decided the event, Tancred—who had not yet attained his majority—was left with little say in the matter. Altrude became the countess of Salerno, and the wife of her mother's first cousin; whether she repented of her decision later, Tancred could only guess.

Tancred had heard that some of the Frankish Crusaders had brought their wives along on the pilgrimage. The idea of women on such a hazardous journey seemed foolish, and indeed, Pope Urban had asked for none but armed men to take the cross. Altrude, like the rest of her family, expressed a desire to see the Holy Sepulcher, but Tancred was relieved to learn that Richard had no intention of taking along excess baggage. "She's better off in Italy mothering my son," said Richard, for their eldest child Roger was sickly and given to fits. "And even if I don't have a wife to lie down with, there'll be women enough in the camp, eh?" he said, giving a wink to his young brother-in-law.

"Just yesterday, a pretty little Greek girl—by my troth, you would like her if you saw her!—asked to take passage in my ship. She said she wanted to see the land of her people. Who am I to say no to a woman's fancy? But the ship's small, I told her, and it will be snug quarters. And that saucy minx looked me straight in the eye and said in that case, she would be quite happy to share my cabin on the voyage…."

Tancred turned away in disgust. If it were not for his sister Altrude and the humiliation it must afford her, he would have found Richard's lechery laughable. But as it was, he had no patience with Salerno's salacious lord.

At the beginning of the Advent season, Bohemond finally pronounced the convoy ready to sail. He had also heard about Hugh the Great's disaster and laughed at the thought that his own fleet might meet a similar fate. "I know the coast of Greece better than I know the paces of my horse!" he said disdainfully. "We shall come to no grief on the sea."

True to Bohemond's prediction, the fleet crossed over with no other mishap than separation. Tancred's force quickly rejoined with Bohemond's on the rocky coast, but Richard of Salerno was detained a day. His small ship had run afoul of a Byzantine harbor guard, and mistaking him for a pirate, they chased him aground until he explained himself and the object of his voyage.

The closest metropolis to Bohemond's landing site was the city of Durazzo. Tancred saw his uncle's nostrils flare with excitement as the city's walls came into sight. The fortress here rivaled the impregnable citadel in Bari with its thick walls and high towers. Over a dozen years ago, when he was Tancred's age, Bohemond had stared out from the other side of those walls. He and his father Robert Guiscard had done the unthinkable, defeating the hosts of the eastern emperor with their intrepid band of Normans. Durazzo had surrendered herself into their hands, and the first step to conquering Constantinople was accomplished.

"Sweet Mary, but that city is as beautiful as last I saw it!" said Bohemond, with all the reverence pious pilgrims have at the shrine of a saint. His eyes lit up with longing and pierced the distance with their stare.

"The emperor's nephew is governor there," said Richard of Salerno. He had learned a few things about the area during his detainment by the Byzantine coast guards. "We must deal with him if we wish to travel through this domain."

"*I* was governor there once," said Bohemond hungrily.

"How did you manage to lose the place?" asked Tancred cuttingly. "It seems that such a strong city could never be breached if her commander were clever enough to hold her."

Bohemond frowned. "The Greek emperor is more cunning than you know. He lured my father back to Rome by hiring the Germans to attack the pope. I was left to hold our conquests, not just Durazzo but all the northern parts of Greece. Shorthanded, I marched out to counter Alexios at Larissa. I lost. Our Norman knights scattered, and it was all I could do to marshal the survivors and lead them back to Italy. We never saw the inside of Durazzo's walls again."

"Nor are we likely to on this expedition," said Tancred callously. The wistful look his uncle cast on the city held no meaning for him. It was Jerusalem, not Byzantium, that had captured his heart.

# Chapter 6

The governor of Durazzo, John Comnenus, spent three days scrutinizing the Normans' landing. When the last of the separated squadrons finally found their way together, he exited the city at twilight and met with the Normans to give them their instructions.

He was a short man, with a dark, pointed beard. His thick eyelids, half veiling his eyes as he spoke, gave him a less than trustworthy air. "Emperor Alexios is pleased that so many of you Latins have come to serve him in the struggle against the Turks," he said, his voice as smooth as the olive oil this region was famous for.

Tancred frowned. *He* had not come to serve the emperor. But before he could object, Bohemond caught his eye and cautioned him into silence.

"We are pleased to offer our swords to your emperor," said Bohemond courteously, towering over the governor by nearly two feet. "How soon can we be on our way to Constantinople?"

"Tomorrow!" said the Greek, excited at the prospect of being rid of them. "My instructions were to send an escort with each party of Crusaders, but so many have come that it is impossible now. Germans, Franks, and now you Normans! I don't have the men to give you a detachment, though"—he looked up at Bohemond slyly—"it is rumored that perhaps you know your way around my uncle's domain quite well enough."

"We've no need of an honor guard," said Bohemond ignoring the man's insinuations, "but our men are beginning to grow hungry." He cleared his throat. "Provisioning us would be in your best interest." It was easy to understand how the Norman army must seek food if none were provided.

"Yes, yes," said the small Greek. "Our emperor has planned for this already. There are storehouses outside Durazzo ready to supply you, and along the way many markets have been laid out so that your men may eat."

"Many thanks," said Bohemond. He bid the governor good evening and returned to the camp. Later, in his tents, he ordered Tancred to organize the procurement of supplies and arrange wagons for transport. "And see to it that it is done before the morning light," he said curtly, pulling off his tunic as he prepared to go to bed.

Tancred waited for the servants to leave before he spoke. "I am not your steward or your quartermaster," he said abruptly.

Bohemond, who had lain down on his pallet, opened his eyes in surprise. "What? Are you still here?" He propped himself up on his elbows and yawned loudly. "What are you babbling on about?"

Tancred's limbs tightened. "Only this—that we have never discussed the terms of our association on this journey."

"What terms?" demanded Bohemond, and his eyes narrowed into slits.

"I think you do not realize that I accompany you not as a subordinate, but as an independent lord. You are my uncle, yes, but not my liege. I have thrown in my lot with you for our mutual benefit, to increase our numbers along the road and protect our men from villainy or ambush. I have not joined with you to be ordered about like a common serving man."

Bohemond sat up straight and tall on the bed. "You think that you are to be accounted a commander of equal rank with me? With the Duke of Normandy? With Hugh the Great?"

"Yes," said Tancred, recognizing the preposterous nature of his own position, but determined to brazen it out. "I have my own company of men, equipped and provisioned with my own money."

Bohemond shook his head. "Tancred, Tancred, you have a mere tithe of the lances I possess. You have never entered a battle save under my command or under the banner of your uncle Roger. You think that these princes, these other Crusaders, will admit you into their councils when we reach Constantinople?"

"And why not since you will be there to vouch for me?"

Bohemond began to laugh, a small chuckle that broadened into a hilarious roar.

Tancred looked at his uncle, then shrugged and grinned, having regained some of the good nature he had been lacking for so many months. "You will see," he said with a smile. "My company may be small, but I wager I'll be the first to take Jerusalem once we've crossed the desert."

"Upon my soul," said Bohemond, "you are the most presumptuous cockerel I've ever heard crow. You'll have to prove yourself better than you did at Amalfi if you want to be the peer to princes. Come, here is what I will do for you. If you will lead our rearguard throughout this journey—and it is a perilous one, despite the sweet smiles of the Greek governor—and contrive to keep our army from any mishap along the way, when we reach Constantinople I will put you forward as your own man, and beseech the other lords to let you have a voice in the deliberations."

"Truly?" said Tancred, surprised at his uncle's magnanimity. Perhaps Bohemond still had some fondness for him, when it did not contradict his own self-interest.

"Yes, truly," said Bohemond wearily, throwing himself down on his bed once more. "Now go see about those supplies, or if you are too damnably proud, find someone else who will!"

Tancred was awake before the morning light came, and by the time the army was ready to set out, he had formed up his company to hold the rearguard. His old servant Ralph watched prudently, chewing a piece of straw, as Tancred put the men in position. "That's right," he said approvingly. "You're wise to keep the lances close together in case it comes to a charge. And for God's sake, send the scullions and camp drabs on ahead of us. We don't want the enemy using them as shields if it comes to a skirmish in the foothills."

Bohemond gave the trumpet signal to advance. The knights pulled forward like colts released from a pen, soon having to check their excitement and their pace to accord with the speed of the ponderous supply wagons.

"This road looks easy for travel," said Tancred, remarking on the broad, paved highway that led east from Durazzo.

Ralph snorted. "Aye, it's fair enough here, but wait a few leagues before you give it any praise. Too many years have passed since the Romans paid gold to repair it, and the ruts make it nigh impassable in rainy weather." He gazed upward at the gray heavens. "Though rain is the least of our worries now. It's coming on to Christmas, and the sky promises snow."

The first day's march was uneventful. Tancred, anxious to succeed in his new command, rode to and fro between the corners of his rear column, exhorting his men to vigilance and constantly surveying the shifting terrain. His horse was tired out before noon, and by the time the sun set, he had spent both of his spare mounts.

At the end of the day, Ralph helped Tancred disarm, but the marquis' mind was too active to rest. "Think you my uncle will keep his promise? If I serve him to his advantage on the way to Constantinople, will he recognize me as an equal?"

Ralph looked up with a furrowed brow. "Are you so worried about your standing before the rest of the Crusaders, young master?"

"No!" said Tancred hotly, then with a rueful smile—"Of course I am. I have made my own promise to Pope Urban that I shall be the first to enter the Holy City. And without a place among the commanders, I have small faith that the expedition to Jerusalem will ever succeed. The road to the Holy Sepulcher is a long one, and what if the rest are like Bohemond? I wager he'll peel off from the Crusade if he sees riper fruit lying on the wayside."

They camped that night outside of a small village, and after posting sentries, Bohemond summoned the remainder of the army to a mass assembly. "Never forget," he told them, "that we are guests here in the land of the eastern emperor. We must treat his people as if they were our own, and their goods as sacredly as the possessions of our Mother Church." In no uncertain terms, he ordered the Normans to refrain from taking any food, clothing, weapons, or gold from the settlements and towns they came across. No villagers were to be manhandled and no women harmed.

"What is this?" said Richard of Salerno, leaning toward Tancred. "My cousin Bohemond grows soft."

Tancred shook his head. "Nay, he plays the prudent man. Why should we anger the emperor with so many leagues still to travel in his land?"

"Perhaps you're right," said Richard with a snort. "But if we cannot live off the land, how are the men to eat? I know that greasy governor promised us food along the way, but I trust him no further than I'd trust a serpent."

"Or no further than I'd trust Bohemond," thought Tancred, though he immediately swallowed the sentiment unsaid. It was a thought best kept to himself.

# Chapter 7

The rain and sleet soon set in, and true to Ralph's prediction, the Via Egnatia was a sorry road in rough weather. The horses, tripping over loose paving stones and up to their fetlocks in mud, tired easily, and many of the knights dismounted to walk beside their beasts. Tancred's shield, usually slung across his back, was often on his elbow now and raised above his head, an umbrella to block the stinging pellets of hail. At night when the Normans pitched their camp, the thick clustered stands of pine trees offered some refuge from the tumultuous sky, but the uneven ground often sent small rivulets across the floor of the tents. Ralph and the other men-at-arms spent long hours by firelight scouring armor and harnesses to prevent the rust from eating away at them.

John Comnenus, the governor of Durazzo, had proved true to his word so far. Every few days imperial messengers would greet the approaching Normans, giving them directions to a stockpile of food and firewood or informing them of a marketplace where they might buy supplies. The people they met in the towns were not exactly friendly, but their sullen glances perked up substantially at the sight of Bohemond's gold. Tancred, vigilant as a mother bear, watched every transaction and interaction with care. He was determined that no scathe would come to the army through any fault of his.

As the old road meandered through the hilly country, many swollen streams blocked the path, some of them with a current strong enough to sweep a foot soldier off his feet. On one occasion, when they encountered one of these overgrown brooks, the main army crossed over with some difficulty. Tancred held the near bank, keeping a sharp eye on the cliffs above, until Bohemond's men had all set their feet on firm ground.

"Cross over in groups of six," said Tancred to his five hundred men. "And let the foot soldiers hold fast to the stirrups of the mounted men in case the water proves too strong." The men set out as instructed, most able to hold their ground against the rushing stream, but a few forced to grab hold of one another when the riverbed proved slippery.

Tancred waited till the last group was ready to cross, and then he too spurred his mount into the stream. His horse plunged spiritedly through the choppy waves, and just as he began to canter up the bank on the other side, he heard a shout. "Look there!" said one of his soldiers with a laugh, and pointed at the river behind them.

As the Norman knights had made their crossing, a wizened, old Macedonian woman had been waiting on the bank, bent double in the rain. When she saw that the soldiers had survived the ford, she put a timid foot into the current herself. The river, frustrated by the stalwart stride of the Normans, gurgled with pleasure to have this weaker victim in its grasp. While Tancred and his men watched, the old grandmother's ankles slipped and sent her sideways. The white caps bit into her body like so many teeth, devouring everything but her head. Within seconds, the unfortunate woman had floated twenty yards downstream, and it was only by catching hold of a low hanging bramble bush—or by it catching hold of her—that she managed to stay her rapid course.

"Sweet Mary!" said the soldier who had spotted her. He was a red-haired, fair-skinned fellow named Turold. "She's in the rocks now. That's the end of her, barring a miracle."

"Why don't you go back in and fetch her?" said Tancred, suddenly moved with pity at the old woman's plight.

Turold stared at his leader, certain that he was speaking in jest. "I wouldn't put my horse in that whirlpool. Not if she were my own mother, I wouldn't."

"No?" said Tancred. "It seems I have a stronger affection for my mother than you have for yours." He turned his horse's head sharply and urged him into the undulating stream. It was a venture best attempted without too much haste, although haste was what the Macedonian woman surely needed, for the brambles' hold on her had begun to loosen. She was in danger of being swept into the jagged rocks and swirling eddies farther downstream. Tancred muttered quietly to his horse as the high-mettled steed picked his way through the stony riverbed.

Once he reached the hapless victim, Tancred leaned sideways and stretched out a hand. But the woman was either unable or afraid to take hold of him. He seized her sopping cloak about the shoulders, and by sheer strength managed to pull her up in front of him without losing his own seat on the saddle.

He had no sooner secured the woman than a great wooden snag came swirling by, the leafy carcass of an upriver tree. Snorting with terror, Tancred's horse reared up, nearly tossing his rider and new passenger into the current. "Gently, gently," said Tancred to the animal, digging his knees into the horse's withers and leaning forward with all his weight. Calmed by his master's voice, the animal's panic abated and Tancred regained control of his steed. The floating hazard spun away downstream. He flicked the reins sharply and steadily compelled his mount to cross to the safety of the farther shore.

Once the peril was past, Tancred had to decide what to do with his new passenger. It was obvious that the woman was old, but how old no one could say for certain. On some faces fifty and one hundred look the same. A dark dress covered her, plain and neat. Her only ornament was a discolored metal star bound tightly over her brow. It might have been silver once, but now it was the same dingy gray as her water-sodden hair. Her shoulders stooped steeply like a wind-plagued sapling, and her brow stood barely higher than the buckle of Tancred's sword belt.

"Where are you traveling to?" Tancred asked the old lady in Greek. She stared at him wide eyed, either mute or uncomprehending. A few more efforts elicited the same unsatisfactory response. "Well," said Tancred, "if you will not tell me where you are going, I must take you along with us until the nearest town." To the surprise of his men, the old lady rode before him until evening, and when night fell, he gave her a place at the fire and a bed on the floor of his tent.

"What's this?" said Richard of Salerno, gawking at Tancred's strange conduct. He nudged Ralph in the ribs. "Your master certainly chooses strange bedfellows. Faugh! What a loathly lady to take into one's chamber!"

Ralph smiled wryly. "That's God's own truth, sir. And what's more, that's the first woman that's been in his tents since his journey to see the pope."

"All the better for me!" replied Richard. He adopted a confidential tone. "My little Greek girl Alexandra seems to have caught sight of our young hero valiantly commanding our rearguard and puissantly protecting us from all the ugly old women that cross our path. The girl is besotted! Question after question she asks me about Tancred— which pavilion is his, what food he likes, what weapons he carries. I gave her a hard beating the last time she said his name and reminded her that I was the one bringing her to Constantinople, not him. If I'm not careful, I'll find her sneaking out of my tent and into his on one of these cold nights!"

Ralph's eyes twinkled and he adopted a tone of exaggerated sympathy. "It's impossible to say why any woman would prefer him when she has you to be her protector."

"Stop your mocking, you old wag!" said Richard, giving him a good-natured shove. "No women for four months? At this rate Tancred is on the road to joining the cloister just like his father, and I can tell you it's the rare wench who prefers a monk to a marquis!"

The army chanced upon a small village the next day. When Tancred deposited his newly acquired charge with the peasants there, the people gabbled excitedly and immediately began to bring out offerings of food and furs. "This is the friendliest village we've met with yet!" said Turold, excited to partake of the local delicacies.

"I do not think this deference is due to us," said Tancred. His suspicion was confirmed when the peasants began to lay their gifts at the feet of the old woman. Despite her humble appearance, she must be a healer or a sage of some sort. The Normans, unfamiliar with the region and its customs, had not recognized the mark that set her apart.

The old crone, lifting her wrinkled face to look full at Tancred, began to pour out a stream of unfamiliar syllables. Apparently, she was not so mute after all. "She says to thank you for rescuing her from the river," said one of the villagers, a young man wrapped in the pelt of a large lynx. He must have traveled some and traded with other villages for he could change the crone's Macedonian dialect into Greek words that Tancred understood.

Tancred nodded in acknowledgement of her gratitude and remounted his steed. As he took the reins, a sudden hush came over the chattering villagers. He turned sharply to find the source of their astonishment.

The old woman—he was scarcely sure that it was the same woman—was metamorphosing before his eyes. Her back no longer bent with age, and she seemed to grow in stature and stateliness. It was like the change from winter to spring, a barren landscape into a garden of blossoms and beauty. The woman still held the appearance of great age, but now she appeared to be in the morning time of her life, with centuries stretching out ahead of her waiting to be walked. Lifting her hands with authority, she began to speak in the measured cadence of a bard or soothsayer.

"What is she saying?" asked Tancred in bewilderment.

The man with the lynx pelt listened fully before he began to translate. "She says that you helped her without being asked, and for that you are blessed. Soon, she says, you will meet a great lady who *will* ask your help. The choice is yours whether to render it, but if you do, you will find great love and also great sorrow."

The woman's words ceased, and once more she shrunk into the silent, pathetic creature Tancred had rescued. She quietly gathered up the offerings the villagers had laid out for her and began to hobble away from the gathered crowd.

"What did she mean?" demanded Tancred, but the young man only shrugged. Everyone knows that a seer does not explain her sayings, and when the wise woman had finished there was no more to be said.

"Lord, what is all this hubbub?" asked Turold, nudging his horse close to Tancred. Few of the men could understand Greek fluently, but the marquis had a gift for tongues. It was a skill of some importance; a man in a foreign land without knowledge of the language is like a man missing pieces of his armor.

"Can you tell us what she said?" asked Turold again, curious about the words of the old crone he had refused to save from the river.

Tancred looked at the red-haired knight and shook his head. "Nothing of importance," he said curtly, and he stuffed the old woman's words down into the recesses of his mind to be remembered at a later time.

# Chapter 8

For several months the Norman army proceeded along the road without encountering anything more hostile than the weather. They kept Christmas at Castoria and neared the Vardar River just prior to the season of Lent. In one town the insolent inhabitants refused to sell them any livestock for food, and Bohemond authorized his men to take the cattle by force. But for the most part, the villagers honored the promise of John Comnenus, the governor of Durazzo, and provided a steady supply of bread and fresh or salted meat.

The first run of bad luck began just after the river came in sight. Bohemond's scouts discovered a small collection of huts beneath a rocky outcropping. On further examination, they found that these were the outlying homes of a small town nestled between two hills. Always in need of further provisions and provender, Bohemond sent an embassy of ten knights into the town. They would show the leading citizens the Byzantine governor's letter of commendation and seek a market to purchase supplies.

When the embassy came back, Tancred was busy conferring with Bohemond. The two men stood on a little plateau, surveying the river ahead of them, swift, swollen, and insatiable as Charybdis. Their vantage point gave them a vivid view of the returning riders. The Norman knights were spurring their horses quickly as if they had just escaped some ghastly peril.

"Sir," said one of the knights, as his fellows reined in their horses and hurriedly unhelmed. "That town over yonder is full of the most dreadful abominations."

"What do you mean?" asked Bohemond, his hand flying instinctively to the hilt of his sword.

"We rode into the place peacefully and asked to see their ruler. They stared at us blankly. Then one of them said they had no such thing, that they were all equals in every way. This confused us a little, but at length, I took out the letter from Comnenus and bade them sell us supplies as their governor had commanded. Several of them laughed at this, the women as shrill as witches. One of the hags spat at my feet and said that they owed no obedience to the Byzantines or any man."

"Merciful Mary!" said Tancred. "Who are these rebels?"

The knight continued. "I pressed them then, not on their duty to their natural lord, but on their duty to Christian brethren. I told them the reasons for our Crusade and showed them the cross upon my arm. And—heaven help me!—they laughed again. They called our crosses idols and us servants of Satan. We told them that we would send them a priest to correct them of their errors, and they cried out fouler blasphemies against us. More and more of these scoffers began to come out of the buildings, some with shards of pottery and others with weapons. I raised my lance and signaled our knights to retreat, for I was afraid they would do us some mischief if they could."

Bohemond shook his head in wonder at this story. "You did well, captain. It were better to withdraw than to lose any men. I think we have put our nose into a den of heretics."

"What shall we do now?" asked Tancred. "I suppose they can hardly harm so large a host as we have here."

"Nay," said Bohemond, "but I would not like to have our backs to them while we are intent on crossing the Vardar—for from the looks of the river, it will be a mighty undertaking to get the men across. And also, it seems almost a sin to overlook these blasphemies."

"My lord," said one of the other knights who had entered the town. "I wish you could have seen the malice in their eyes, the contempt they had for the cross. Such heretics are not fit to live!"

"Should we send them a priest?" Tancred asked his uncle.

Bohemond shrugged. "I do not think there can be any use in that. All the clergy we have brought with us are simple folk. They can mumble a mass and grant confession, but I doubt that any of them could reason with these rebels. No, we must deal with them in another way."

Without any further discussion, Bohemond gathered two hundred picked lances and thundered off toward the village of heretics. It was too far away to hear any screams or clashes of weapons, but soon a pillar of black smoke ascended into the white winter sky. In less than an hour, Bohemond returned, leaving only a pile of ash and charred sticks where the town had once been.

Now he could order the main body of the army to proceed on its way to the Vardar. There would be no vengeful villagers lurking in the hills behind them—the two hundred lances had made sure of that.

The Vardar River was as engorged as the earlier view from the plateau had augured. The brown, turgid water swept through the valley like a despot, ordering everything in its path to stand aside. It was too deep for a stallion to cross without being swept off his feet, and a man on foot would stand little chance in the current. The Normans staked out a hasty campsite a quarter mile from the torrent while their leaders devised a strategy to conquer the river.

"We must have boats—there's no way around that," said Bohemond.

"And where would we be finding those?" demanded Tancred's brother-in-law, Richard of Salerno. He sat on a stump, rolling his dagger back and forth between his hands. "Recall that you just burnt the nearest village, along with any watercraft they might have had."

Bohemond shot a withering glance at his cousin. "There are bound to be other settlements along this river. Take a company of my men, Richard. You'll go upstream and I'll go down. Seize barges, rafts, fishing boats—anything you can find. And one more thing, sweet cousin: leave your strumpet here. I wager it will make you hurry more on your mission knowing there will be no women for you till you return."

Tancred was left with the bulk of the army to guard the camp. He quickly put his men in defensive position and ordered all the knights to be on alert. Most of the men instinctively planted themselves with their backs to the river, afraid of the country they had just passed through and keeping a wary eye on the dissipating smoke of the smoldering fire.

"Is that where you think an attack would come from?" asked Ralph, glancing in the direction of the heretic village. Perhaps there were more of those folk in the hills, gathering arms to come down and avenge their brethren.

"Not necessarily," said Tancred. He looked beyond them at the opposite bank of the Vardar, craggy and uneven with only a few forlorn pine trees braving the sandy soil. The eastern hills rose ominously in the background, looking like the back of a mangy dog with their scattered stands of evergreens.

"We know what is behind us, but the land that lies ahead is not so sure. We'll keep a good watch riverward as well as in the rear. I've a suspicion those eastern hills are not as empty as they look."

The men grumbled a little when Tancred ordered a double watch over the camp. Their grumbling ceased around midnight when the first of the beacons appeared across the river. It changed to uneasiness when the beacons multiplied and to trepidation when the glow filled the whole far side of the riverbank. "Where is Lord Tancred?" shrilled a nervous sentry, running to the marquis' tents with his report.

"Yes, man, I've seen the fires," said Tancred curtly as the tent flap opened. He was fully armored and had not lain down for more than an hour that night. Seated on a chest and holding a guttering candle, he was perusing some maps that delineated the rest of the route to Constantinople.

"There are hundreds of them! What are we to do?" asked the frightened soldier, his Adam's apple bobbing up and down like a man trying to swim in choppy seas. Tancred looked at him pityingly. This must be his first campaign.

"Wait till morning's light," said Tancred, "and see if they're friend or foe. We cannot cross that torrent, and I wager that even if they have boats, they'd never dare to float them in the dark."

The callow sentry left, impressed with his leader's unflappable demeanor. Alone again, except for his sleeping manservant, Tancred sighed heavily and forbade his mind to speculate on the identity of the men across the river. He must take his own advice and wait patiently for the morning.

As the marquis sat up in the darkness awake and alert, a subtle combination of outside sounds afforded him the singular sensation that someone was prowling around the perimeter of his tent. Could the owner of one of those campfires have swum the river and snuck past the sentries? Or was a member of his own entourage lurking in the shadows outside? He looked over at Ralph's quiet form and considered waking him to go investigate, but the peaceful rise and fall of the old man's wrinkled chest decided him against it. Even though his own nerves were on edge, there was no reason to spoil another's sleep.

Standing up quickly, Tancred jerked open the flap of the tent. No monsters materialized. He walked the perimeter carefully. Nothing attacked him besides a light sprinkling of winter rain. Shaking his tired head with annoyance, he went inside and, by force of will, constrained himself to lie down.

And at the same time, a darkly cloaked figure crept out of the shadows nearby and silently slipped away. The marquis was too vigilant now, but there would be another time and another opportunity.

# Chapter 9

The gray, misty morning broke to reveal rank upon rank of mounted men on the far bank of the Vardar, ranged in tight rows like the teeth of a shark. Tancred's keen eye told him that they were light cavalry, armed with bows and arrows and with only a few pieces of chain mail amongst them. But though their quality was doubtful, their sheer quantity was indisputably daunting.

"Turcopoles," said Ralph with a condescending snort. "An armed knight could take on five of them and win."

"Good to hear," said Tancred sarcastically, "since they outnumber us by that much or more. Do you think they are the emperor's, here to punish us for the burning of that village?"

"Unlikely," replied Ralph. "If they do belong to Alexios, he would sooner thank us and give us gifts. He's been trying to root out those heretic Manichees for years. Perhaps they are friendly. An imperial escort to Constantinople?"

A barrage of pointed arrows quickly dispelled that notion. Tancred ordered the Normans to fall back, putting them beyond the short range of the Turcopoles' curved bows. After that, things were at a standstill. The enemy seemed to have no intention of entering the swollen river but also no intention of departing. But if the Norman army was to reach Constantinople, the Vardar must be crossed. There was no way around it.

"Let us hope that my uncle and brother-in-law have not run into this same hornet nest," said Tancred. He was forced to acknowledge to himself that he would be a little relieved when Bohemond returned to resume command of the army.

"Let us hope so indeed," replied Ralph. "I assume you'll order no action until your uncle returns?"

"Certainly not," said Tancred. "Until then, we wait—wait and go to confession. I'll have the men take shifts on guard and in going to the priest. Ash Wednesday—fitting that this day should be the beginning of our sufferings. We have met the first true obstacle on the road to Jerusalem."

It was another two days of deadlock before Bohemond and Richard returned from their scavenging. Richard's group was virtually empty handed, but Bohemond had secured several watercraft suitable for transporting horses and men.

"Well met!" said Tancred, raising an arm to salute the approaching party.

"I see you've been busy," said Bohemond, sliding hurriedly off the side of his giant charger. His face, usually clean-shaven, had the light scruff of four days' beard on it. He cast darting glances over the river at the enemy forces. "Have they made you any overtures?"

"Only a volley of arrows," said Tancred. His eyes were bleary. He had hardly dared to sleep during those last few days, for he knew that he must render an account to Bohemond for the army. "We've sat two nights under constant guard, but they've made no move to cross the river."

"Why should they?" demanded Richard of Salerno. "They're doubtless meant to hold us here till another group can find a shallow crossing and circle around our camp. We'll have Turcopoles behind and before!" He spoke loudly, and several of the men-at-arms standing nearby exchanged furtive glances with furrowed brows. They began to talk quietly among themselves.

"Idiot!" said Bohemond, slapping Richard on the shoulder with his glove. "There's no need to alarm the men."

"If there is cause for that concern," said Tancred, "then we should act now. Cross the river with the boats you've brought! Let's chase away their scrawny mounts before they can surround us."

Bohemond frowned and scratched the stubble on his cheeks. Tancred could tell that he was weighing the odds in his mind. "It were better to wait," he said slowly. "I would not risk an assault in open boats and against such numbers."

And so, despite the growing fear of a stealthy attack from behind, the Normans circled their tents and bided their time. The Turcopoles on the far bank of the Vardar showed no signs of abandoning their position. They rode their small horses up and down the bank letting out unintelligible yells of challenge, but they made no move to enter the swirling brown waters.

After another half week of irritable inactivity, Tancred could bear it no longer. He went out to the river to see what could be done. Pacing the shore, he found that the spring flooding had receded slightly. The river, instead of rushing precipitously through the valley, hemmed and hawed a little like a phlegmatic schoolmaster. And furthermore, the Turcopoles after so many days of idleness seemed to have grown lax in discipline. Tancred saw many of their horses untethered, grazing haphazardly on the hills while their masters napped.

The gray afternoon had just begun to take on the chill of evening when Tancred descended upon his tent. "Unfurl my pennant, Ralph," he commanded. "I mean to ride into battle before night falls."

"Your uncle's orders?" asked Ralph hesitantly, as he unwrapped the great blue cloth checkered with red and white.

"My own," said Tancred with a grunt.

Ralph clucked his tongue and drew in a great breath. In former days, he had been quite free with his advice to the novice commander. But this new Tancred, with his abject contrition of soul and absolute certainty of mind, eluded the old warrior's understanding. "I thought the job of a rearguard captain was to go *behind* the army," Ralph said circumspectly.

"Not today," said Tancred definitively. He fastened the straps on his helmet. From underneath the metal noseguard he issued a clipped order for his men to assemble. Ralph, seeing that it would be dangerous to beard the lion that had awoken, held his peace and muttered a short prayer for divine favor.

The Norman knights in the young marquis' contingent responded to his orders with incredulity. "Cross the river into that horde?" asked red-haired Turold. "Why, it's madness!"

"Madder to remain planted on this riverbank, waiting—nay, begging—for them to encircle us," said Tancred. He quelled their grumbling with an angry look and forbade the men to speak another word. Losing no time, he commandeered Bohemond's boats that lay listlessly on the shore like so many empty husks. "Half of you dismount and fill the bottoms of these boats," Tancred told his men. "The rest of you enter the river on horse—the current has abated enough for your beasts to swim."

True to Tancred's pronouncement, the waters had lost some of their turbulence. Only a few knights suffered mishap when their frightened horses began to flail their hooves, but even these managed to keep afloat by holding onto the tails of their animals.

The boats had nearly reached the far bank before the ignorant Turcopoles sensed their danger. A jabber went up from the enemy camp as the irregular troops scrambled to collect their shaggy ponies. Wearing only light armor and carrying bows, these hill warriors had a much easier time mounting than a Norman knight would have. Several of them had swung into the saddle by the time the boats scraped to a halt on the rising riverbed.

Tancred, having swum his charger across the stream with little difficulty, reached the far bank at the same time as the watercraft. At the marquis' command, the soldiers in the boats threw up a roof of shields, screening themselves from the whirring arrows as they disembarked. Authority radiated from Tancred like heat from the summer sun, and, recognizing this, the Turcopoles pointed their bows in his direction trying to bring down the leader and his horse. All around the bank of the river the arrows fell like hail and the shafts planted themselves in the dirt like a field of grain.

But though the Turcopoles could fire with great speed, they were poor judges of distance. Alert as a hunted fox, Tancred watched where each previous volley had fallen. With a quick dig of the heels, he led his horse to that very spot, trusting that the next volley would fall behind him on the ground he had just left.

While the enemy archers were thus distracted with Tancred's nimbleness, the rest of his troop was able to cross the river. Once the Norman knights closed quarters with the Turcopoles, the fight was as good as over. The leather jerkins of the enemy were no match for the lances of the heavily armored Norman knights. Yelping like frightened dogs, the enemy took to the hills leaving the Vardar valley clear for the army of Crusaders.

Bohemond had been almost as slow to realize his nephew's intentions as the Turcopoles themselves. When he finally became aware of the sortie, Tancred's troop had already passed the point of recall. Bracing himself for the worst, Bohemond quickly ordered the remainder of the army to form up in ranks on the near side of the river. He assumed that once Tancred was cut to pieces, the Turcopoles would cross the water and wreak vengeance on the rest of them.

To Bohemond's surprise, however, he soon saw the enemy cavalry retreating. His squinting eyes noted with pleasure the bloody wake that Tancred had hewed through their host. Now was the time to advance and press the victory home. Bohemond's knights, following the example set for them, plunged into the river with their steeds and allowed the high-mettled chargers to bear them across the waves. Bohemond himself arrived on the far shore in time to witness a total rout.

There was Tancred, streaked in blood, calmly ordering the disposal of the enemy prisoners and their gear. He greeted Bohemond with a smile, his teeth glowing like polished ivory amidst the gory grime that speckled his face. "God give you good den, uncle!" he said triumphantly. "The spoil has been collected, and I await your orders to determine the fate of our prisoners."

# Chapter 10

Before the light had completely gone, Bohemond interviewed the two dozen prisoners taken by Tancred's men. They were warriors by trade, originating in the northern lands beside the Black Sea. When the Byzantines overran their land, they had made shift as best they could, hiring out their bows and arrows to their conquerors. In mongrel Greek they assured Bohemond that they had no ill will toward the Norman host. They had intercepted them solely on the orders of Alexios, the Emperor of the Byzantines. "That king promise us many coin, if you Normans never reach great city," said one of the captives, a chubby fellow with a dirty sash wrapped several times around his waist.

"Treachery!" cried Richard of Salerno. He leaped on the poor man whose lips had made the confession. His dagger was out and he would have slit the Turcopole's fleshy throat if Bohemond had not pulled him off.

Tancred was more restrained than his brother-in-law but no less displeased. The emperor who had called for their aid had dealt them a blow from behind. What further perfidy could they expect when they reached Constantinople? Tancred loosened the chainmail coif from about his neck. His nostrils flared as he scraped the dried blood from his cheeks. Angrily, he demanded what Bohemond intended to do now.

"Do?" asked Bohemond coolly. "Why, I shall dismiss them to return to Alexios with my sincerest apologies. We cannot afford to be making enemies of the emperor."

Tancred's weary limbs sank into a chair with disbelief. "Enemies? Has not the emperor already proclaimed that we are such with this ambush!"

Bohemond shook his head. "You are making too much of this skirmish. A simple misunderstanding! And if we take no offense, why then there is no harm done. We will release these prisoners and proceed in peace. Alexios will thank us when we reach his capital."

"Why do you wish to curry favor with him?" demanded Tancred. "He is not the leader of this Crusade—Pope Urban has appointed a bishop for us to follow."

"Truly, Tancred, you are still as simple as a peahen. Alexios' goodwill is paramount. It is he who has asked for our aid, and it is he under whom we will serve."

"You will serve the eastern emperor?"

"Yes, as will you. When we arrive at Constantinople, he will doubtless require our allegiance. You *will* render it."

Tancred laughed harshly. "I have already sworn my fealty. The bishop of Rome is my liege, and I am bound to him body and soul. I am here to fulfill his commands and regain the Holy Sepulcher."

"A noble goal," said Bohemond dryly, "but Jerusalem is only one city among many. There are other kingdoms to be had in the East, and with the help of Alexios we can make them our own!"

"And when you have had Alexios' help, what then? Will you continue to serve him faithfully as your lord?"

Bohemond was silent.

"So this is your plan then," said Tancred, "to wheedle your way into the emperor's good graces, carve out a kingdom—perhaps from his own territory—then show him the fig to his face. And what of Jerusalem? I suspected that you never cared much for her, and I was right." He spat. "God keep me far from such false-hearted schemes."

He would have walked away then, but Bohemond's piercing eye caught his. "Tancred," said Bohemond levelly. "It is better that you should stay friends with me."

"So says my mother," said Tancred, bitterly remembering the promise he had made back in Bari. "Very well, we shall continue on together. But know this, uncle—the day you forsake the road to Jerusalem is the day that we part ways."

"And until that time will you do as I bid, as my lieutenant and my right hand?"

"I will obey you in all things, saving what touches upon my honor and upon the success of this crusade."

"So be it," said Bohemond. And thus a truce was brokered between them.

Bohemond, as he had indicated, released the prisoners and sent them away with their horses, under pledge that they would convey his compliments to the emperor of Constantinople. The Norman army continued its march through the eastern half of the Vardar basin, and Tancred resumed his position in the rearguard.

Still piqued that the Turcopoles had been intentionally set upon them by the emperor, the young marquis increased his vigilance. In the months since their departure from Bari, his body had grown harder, used to the cold of this eastern countryside and inured to the deprivation of sleep. He was the first to wake each morning and the last to lie down after the tent stakes had been driven.

Tancred's own men, seeing that he never asked any hardship of them that he did not undergo as well, had grown a new respect for their young commander. Following his example, they had filed their own readiness and mental awareness down to a sharp point. By day each of the marquis' five hundred lances watched the horizon like an unhooded hawk. By night they sniffed out the camp perimeter like a pack of bloodhounds.

But if Alexios had indeed wished to forcibly halt their march, the return of his humiliated Turcopoles must have changed his mind. There was no recurrence of the riverside ambush.

With the Vardar River conquered, the landward journey was more than half completed and the roughest of the terrain had been crossed. As the men threaded their way through the foothills of the

Balkan Mountains, they encountered few inhabitants. The stolid Bulgars ignored their presence. When pressed, they provided plain food for honest coin but more often they retreated behind the walls of their stick cottages or hillside forts.

Tancred, who often went out to forage, learned that Hugh the Great had passed this way several months ago before the winter rains had begun in earnest. Once again, there was no word of William, and Tancred could only hope that he had met with no misfortune along the way. Ralph was reassuring in that matter. "I think you'll find," said the old man dryly, "that when you're not there to coddle him, your brother William is quite able to care for himself."

A few of the more loquacious Bulgars also told of a larger army, approaching from the north, that had already reached Constantinople. "They say that it is led by three brothers—Germans," reported Tancred to his uncle, "and that they have been camping outside the great city since Christmas."

Bohemond frowned and, soon after this intelligence, bade the company increase their pace. Richard of Salerno laughed at this sudden change. "My cousin is afraid that these Germans will ingratiate themselves with the emperor before he has had time to exercise his own charms. We must hurry, hurry, hurry, eh, Tancred?"

The breakneck pace that Bohemond had set for them left little time for rest. Tancred retired to his tent each night exhausted, his thighs and buttocks aching from so much time in the saddle and his eyes attempting to close of their own accord. If it were not for Ralph's ministrations he would often have fallen asleep in his boots and his chainmail, too tired to be bothered by their presence.

On one blustery night Ralph was taken sick—he had dined that night at the mess in front of Richard of Salerno's tent, and something rotten in the campfire stew had left his bowels in agony. Instead of sleeping on the floor of Tancred's tent as was his wont, he had taken himself off to the corner of the camp that served as the infirmary. God willing, one of the priests knew an herb that would alleviate the pain. Left to fend for himself, Tancred did very little fending. Without even taking the time to wash the grime from his stubbly cheeks, the marquis fell upon his pallet, covered himself with a woven blanket, and closed his throbbing eyes.

When lying down to slumber in a well-disciplined camp, a soldier usually expects to be awakened by the soft gray light at dawn. For Tancred that night was full of the unexpected.

All was silent in the camp save the wild wind. The only feet that should have been moving were the sentries' as they stamped them to keep warm. But strangely enough, a pair of unexplainable footsteps was tracing a line from one side of the Norman camp to the other. They stopped at the marquis' pavilion where—thanks to Ralph's mysterious malady—Tancred lay sleeping alone.

His body comatose with exhaustion, Tancred registered none of the sounds of the intruder's tiptoes or his shallow breathing. The figure, heavily mantled, paused at the side of the bed. Perhaps he had second thoughts about the enterprise at hand. Perhaps he was just waiting for his eyes to acclimate to the blackness in the tent.

The intruder carefully discerned the outline of Tancred's body under the blanket. Slowly—ever so slowly—he slid back the right side of his mantle where an unsheathed dagger waited in his hand. He raised the weapon high, like the sacrificial blade of some ancient priest. Then, driving it with calculated force, he thrust the dagger sharply through the corner of the blanket that covered Tancred's heart.

But the assassin had not counted on the chainmail corselet that was also covering the same spot. The blade tip turned on the metal rings, and what was meant to be a deathblow left only grazed skin and an eventual purple-yellow bruise.

Although the armor bore the brunt of the attack, the shock that beset the sleeper was still acute. Tancred bounded to his feet with a yell. He struck out instinctively with his powerful arms, caught the intruder in the jaw with his fist, and nearly knocked him to the floor of the tent. Screeching like a parakeet, the unwelcome night guest made a wide swing at Tancred with the dagger. But Tancred caught his wrist, and spinning him around, pinioned his arms to his side while enveloping him in a close hold from behind.

It was at that moment that the marquis came to realize that the man who had come to kill him that night had a distinctly womanly body beneath the mantle that he wore.

# Chapter II

"Hold still," said Tancred roughly, removing the dagger from his assailant's hands as one takes a toy from a naughty child. He shoved the unarmed creature into the corner farthest from the tent flap while he fumbled in the darkness to strike a light. The flint sparked, the beeswax candle accepted the flame from Tancred's tinder, and immediately his quarters were bathed in a yellow glow. Now the marquis could see his would-be assassin, kneeling by the edge of the tent, trying to loosen one of the stake-fastened ropes so that she could wriggle under the side and out to freedom.

"Stop that," said Tancred. He pulled her away from the thin wall and yanked off the voluminous hood of her mantle. Underneath was the face of a young woman not long out of childhood. Her cheeks still curved with the roundness of youth and her lower lip jutted out with a petulance unbecoming in a more mature lady. Several scratches and bruises, besides the one Tancred had just recently planted on her jaw, added even more color to her warm toned skin. She had seen her share of mistreatment in this world—that was evident.

Her dark chestnut hair, left to its own devices, would have sprung wildly with curls, but she had pulled it back tightly and bound it in a rigid knot at the nape of her neck. The masculine clothing she wore—a belted tunic and hose—was obviously sewn for someone of larger build. It bagged upon her like St. Bartholomew's empty skin. She was as unlikely an assassin as Tancred had ever set eyes upon, and yet not five minutes ago she had tried to stab a dagger through his breastbone.

"Who are you?" demanded the marquis, holding her by her shoulders at arm's-length, and looking down upon her sternly.

She pressed her lips together tightly to forestall any possibility of the answer slipping out. Her brown eyes flashed like the sky in a thunderstorm, and tilting her face upward to front his, she spat as hard as she could.

Annoyed, he wiped his face on his sleeve and dug his fingers into her arms more tightly. "I have seen you before," he said, his mind running through the catalogue of female faces that had accompanied the Normans on their journey. Most were strumpets who had formerly plied their trade in Bari, smuggled aboard the ships by soldiers who found the prospect of a lengthy pilgrimage too lonely an undertaking. This one's round face had a warm olive tint—she was clearly bred in southern lands, and Tancred surmised that she was Greek in origin. He remembered that Richard had boasted of giving passage to just such a girl, and pulling a dragnet through his recollections, he dredged up an image of her in the company of Salerno.

"You are my brother-in-law's doxy," pronounced Tancred. "Is that so?"

Still she made no answer.

"If you'll not admit to it, I'll send for him and see if he can put a name to you." Releasing the girl, he walked toward the opening of the tent, ready to summon a guard who would in turn summon Richard.

The girl had shown little fear up until now, but seeing that Tancred intended to make good his threat, she flinched visibly like one who puts his hand in the fire. Darting like a swallow, she overtook Tancred before he had time to whistle for one of the sentries. Pleadingly, she grabbed hold of his arm. Her sullen countenance had reshaped itself, and she gave Tancred a smile intended to be beguiling. "Please, my lord, there is no need to tell him that I have been here. It will be much the worse for me if he hears of it."

Tancred stared at her beseeching eyes and burst into astonished laughter. "You creep into my tent to murder me in the dead of night, and then ask me to do favors for you afterward?" He shook off her hold on him and sat down cross-legged on his pallet, his scornful glance showing how harmless he rated her.

Her eyes narrowed. She did not like to be made light of. "But I did not murder you, did I?" she said, a little bitterly. "In fact, you do not seem to have suffered the slightest scathe."

"What possessed you?" asked the marquis, leaning back with a weary groan. "In sooth, unless you are a madwoman, I cannot think why you would attempt such a thing!" His voice became short and clipped. "Tell me now or I will take you back to Richard's tent and have it out with you there."

She took a deep breath as if she were weighing the terrible consequences of speech against the awful cost of silence. "Will you promise not to harm me—or let him harm me—if I tell you?"

"On my honor, you shall be as safe in this camp as my lady mother would be," said Tancred perfunctorily, too curious to forgo the pledge she desired. "Now, come! What causes have conspired to make you desire my death?"

"It is a long story."

"There is half the night left to hear it. Sit down. I am determined to hear this out."

Compelled by the eloquence of his threats, she sat down, sighed, and began her tale, adopting the formal tone of a traveling storyteller.

"My father was born in Bari in the days when Byzantium still ruled. His name was Alexander, called that after his own father who was a respected merchant there. The old man had shares in half a dozen ships that sailed to Constantinople, Cyprus, Jaffa, and Alexandria. When he died, Alexander and his young brother Nicholas inherited the business. Through industry, Alexander increased the family holdings until he was one of the richest merchants in Bari.

"But such prosperity was not long to last. Your people, the Normans, had been as busy as bloodhounds putting the Byzantines at bay in Italy. Not long after my grandfather's death, Robert Guiscard took Bari with an iron fist and brought it under the Norman yoke...."

"Guiscard was *my* grandfather," said Tancred proudly.

Her brows contracted into a thick line. Tancred could not tell if she were more angry at his ancestry or at the interruption. "If you want to hear my story, you had best keep quiet!" she ordered, as autocratic as a bailiff to a tenant in arrears.

The girl cleared her throat. "My father was permitted to continue his trade, but the greedy taxes of our new overlords left little enough to live upon once the ships' wares were sold in the marketplace. My young uncle Nicholas, about to come of age, saw that the family business was not to be depended upon and so he ceded his share over to my father and apprenticed himself to a goldsmith.

"In the course of time my father married. She was a native of Bari by the name of Constantina, a beauty but with no dowry to speak of. She bore to Alexander seven children, but all of them wenches and worse than worthless at increasing the family's fortunes."

"Which one of the seven are you?" asked Tancred, giving an involuntary yawn.

She withered him with a glance. "The eldest, of course."

"Little Constantina, no doubt," he said with condescension.

"Alexandra," she replied haughtily, "after my father." Swallowing her annoyance, she continued the tale.

"When I was still a little girl…"

"You're hardly more than that now," objected Tancred. He was really beginning to enjoy tormenting her with his constant interruptions. It almost made up for the throbbing bruise on his left pectoral.

Alexandra raised her voice to drown out his. "When I was still a little girl, I used to go sit with my father at his stall in the market. He would let me lay out the skeins of colored silk and unstop my favorite perfume bottles for a quick sniff. The people of the town would gather round to feel and smell the luxuries on our table, and strangers too who had come to Bari by land or sea.

"One day, a young oaf of a Norman—tall and blond and thinking himself the owner of the whole world—strode up to our booth and began to finger the gold and silver chains that glittered proudly on display. He was careless with his money, or at least seemed that way, for when he chose the bauble he wanted, he tossed my father his whole purse and bade him take what he needed in payment."

Tancred frowned. He was beginning to resent the shape that this story was taking. "And what did your father do?" he asked, his low voice acquiring the hint of a lion's growl in it.

"He took the purse and emptied it, separated out two bezants for the price of the chain, and then gave the money back to you!"

"And what did I do?" asked Tancred, his voice rising a little to meet hers. The pretense was up now. The girl was about to make her accusation plain.

"You looked in your purse and said that he had cheated you. Then, pulling a knife out of your belt, you stabbed him where he stood!"

Tancred looked at the young, impassioned face, inflamed with the disease of bitterness. Compared to hers his countenance was old and worn, and God knows that tonight he was tired enough to have lived half a century. He had an explanation—a good one in most men's minds—for what he had done. He knew that if he told it to her she would not believe him; or even if she did, her hate was so powerful that the explanation would not matter.

"You said he had not given you back the right change!" she said hotly. "But he did, I saw it! I watched him count the coins back into the bag."

Tancred shook his head. "The number of coins was correct, but they were not the same coins that I had given him. He switched them out with other bezants that contained only a fraction of the gold that they ought to have carried."

"What?" she asked in outrage. "Do you say he gave you counterfeit coin?"

"Aye," said Tancred simply. "I know he did."

The thought of such fraudulent dealing on her parent's part had never entered her head. "Where would my father get counterfeit coin? He had not the means!"

"How should I know where?" asked Tancred shrugging his shoulders helplessly. "Although you did say that his brother Nicholas was apprenticed to a goldsmith. Your uncle would have had the knowledge to make false bezants or the access to obtain them."

She opened her mouth to protest, then closed it again in silence. Her full lower lip began to tremble. A counterfeiter was sure to be found out more times than once. Tancred suspected that sometime in the past a similar accusation had surfaced against dear Uncle Nicholas. This concatenation of evidence was starting to topple her time-honored version of events.

Red marks appeared on her cheekbones and her voice shrilled higher. "It does not matter! Whether he tried to cheat you or no, it was not a killing offense. His blood is still upon your head! If you die, God will require it of you."

"Yes," said Tancred quietly. "That I know." He was sitting on the edge of the pallet now, no longer deriving enjoyment from chaffing his would-be executioner.

"Oh?" said Alexandra, somewhat taken aback. She had never expected him to agree with her.

"I am reminded of it every moment my mind is at rest and more often than not in my dreams as well. It is one of the reasons I came on this Crusade, to receive remission of my sins and save my soul eternally."

"Remission of your sins?"

"If I devote my life to deliver Jerusalem, the mortal sins I have committed will be wiped away from the scroll of judgment. The blood-guilt I bear for your father will pass away like the evening shadows when morning comes."

"How can you be sure of this?" she asked with perturbation. The prospect seemed to occasion as much distress for her as it did hope for the marquis.

"Pope Urban has promised it," said Tancred, "to me and to the other true pilgrims on this venture. That is why I seek Jerusalem without delay."

Alexandra bit her lip in vexation. A few chestnut curls had escaped from the tight knot in which they were bound and fell, Medusa-like, across her face. "Well then," she said angrily, confiding too much of her intentions in the manner of youth. "I see that I must make the most of the journey ahead of us and end your life before Jerusalem is reached. I would not want you to die *after* your guilt is purged away." Her gaze wandered over to the table with the candle where Tancred had laid her deadly weapon. She made a dash for it.

"Not again, you little hussy!" said Tancred. Surprisingly agile for a man of his size, he leaped up from his bed and reached her just as she reached for the dagger. Trapping her two slim wrists in one hand, he grabbed the candle in his other. "Back to your den, viper," he said, preparing to haul her out of the tent and across the camp to Richard's quarters.

"No!" she shrieked. "You promised you would not bring me back there!" She refused to walk in front of him, and small as she was, her struggling frame was more weight than the marquis could carry comfortably all the way to Richard's tent. "You promised I would be as safe as your own mother in this camp! You know what he will do to me!"

Tancred did know. He would beat her within a finger length of her life and enjoy it as roundly as a Christmas dinner. The marquis dropped her like a slippery eel, and ran his hand through his hair wearily. "God help me! This is the devil's own dilemma. If I bring you back to Richard and allow him punish you like you deserve, I am forsworn. If I let you stay here, I am liable to be murdered the minute my back is turned. And all I want, all I really want right now, is for you to vanish like an Arab jinn so I can close my eyes and get some sleep."

Alexandra shrugged, indicating that the problem was none of her own making. "I suppose you'll have to stay up all night and keep guard over me."

Tancred glared at her coldly. "I have a much better solution than that."

# Chapter 12

When Ralph returned to Tancred's tent in the morning, tired and gray but rid of his gripes, he found a mass of ropes encircling the center pole of the tent with what looked to be a young lady all knotted up inside the tangle. The marquis, normally no layabout, was still sprawled in a sleepy stupor. His face was buried in the straw pallet while his right hand perched atop the hilt of the naked sword that lay beside him.

Confused by the peculiar scene, Ralph immediately set about shaking Tancred awake. He realized his mistake when the marquis' fingers folded instinctively around the sword hilt. Startled into action, Tancred began brandishing it bleary-eyed at the old retainer.

"It's only me, master!" said Ralph hastily, averting disaster by jumping clear of the blade's arc.

"Oh, Ralph," mumbled Tancred, his head beginning to clear. Briefly, he related to his manservant the story of his midnight adventure with Alexandra: the bungled assassination, her family history in Bari, and her continued determination to put an end to his own life.

Ralph assessed the situation and identified the easiest way to rid themselves of this dangerous damsel. "I shall return her to your brother-in-law."

"No," said Tancred. "She took passage with Richard merely because she thought it would be a convenient way to follow me and wreak her revenge. But I think, by now, she's found out the folly of throwing in her lot with strange men. She begged me not to bring her back to him, and in a moment of stupidity, I pledged my word that I would see to her safety."

Tancred lowered his voice. "Though between you and me, I'd be loath to return any woman to his care—my own sister included. This one is covered with welts and bruises as far as the eye can see, and I'm sure there are more under that oversized tunic she's wearing."

A movement from the center of the tent caught his eye. Someone was listening to their conversation. "Not that you don't deserve to be beaten!" said the marquis, raising his voice and looking at his prisoner ferociously.

"Beat me all you like," said Alexandra petulantly, "as long as you untie me first. I've never spent a night in more discomfort!"

"False!" replied Tancred. "I heard you snoring in those ropes long before I could convince my eyes to close."

"I fear I must claim the most discomfort out of the present company," said Ralph with acerbity and with good reason. He turned to Tancred. "Your sweet guest is about as successful a poisoner as she is a knife-wielder, but even her failures do leave some painful results."

Poison is a weapon particularly distasteful to a man of action, for it is the one weapon he can least defend against. Tancred looked at Alexandra in disgust, but she did not even have the grace to blush. It had not been easy for her to think of a way to incapacitate the marquis' servant—and ensure that she would find Tancred alone in his tent. She seemed quite proud of the result she had produced.

"What's to be done with her then?" asked Ralph, perplexed.

"I suppose we'll have to bring her along with us," said Tancred with a sigh, "and keep her well hidden from Richard if I'm to keep my promise. When we reach Constantinople I'll find a ship to stow her in that will take her back to Bari, but until then, we'd best watch her like Argus and keep her clear of the cook pot."

By day, Tancred assigned Ralph to keep watch over Alexandra, and the manservant, somewhat vengefully, sequestered her in a supply wagon full of pickled fish. When she complained about the noxious stench of the herring, Ralph told her it was for the good of all concerned. "With pickled fish as your perfume, sweetheart, men will be able to smell you coming and know when to take to their heels."

By night, Tancred cautiously committed the girl to the ruthless care of the rope. She had made no pretense of giving up her quest for revenge, and Tancred knew it was not safe to let her roam about untrammeled. He had taken away her dagger, but in a military camp, there were plenty of sharp implements lying about unguarded.

Not many days elapsed before Richard of Salerno came to inquire about his wench. It was evening. The day's march was done and Ralph had just ushered Alexandra into Tancred's tent fresh from the fish wagon. "Your brother-in-law's on his way here," he said urgently, "and he's not strolling about with his usual loiter. Someone must have told him some falderol about you stealing his girl!"

Without further ado, Tancred bustled off Alexandra to hide behind some wine barrels in the back of the tent. They were his own private store of the dark red Italian vintage, and to keep the overeager men-at-arms from tapping the bunghole, he had ordered Ralph to keep them with his personal effects. "Keep quiet!" the marquis hissed at the girl, and strangely enough, she complied. He lay down on his bed and prepared himself to lie through his teeth when Salerno came to collect her.

He did not have long to wait. Within minutes, Richard's large, aquiline nose was poking itself through the flap of Tancred's tent, and his slight frame stepped inside without so much as a by your leave. "Where's my woman, Tancred?" he said brusquely, forgoing any of his usual crude pleasantries.

"I believe you left my sister Altrude behind in Italy," said Tancred in clear, crisp tones. He quite enjoyed playing the moralistic brother-in-law with his rakish relative.

"And last I heard she is thriving beautifully with me gone and my money there," said Richard, playing along with Tancred's quip. He adopted a more ingratiating tone of voice. "But to come to the point, rumor tells me you've been enjoying yourself with my little Greek girl, Alexandra—which I don't begrudge you in the least. But when you're done with her, I do want her put back where she belongs."

"In Bari?" asked Tancred, with raised eyebrows.

Richard laughed. "Of course not—in my tent!"

Tancred stared at him, refusing to join in his mirth. "No," he said with the firmness and finality of a royal decree.

"What do you mean?" asked Richard, his eyes narrowing with apprehension.

"I mean that even if I did have this girl—what do you call her? Cassandra?—I'd be of no mind to hand her over to you."

The frown that suffused the lord of Salerno's face was as dark as Burgundian wine. "Now, see here, Tancred…."

"What is there to see?" asked the marquis.

Richard opened his mouth and closed it again, looking for all the world like the carp in his castle's moat.

"Go on, tell me!" said Tancred, "You're brave enough with your dogs, your horses, and your half-grown women!"

It was easy to bandy cross words with a man who weighed four stone less than himself, but then, to Tancred's credit, he had never scrupled to cross men of his own size as well. The marquis' bravado might have served to send Richard away disgruntled had not a vociferous—and distinctly feminine—sneeze suddenly erupted from the back of the tent. The old wine barrels had proved too dusty for Alexandra's sensitive nose.

"Ha!" said Richard triumphantly. "So she is here, you villain!" He pushed past Ralph, intending to seize his fugitive by her tangled curls and drag her out into the open. But before he had gone far, he found his brother-in-law's broad chest blocking his way.

"Get out of my quarters!" said Tancred with vehemence, his tongue adopting a tone that no one could mistake for jocularity.

Richard snorted contemptuously. He tried to duck past the younger man, but the marquis' fingers closed on his forearm like the jaw of a lion. Richard was affronted by this ill usage. He roared to be released. Tancred smiled and refused. And that was when the lord of Salerno used his free hand to draw the double-edged misericord that lay hidden in the folds of his tunic.

Tancred, who had not expected sharp points from his relative, drew back instinctively at the flash of the blade. His right hand leaped to his own dagger hidden in his boot. He whipped the weapon out of his scabbard while twisting sideways to avoid Salerno's stab.

"Who is the villain now?" asked Tancred hotly. They faced each other with intensity, little more than an arm's reach apart, daggers out, knees slightly bent, and pulses quickening. Alexandra, her olive skin having paled considerably, peered over the rim of her hiding place while Ralph positioned himself to intervene if it appeared that Tancred was getting the worst of it.

But as it turned out, there was no need for the old man to interfere. It was Richard who had drawn his weapon first, and it was Richard who threw down his misericord unbloodied making a dull thud on the hard packed earth. An unfamiliar observer might have ascribed this capitulation to fear over Tancred's greater speed and longer reach. But, for all his faults, Salerno was no coward.

He was, however, a pragmatist. His facile mind recognized that Tancred had no intention of yielding the argument, and that there was nothing to gain by creating an irreparable rift between them. Alexandra was a pretty little gem, but there were others about the camp with almost as much sparkle. "What is a wench between two friends?" he said gesturing widely with open palms. "Put back your blade, Tancred. I wish you joy of her."

If Richard had expected his brother-in-law to reciprocate with expressions of thanks, he was sorely mistaken. Tancred, still hot behind his ears, kicked aside the fallen dagger and ordered the man out of his tent with ill grace. The lord of Salerno voiced a sarcastic farewell and departed. Alexandra, who had been unconsciously holding her breath through the entirety of the encounter, exhaled violently as the tent flap fell closed.

"Do you think he'll be going to Bohemond to complain?" asked Ralph.

"Perhaps," said Tancred carelessly, sitting down and allowing his anger to dissipate. "But my uncle will not interfere between us.

He's too busy hastening to make friends with his precious emperor. Richard will find some new baggage to warm his bed, and in a week he will have forgotten the whole matter. I only wish his anger *would* last and he would take pains to avoid me out of pique.

"You can come out of your hole now, Cassandra," said Tancred, giving a whistle to the pile of wine casks in the corner.

She crawled out from her hiding place indecorously on all fours, the oversized tunic puddling around her. "My name," she said, dusting off her clothes with vigor, "is *Alexandra!*"

"Oh, is it?" replied Tancred. "I'd forgotten already. But never mind that—it's late! I've nearly been stabbed again, thanks to you. And now that I've sent your paramour packing, it's time to strap on your leg irons." He held out a rope invitingly.

She sniffed, holding her head high. "I suppose that in consideration of the good deed you did by driving that monster away, I could promise—just for tonight—to forgo my vengeance." She looked at him through a veil of eyelashes, eager to discover how he would respond to her magnanimity.

"I suppose that in consideration of your promise—just for tonight—I could forgo your restraints," said Tancred, mimicking her girlish accents. He tossed the rope into the corner. "But in case milady should have second thoughts come midnight, I'm wearing my armor to bed."

"I'd wear your helmet too," advised Ralph.

"That won't be necessary!" said Alexandra huffishly. "I gave you my word, did I not?" She curled up on the hard ground and, almost immediately, began to snore, her full lips parted attractively with her soft breathing.

Tancred and Ralph exchanged glances. "That one doesn't need any goose down to soothe her to sleep," said the old manservant. His voice sounded almost grandfatherly in tone.

Tancred looked at him sharply. Apparently, Ralph had spent too much time in the fish wagon with his charge, and unlikely as it seemed, the olive-skinned girl had cozened the old man into a modicum of affection for her. "The sooner we put her on a ship to Bari the better," Tancred reminded him.

"Yes, yes," agreed Ralph hastily. "But Constantinople's still aways off."

"Not so far as you might think," said Tancred morosely. He frowned like a skipper who sees storm clouds on the horizon. As much as he wished to wash his hands of Alexandra, he also knew that their nearness to Constantinople augured an audience with Alexios. Of his own conduct toward the emperor, he had no fears. It was what Bohemond might say and do that worried him.

# Chapter 13

The Norman army was a fortnight distant from the Golden City when Alexios' envoy arrived. They had received messengers from the emperor before now, directing them to certain markets and routes, but this envoy was clearly a man of rank, a man who had stood before the Byzantine emperor in council. He was young, smooth skinned, richly robed, and with the oily demeanor that Tancred had come to recognize as characteristic of the Byzantine nobility. He introduced himself as Michael Podromos. "Our emperor has been watching your progress for some time now," the Byzantine said politely. He held a little golden ball that he played with in his fingers, refusing to set it down even when he spoke.

"Watching how he can thwart us, you mean!" burst out Tancred. Michael Podromos looked from Bohemond to Tancred in consternation. Such plain speaking was not the style of the court from which he came. "Whatever can you mean?" he asked.

"My nephew is overhasty," said Bohemond reassuringly, gripping Tancred's shoulder with a warning hand. "We encountered a few unfriendly horsemen at the Vardar who claimed to be in the emperor's employ. However, I am not so sure that they were telling us the truth."

"Ah," said Michael Podromos, as he spun the little golden ball on his fingertips. "We in Constantinople have heard of this encounter. Our emperor greatly deplores that you were inconvenienced by rogue bandits in his territory. They were certainly none of his sending. Indeed, this letter will show you in how much favor and esteem the emperor holds you."

He handed Bohemond a stiff scroll. The tall Norman instantly unrolled it and his gray eyes scanned the contents. He could not make out all the Greek flourishes, but what he understood satisfied him. He grunted and handed the document to Tancred. "There, you see how well the emperor regards me."

Tancred took the letter and, having imbibed some learning from his scholarly father Odo, read it with less difficulty:

> King Alexios to Bohemond, greetings. I have received news of your arrival with paternal pleasure since you have now undertaken a task worthy of your heritage by turning your eagerness for war against the barbarians. As I see it, God has favored the undertaking of the Franks since he undertook to strengthen them with such a great companion. Your approach promises in its own right an answer to my desires. The very prophets of the Turks foretell your victory over their people. It is well, therefore, for you to hurry, my son, and by coming bring an end to the delays of those leaders with me who await you. The leaders and the magnates and all the people long for you.

Here Tancred stopped and looked up in some disgust. These fulsome praises of Bohemond seemed extravagant and unwarranted.

But were they? Tancred had only been a boy when Bohemond and his father Robert Guiscard took the Byzantine Empire by storm. He did not know firsthand how great a role his uncle had played in that adventure. Tancred had always rolled his eyes at Bohemond's tales of Durazzo and Larissa. Stories grow in prowess with the passage of time, and he had assumed that his uncle had gilded his early conquests and battles in far more glory than they deserved.

Tancred looked down at the Greek words again. Alexios was not rolling his eyes at Bohemond. These compliments indicated three things: that he respected him as a warrior and feared him as an enemy, and also, feared him as an ally. When Alexios had asked for help from the lords of the West, he had not reckoned with Bohemond answering the call. Perhaps the attack by the Turcopoles had been his feeble attempt to send the Norman giant home again. When that maneuver proved futile, he had turned to a more conciliating stratagem sending Podromos with this flattery-filled letter.

Shocked, Tancred realized that Alexios was as anxious to be on good terms with Bohemond as Bohemond was to curry favor with him. He glanced over at his uncle, his head whirling with these new discoveries, then resumed his reading of the letter.

> The Latin heroes are with me and they have been granted generous gifts. But as you are so much better known to me than they, so too you, who have remained behind, will receive even greater gifts. Here, there are garments, gold, horses and all the remaining abundance of the treasury for you. Whatever you have seen anywhere else, it is as nothing in comparison to what is collected here. You should know that everything here is ready for you as if for a son if you are ready to be good and faithful to me like a son.

"Ah," thought Tancred. "There's the rub. 'Good and faithful to me like a son.' He wants Bohemond and the rest of us to bind ourselves to him to serve the good of the Byzantine Empire. But I am here to serve another master, to further the good of Jerusalem, not Constantinople." He pressed on to the conclusion as Alexios set out some private instructions for Bohemond.

> If you begin to set a faster pace, content with only a few men, you will finish your journey more easily. Leave behind the other forces and commanders and the road will be easier. Do not forget the many gifts waiting for you in the city.

The letter ended with some closing salutations. Tancred rolled up the scroll in a tight cylinder with his broad hands, feeling his throat constrict as he did so. The emperor intended to cull Bohemond from their company and then bribe him into the service of Byzantium. The sickening feeling in the pit of his stomach was the knowledge that Alexios' plan would assuredly succeed.

He looked over at Bohemond who was talking animatedly to Michael Podromos. The envoy had reiterated to him all the instructions that he had but vaguely understood from the emperor's letter. On his uncle's face was a smile of supreme delight and gratification, the grin of a wolf who has just had his way with the sheepfold. The treasure house that he had fought so many years to obtain now promised to open of its own accord and shower unlimited wealth upon him.

"So," said Tancred to himself, "my uncle is seduced by the emperor's promises of gold. He will go on ahead and sell himself like the veriest whore for the contents of Constantinople's treasury. Well, I shall remain behind with the army—and no matter how many of the Latin lords swear fealty to that Byzantine snake, I pledge on my father's soul, that I will never say those words."

# Part II

# Alexios

# Chapter 14

I t was the middle of Easter week when Michael Podromos, the Byzantine envoy, had arrived in the Norman camp bearing his sweet-smelling letter from Emperor Alexios. The next day Tancred rose early to celebrate the offices of Holy Thursday. After washing himself and shaving his cheeks cleanly, he went to mass and made confession beside his own knights. The priest, a large, bluff man with only enough learning to administer the basic rites, girded up his robe and prepared a basin of fresh water. Then, in the manner of Christ, he knelt before them and washed their feet with his own hands.

At the priest's prompting, Tancred recited: "I will not give Thee a kiss like Judas, but like the thief I will confess Thee: Remember me, O Lord, in Thy Kingdom." He crossed himself devoutly. This was the first Easter week he had ever celebrated the rites with more than a perfunctory observance. "Remember me, O Lord, in Thy Kingdom." If he could fulfill his vow and be the first to retake the city of Jerusalem, then there was indeed some hope that Christ would remember him.

Upon leaving the mass, Tancred found Bohemond already dressed, armored, and ready to depart. Michael Podromos, still toying with his little golden ball, stood beside him with a satisfied smile. The fish had taken the hook.

"So, you are off to Constantinople," said Tancred.

"Yes," replied Bohemond. "I will take only a dozen men on fast mounts and reach the gates perhaps within the week. The army I leave in your charge. Proceed on apace to Constantinople and meet me there. Richard will advise you if you encounter anything beyond your experience."

Following these words, Bohemond gave his nephew a long look as if he expected some argument or petulance, but Tancred only inclined his head stiffly. He would keep his opinions to himself until the proper time came to voice them. Bohemond continued to give his instructions. "Michael Podromos has graciously agreed to remain behind as your guide. He will direct you without mishap to the Golden City."

Tancred nodded again impassively. He was surprising himself at how well he could make his countenance conform to his will. In reality, the news that Podromos was to be left behind—doubtless to monitor his every action—filled him with boundless rage. So Bohemond had guessed his resolve, never to enter the city of Constantinople and stand before the emperor. Michael Podromos was to be his watchman and jailer to ensure that the young marquis was delivered to Alexios to pay the shameful homage.

Stuffing these thoughts deep down into his chest, Tancred saluted his uncle with a cordial farewell. He would hold his tongue, bide his time, and seize his chances. He had not been Bohemond's pupil these ten years or more without learning something from him.

As soon as Bohemond's miniature column disappeared into the distance, Podromos turned to Tancred. The dark, small-boned Greek stood half a head shorter than the Norman. His sloe-colored eyes were hooded like a cobra, but any venom they might contain was well concealed. "You are most fortunate," he said insinuatingly, "to have such a valiant and distinguished relative as Bohemond."

"Fortunate, indeed," said Tancred shortly. He looked disdainfully at the man's soft hands, interminably occupied with their golden toy. "If you will excuse me, I must see about the affairs of the army and order the men forward for this morning's march."

The morning march was made to wait a little longer, however, for Tancred had another, more pressing affair to attend to. Once he was out of earshot of the envoy, he called abruptly for Ralph. "I have a task for you," he said, "and it will not be easy."

The old man's eyes lit up like coals fanned by a breeze. He put aside the dagger that he was sharpening and listened attentively.

"I must find out the real state of affairs in Constantinople," said Tancred hurriedly. "I cannot trust either my uncle or this Byzantine lackey to speak me true. And I must, at all costs, avoid entangling myself in any service to the emperor. Tell me, do you think that you can follow Bohemond unobserved and spy out the doings in Constantinople?"

Ralph nodded without hesitation. "The way is clearly marked. There are many Latins in the city already, and it is easy to lose oneself in a crowd—one foreigner looks much the same as another. My Greek is good, and I shall contrive to learn as much as I can without awaking suspicion."

"Good. Take two men then—trusted ones from my own company—and when you have discovered as much as you can, come back and give me the particulars. Then I shall not be as a blind man groping in the dark in this den of deception and intrigue."

"And who will supervise my tasks here in camp while I am gone?" asked Ralph pointedly.

"You mean Alexandra? I suppose I could tempt my fate and let her supervise herself. I've had not a single threat of vengeance from her in over a week, and she's been as quiet as a convent-bred lady these last few days—homesick, no doubt. At any rate, she's lost interest in *me*. I daresay she'll be as happy to embark at Constantinople as we will be to put her aboard ship."

"That's as may be," said Ralph hesitantly. If he had spoken his mind, he could have told Tancred that the little Greek most definitely had not lost her interest in him. Her dark brown eyes followed him everywhere he rode, or walked, or supped, or slept. It was the same keen watchfulness with which she had observed him when planning his demise, but after Tancred's rebuff of Richard, there had been a subtle alteration in Alexandra's attentions. Her vigilance had not relaxed but Ralph surmised that it was now rooted in a different ground than vengeance.

The first signs of the change were her new exertions to please the marquis, although nearly all of her overtures were met with suspicion.

When she washed Tancred's second best tunic and dried it in the few hours of spring sunshine, he caustically inquired if some centaur had given her a poison paste to spread on the cloth. "If my skin goes up in flames when I put this on, at least I have the consolation of dying like Hercules." When she cooked him a hot stew on a cold night, he refused to eat it, even though she swore up and down that Ralph had examined every herb and bit of meat that had gone into the making of the broth. When he came to his quarters rain-soaked and mud-caked, she heated water for washing and wiped down his armor as best she could. When he rested his favorite mount and rode a spare one, she curried the beast until his coat shone.

She would not bring herself to admit, even to herself, that she had given up her vengeance entirely, but Ralph conjectured that in this conflict of emotions that beset her, her hatred would soon be vanquished. It was one thing to kill a man who had killed your father; it was another thing to kill a man who hated himself for doing so and was willing to travel two thousand miles to atone for it. And when this tall, handsome nobleman undertakes to protect you against a wretched miscreant like Richard of Salerno, what more could be needed to win over an impressionable young girl?

Tancred had said the girl was homesick. Lovesick was more likely, thought Ralph to himself. But since these speculations were not ones that Tancred would have welcomed, the old man kept them closeted inside his mind.

"You think the girl will be glad to leave us?" repeated Ralph. "You may have read the signs aright."

"Aye, some of the time I actually do," said Tancred with a grin, "although you seem to forget that oftener than not." With the new plan for Alexandra's custody settled, he tossed his servant a bag of coins. It was nearly the last of the meager monies that he had brought with him, the amount totaling even less than his mother's jeweled girdle. "Now get you gone on Bohemond's trail, and learn some news worth bringing back."

Putting his trust in Ralph's intelligence and intuition, Tancred brought the rest of the army on slowly and obeyed Podromos' every direction like a docile pack animal. On Easter Day he halted and would not allow the men to travel. They celebrated the feast of the resurrection with as much pomp as they could muster. Their Byzantine guide, although he viewed their Latin observances a little superciliously, generously found them a market to purchase both sheep and oxen to keep the feast.

It was a fortnight later when they first saw the face of the city rising in the east. Even from such a distance, the Normans could see the two great rings of walls and the countless towers and spires that soared above them.

"Tell me," said Michael Podromos proudly. "You have seen Rome, yes? How does our fair city compare with her?"

Tancred squinted his eyes at the navel of the east, fully cognizant that it was at least ten times the size of dilapidated Rome. "In truth, I have hardly had opportunity to gaze on your city, though she does seem to be of remarkable girth."

"Yes, indeed," said Podromos, letting go a little his languid air of nobility to wax eloquent about the metropolis. "She is remarkable in both size and workmanship. Never will you see such an array of monasteries and palaces in one place. It is almost a nuisance to catalogue the opulence that overflows in every street: gold, and silver, and embroidered cloth, and the holiest of relics."

"Most remarkable," murmured Tancred, determined not to show excessive astonishment.

"The population, I have heard, is the largest in the world. Just think, that at any given time, we have almost twenty thousand eunuchs serving in the city."

Tancred's lip curled a little and he tried not to laugh. "Truly? Twenty thousand eunuchs at once? That is not a boast that any city in the West could make." Nor would it wish to, he thought in silence. He looked at Michael Podromos curiously. He had heard that many of the emperor's servants were eunuchs. Podromos himself did not seem overly effeminate, but perhaps he too had undergone the knife.

On the same day that Constantinople was sighted, a Byzantine rider approached the camp bringing with him a scroll from Bohemond. Tancred found no surprises in the letter. Alexios had received Bohemond as Solomon did the Queen of Sheba, bestowing on him every luxury imaginable. "There are similar gifts," said Bohemond, "for you who are following behind me. I have spoken to the emperor about you, and he greatly desires an audience with one so young and so courageous." Tancred was certain that this audience could portend only one thing, and he noticed that Bohemond had omitted to mention whether he himself had sworn an oath of homage to the emperor.

Podromos, hovering intently in the background, could not resist inquiring about the contents of the letter. "Your uncle is well, yes?" The golden ball slipped from his fingers and rolled between the Norman's feet.

"Assuredly, thanks to the kindness of your emperor." Tancred knelt down and picked up the golden toy. "They are expecting us tomorrow at the palace," he said, and firmly deposited the bauble in the Greek's outstretched hand.

"You will be greatly blessed to learn more of Constantinople!" said the Byzantine.

"Indeed I shall," said Tancred. He smiled. There was someone waiting on the outskirts of the camp who would give him all the learning he needed.

# Chapter 15

Ralph, chary of making an ostentatious entry into the camp—and thereby giving Podromos cause for suspicion—had sent quiet word to Tancred that he was returned from his mission. He had infiltrated Constantinople, learned news of Bohemond and the other Crusaders, and returned to give the intelligence to his master before the marquis walked into the wolf trap.

As the sun was setting, Tancred strolled out to the perimeter to meet with Ralph. The old man was seated cross-legged on the ground, munching on some hard bread.

"So?" asked the marquis, glad to see his manservant, but even more eager to hear the news. "What of my uncle and the other Crusaders? Does Alexios have them all in his toils?"

"Sit down, master," said Ralph with an expansive gesture to the empty ground beside him. "I've more news than can be told in a moment if you will have the stomach to listen." Tancred settled his long legs under himself on the ground, and Ralph, rubbing his wrinkled nose, launched into his tale.

"We trailed Bohemond at a goodly distance for the seven days it took to come unto the city. When the hustle and bustle outside Constantinople grew, we lost him altogether. But your uncle's not one to lie low in great places amongst great doings—I reckoned we'd find him again whenever we laid eyes upon the emperor's court.

"The whole city juts out into the Sea of Marmara like a giant thumb, and on her right side a little finger of water called the Golden Horn gives shelter to the fleets in port. The number of ships I saw tied up at anchor astounded me. If your grandfather had had a fleet of that size to support him in his campaign, I think it would be the flag of Robert Guiscard on the walls of Byzantium now. There's more than one merchant making for Athens, Venice, then Bari, so it should take only a handful of silver to secure passage for our little Greek friend.

"You're close enough upon Constantinople now to see how massive and well-fortified she is on the outside, but let me tell you, that the hide is nothing compared to her innards. Outside are manors and villas, the like of which you've never seen in Italy, but once you pass through her gates—and the walls are five horse lengths of stone or more—why, it is like entering the New Jerusalem! Marble in a multitude of colors, great pillars rising into the heavens, and more churches than you can count on a dozen hands. It took me all of a morning, once I had passed the gates, to cross the metropolis to the palace of the royal court!"

Here the storyteller stopped his rhapsodies to take a drink from his skin of water. Tancred, although attentively absorbing every descriptive and geographical detail, began to redirect Ralph to more pressing concerns. "But you have not explained yet how you entered the city? And whom did you see there? What of Bohemond?"

Ralph fingered his long moustache and his wrinkles parted in a smile. "I saw a great many people, your uncle among them. But patience, and I will tell you all!

"It was when we first came into the suburbs of the city that we lost the track of Bohemond and his men. Truly, if I had not seen those towers looming ahead of us, I would have thought we were already inside the place, for there were so many mansions and merchant shops outside that it was like a city unto itself.

"Some of the buildings showed marks of recent violence with overturned columns and black-burned trees. I asked one of the merchants what was the cause of this disrepair, some of it seeming only a few days old. The merchant looked at me a little suspiciously—indeed, our Western appearance caused most of the Greeks to narrow their eyes and stiffen their shoulders. 'I wonder you need ask me that,' he said, 'when, God knows, you Latins have been the source of all this wreckage. Ask the rabble that your hermit brought why the fountains are broken down! Ask the Germans from Boulogne why the market stalls are overturned!'

"He would tell me no more, but by persistent questioning of some other reluctant natives, I learned that the Germans, led by three noble brothers, were camped a quarter of a league to the south beneath the outer wall. They had been pitching their tents there for several months since the emperor had denied them admittance into the main city. 'Filthy brutes!' remarked one tall Byzantine woman with gold bangles on her wrists. 'They'd loot the Church of Holy Wisdom herself if the emperor let them anywhere near her.'

"We headed south and found the brothers from Boulogne with little trouble—the scowls of the Byzantines pointed the way. The Germans possessed an impressive congregation of tents and pavilions, though even they were dwarfed by the masterful masonry towering above them."

"How many Germans would you say there are?" asked Tancred, leaning forward with interest.

Ralph pursed his lips thoughtfully. "Methinks ten thousand men, although I could not say for certain."

Tancred whistled. It was no small number—four times the men that Bohemond had in his train.

"The Germans recognized us immediately as men of the West. One of them offered us food—there seemed to be plenty of that—and we had as much barley cake and fish as we could eat. 'What is the name of your lord?' I asked. A great bearded fellow with long hair told me that he served Baldwin though most of the others standing around in that circle said that they were for Godfrey. 'Is Godfrey the eldest of the three then?' I asked.

"'No, Count Eustace is the eldest,' said the bearded man indulgently, 'but he's of no temperament to lead and he takes no part in the councils of war.'

"'That's right—Godfrey's the man we follow!' said one of the men-at-arms who had already proclaimed his allegiance to the second son. 'He's left all his lands in Lorraine to rescue the Holy Sepulcher. He's a fair fighter and the most holy man I know. On our travels to Byzantium, the whole column would be delayed—oftener than not—because Godfrey was at his prayers and could not be disturbed to take to horse.' The men nodded like rag dolls, obviously proud of their leader's piety.

"The great, bearded man, sworn to the youngest brother Baldwin, grinned irreverently. I could see that he had not joined the cult of veneration for Saint Godfrey. 'It seems that your master should have joined the Church,' said he to the others, 'since he feels so much at home inside one.'

"'Ha, Rudolph!' shouted one of his fellows, 'He certainly would have taken to it better than your master Baldwin did!' The whole company of them laughed then, and they explained to me that Eustace, as the eldest son, had inherited his father's county, Godfrey, as the second son, had inherited his uncle's estates, but Baldwin, as the third son, had been apprenticed to the Church.

"'And mighty poorly did he take to that profession,' said one of the Germans.

"'Like a lead weight to the water,' said another. 'The benefices he had throughout the Frankish territory were nothing to blush at. But he could not stand the books, and the councils, and the doctrinal wrangles, and the new regulations of celibacy. Before he was thirty he had given up the Church entirely.'

"'And why shouldn't he give it up?' demanded the bearded one whom they called Rudolph. 'If you've ever seen a man built for war, why, it's Baldwin! He has the strength of an ox, the cunning of a fox, and the command of the lion. Such a man should not be wasted on the clergy!'

"The other men assented grudgingly, but I could see that the landless Baldwin was not such a favorite with them as was pious Godfrey. They asked me questions about myself and my two men. I told them that we were Normans but hinted that we had come alone on our pilgrimage and needed an army to attach ourselves to. Those long-haired fellows became even friendlier at this, for a Latin of any kind is still a Latin when all around you surges a sea of foreigners. They bid me eat up and gave me more barley cakes and some spiced wine.

"'Gentlemen,' I said, determined to turn my chance acquaintance with them to some advantage. 'How is it that you are still outside Constantinople when you have been here for so many months?'

"At this, they all scowled. One of them kicked up dirt clods roughly and let out an oath. 'These back-stabbing Byzantines!' said Rudolph between his teeth. 'First, they send word asking for our aid, and then when we're here to render it, they make caveats and conditions and bid us grovel.'

"'At least they have provided you well with food,' I said, licking the honey from the barley cakes off my fingers with enjoyment.

"Rudolph leaned forward confidentially and shook his head. 'You see the feast today, but not the famine of last week. When we first came at Christmastide, the emperor was all bounty and largesse. He showered us with food and gold and raiment and lodged us in the finest villas we had ever seen. He promised us access to the city as soon as preparations had been made and gave us sweetmeats to while away the time. But then we learned the key element of preparation, the key that would open Constantinople to us: Duke Godfrey must swear fealty to him and render homage. It was a hard thing to ask, and Godfrey'—here he lowered his voice so the others would not hear or contradict him—'is as indecisive as the summer breeze. He did not know whether the other Crusader lords would swear the oath when they arrived and so he did not know whether he should swear it himself.

"'I asked Lord Baldwin at that time whether he himself would swear the oath of homage. He told me that he would do so without any hesitation. Alexios would clearly not cooperate without the words being said, and so what was the point of refraining? A clear-sighted man, Lord Baldwin.' Rudolph nudged me familiarly. 'If you take service with him, instead of his brother, you'll show much wisdom in your choice.

"'Alexios, tired of Godfrey's delaying, sent out his mastiff Hugh the Great. That one is the brother of the King of France, though if his mother mated with an ass, it couldn't have had worse results. This Lord Hugh had taken the Italian route and the road through Greece, and reached Constantinople a few weeks before us. He had no scruples about the emperor's demands—he said the words promptly and ensconced himself in one of the Byzantine palaces. So Alexios sent him out as his herald, and he shook his great jowls at Godfrey, assuring him that if someone so magnificent and exalted as himself had sworn fealty to the emperor, there could be no shame in doing likewise.

"'But Godfrey had not enough strength of purpose to be persuaded either way, and Hugh left in a huff of wounded dignity. The matter dragged on, and after several months, finally losing his patience, Alexios' heart grew hard toward us. The stream of glorious gifts ceased. He suddenly revoked all our marketplace privileges and the people refused to buy or sell with us.

"'What were we to do? It was Easter Day, but there was no feasting in our camp. Liable to starve, we armed in companies and raided the outlying suburbs for food. Many of our men claimed that Alexios had lured us here expressly to kill us with hunger. In a fury of madness, several knights lit fire to the luxurious villas that had been lent us, and a whole quarter of the outlying city became a forest of charred stone. A few Greeks were harmed—that enraged the emperor even further. He waited until the holy day had passed, then sent out his Turcopoles to chastise us. My master Baldwin, quickest to sense the danger, gathered a few of us who had not scattered for plunder. Our heavy mail staved off the pinpricks of their archers, and close ranks kept them back in time for Godfrey to rally the men and repel them altogether.

"'After the Turcopoles showed us their horses' tails, the emperor recovered some of his good humor and reopened negotiations with us. At Baldwin's prompting, Godfrey accepted Alexios' invitation to visit the city. They were allowed only a few men in their bodyguard, but they met with no harm and came safely to stand before the emperor's throne. Then Godfrey did what he should have done months ago.

He swore the required oath. The river of gifts began to flow again and our marketplace privileges were returned.'

"'But how is it that you still lodge outside the city?' I asked Rudolph.

"He snorted. 'By the will of the emperor. He claims that our wildness may deface the ancient monuments inside the walls. Oh, he allows a few of us in, but only a set amount each day, and you must show your pass to his officers at the gate. Our commanders partition out the visits by lot, for nearly every one of the soldiers longs to see the sights in the Golden City.'

"I thanked the long-haired German for his information and stored it away in my mind. Then I drew back a little from the camp of Godfrey to collect my thoughts and see how I might gain myself one of those fortunate pieces of parchment that would allow me to pass into the city of the emperor."

# Chapter 16

"It was easier to contrive entrance into the city than I thought it would be," continued Ralph. "I had a handful of *denarii* about me, thanks to you, my lord,"—he smiled broadly at Tancred—"but you must know that I used them only out of necessity. I know how empty our strongbox is.

"As we were leaving Godfrey's camp, we came across a table of Germans playing at dice with one another. They hailed us and I repeated the same story I had told Rudolph, that we were Normans looking to take service with one of the great Crusader lords. They asked me to join in their game. 'Why, what are the stakes?' I said. They answered that it was gold, although one fellow who had none had staked his pass to enter the Golden City on the morrow. Just the thing I needed! I shrugged and sat down with them. My heart fluttered a little to think that this was the most important game of dice I would ever play.

"My first throws were not lucky and I lost more than half of my purse. Then I said a little prayer to Saint Martin and the dice began to fall my way. But the other fellow, the soldier with the pass into Byzantium, must have been praying too, for he had won as much as I until the two of us were the only gamblers left at the table. 'Come, fellow,' I said. 'Let us trust all to one last hazard of the dice, your pile of winnings and that pass for the great heap of gold I have here.' He grunted and agreed to it and so I staked my mission and all our means on Lady Fortune.

"And what do you think happened?"—Ralph paused here for dramatic effect until Tancred's impatient scowl forced him to go on. "She smiled on us! I won the lot of it! The fellow was a little angry with me, for he had been sure that the lady was on his side. But I called for a stoup of wine and drank with him until his choler abated.

"The next morning, I left my two men outside the walls and presented my pass at the gate. The officer in charge wrinkled his nose a little, but his duty required him to let me through, and so I entered into the Golden City intent on finding your uncle and ferreting out his doings.

"From the size of the outside walls, I had expected immensity within, but even my expectations were dwarfed by the splendor that surrounded me. The city seemed to be nothing but a vast market stretching for miles in every direction. All around me hawkers called out the price of raisins, rice, saffron, and slaves. Women waved silks as bright as polished bezants and shot through with golden thread. White pottery, as smooth and delicate as a lady's hand, held up fruits and sweetmeats from southern lands.

"Here my knowledge of Greek stood me in good stead. Most of the Byzantines were so astounded to hear a 'barbarian' speak their language that they answered my every question without delay. They bade me follow the main way past the Forum of Theodosius and the Forum of Constantine till I came to the palace quarter. The further I pressed on, the older and grander the buildings became. It was half a morning of slow walking through the crowds before I saw the dome of their Church of Holy Wisdom. Across from it stood the Hippodrome, a great arena shaped liked a long horseshoe. I could see four golden stallions perched on the roof of the grand entrance, a token of the chariot racing inside. I did not go in myself, but one boastful wine merchant told me it holds a hundred thousand people or more.

"Behind the Hippodrome, and indeed, connected to it, stood the great palace of Emperor Alexios. It was there that I encountered my next obstacle. How was I to receive word of Bohemond without him receiving word of me? I knew, my lord, that you did not wish him to know of my presence in the city. I could hardly ask *him* for admittance to the royal quarters. For the rest of the afternoon, I hung about the gardens and bathhouses, plying passers-by with questions. Some admitted to having seen your uncle enter the palace—his height had made quite an impression—but no one knew what had transpired inside.

"I was nearly at my wits' end when I caught sight of a familiar shock of blond hair. Its owner, gazing about the streets with a curious, childlike stare, did not see me at all until I plucked him by the sleeve. 'Well met, Master William!' I cried, for it was none other than your brother who left us behind at Bari.

"'What? Is it Ralph?' he said, and threw his arms around me in an embrace. We stepped into an empty portico and chattered excitedly, for there was much to learn of each other's story.

"William, as you know, went to sea with Hugh and his Franks, but there were few proper seamen in that fleet. A storm overset them, and nearly half of Hugh's company was lost in the Adriatic, or so bedraggled that they begged leave to go home again. A poor start for them, but thankfully, the journey through Macedonia was without mishap. Durazzo's governor, John Comnenus had given them a large escort—a virtual army—led by Manuel Boutoumites, one of Alexios' favorite generals. They had no trouble from the local villages or from assailants.

"When they arrived at Constantinople, Hugh—far from being daunted by the emperor's splendor—was concerned only that he, as a king's son, should be properly received. He had sent William ahead as one of his emissaries to Alexios, and this was the greeting he was instructed to bear: 'Know this, O Emperor, that I am King of Kings, the greatest of all beneath the heavens. It is my will that you should receive me with all the pomp and ceremony due to my noble birth.'

Here Ralph broke off his tale with a laugh as Tancred stared dumbfounded. "By all the saints, what a peacock!" snorted Tancred. "And how did the emperor rate him for this effrontery?"

"Your brother said that Alexios seemed more amused than angry at this greeting. He smiled in his beard and made Hugh welcome in the city. Then he showered the puppy with ten times the gold that the Frankish king has spent on his mistress Bertrade. And as a result of this luxurious treatment, Hugh could not bend the knee fast enough to become the emperor's vassal. He has become the emperor's strongest advocate and

ROAD FROM THE WEST | 99

adherent among the Latins—it was he who tried to persuade Godfrey to swear the oath of homage. I think he will be a sad hound to leave these royal kennels when the order to hunt is finally given.

"William was overjoyed to hear me tell how near you were to the city although, in truth, he had already learned that much from your uncle Bohemond. I told him of your quandary about the oath of homage to Alexios. He nodded worriedly, already having developed some inkling of what your thoughts would be on that matter. For his own part, he had not been obliged to bind himself in any way since he is only one lance with no company of his own.

"I asked him then concerning Bohemond's whereabouts and doings, since those were your primary instructions regarding my mission. 'Oh,' said William quite simply, 'our uncle has sworn the oath already.' Bohemond had exhibited none of the bravado of Hugh the Great and none of the wavering of the German Godfrey. When he entered the city, he was admitted to the emperor straightway. Alexios cautiously complimented him on his past exploits at Durazzo and Larissa. Bohemond returned the praise, assuring Alexios that he was the most skillful tactician he had ever encountered.

"'They sat down to a feast then,' said William, 'and I was at my uncle's right hand. He expressed great joy to see me after a separation of so many months, and at first, I thought him exceptionally considerate toward me since he passed down many of the delicacies from his own plate so that I might enjoy them. Later, he asked me if I had suffered any ill effects from the meal, and I realized that he—in concern for his own life—had eaten nothing from the emperor's table. I admired his shrewdness, but thought it a little hard that I should be the slave to taste his food for him. The emperor, it seems, also noticed my uncle's forbearance, for afterwards he sent a great side of raw beef to his lodgings and begged him to have it prepared in whatever manner best suited his digestion.

"'So as you see,' continued William, 'there is no trust between the two, however polite they might be upon the surface. The next day, Alexios proposed that Bohemond become his vassal, fighting to reclaim the old borders of Byzantium and returning anything won by his sword there into the jurisdiction of the empire. In return, Alexios promised to aid the Crusaders with his fleet and his own men. It did not take Bohemond more than a minute to respond to the emperor's offer. I think he had turned it over many times in his mind before it was even made. He accepted and swore the requisite oath. Alexios was pleased at his compliance, and bid him ask for a gift in return.'"

"What did my uncle ask for?" interrupted Tancred.

Ralph shook his head in chagrin. "Something that not even Hugh the Great had the gall to demand. Your brother says that Bohemond asked to be named Grand Domestic of the East."

"Grand Domestic?" Tancred lifted an eyebrow. "That post is second in command only to the emperor! He asked to become the head of the Byzantine army?"

"Yes," said Ralph dryly. "It was a bold request, and the emperor did not grant it outright. He said only that Bohemond was surely a worthy man to hold such a post. Once your uncle had proved himself against the Turks, the title might very well be his."

"So," said Tancred. "My uncle might find a way to rule the empire of the Byzantines after all. But there is one more thing I must know. Was anything said concerning me? Will the emperor require my oath?"

"I quickly asked your brother that when he had finished his tale," said Ralph. "It was growing dark, and I knew that I must soon leave the city before the gates were barred. The answer is: yes, Bohemond did speak of you. He mentioned that his cousin and his nephew led bands of their own beneath his ensign."

"And what said Alexios?"

"That any man with a troop of his own must swear homage to him before leaving Constantinople. His company may pass over the strait, but he must stay until he speaks the oath."

Tancred cursed beneath his breath. But before too many seconds had passed, an idea took shape in his mind proving that he had his grandfather Guiscard's head on his shoulders. "There may be a way for me to avoid this entanglement," he said, and he went on to outline a plan whereby he might continue on the Crusade without being constrained into homage to the emperor. It was daring, difficult, and dabbled with duplicity. It was expressly tailored to the needs of the moment.

"That is easier concocted than carried out," said Ralph giving a low whistle, "especially since Bohemond will be keeping watch on you like a wheeling falcon. And furthermore, it leaves you scant time to arrange a ship for Alexandra."

"Then I'd best find someone else to make those arrangements in my stead." Tancred fixed his eyes mischievously on the old servant. "You've already demonstrated that your Greek is good and that you know your way around the city. And though it proves you're in your dotage, you actually seem fond of her." He clapped the wiry, old man jovially on the shoulder. "I count on you to settle the matter in my absence."

# Chapter 17

Bohemond came out to meet his army the next day wearing the gold and purple panoply bestowed on him by the emperor. Michael Podromos, the Byzantine envoy, congratulated him on his appearance and felicitated him on the wonderful understanding he had reached with the emperor. "The marquis has been most dutiful in your absence," he reported smoothly. "You must be proud to have such a nephew in your following."

"Proud indeed," said Bohemond. He clasped Tancred's sword arm in greeting, and Tancred realized incredulously that as much as he mistrusted his uncle, he had missed his company during the last fortnight. "I saw your brother William in the city," said Bohemond cheerfully.

"Truly?" said Tancred, feigning surprise.

"Yes, I dined with him at the emperor's table," replied his uncle, omitting to mention that he himself had eaten nothing and William had supped on his own suspicious food. "He is well and happy and longs for me to bring you to see him. Tomorrow, I'll show you the sights of the city and take you to William at the emperor's court."

"And the army?" asked Tancred.

"They will cross over the Strait of St. George at first light," said Bohemond. "It is the closest crossing into Asia and begins where the city ends, directly west of the palace. The channel there is so narrow that they say a strong man might swim it. Across that strait lies the country of the Turks which they snatched from Byzantium not so many years ago. That is the bulk of the land that Alexios wants to reclaim. The main city in that region is Nicaea, only a few days' easy journey from the coast.

"The emperor has arranged a great convoy of ships for the knights and men-at-arms. He is ready for us to begin this campaign against the Turks as soon as the rest of our number arrives. His scouts report that the remainder of the Frankish host is but a day's march behind you. Count Raymond of Toulouse is leading them along with Bishop Adhemar, the pope's envoy."

"Well then, if it's an early start, I must tell my men to make ready," said Tancred. He inclined his head respectfully as he turned to take his leave.

"Good, good," said Bohemond. "When their gear is packed, Podromos' men will direct them to the docks in the morning. And then you and I, and Richard too, will ride our mounts into the city. Tomorrow holds surprises that not even you can imagine!"

Tancred smiled. He had surprises of his own in store for the next day.

By the time the morning sun had spilled over the eastern horizon giving the blue waters of the Golden Horn a rosy glow, the Norman host was ready to embark. The Byzantine guards directed them through a narrow northern gate to the western port. There the flotilla Alexios had prepared lay at anchor, some of the ships already full with Godfrey of Boulogne's men. A few of the Norman knights complained about not being allowed to tour Constantinople, but others scornfully declared that Jerusalem was the only city they cared to see the inside of. They would camp that night on a new continent, one waterway closer to the fulfillment of their pilgrimage.

Bohemond, as soon as he had seen the last of his men safely on their way to the port, scouted the empty campsite sharply for signs of Tancred. His nephew's tent had been folded with the others and sent on with the baggage. The nearby suburban streets and inns were empty of all but a few frowning Byzantines. Richard of Salerno watched silently as Bohemond strode to and fro. It was not often that the great Bohemond could be disconcerted, and Richard was gaining immense enjoyment from the frustration welling up in his cousin.

"Come, Richard, do you know where he is?" demanded Bohemond, seeing the smirk on the other's face.

"Not I," said Richard, lifting his hands in protest. "But look, there's his manservant Ralph coming across the square. He knows where the boy is to be found, I'll wager."

"Where is Tancred?" demanded Bohemond, looking down at Ralph's wizened face with displeasure.

"At his prayers, my lord," said Ralph composedly. He gestured toward a small chapel erected nearby, one of the buildings outside the walls that had escaped the ravages of the enraged Germans on Easter Day. He led two horses, his master's and his own, up to the post to be tied. Tancred's blue shield was fastened securely to the pommel of his saddle and his sword belt hung heavily with a full scabbard. The marquis had not taken his weapons inside the church.

Bohemond snorted and sat down on a nearby stone bench. He had an appointment arranged with the emperor and he was eager to be punctual, but now there was nothing he could do but bide his time.

"At least he does not keep us waiting for a less important person than the Almighty," said Richard sardonically. It was all the same to him whether they went into Constantinople or not. He leaned up against his stoic horse and amused himself by pulling single strands of coarse hair out of its mane. Bohemond did not respond to his cousin's jibe.

A cool spring breeze wafted the scent of the sea air through the square, and Ralph began to whistle blithely. The sun inched its way upward along the horizon, but there was still no appearance of the young marquis.

After half an hour or more, Bohemond rose suddenly to his feet and strode over to Tancred's manservant. "Are you certain he is in the church?" he demanded, collaring Ralph a little roughly.

"Why, yes! Yes, lord!" protested Ralph, shaking himself free and dusting off the places where Bohemond had laid hands on him. "See for yourself if you must."

Bohemond took the three stairs up to the church porch in one stride. He shoved open the doors vehemently, like a jealous husband determined to discover if another man is hiding in his wife's bedchamber.

The church was empty save for one soul. At the foot of the altar knelt a Norman knight, clad in chain mail of the finest quality and wearing a blue surcoat with a stripe of red and white checkered squares. His head, covered by the mail coif, was bowed reverently before the crucifix.

The painted icons, mounted on all four walls of the building, seemed to stare reproachfully at the trespasser. What cause could there be for such a rude intrusion into this holy place? Bohemond, recognizing his nephew's coat-of-arms and a little confounded by the solemnity of the sanctuary, almost turned to leave. But then he remembered his appointment with the emperor and thought better of it. "Ho there! Tancred!" he said brusquely. "You must continue these prayers at a church inside the city. The horses are outside and Constantinople awaits."

The prostrate man said nothing. Indeed, he made no movement to even acknowledge the intruder's presence. Bohemond stared at him for a moment, and his eyes narrowed to cold gray slits. Walking purposefully between the pews, he came up behind the praying man and jerked off the metal coif that covered his head. A pile of curly hair—red, not blond—tumbled out. The owner flung up his arms in front of his face, as if afraid that Bohemond would strike him.

"I beg pardon, my lord," stammered Turold, for it was he inside Tancred's suit of armor.

Bohemond barely refrained from blows. "Where is your master? Tell me if you value your life!"

Turold's fair face went a shade whiter than its usual cast. He had been strictly warned not to reveal Tancred's whereabouts to anyone.

"There's no harm in saying where now," said a wry voice. Ralph, fingering his moustache with satisfaction, had peered inside the doors of the church. "I'm sure the fleet has sailed by now."

"What fleet?" said Bohemond, his voice as sharp as the edge of a knife.

"The Byzantine fleet," said Turold hurriedly. "He dressed in my armor and went into Constantinople at morning's light to cross the strait with the rest of the men. He bade me switch places with him—it was none of my doing."

"They're halfway to Nicaea by now," said Ralph with a shrug of his shoulders. The old man was feeling triumphant at the success of this deception, especially delightful since it had duped the seemingly omniscient Bohemond.

The Norman count pressed his lips together tightly. He would not stand here to bandy words with Tancred's pawns. He exited the small chapel as determinedly as he had entered. "Mount up, Richard," he said, throwing a long leg over his tall steed. "Tancred thinks himself as clever as a sparrowhawk to skirt the city and miss the fowlers, but he will land himself in the lime sooner or later. Let us to the emperor straightway to make sure that he does not mistake Tancred's contumacy for our own."

# Chapter 18

While Bohemond was making his nephew's excuses to the emperor, Tancred was pacing the deck of a Byzantine warship on the Sea of Marmara. The dull sheen of Turold's armor and plain black shield screened his identity from even his own men. They supposed that their commander was in Constantinople, consorting with courtiers and royalty. Tancred smiled to think of Bohemond's surprise when he discovered the cheat in the chapel.

The Strait of St. George was placid today, the gray water as still as a frozen lake. It would not take half the morning to reach the far shore in this fast warship. Double-masted and sleek-hulled, the ship's deck had been cleared for transport of men and horses, but even with its fighting gear stripped down, Tancred could see that a dozen of these ships would make a formidable fleet.

"How many men can this ship carry?" he asked one of the sailors in Greek.

"Three hundred or more," replied the man, "if all the rowing benches are full."

Tancred gestured at the bronze decorations on the prow and stern. "And these lion and leopard heads—what do they symbolize?"

The sailor scratched his head. "Why, I suppose they symbolize the might of our emperor, but they are more than just symbols, of course." Eager to show off the splendors of the ship, the sailor took Tancred up to the prow and showed him how the leonine heads were, in fact, machines of war. The Byzantines used them to shoot out a mysterious, pitchy substance that would spread flames over enemy ships. It could not be put out with water like any ordinary fire, and would burn and burn until there was nothing left to destroy.

Tancred took in the information attentively, realizing how useful it would be to the Crusade to have a fleet such as this. He would rather they had ships of their own, however, than ships of the emperor's lending. The nearing coast of Asia Minor soon claimed his attention. "Are we in Turkish territory once we land?" he asked, turning again to the Byzantine sailor for information.

"Aye," said the helpful sailor, more ready to chatter to an eager listener than to haul ropes or take a turn at the oars. "Although we do have a fortified port here, and the infidels will not press you so long as you remain on the coast. Nicaea is the capital of this region, a few days' journey from the water. The sultan there is a young Turk. He's barely grown his first beard—but he is no child in warfare or treachery. They say he killed his father-in-law by deceit, and even now he wages war with the Danishmend Turks to the east of his province. Kilij Arslan is his name, and I warrant you'll meet his host in battle before the month is out."

"So we are the first of the Crusaders to be set ashore here?" asked Tancred.

"The first?" responded the sailor in surprise. He grinned a toothy smile. "Oh no, sir. There was a huge host of Latins that came to Constantinople last summer, nasty, vulgar men, and no true knights like yourself."

Tancred remembered how Pope Urban had told him of a great company of people stirred up to frenzy by a hermit named Peter. Farmers, women, children—the pope had not been able to restrain them from taking the road to Jerusalem, and so they had set out before the fighting hosts were ready, a disorderly, unprotected band.

"The emperor," continued the sailor, "counseled them to wait for the remainder of the Latin army, but these brutes would listen to no reason. They grumbled and clamored and pillaged the outskirts of the city so violently that he was forced to send them over the strait. He warned them again to remain at the coast and not to venture toward

Nicaea. But again, they had no ears to hear. They thought they had the will of God with them, and they went against the Turks with only their scythes and stones and dirt clods. It was a slaughter. You will see their bones on the hills as you march." He smiled a little at the thought of their destruction, for the behavior of that pilgrim crowd had been as detestable as the men of Sodom and Gomorrah.

"And what of Peter the Hermit?" asked Tancred. "Did this fanatic die with the rest of his crew?"

"No, he was a better man than the others," said the sailor, grudgingly acknowledging some good in the matter. "He tried to restrain the multitude from their outrages and follies—to no avail. Before they marched on Nicaea, he had returned to Constantinople, begging the emperor to send our imperial troops to salvage these unworthy people. And so he escaped the destruction that beset the rest. The hermit is still in the city. Perhaps he'll come over with your leaders when they take ship."

The harbor across St. George's Strait was a smaller version of the stone docks on the Golden Horn. Surrounding walls marked the border of the abridged Byzantine Empire that had shrunken so shamefully in recent years. The land close to the shore was as densely wooded as the French countryside, but beyond the gray stones of the harbor fortress, the landscape rolled away in a series of green plateaus, still verdant from spring rains.

"I was expecting a desert," said Tancred in surprise. "This land is lush and full of food for the horses."

"Press on a little past Nicaea and you'll see desert sure enough," said the sailor. "Godspeed to you, sir!"

The knights and men-at-arms disembarked, beset by a barrage of orders from the Byzantine harbormasters. The emperor's men wanted them out of the ships as quickly as possible. They directed them to gather their gear then herded them like cattle toward a campsite under the auspices of the harbor walls. Several of the Normans knights bridled at the curt and uncivil treatment they were receiving. "Where are

Bohemond and Tancred?" demanded one of the flaxen-haired giants. "They would not have stood for this."

The Germans, accompanied by their leaders, the three brothers from Boulogne, held a better state of order. Baldwin, issuing commands for his brother Godfrey, was organizing the men into companies. Tancred caught sight of the tall German for the first time, his equal in height and breadth. Both men's complexions were as fair as honeyed milk, but while the Norman's head displayed close-cropped yellow hair, the German's dark locks hung long. The thickness of Baldwin's beard showed him at least ten years Tancred's senior. His nose curved sharply like the arch of a gatehouse and his upper lip jutted out strongly like the parapet of a tower. There was no mark of a tonsure about him now or, indeed, any sign to show that he had been raised and trained as a priest in the house of God. He had brought along a wife, Godvera, a tall, handsome woman whose round breasts may have contributed to his distaste for holy orders.

"Pitch our tents here," called out Baldwin firmly, directing the men to stake out ground for themselves on the western corner of the embankment. Godfrey, a head shorter than his brother and much slighter in build nodded his assent at the choice of campsite.

Tancred saw immediately that Baldwin had chosen all the level ground and that which was closest to the water source. He also saw that his own people, the Normans, were milling about confusedly while a few of the bolder knights uttered contradictory orders. They had only a third the strength of the German host and were leaderless to boot.

Tancred took off his helmet. He had dissembled and disguised himself for long enough. It was time to take back his pedigree and position. "To me! To me!" he shouted loudly, the golden stubble of his bare head shedding light like a lantern.

His own men, and Bohemond's too, recognized his face immediately. "It's the marquis!" they began to shout excitedly, and before half a minute had passed they began to cluster around him like hounds waiting for food from the kennel master. "Where are we to camp?" they demanded. "And who is in charge of the provisions?"

Tancred held up a hand to quiet them then, casting a glance in the direction of the Germans, strode off to confront their leader. "Ho there, man!" he said, saluting one of the German knights. "Bring me to your Duke Godfrey."

The knight looked at Tancred's dingy armor and lack of a crest and almost refused his request, but the Norman fixed his eye upon him and the imperiousness of his bearing could not be denied. Within moments, Tancred found himself standing before Godfrey's tent. He inclined his head, as to an equal, and spoke out boldly before anyone could question him. "Well met, Lord Godfrey. I am here to settle with you about a campsite for my men."

Godfrey looked up at him in wonder. His hair and beard were lighter than his brother's and his eyes held a peculiarly beautiful shade of blue, bright and clear like the tiles of a Byzantine mosaic. "And who might you be, sir?" inquired Godfrey politely, taking Tancred's bravado at its face value.

"I am the Marquis Tancred, nephew of Count Bohemond and co-leader of the Norman host from Italy."

"Well met, indeed!" said Godfrey in a friendly fashion. He clasped Tancred's hand with warmth and kissed him upon the cheek.

Baldwin, who had witnessed this extraordinary intrusion from afar, stalked over to his brother's tent to forestall any trouble. His dark mantle hung down to his calves and fell across one shoulder like the mane of a horse.

"It would be kind of you," said Tancred, "to move your men to one side of the western springs so that we may have easy access to the water as well."

Godfrey smiled and seemed ready to agree, but he was interrupted before the words could be spoken.

"What is this? What is this?" asked Baldwin hastily. "We have already established our camp. There can be no good reason to undo our labor and move it."

"Why, yes, there can," objected Tancred. "You are hoarding all the water supply within your borders and my men will find it a hard task to water themselves and their animals with the stony ground you have left us."

"Your men?" asked Baldwin with a sneer. He looked Tancred up and down contemptuously, for in truth, Turold's armor which he wore was a sorry sight. The straps on one of his leg greaves were frayed through and his surcoat was ripped and patched and so dirty that its color could barely be determined. "I do not think you are the grand war leader you think you are," said Baldwin. He ran a hand through his dark beard and laughed insultingly.

Tancred's fair face flamed red, but he channeled his fury into a cool, measured voice. "The same might be said of you, Lord Baldwin, which is why I have put my request before your brother Godfrey." Tancred had heard—quite reliably—that the German company was sworn to follow Godfrey, and that his younger brother had only a handful of men in his service.

Baldwin's throat filled up with the beginnings of an angry growl, but Godfrey spoke quickly to forestall his outburst. "Come, come Baldwin. It would not be so much trouble for us to move a corner of our tents. The Holy Writ says that it is good for brothers to dwell together in unity, and we are surely all brothers on this sacred endeavor."

Baldwin, seeing that Godfrey was against him in this matter, set his face stiffly like a mask. "Very well then," he said gruffly. "I shall give the orders to remove some of the pavilions." He looked at Tancred with distaste. "You Normans may have the green space on the leeward side of the springs. We would not have our *brothers* suffer thirst."

Tancred, deciding to ignore his tone and take his words at their face value, thanked him courteously for his pains. Godfrey, overjoyed that the matter had been settled, clapped the young marquis on the shoulder. "You must dine with us later, young man," he said genuinely. "I have heard much of your famous uncle, and I long to learn more of you. We are companions-at-arms now, the first of the holy brotherhood to make the crossing into a pagan land. I must go to my prayers now, but find me when you have disposed your men and we will sup."

# Chapter 19

Tancred had more occasions than one to sup with Godfrey as they continued to wait on the coast of Asia Minor. Franks and Flemish knights were ferried over the strait daily, but their leaders remained behind in Constantinople. Alexios would not let the lords leave till he had exacted an oath of fealty from each of them. It would be more than a fortnight before the matter was settled to his satisfaction.

Ralph was in one of the companies that came over the following week, bearing with him a glad Turold, eminently relieved to be out of the orbit of Bohemond whom he had so unforgivably deceived.

"I hope you've kept my arms in better condition that I've found yours to be," said Tancred, approaching the newcomers with a laugh and laying a comforting hand on his warhorse's nose. He had missed his steed almost as much as his armor and weapons.

The red-haired knight dismounted and eagerly shucked off the blue surcoat and borrowed sword. "Here, take them back!" said Turold pleadingly. "I've never in my life wanted so much to be rid of good armor, a good horse, and a good name. You know it yourself already, my lord, but your uncle Bohemond has an eye that pierces like the nails of the Holy Cross. God's blood, I almost believed that he would murder me in that chapel when he learned that I was not your lordship."

"You've served me well, and I'll not forget it," said Tancred soothingly. Then, turning to Ralph, he bade him recite how matters stood in the Golden City.

"Most famously!" said Ralph, twirling his moustache with delight. "You had no sooner crossed the strait than the main body of the

Frankish army arrived. I would you could have been there to see them. Bishop Adhemar, the pope's legate, is a bull of a man, with arms like a blacksmith. I'd reckon he's mighty in more than just mouthing a mass."

"A churchman *and* a warrior?" asked Tancred doubtfully. His own father had joined the Church because he was no warrior. The marquis had met few fighting priests.

"Aye," said Ralph. "They say he's fought the Moors in Spain and can wield a battle-axe with the best of men. And what's more, he's prudent and cunning and well able to deal with men like Hugh the Great or even your uncle."

"Pope Urban would not have picked him if he had no discretion," said Tancred staunchly. At the same time, he felt greatly relieved that the governance of their pilgrimage was in the hands of so redoubtable a bishop.

"And along with Bishop Adhemar came a certain Count Raymond of Toulouse," said Ralph. "Alexios bade him make the same oath your uncle swore, and that is when the trouble started."

"Trouble?" Tancred's nostrils flared with interest.

"It seems that this Count Raymond is of the same mind as yourself. The oath liked him not. He refused to swear it and would stomach no remonstrance from Prince Hugh, Bohemond, or the rest."

"Better and better!" said Tancred smacking his palms together with joy. "I begin to like this count already. And what says Alexios to the refusal?"

"Why, he claims he will keep Count Raymond there until he bends unto his will."

"More delays! Are we to be kept here on this wretched coast till doomsday? Jerusalem will not wait forever. I will not wait, and neither will Duke Godfrey." Casting aside the last of Turold's mail, the marquis began to pick up the burnished pieces of his own newly returned armor.

"You've made the Germans' acquaintance then?" asked Ralph. He knelt beside Tancred and began to fasten the points of his mail.

"Yes, all three of the brothers," said Tancred reaching for his blue surcoat with the red and white squares. "Eustace is such a fainthearted scrub of a man that I do not see what possessed him to come at all. Godfrey is as you described him to me, mild-mannered and well spoken. But though he lacks force there is a kind of ardor in him that my soul admires. We have spoken often with each other, and it is his dearest wish—as it is mine—to see the Holy City liberated from the infidel. *There* is one man at least who is pure of heart and not greedy for gain."

"And Baldwin?"

"He is another matter entirely," said Tancred, a scowl creeping over his smooth face. In the week preceding he had had more conflicts with Baldwin than their initial dispute over the campsite. "He is strong and ruthless, though not as cunning as my uncle, and he has no affection for me. I think he may do me ill-service on this adventure."

Ralph grunted and rose to his feet wiping the dust from the knees of his hose. "Thank God we are forewarned and can prepare for it," he said. "I shall keep my eyes open and my ear pressed to the tents of his followers."

"I shall thank you to do as much." Tancred slipped his blue surcoat over the mail and felt like his own self once more. "There's one piece of news you've neglected to mention, Ralph."

"What's that?" asked the old man apprehensively. His neglect had not been unintentional.

"Alexandra. Did you put her aboard a ship to Bari?"

"In a manner of speaking…as matters came about, my lord…." Ralph equivocated a little then settled on the plain approach. "No."

Tancred stared like a woolly calf. "And why not, for God's sake?"

"She proved difficult," said Ralph, clenching his teeth with exasperation. He omitted to show Tancred the bite marks on his wrists from when he had tried to force her down to the quay. "It was hard to find a sea captain willing to take such an unwilling passenger. But do not fret," he said hastily. "I explained the whole state of affairs to William and left the girl with him. He will set all to right before he crosses the strait."

Tancred groaned. "I wish I had your confidence in the lad's abilities, but alas! I fear our next news of Alexandra will be that she murdered a marquis' brother in lieu of a marquis."

After Ralph's arrival, three more days passed without the appearance of the other leaders. The camp became as restless and cantankerous as a chained bear. "Tancred," said Godfrey, catching him by the sleeve in the morning shortly after he had attended mass. His bright blue eyes were infused with an intense longing—like a man on a promontory straining every fiber to look across the sea but unable to discover the vessel he awaits.

"I cannot tarry here another day without falling into mortal sin," Godfrey said. He tapped an anxious finger on the red cross sewn upon his shoulder. "We have sworn to pursue a course to Jerusalem, and this continual delay is nothing more than a stratagem of the devil to keep us from our purpose. Three months wasted at Constantinople! And who knows how long diplomacy and disputations will keep us here?"

"What would you have us do?" asked Tancred. He chafed as well under the delay but knew no remedy for it.

"I have spoken to my brothers," said Godfrey, linking arms with Tancred and leaning in confidentially, "and we are agreed that—with or without the other dukes—we will take the road for Nicaea this very afternoon. The emperor cannot be displeased with us, that we are so eager to fulfill our obligations to him. And the sooner we reclaim his lands in Asia Minor, the sooner we can press onward to the land I truly love."

Tancred cocked his head in thought. The flower of the army was with them on this far side of the strait. And if this Count Raymond were as much of a man as his refusal portended, his deadlock with Alexios would continue indefinitely. Perhaps once the other leaders learned that their men had invested Nicaea, they would leave the eaves of the emperor's court like so many sparrows and wing their way to the south. Bohemond, Tancred knew, would be loath to lose control of his own army. When he heard they had marched on, he would desert the delights of Constantinople and take ship immediately.

"Very well," said Tancred. "I will undertake to join you with my knights and with my uncle's men as soon as we can obtain provisions. We shall alert the emperor of our purpose, and when he sees that we have addressed ourselves to the Turks, he will send on our companions to join us."

Nicaea was an easy march from the coast, or at least so it appeared. Godfrey and Baldwin took their troops on ahead, while Tancred waited two days till sufficient supplies could be gathered for the road. When Alexios learned that the impatient Crusaders were on the move, he quickly dispatched some Byzantine scouts to accompany them. A corps of engineers came over the strait as well, bringing materials to construct battering rams, mangonels, and trebuchets.

At the head of this Byzantine detachment was Manuel Boutoumites, the general who had escorted Hugh the Great from Durazzo to Constantinople. Boutoumites, it was said, was one of the few Byzantine nobles to have the ear of the emperor. The emperor trusted him with secrets spoken before no others but deaf and dumb servants. Perhaps it was because Boutoumites was almost as silent as they. On the whole journey down from the harbor to Nicaea, he hardly spoke one word to Tancred, though they were often in company.

Godfrey and Baldwin had camped at Nicomedia, the halfway point to their destination, and it was there that the Normans caught up with them. "After this the road narrows exceedingly," said Godfrey to Tancred with a worried frown. "We must march through a crevasse of sorts, and all around the place are dead men's bones."

Boutoumites, listening to the Latin lords converse, lapsed into a rare moment of speech. "Those bones are your people," he said, the soft sounds of Greek coming out in deep rumbles.

"What does he say?" demanded Godfrey. Tancred translated the statement and besought Boutoumites to explain himself, but the general had exhausted his supply of words for the day. He shrugged and turned away.

"I know what he means," said Baldwin, coming upon them abruptly. He pulled aside his dark cloak and held out a shoulder bone that he had picked up from the pile of carcasses. It was stripped of all flesh and bleached by the sun, but wrapped around it was a ragged piece of fabric with the remnants of a red cross. "The animals and the elements have left little enough of their bodies, but there were Crusaders here before us, methinks."

"Peter the Hermit," said Tancred slowly, "or, at least, his followers."

"They were slaughtered in between these cliff faces," said Baldwin, "and their corpses stacked here at the entrance to the ravine as a warning to others."

"Yes, I heard tell of this from a sailor," said Tancred. "He said that they were untrained men, undisciplined, with few weapons, and no match for the Turks."

"I saw the bones of several children in the pile," said Baldwin bluntly. "There are more skulls in that graveyard than there are heads on our men. Fools! They ought to have waited for the army."

"We must send scouts ahead," said Tancred. "The Turks have doubtless heard of our coming. They may be waiting to ambush us here as well."

"And let us not forget," interjected Godfrey, "to set up crosses here in remembrance of the fallen. We must pray for their souls before we depart."

The sight of that grim graveyard caused the pace of the army to drop to that of a lame horse. As they wended their way through the defile, the knights sent apprehensive glances overhead as if they expected fiends to pop out from behind every rock. In places where the path was too narrow for more than two to go abreast, the army halted, secured the area, and waited for the engineers to clear a wider path. Tancred fretted at the waste of time, but Ralph reminded him that the others would have an easier road to tread when they finally left the comforts of Constantinople to join them on the journey.

The ravine stretched on and on but could not last forever. Eventually, the canyon walls opened up into a green valley, and there, nestled against a freshwater lake, sat Nicaea. The western wall of the city butted up against the water, providing protection from siege and a source of supply that would be nearly impossible to sever. Walls six times the height of a man ringed the city, surmounted by over two hundred high towers. A double-ringed trench surrounded the three landlocked sides of the city, and the three large, landward gates were the only points of egress or ingress.

A moment of silence overcame each of the Crusade commanders as they beheld the task that awaited them. Save the walls that surrounded Constantinople itself, they had seen no defenses the equal of this. "How shall we ever take it from the Turks?" asked Ralph, shaking his head in awe.

"What I would like to know," said Tancred to Manuel Boutoumites, "is how, in God's name, the Turks ever managed to take this fortress from you Byzantines in the first place?"

But Boutoumites only grunted and urged his horse ahead. He had work to do laying out the engines and he would not waste his breath in idle conversation.

# Chapter 20

The Byzantine engineers unloaded their carts of timber, rope, weights and counterweights, and the Germans and Normans quickly disposed themselves about the walls of Nicaea to establish the beginnings of a siege. Godfrey and Baldwin encamped outside the northern wall. Tancred directed his men to the eastern side, with the city between themselves and the lake.

The Turks inside the city had a full view of all these operations, but they made no sortie outside the city to stop the Crusaders from encamping. If they had a large garrison, they were keeping that fact well hidden. A few helmets and spears jutted up from the walls like the bristles on a boar's snout, but for the most part, the city was as silent as a pile of stones. Tancred remembered what the Byzantine sailor had told him, that the sultan Kilij Arslan was away on a campaign against the Danishmend Turks. Probably, he had left only a skeleton force behind to guard Nicaea. He would bring back his army soon enough when he heard that his capital was under siege.

Tancred lay down that night with more excitement than he had felt since his interview with Pope Urban. The Crusade had been consummated. He was in sight of the infidels and who knew what battles the morrow would bring? The road from Bari to Constantinople, all that toilsome journey, had been but a prelude to this, and now the road to Jerusalem had begun in earnest.

That night a dream overtook Tancred that had not invaded his sleep since the siege of Amalfi. While his body lay asleep, his other self walked barefoot through the desert, girded only with the lightest of linen tunics and armed with a sword in its sheath. Every step in the hot sand burned the skin from his soles and sent fire into his sinews. The sun beat down on him with the heat of a bread baker's oven. His lips cried out for water.

A river rose up before him, but when he knelt down to plunge his face into its coolness, he found that it was not a river of water but of blood. And the blood was boiling—even hotter than the desert around him. Parched and despairing, Tancred knew not where to turn. Then a city appeared in the distance, white and fair with golden gates like the Jerusalem of John the Revelator. He began to run toward it, but with every other step he stumbled and fell. All around him were bones— bare, white stacks of bones like the remnants of Peter the Hermit's army. He could find no clear ground on which to set his feet.

Still he staggered onward. As he neared the heavenly vision, a crop of black ants sprung up before him from the dragon's teeth some fool had sown. The insects were huge, each the size of a man. Their mandibles swung like scimitars, and their shrieks filled the air like the cries from a thousand minarets. They besieged the beautiful city and began to climb its walls. Tancred watched in horror as their impious legs scuttled up the white stones, leaving black stripes of filth on the alabaster towers.

Suddenly, a man was at his elbow—a knight rendered faceless by his helmet but dressed in the garb of a Frank. "We two together," said the man, "together we can stop this impiety." He drew his sword and gestured for Tancred to do the same. It would have been easy to obey, and yet Tancred hesitated. He looked from the knight to the city, to the knight, and then back again.

From inside the city rang a scream of a woman in anguish, terrible and piercing as the lance that tore Christ's side. One of the golden gates flew open and a veiled woman walked out. Tancred yearned to run to her and press her against his breast. But when she tore off the veil with a swift motion, the yearning died. She was not the woman he had expected.

"Tancred," she said solemnly. "Tancred!" Her form withered from a slender beauty into the stooped old woman from the Vardar River.

"The choice is yours whether to render your help, but if you do, you will find great love and also great sorrow."

The Macedonian crone replaced her veil and shuffled backward into the city. The gate swung shut behind her. And then it came again, that woman's scream that threatened to rend the vault of heaven. The black stripes on the white walls began to thicken.

"Draw your sword!" said the Frankish knight who had continued at Tancred's side all this while. "Draw your sword and together we will stop this impiety!" Tancred stared at the knight and slowly placed his hand on the hilt of his sword. But as each finger felt the warm metal of the pommel, an overmastering hatred of the Frankish knight filled his bowels.

Tancred drew his sword as the knight had told him. But instead of advancing on the city, he swung the blade back over his head and then forward again. It sliced through the knight's helmet and clove his head in two all the way down to the neck. The mutilated body fell backward like a tree split apart by lightning. Tancred pulled back the sword and tried to wipe it off, but the blood would not come off the blade. The more he rubbed it, the redder it became. The task was useless.

Looking up at the city once more, Tancred saw that the entire face of it had been covered by the swarming, man-sized ants. The walls, once alabaster, were now as black as pitch. Not a hint of gold could be seen on the swarthy gates. From behind the walls came up a great many wails and cries, no longer just the voice of one woman, but of a multitude.

A hand gripped his shoulder ominously. Whirling around, Tancred found himself face to face with a black-cowled man. Guilt overwhelmed him like a wave. He hid the bloody sword behind his back, but it was too late. The other man had seen it all. Stretching out a cadaverous hand, the black-cowled man pointed accusingly at the dreamer. "All this misery has come about because of thee, sinner. And thinkest thou wilt escape the judgment of thy God?"

Tancred awoke in a feverish sweat and crossed himself convulsively. The events of the dream were enigmatical, but the terror they evoked was undeniable. He shuddered. He had begun his penance, but it was not enough. If he wished for remission of sins, he must retake Jerusalem as he had vowed. Rising from his bed, the marquis paced his tent in the darkness. "No more delays," he pleaded, his chest heaving distractedly. "We must capture Nicaea and press southward!"

But however much Tancred might deplore it, delay was inevitable with such a diverse and disjointed fellowship. It was another week before Bohemond arrived at Nicaea. With him was a whole cohort of Crusade leaders, and thousands more men both Frankish and Flemish.

Robert of Flanders was one of the lords who arrived in concert with Bohemond. He rode into the camp on a sturdy warhorse caparisoned in rich livery. His shield was a mustard yellow emblazoned with a lion rampant. Tancred would learn later how difficult it was to find a man more doughty in battle or more sensible in council than Count Robert.

This count had set out on his journey in company with Robert, the Duke of Normandy, and Stephen, the Count of Blois; they were neighbors, the three of them, all hailing from the north of France. But though they possessed adjacent lands, they did not possess similar temperaments. The Count of Flanders soon found that his companions preferred to travel at a leisurely pace, and indeed, Count Stephen hardly wished to travel at all.

It was rumored that Stephen had joined the Crusade against his will and that his wife Adele had compelled him to come. Adele was sister to the Norman duke and daughter to the great William the Conqueror. Desperate that her husband's honors should equal those achieved by her father, Adele had vexed Stephen night and day till at last the poor, henpecked man had taken the cross. Whether or not that story was true, the Flemish count could at least bear truthful witness that Count Stephen was in no hurry to reach the Holy Land.

The three northern leaders had entered southern Italy just after Bohemond and Tancred had left it. Diligently, Count Robert of Flanders began the task of securing ships for the crossing. Deliberately, his feckless companions delayed. The winter weather in the Macedonian passes frightened them. They determined to spend Christmas—and also the two succeeding months—in the comfort of the Italian countryside where wine and olives were ready to hand.

Robert of Flanders snorted in disgust and continued on alone, if a man with several thousand soldiers at his back can be called alone. He took ship from Bari, following the same route as Bohemond, and arrived in Constantinople during the Easter season. His men had been ferried over St. George's Strait in the same flotilla as Tancred while the count waited in the city for Alexios to dismiss him.

Another leader also arriving at Nicaea was Peter the Hermit. His steed, no warhorse like Robert's, was an ill-tempered mule that would take orders from no one but his master. The hermit himself was a curious sight. He wore a simple woolen tunic that came down to his ankles, and over that a hooded cape. The thick calluses on his bare feet proclaimed that they were unused to shoes, and his skin was as brown and creased as a walnut shell. Some said that he had been captured and tortured by the Turks long ago, and that this was why he had so fervently preached the need to liberate the routes of pilgrimage to Jerusalem.

Tancred wondered what the hermit had thought upon seeing the cache of carrion corpses in the ravine. Those were the only remains of the unruly peasants that Peter had led to this land. Did he feel responsible for their deaths at the hands of the Turks? Or did he deem that their blood lay upon their own heads since they had refused to follow his orders? Though he had certainly lost his followers, he had not lost his own faith in the cause of the Crusade. He had crossed over from Constantinople to serve in whatever capacity the Crusader lords might ask of him. Perhaps his enthusiasm could keep up the morale of the men in the difficult times ahead.

Riding along with the Count of Flanders and Peter the Hermit was the heavy-jowled scion from the royal house of France. Hugh the Great was great-grandson to the first Capetian king. He had lived his life as a second son, subordinate in all things to his philandering brother King Philip. Alexios, adept at discerning men's foibles, had bestowed on him all the pomp and prestige he desired, and grateful

Hugh had become the staunchest supporter of the Byzantine cause. It was with great reluctance that he had abandoned the magnificence of Constantinople to brave the hardships of the campaign.

In Hugh's train came William. His face glowed with unmitigated pleasure to see his older brother once again. They embraced joyfully and exchanged rapid greetings.

"Why could you not wait for me?" demanded Tancred.

"Why were you so slow on the road?" returned William. Then both of them laughed heartily and clapped each other on the back. There would be many stories to share from the months they had spent apart.

At Tancred's suggestion, William now took leave of his Frankish traveling companions and brought his pennant back to the Norman camp. "Now your lance is where it belongs," said Tancred approvingly, and he ordered his brother's tent placed beside his own.

As William unloaded his gear from the supply wagon, Tancred caught sight of an unwelcome surprise atop his brother's spare mount. "You seem to have brought some baggage that was better left behind at Constantinople." William looked up in surprise to see his older brother glaring at Alexandra.

The little minx cast down her eyes demurely and held out her hands for William to help her dismount. She had changed her oversized, masculine clothes for a tight-fitting dress of leafy green that brought out the brilliance of her chestnut curls. An impartial observer would have called the girl a beauty, and even Tancred grudgingly admitted to himself that the change in attire was a vast improvement. Where she had come by the dress was entirely open to question, though the marquis speculated that softhearted—and soft-headed—William had paid good coin for it at some Byzantine bazaar.

"Did not Ralph tell you that my orders were to put her on a ship back to Bari?"

William smiled frankly at his older brother. "Aye, he did. But when I went to arrange passage for her, I learned something that compelled me to countermand your orders. She has taken the cross!"

Tancred stared at him blankly. "What does that matter?"

Undaunted by Tancred's obtuseness, William patiently launched into an explanation. "It matters because she must finish what she has begun. Do you not know that it is excommunication for all who turn back from the Crusade? I would not—nay, I could not—force her to default through no will of her own. The breach of faith would undoubtedly devolve upon my own head." William's innocent brow puckered with dismay at such a thought. "And in sooth, she wishes to make the pilgrimage to the Holy Sepulcher just as much as you or I do. If you do not object, I intend to take her under my protection and let her continue on with our company."

Tancred glanced at Alexandra. She stood behind William carefully listening to the exchange between the two brothers. When she saw the marquis' eyes upon her, she turned her shoulder conspicuously, in order to better display the red cross that had been newly stitched onto her wide-sleeved gown.

"Is this true?" demanded Tancred.

"Every bit of it," she said, her chin tilting upward with resolution as she returned his stare. "I am bound for Jerusalem the same as you are."

"And does a blood feud still lie twixt you and me?"

She hesitated. "No, that is cleared." Her gaze fell to the ground. "You have done penance enough."

"So be it," said Tancred. "I will not compel you to return the way you came. Although I warn you—this pilgrimage has little place on it for women or children, and if you fall into the hands of the Turks, worse things may befall you than my brother-in-law's brutish behavior."

He turned to William. "You are over-generous to take this wench under your protection. It is my fault that our camp is encumbered with her, and I would not pass her off to you like a flagon of soured wine."

"Oh," said William, his cheeks reddening like a village lad who has just run races with his fellows. "It is no trouble at all!" He glanced shyly at the green kirtled girl, but Alexandra, with her luminous brown eyes fixed firmly on the marquis, had no opportunity to perceive his confusion.

"Very well then," said Tancred curtly, and dismissed the matter from his mind. The girl and her preferences were not consulted, although had she been given a choice of guardian, she might have picked the elder brother—despite his inveterate indifference—over the younger brother and his obvious admiration.

Tancred had no sooner dealt with Alexandra than he was obliged to face another unwelcome interview—this one, however, came as no surprise. Bohemond, finding that his troops were disposed by the eastern wall, spurred his horse to that quadrant immediately, eager to resume the mantle of command. "Well met, nephew," said Bohemond as he reunited with Tancred. His clear eyes ranged over the Norman encampment, surveying its strength and soundness as a physician surveys the anatomy of his patient. "The siege lines are well placed," he said, "and I see you have already begun a bombardment with the catapults."

The approval in his uncle's voice caught the marquis off guard. Perhaps the intervening fortnight had dissipated his anger at Tancred's deception. Or perhaps he simply knew it would serve no purpose to quarrel with him now.

"Yes, we have the city cordoned off in the north and the east. A few boats may slip in from the lake on the west, but the southern wall is the major gap right now. It would take more men than you and I have to hold that stretch of land, yes, and more than are with Robert of Flanders."

"No matter," said Bohemond. "Raymond, the Count of Toulouse, rides only a couple of days behind me. He has an army big enough to rival Godfrey's, and I'm sure he'll be well pleased to have his men piss on the southern wall."

Tancred looked at his uncle sharply. "You do not like this Raymond, I think?"

"On the contrary," said Bohemond with a smile that showed a little too much of his teeth. "I think he will be a famous addition to our numbers. One can never have enough men ready to lecture their fellows at any moment on duty, morality, politics or practicality."

"He refused to swear the oath to Alexios, did he not?" asked Tancred, for in Tancred's mind, that one fact was enough to recommend the count, whatever else his failings might be.

"Why, that's more than I know," said Bohemond snidely. "He made a great show of refusal at first, but he had so many private conferences with Alexios over the last fortnight that he had ample opportunity to swear it in secret. Indeed, the emperor seems well enough pleased with him now."

Tancred wrinkled his nose and said nothing. His uncle was as jealous as a sultan's second wife. His hopes of being appointed Grand Domestic of the East had been dramatically shaken by Raymond's arrival. Raymond had the experience, the silver hair, the silver coin, and the connections to assume leadership over the whole Crusade. Bohemond knew this and was determined that it should never come to pass. It was not for mere courtesy's sake that he had hastened his pace to Constantinople and played the courtier to Alexios.

But all this was forgetting one thing, that Pope Urban had already selected a leader for the Crusade.

"Is Bishop Adhemar en route as well?" asked Tancred.

"Yes, he is with Count Raymond," said Bohemond, "though I do not think he is *with* Count Raymond in all things, if you understand my meaning. He is a fair-minded clergyman and sensible as a soldier." And that, from Bohemond, was praise indeed.

"I look forward to meeting him," said Tancred sincerely. To deal with Godfrey the idealist, Baldwin the unscrupulous, Hugh the incompetent, and Bohemond the opportunist, this army would need an extraordinary leader. Adhemar must needs be as wise as a serpent and as innocent as a dove.

# Chapter 21

On the morning of the following day, Count Raymond rode up at the head of an enviable company. He sat tall in his saddle, guiding his horse easily with one hand. His iron gray hair flowed out freely from beneath his helmet, adding a wisdom and dignity to his martial air. The wagons that came with his company were well stocked from the Byzantine emperor's larder, and Tancred saw several carts dedicated to nothing but treasure and costly ornaments. Tancred glanced down at his own purse, nearly empty and likely to remain so for some time unless he forsook his principles and received the emperor's gifts. But surely Raymond had not received those gems and gold from Alexios, for had he not also refused the oath of fealty?

At Raymond's side rode Bishop Adhemar of Le Puy. Ralph was guilty of no exaggeration when he had said that Adhemar was a bull of a man. Tancred reflected that it was well that the clergy nowadays must remain unmarried, for he doubted whether any woman could reach her arms around the broad chest of that churchman. His brown face betokened a life much lived outdoors, not spent in the dank halls of a cloister. He conversed easily with Raymond as their horses came to a stand but made no motions to direct the actions of Raymond's troops. Urban had sent him to lead the leaders of the Crusade, not their men.

Carrying Adhemar's cross, the sign of his office, was a thin, clean-shaven man in a black robe. His lips were clamped together in a determined fashion, like a boy who has been set a task for the first time and is eager to complete it well. Tancred learned later that this black-robed cross-carrier was Adhemar's chaplain, Bernard of Valence. What

Manuel Boutoumites was to the emperor, Bernard of Valence was to the bishop: his servant, his confidant, and his right hand.

The Franks paraded around the perimeter of the city with all their host till they came to the gap in the siege line. Count Raymond, as Bohemond had predicted, was delighted to use his knights to fill the vacant space outside the southern wall. With his tents pitched, the ring of besiegers was complete, and just in time too.

The expected arrival of the Frankish army coincided very nearly with the unexpected arrival of another host. Count Raymond had no sooner disposed his troops than a sheen of armor glittered on the horizon. An unaccustomed hubbub arose from the hitherto quiet city. Nicaea's garrison had seen it too—the reinforcing army sent by their sultan.

Between the sighting of the enemy soldiers and the sounding of the alarum there was barely a breathing space. The Turks poured over the southern hill like water over the rim of a bowl. If Raymond's army had not just arrived to fill that place, they would have penetrated the gap and entered the gates of the city.

Tancred, seeing that the clash would come at a distance from his post on the eastern wall, hurriedly mounted up a squadron of knights. Some were in their full armor, others in various degrees of undress, but all were of one mind with Tancred—they desired the glory of inflicting the first wounds upon the enemy. The Normans veered to the left around the city wall and thundered towards Raymond's hastily constructed battle line. The Franks, weary from travel, had adopted a defensive position, but the impetus of Tancred's charge carried some of them forward into a rush at the descending Turks.

Tancred gave a lusty yell and spurred forward to meet his first foe, a grizzled Turk riding a few paces ahead of the rest of his comrades. The odds were entirely in the marquis' favor. Covered in chain mail and bearing a long lance, he ought to have bowled the lightly armed Turk off his horse with little trouble. But the Turk, with no other weapons than a bow slung over his back and a curved scimitar in his right hand, would not be unhorsed so easily. A jagged scar across his forehead showed that he was a veteran of many battles, and indeed, he had been with the father of the current sultan when the Turks first took Nicaea. His dark eyes sized up the Norman's charge, and he swiveled in his saddle to avoid the lunging head of Tancred's lance. The gap closed between their horses.

Tancred, unable to use his weapon at such close range, now felt the disadvantage descend upon him. While his left arm blocked the storm of blows that the black-mustached Turk rained down upon his shield, his right hand jettisoned the useless lance and fumbled to extract his own sword from its scabbard. Once his sword was in his hand, Tancred had hope again. His long arms and longer blade pierced the Turk's defenses. He dealt the Turk a deadly buffet upon his pointed helmet, and using his shield as a bludgeon, knocked the dying man from his saddle.

By now, Tancred was in the press of the battle. His next few assailants met with much quicker deaths, and Tancred recognized that the enemy's resolution had begun to falter. The Turks, who had hoped to pound through Raymond's unprepared army like a tent spike, were dismayed to face such a fierce onslaught. Their only interaction with Latins up till now had been the massacre of Peter the Hermit's wretched band in the northern pass. That event had taught them to despise the fighting power of the Westerners and to account them as weak as women. These few short moments in front of Nicaea disabused them of the error they had held for so many months.

The combined lances of the Normans and Franks pushed the Turks back into the nearby hill. Turning tail, the lightly armored Turks abandoned the conflict and returned the way they had come. They knew now what they did not before—that to succor Nicaea would take more manpower than a small relief party. The survivors would tell their sultan that he must come himself if he wished to extricate his capital from the siege of the Latins.

After the enemy had evaporated into the hills, the victorious knights picked their way slowly back to their campsites. Here and there, they would stop to pluck the curved blades from their fallen enemies, souvenirs of the first battle in this holy endeavor. Red-haired

Turold, less afraid of the Turks than he had been of Bohemond, excitedly stripped an arm ring from one of the corpses, and many of the other Normans found similar articles of plunder.

Tancred, striding over to his own first kill, picked up the curved scimitar that the fallen man still held in his grip. Ralph, never far from his master's heels, looked at the sword with interest. "I heard a man say that the Turks call that blade a *kilij*, the same word as the name of their sultan." He looked up at Tancred. "What will you do with that sword?" he asked.

"This," said Tancred curtly, and with one swift motion the blade arced through the air and severed the dead Turk's head from his shoulders. "So perish all who would threaten the Christian cause." Then, taking the head, he mounted it on the broken shaft of a lance. "Plant this outside my tent," he said, handing it to Ralph. "This is the firstfruits of our war with the infidels. By the time we reach Jerusalem we shall have as many bleached bones as are piled outside yonder pass."

After the skirmish was concluded and Raymond had a little time to establish his position, the Frankish count wasted no time in summoning all the Crusader leaders to a meeting to discuss a joint strategy for the siege. Bohemond grumbled that Raymond had no authority to call such a meeting. Tancred agreed with his uncle—was it not Bishop Adhemar's prerogative to call an assembly of war?—but he was still inwardly delighted that Raymond had invited him by name. He had been recognized as a leader in this endeavor, on his own merit and without Bohemond's interference.

As requested, the leaders assembled before Adhemar's tent: Godfrey and Baldwin, Hugh the Great, Robert of Flanders, Bohemond and Tancred, Raymond, the Byzantine general, the hermit named Peter, and of course the bishop of Le Puy himself. Tancred noted that Bernard, the bishop's chaplain, stood behind Bishop Adhemar's chair, leaning forward every so often to whisper in his master's ear. At one point Bernard gestured with a bony thumb in his direction, and Tancred knew that the clergymen were speaking of him.

"So," said Adhemar to Tancred as they waited for the other leaders to take their seats, "I hear that we can ascribe the first kill of the Crusade to your hands."

"God favored me with the opportunity to reach the line of battle first," said Tancred. "I can only hope He shows me the same favor when we breach the walls of Jerusalem, for I have sworn to be the first to enter the gates of the Holy City."

"A noble goal. May God reward you with the opportunity to fulfill this vow." The bishop's voice resounded mightily like the rushing of underground waterfalls. His large shoulders could barely be contained in the white vestments he wore. In appearance and sound he was as like Pope Urban as summer is to winter, but Tancred felt the same thrill of exultation as when he had pledged his sword to the Roman pontiff so many months ago. Here was a man who knew the true purpose of the Crusade!

The council had formed itself by now, and Adhemar stood to address the group. "My lords, as you know our beloved Pope Urban has appointed me the leader of this endeavor. In matters where one must decide our course, that word will come from me. But in matters of military strategy, I think it better that we decide such things in council. You are not here because you are novices at war. Each of you knows best the strengths and weaknesses of his troops, and each of you will retain command of your own men. But we must act in concert or we have no hope of overcoming our enemy, and that is why I say that we must decide our strategy in council. And furthermore," he said, pausing and fixing his eyes solemnly on each member of the group, "you must all swear to abide by the decision of the council once it is reached."

The counts and dukes nodded receptively and gave the pledge that Adhemar required. A threefold cord is not quickly broken, and each saw the wisdom of maintaining a united front against the Turks. As Tancred knew, several of the leaders were ambitious for personal gain, but at this point on the journey, such ambition could best be served by cooperation.

With these preliminaries concluded, the council began in earnest.

"We've shown the sultan today that we're a force to be reckoned with," said Count Raymond enthusiastically.

Peter, bronzed and barefoot and seated on the ground, broke in mournfully. "Would to God that you had been here nine months ago!" A tear trickled down his cheek. "All those unhappy souls...." His voice trailed off into incoherence.

"Today we saw only an advance detail of the sultan's army, of course," said Baldwin, ignoring the hermit. He was determined that Raymond should not make too much of the little victory that his men, and the Normans, had accomplished that day. "When Kilij Arslan hears of our numbers, he'll give up his petty quarrels in the east and come in full array to lift the siege. Then we'll see a real battle."

"That may be so," said Robert of Flanders thoughtfully. "We must prepare for his arrival, but in the meantime, we must also decide the best way to conduct this siege. Nicaea is one of the greatest cities I have ever seen."

"Perhaps we can starve the Turks out!" said Godfrey, his bright blue eyes catching the sunlight like gemstones. He looked at his younger brother Baldwin for support, but the tall, dark-haired German only shrugged doubtfully.

"How can we starve them out when they can easily bring in supplies from the lake?" said Bohemond perceptively.

"Well put, sir!" inserted Raymond, in the tone that one would use to congratulate a young pageboy. Bohemond stared at the Count of Toulouse coldly as the Frank began to offer his own plan. "We must ask Alexios to send some ships overland. They can cordon off the waterway on the western wall of the city. Boutoumites could convey this message to the emperor for us...." He looked over at the Byzantine general, but the man was staring at his feet with as much animation as a rock wall. "Alas, I speak no Greek," said Raymond.

Without any further invitation, Tancred spoke up immediately and explained the situation to Manuel Boutoumites. Grunting in monosyllables, the Byzantine general promised to relay their request for ships to the emperor.

Raymond thanked Tancred courteously for serving as their interpreter and commented on how valuable a skill the knowledge of tongues was. "You inspire all of us to greater diligence to make such knowledge our own." The young marquis blushed a little, confused by so much praise for so small a service.

"So, with these ships you think we can starve them out?" asked Robert of Flanders, seeking to return to the discussion at hand and to make the plan clear in his own mind.

"Not before Kilij Arslan comes," said Bohemond, and most of the others nodded in agreement. "We'd best build ourselves houses and plant vineyards if we intend to wait for Nicaea to come to her knees through hunger."

"Come, come," reproached Raymond. "O ye of little faith! A blockade of ships is a good first step, and there are other measures we can take. I, for one, will set my men to digging mines. A well-dug trench can overset the thickest of walls. I've seen it done time and time again."

"Do as you like," said Bohemond confidently, "but I say that those walls will never be breached except through betrayal or surrender."

# Chapter 22

Manuel Boutoumites, though he would hardly hold one minute's worth of conversation with the Latins, was a great letter writer. Every day Tancred saw several special envoys leave his tent bearing sealed letters. Most were bound back through the ravine and up to the Sea of Marmara; there they would hand over detailed daily reports to Alexios concerning the progress of the siege. But a few of the messengers—though Tancred could not swear to this—seemed to set out away from Nicaea at first, then double back through the camp. There were unguarded places where a single man could slip through the siege line, and Tancred thought it entirely likely that Boutoumites was in correspondence with the Turkish garrison as well as with Alexios. The subject of that correspondence he could not say for certain, but he liked the whole matter not at all and the circumstances smacked of treachery.

In response to the Crusaders' request, Alexios did send several ships overland, and the lake outside Nicaea's western wall was now as secure as the rest of the line. The siege could commence in earnest now, and for almost a week the Crusaders had the satisfaction of holding Nicaea like a bird in a cage.

Baldwin had been correct when he said it would not take long for Kilij Arslan to leave his warmongering in the east and come back to deal with the invaders. Nicaea was his capital, and what is more, his young wife great with child was immured within her walls. Lose Nicaea and he would lose both his future heir and the plum of his inheritance. Once again the sultan's men came up from the south, and once again it was Raymond's men that bore the brunt of the attack.

It was a little after daybreak when the Turks descended upon them. It was a little after sunset when those who survived the battle limped tiredly back to their tents.

Tancred, eager to participate in the fray, would have taken all his knights to join with the Franks, but Bohemond forbade him to leave his post. "Can you not see that if we do not hold the eastern wall and Godfrey the north, then the Turks will circle round and enter the city by another gate?" Checked in his impetuosity, Tancred was forced to acknowledge his uncle's greater wisdom. But oh, how it galled him to lean on his spear while the Frankish lances were couched in battle!

Surrounded by all the knights of France, Adhemar and Raymond stood out against the superior numbers of the Turkish host. The bishop of Le Puy commanded Raymond's right flank. They had often fought together, these two, against the Moors in Spain in their younger days. The battle was a fierce one. Kilij Arslan fought like a mother bear against a hunter who has captured her cubs—and so did his men, for nearly all of them had wives and children within the city. In the end, it might have gone hard with Raymond had not Robert of Flanders brought up his doughty Flemish knights to spell the Franks. The fresh fervor of the Flemish lent heart to the Franks, and they were able to push the Turks farther and farther away from the walls of the city.

All day the battle raged forward and backward across the southern valley. Both sides lost hundreds of noble warriors. But as night began to fall, Kilij Arslan abandoned the field. The Franks would not budge from the southern wall, and he no longer held out any hope of uniting his army with the garrison inside the gates. The red sunset lit up the blood-soaked sand of the battlefield leaving just enough light to reveal the departure of the sultan.

The Turks inside Nicaea had watched the battle intently, biting their nails down to the quick with each change of fortune, cheering on their countrymen with eager anticipation. Now they saw the dark shadows of a discouraged army retreating into the hills. The younger sentries wondered anxiously whether their sultan meant to renew the assault tomorrow. The older men knew that he had gone for good.

Even with his wife just recently brought to childbed inside the besieged city, Kilij would not hazard his entire army again against a foe that had proved so formidable. There were other cities besides Nicaea in the sultanate of Rum. Kilij would retreat into the heartlands and bide his time till the Crusaders had passed through his domain.

Nicaea's garrison, although disheartened at the sultan's desertion, refused to capitulate. Even without Kilij Arslan, they were not without resources. Their stonework walls were nearly unscalable in height. Their towers bristled with stone-throwing ballistae. Their moat, fed from the western lake, prevented any sudden charge around the three landlocked sides of the city.

The Crusaders braced themselves for the long siege Bohemond had predicted. It soon became apparent that the scarcity of provisions would harm those without the city as well as those within. The valley in which Nicaea was situated had just enough provender for the horses, but it offered no easy provision for the needs of the men. Before bringing the Norman army down to Nicaea, Tancred had gathered as much food as he could lay hands on. That food was long gone. Bohemond had brought more supplies when he came a fortnight later and those too had been devoured by the horde of lance-bearing locusts.

Alexios, who had provided for the Crusaders so liberally while they were at Constantinople, saw the chance to recoup some of the gifts that had left his treasury. The oxen that had carted the ships overland for the blockading of the lake were accompanied by several caravans of victuals. Manuel Boutoumites set up a market aboard the ships. There the Crusaders who had money could buy high-priced raisins, figs, grain, and meat.

Most of the Crusader lords were well equipped to look after their own men. They had brought heavy strongboxes from the west whose weight had only increased from the emperor's gifts. But Tancred's purse was as empty as a widow's cupboard. "My lord," said three of his knights approaching him as he surveyed the sentries' positions one morning, "When will we have grain again in our camp? Last night we ate the boiled head of a donkey, and soon—if nothing is done—we shall be compelled to eat the flesh of our horses."

Tancred's eyes clouded over with concern. He was aware that food was low but he had not known that things were come to such a pass as this. A knight without a horse was of little value—the glory of the Latins' battle line was in the armored charge and lowered lances of mounted men. The horses must be preserved at all costs. "You will have food tonight," Tancred promised them, and pulling sharply on his horse's reins, he cantered northward around the city until he came to the shores of the lake.

The Byzantine floating market was well stocked with bread and fish and cattle on the hoof. "How much for this? How much for this?" Tancred asked several of the merchants. The price they quoted him for a head of mutton was as much as a warhorse would have cost in Bari. A cake of raisins cost as much as one of his mother's fine bracelets. The marquis' light eyes darkened, and he strode angrily across the deck of the ship until he found the cross plank to come ashore again.

The tent of Manuel Boutoumites lay nearby and Tancred entered it without ceremony, surprising the laconic general into a hasty exclamation of surprise.

"My men need food," said Tancred curtly.

Boutoumites shrugged and gestured in the direction of the lake. "The market is open for them."

"They have not the money to buy your usurious fare!" said Tancred. He swallowed painfully. "*I* have not the money to buy it."

Boutoumites stared at him. "That is to be pitied," he said without a flicker of emotion in his dark eyes.

It was no use to beg. Tancred saw that Boutoumites was of no mind to dispense food without the receipt of coin. Indeed, if he had seen the whole of Boutoumites' mind, he would have known that Boutoumites was relishing every moment of this situation. This young Norman upstart had refused to make his obeisance to Alexios. His uncle Bohemond had tried to smooth the matter over with excuses and pleasant-faced lies, but

Alexios' spies had ferreted out the truth of the matter. Let the marquis and his men starve. It was no loss to the emperor.

Tancred stumbled out of the Byzantine's tent, almost blinded by the bright-beamed sun and his own growing sense of helplessness and rage. "Have a care there!" said a sturdy French voice. Tancred looked up to see that he had almost walked directly into Count Raymond.

"Why, Lord Tancred!" said Raymond, putting a hand on the young marquis to steady him. "You look overheated from this hot weather. Are you bound for the market? The cool breeze on the lake will do you good."

"No," said Tancred, a little churlishly, "I've seen enough of the market and these Byzantine Jews. They'd charge a man a bezant for a bowl of cow dung if they thought they could make us pay it!"

Raymond had heard rumors of scant rations in Tancred's camp and was well aware of the reason behind the young marquis' diatribe. "Listen," he said sympathetically. "It does not become a man to boast of his wealth, but I may say without boasting that I have much gold and more than I need. Let me lend you a little until you have the chance to gain your own prize money on this campaign."

The same pride that had compelled Tancred to pay for his own men's equipment at Bari welled up in his breast now at the Frank's words. "I need no man's coin," he said coldly, rejecting the offer that had been made. He pushed past the count without so much as a farewell leaving Raymond with a furrowed brow of concern. Then, mounting his horse, the marquis completed the circuit of the city and returned to his own camp.

It was noonday by now and Tancred's manservant Ralph was awaiting him at his tents. "How fare our Byzantine brethren?" asked Ralph sardonically, for he knew that Tancred had been to the lake where Boutoumites was camped.

Tancred spat. In rough, uncensored language he told Ralph what he thought of the Byzantines and their price gouging. When the marquis bitterly mentioned his encounter with Count Raymond, Ralph grew thoughtful. He waited until Tancred had drunk down a goblet of wine—the last dregs of the last barrel—before he spoke.

"Master," he said. "If your men were in danger, what would you give to save their lives?"

"My own life."

"Would you give your pride?" asked Ralph.

Tancred's brows melted together in confusion. "What do you mean?"

"Why, only this," said Ralph, his voice growing in confidence, "that your men's lives *are* in danger…from hunger. And it is nothing more than your pride that stands in the way of feeding them."

If it had been any other man besides Ralph to say those words, Tancred would have struck him. As it was, he glowered terribly and sent killing thunderbolts with his eyes. Ralph, unashamed of his words, shrugged carelessly in the face of the marquis' ill temper. He turned aside and took up his tools to mend the leather straps of a well-worn saddle. When the silence became unbearable, he began to whistle, a lively tune from sunny Italy and one the soldiers were fond of singing.

Tancred, knowing that Ralph was in the right of the matter, could not stay angry for long. He debated within himself, remembering how he had never taken any man's coin before now but also remembering the promise he had made to his knights—"You will have food tonight." That promise must be kept at all costs. "And after all," he reasoned to himself, "if necessity constrains me to borrow from any man, I would fain choose Count Raymond. He, at least, did not abase himself to swear the oath to Alexios."

# Chapter 23

Later that afternoon, Tancred betook himself to the southern side of the city to seek out the Count of Toulouse. He found him seated in company with the bishop, the bishop's chaplain, and a curly-haired, stocky young man with whom Tancred was unacquainted. At the sight of their approaching visitor, Raymond's eyebrows lifted. "Here comes the young marquis," he mouthed audibly, and all eyes turned to Tancred as he dismounted and approached the Frankish leaders.

Recalling his earlier rudeness—and realizing that he now came in the position of a supplicant—Tancred's cheeks reddened a little. He made his obeisance to the bishop, taking his right hand and pressing his lips to a worn signet ring with the reverse image of the Virgin Mary. The image was different, but the ring itself was of the same workmanship as Pope Urban's signet that depicted the Apostle Peter. After he had greeted Adhemar respectfully, he turned to the Frankish lord. "Count Raymond, I believe I was uncivil to you earlier. I would make amends."

Raymond waved his right hand dismissively. "It is forgotten already. Will you sit with us? We have just tapped a good cask of wine and are in need of good conversation."

"Yes," said Adhemar dryly, his thick forearms bulging out of the rolled up sleeves of his habit, "I'm afraid the brave count and I have known each other for so long that he finds my own conversation dull."

"Not so, not so!" protested Raymond with a smile. "Have you met my nephew?" he asked Tancred with enthusiasm. Tancred shook his head and Raymond presented the stocky, curly-haired young man to him. His name was William-Jordan, and if his face did not lie, he was just a few years older than Tancred. The only son of Raymond's sister, he did not seem as fond of his uncle as Raymond was of him. He acknowledged the introduction very aloofly, and looked away from Tancred as soon as he could without giving obvious offense.

Pressed by the count's hospitality, Tancred sat and took a goblet of wine, a vintage considerably better than the vinegary dregs he had swilled in his own tent. Raymond beamed at their visitor and expatiated at some length on the beauty of unity between soldiers in arms. "And with such goodwill between us, God cannot but bless us in our endeavors. We are making decided progress on the siege," he pronounced confidently.

Adhemar cleared his throat. "Yes, we have achieved two failed mine shafts and three burned siege towers. That is progress, is it not?"

Raymond shook off this pessimism like a wet dog drying his coat. "Preliminary attempts," he declared. "Our third mine is in much better ground. We've discovered the weak places in their defenses. It's only a matter of time before the cross flies over the walls of Nicaea."

Tancred, trained in realism by his uncle, kept his doubts to himself. He was monitoring the count's conversation closely waiting for a favorable interval to make a beggar of himself. How he wished that the bishop had been absent from this interview, both the bishop and that chaplain of his who stood behind him like a deaf and dumb statue! Adhemar was the viceroy of Urban, his liege, and it increased Tancred's shame to admit his poverty before him.

The marquis' attention was so taken up with his own predicament, and the shame of it, that he barely noticed when the bishop addressed him.

"Pope Urban has told me something of you," said the low bass tones of the clerical leader.

"Indeed?" asked Tancred, turning his head sharply in surprise. It pleased him to hear that the pope had remembered him.

"Aye," replied Adhemar. "He said that many had shown enthusiasm for this adventure, but that you seemed to truly embrace the sacredness of the cause." The big man's searching glance moved from the red badge on Tancred's shoulder to the frank blueness of his eyes. "He is right, I think. You have not taken the cross lightly."

"How could I," asked Tancred with sincerity, "when my sins lay so heavily upon me?"

"You must write to him as soon as you enter the gates of Jerusalem. It will gladden his heart to know you have completed your promise."

"I shall put pen to parchment as soon as I have sheathed my sword," said Tancred exultantly. The jubilation did not last long, for the present worry, which had retreated from his mind momentarily, came back with renewed vigor. However much Urban trusted him to batter down the gates of the Holy City, that trust would assuredly be misplaced if he could not feed himself and his men on this first stage of the journey.

Tancred turned from the bishop to the Frankish nobleman. "Count Raymond," he said formally, "I did not come here solely for the good pleasure of your company. You made me an offer earlier today...."

"Say no more, say no more!" said Raymond interrupting him with a lifted hand. "My coffers are open to you, marquis. You shall take what you need and render me an account of it when you can."

Here was the offer again, before he had even abased himself to make the request. Astonished at this generosity, Tancred stammered out his gratitude. Others, including Count Raymond's nephew were just as astonished. William-Jordan stared at his uncle with as much confusion as if he had just seen a snake grow wings. Instead of remonstrating with Raymond, however, the young man merely raked his fingers through his tangled curls, bit his lip, and said nothing, showing a restraint that Tancred was learning to use with his own uncle. Perhaps William-Jordan's entire fortune was dependent on Raymond's good will, in which case, it was best to humor his every whim.

"Take this, Bernard," said Count Raymond, tossing a plump purse to the black-robed cleric behind Adhemar's chair. "Accompany the marquis to the market and pay for whatever he requires."

The thin-faced chaplain looked to the bishop, perhaps resolved that he would take orders only from his own master. Adhemar nodded impassively, giving Bernard permission to go. Setting down his wine goblet, Tancred arose. He lifted the tent flap for the chaplain, and they stepped out of the pavilion.

As the marquis and the chaplain exited, an almost imperceptible frown fell over the face of the bishop. "You are most generous in your money lending," he observed coolly. "Why is that, Raymond?"

But by the time the count made his response, Tancred was too far away from the tent to hear anything of it.

Tancred was soon astride his horse, but Bernard mounted his own steed most clumsily. The animal was a broad, raw-boned nag, and it took all of the chaplain's power and concentration to turn her where he willed.

"You were not trained to the saddle," Tancred stated matter-of-factly.

"No," said Bernard with a wry grin. "And all of these months traveling have not served to remedy that."

"But surely the bishop has taken you on many journeys with him?" asked Tancred. Up until this moment, the tonsured priest had been as mute as Boutoumites, but now it seemed that he had a tongue after all and a ready sense of self-deprecating humor.

"No, not at all," said Bernard. "When I entered the priesthood at Le Puy, I thought I entered Le Puy for good. The church was on the hill, the town was down below, and I never hoped to go anywhere besides the two of them."

"So you did not go to Spain with Bishop Adhemar as his chaplain?"

Bernard shook his head. "I was a canon regular at the time, having not yet been promoted to the prestigious position in which you see me today."

Tancred laughed. "What made you come to the East?"

Bernard snorted. "Bishop Adhemar made me come. I had resolved that nothing would drag me from the confines of our community on the hill. I would stay there as faithfully as Saint Simeon atop his pillar.

Even when Pope Urban passed through our place preaching the 'will of God' and the need of Jerusalem, that did not sway me.

"But when Adhemar's previous chaplain died right after Urban had departed, the bishop offered me the vacant position. 'I will be your chaplain as long as you remain at Le Puy,' I told him, for I knew him of old, how likely he was to wander about the countryside on pilgrimage or in pursuit of some holy cause.

"He feigned astonishment at my proviso—feigned, I say, for it was well known to all in Le Puy that I was as rooted there as the old oak trees. 'How now!' Adhemar said to me. 'Am I to understand that you would choose the part of Orpah rather than the part of Ruth?'

"'You may understand it as you will,' I said, perhaps a little more impertinently than I ought, 'as long as you understand that no promotion or earthly treasure will take me away from Le Puy.'

"He said nothing to this, merely folded his big hands and turned away from me. The following day he told me that he would accept me as his chaplain at Le Puy and pledged to make no demands that I accompany him outside its environs.

"Over the next six months I discovered that to be Adhemar's chaplain was more than to conduct a few masses now and then. I was his scribe, his messenger, his porter, his pupil. Le Puy and all the surrounding region owes fealty to him, and I became his constant attendant as he dealt with complaining tenants, visiting dignitaries, and ecclesiastical disputes. To those who do not know him, the bishop's physical appearance mayhap belies his mental sharpness and pious benevolence. In body he looks as brash and bullish and overweening as any baron who has achieved his lands by brute power. But in speech and thought he is ever courteous, kind, peaceable, just, and true.

"When the time had elapsed that Pope Urban had prescribed for the Crusade preparations, Count Raymond came from Toulouse to take Adhemar with him on the long journey. Bishop Adhemar began to make arrangements for another chaplain to accompany him on the journey. He did not reproach me for a lack of desire to go, but neither did he ask me to attend him—I had made myself clear on that point. In a few more days they would be away to the east, perhaps away forever.

"As I contemplated Adhemar's departure, a strange feeling welled up inside of me. I found that as much as I could not bear to leave Le Puy, even more, I could not bear to part with the Bishop Adhemar. The night before his departure, I made my confession to him and besought him on bended knees not to leave me behind like an unwanted stepchild.

"'Ah! You are Orpah no longer then?' he said with a sparkle in his eye, and I knew then that he had foreseen that such a transformation might come about in me. I had little to pack—a priest owns hardly more than his habit—and on the morrow I set out with the bishop and the count on this adventure I never desired, on a quest I never dreamed to undertake."

"You travel in a worthy company," replied Tancred cordially. "Of all the leaders encamped before Nicaea, I think your master and his friend are the most honorable by far." Tancred slowed his horse to match the uneven pace of Bernard's mount. "The bishop and Count Raymond seem as close as brothers in fellowship," he observed.

Bernard's thin face smiled knowingly. "So it would seem," he said. "Though"—he could not resist adding—"the Holy Scriptures themselves provide many examples of brethren whose fellowship was easily broken."

"But you yourself attest to the qualities of your bishop, and Count Raymond appears extremely worthy and amiable," objected Tancred.

"Yes," replied Bernard vaguely, "So he appears." Tancred shot him a questioning look, but the chaplain's horse began to shy and buck as a dust-covered snake casually crossed the path in front of them. It took all of Bernard's efforts to calm the beast and avoid being thrown. By the time the reptile had passed and they had resumed their conversation, the lake and Boutoumites' floating marketplace was only a field-length away.

They came to the docks and dismounted. Bernard pulled out the heavy purse from the breast of his habit, and Tancred heard the coins clink against each other. "Listen," said Bernard softly, before they came within earshot of the Greek merchants. "I know you are compelled to take this gold for the sake of your men and their hunger, but be advised that such a debt will take more repayment than you anticipate. Raymond is the head now, and you are the tail. Have a care that he does not turn you and wag you about wherever he pleases."

"I thank you for your advice," said Tancred, a little confused by Bernard's low-spoken confidence, "but have no fear that I will do anything contrary to my honor. And what is more, I am certain that Count Raymond would not ask such a thing of me."

"That is as may be," said Bernard with a shrug of his thin shoulders. He dropped the heavy bag of metal into Tancred's outstretched hands. "Only consider yourself warned, my friend. Esau sold his birthright for a bowl of pottage, and what would he not have given afterwards to have that inheritance back again?"

# Chapter 24

Thanks to Count Raymond's munificence, Tancred procured enough food for his men to last them several weeks. It was a good thing too, for the Turks inside the city still showed no sign of yielding. The Crusaders had piled the heads of the sultan's fallen men outside the walls, but the infidels refused to be terrified. Both sides knew that Nicaea had been built and fortified by the greatest architects in the world. Byzantine construction was unparalleled, and so far both the sappers and the catapults had failed to make a dent in the Turkish defenses.

The month of June began. Robert of Normandy and his brother-in-law, Stephen of Blois, finished dallying on the road and arrived at long last before the walls of Nicaea. With little military action to occupy them, Bohemond, Tancred, Richard of Salerno, and young William spent several hours scrutinizing and studying Robert. As Duke of Normandy he was the acknowledged head of their race, but Bohemond had determined, even before his arrival, that he would yield no precedence to him in the Crusaders' councils.

"I've heard that he's mortgaged his realm for ten thousand marks," said Tancred, "to raise the money for this adventure."

"Who gave him the money for it?" asked William.

"His brother William the Red, the king of England," replied Tancred. "Robert thought it a fair trade and he plans to acquire enough plunder in the east to buy it back on his return."

"The more fool him!" burst in Bohemond. "Red William has had his eye on Normandy ever since their fat father found a pauper's grave.

He'll never give it back to Robert, and, in any case, the people there will not desire him to return it."

"Is Robert such an evil man?" asked William. As a single knight instead of a company commander, he took no part in the Crusader councils of war and thus had less opportunity than the others to observe the Duke of Normandy face to face.

"Just the opposite," replied Tancred. "He seems to act with such piety and mercy and devotion that I've never seen the like in all my days—unless you look to Godfrey of Boulogne who spends more time at his prayers than in his bed. But Robert's very mercy is in itself a cruelty for it is utterly devoid of wisdom. They say that when a thief or ravisher or murderer is brought before him for judgment, the criminal has but to burst into tears—Robert's heart will melt and he will pardon him straightway. Think you the common people like that, to have murderers running loose among them?"

"And what's more," said Bohemond, eager to find fault with one whom some might account his superior, "he's hopelessly extravagant. He'd empty his treasury to purchase some pretty dog or sparrow hawk. And when the coffers are bare, the peasants must pay and pay again to have them filled. No, they'll not be pleased to have him back if he ever returns from this Crusade. King William has the land for good, I'll wager."

Richard of Salerno, who had been in his cups all day and now lay prostrate on the floor of the tent, sat up suddenly to add his tidbit to the conversation. "I've heard his men call him Robert Curthose," he giggled. "But only behind his back!"

"What does that mean?" asked William.

Richard hiccupped and lay down again, putting a hand to his muddled head. "More wine," he mumbled and reached for the cup that was near him.

"Short stockings," replied Bohemond, indulgently filling his cousin's cup. "They say his father dubbed him that when he was a lad, knowing that he would always be a small man in many ways, that he'd never measure up to the glories of the family name."

Hearing Bohemond's explanation, Richard's giggle turned into a hearty laugh. Inevitably, he choked on his wine and fell into a vigorous bout of coughing.

"Why such mirth?" demanded Tancred after he had slapped the breath back into his brother-in-law.

"Why, I was thinking of the name Bohemond's father gave *him*." said Richard. "Bohemond. The giant! Truly, coz, *you* should have been the Duke of Normandy and not this Robert fellow. Your father knew that when he named you after a giant troll!"

"I should have been not only the Duke of Normandy, but also the emperor of the East," replied Bohemond calmly, "and would have been too if we had not lost Durazzo through the impious treachery of the Germans. But it is no matter now. The East has many opportunities in store for me—for us all!" He included the whole room with a generous gesture of his hand.

"But nephews," he said, training his eyes on both of them, but on Tancred in particular, "if you would fly high in this world, you must take care to imp your wing on mine and mine alone. Others will coax you with favors and blandishments, but once they have used you for their own ends, what then? They have no natural affection for you and will cast you away like a handful of chaff. But I—I will do my duty by my kin as long as they do their duty by me. Do not forget it."

"Yes, uncle," said Tancred and William simultaneously, their response an instinctual relic from childhood when Bohemond had been life's schoolmaster and they his pupils.

"So," thought Tancred inwardly, "Bohemond has heard of my borrowing from Raymond and it does not please him. Well, let him storm. It is better to be indebted to an honorable count than to an intriguing uncle who will give his word and break it when it suits him."

While the Normans from Southern Italy spent their time finding new reasons to despise Robert of Normandy, that Duke pitched his camp on the north side of the city. His army greatly added to the Crusaders' numbers, but in the current food shortage this was no boon. It was ingenuity that the army needed to get inside Nicaea, not reinforcements.

As the month of June wore on, Count Raymond of Toulouse optimistically continued his efforts to undermine or over-climb one of the towers. He was frequently in conference with the Byzantine engineers, trying to communicate with them as best he could how to build the siege equipment that he desired. Following a crude drawing made by one of the Frankish knights, the engineers had constructed Raymond a mobile shed, called a penthouse, that could be pushed up against the base of the wall. While the armored roof deflected missiles from above, the men inside could dig furiously under the foundations of the city. Hopefully, they would weaken the wall enough to cause a collapse and effect a breach.

Unfortunately, the first penthouse that the engineers constructed was an utter failure, and a fatal one at that. Perhaps they misunderstood the design, perhaps they were overhasty in their construction, or perhaps, as some said, the Byzantine engineers were as happy to see the Latins humbled as were the Turks. Whatever the cause, after the penthouse was rolled up beneath the city and the sappers had begun their work, the armored shed mysteriously collapsed killing all the Franks inside.

Raymond harangued the engineers and they tried again. This time they were more careful with their hammers. The penthouse did not collapse; the sappers did their work, but the digging was slow and difficult. Darkness fell just as the Franks had made a small breach in the wall, and they were forced to leave any assault till morning's light. The Turks were no fools. During the night they closed the breach and burned the equipment that lay at the foot of their walls. In the morning, when one French knight approached the site to reconnoiter, they captured him, killed him, and hung his body from the newly reinforced wall.

After this the Frankish knights grew warier of attempting any kind of assault. Raymond exhorted them to persevere. "That wall is tottering!" he insisted. "Do you think they had time to build it anew with stone and mortar? A heavy wind could knock it over, to say nothing of a charge from the best knights in Christendom!"

But the men were not convinced, and nothing was done until a third penthouse could be constructed. Once the armored shed had been pushed across the ditch and placed against the wall, the diggers found that the Turkish repairs had been superficial at best. Sweating like field hands in the small enclosure, they swiftly undermined a short section of the wall. But instead of allowing it to fall—and alerting the Turks to their danger—they supported the heavy stones with wooden props from underneath. "They'll think we've failed to make any headway," said one of the diggers, covered in sandy dirt from head to toe. "But when night comes we'll set fire to the wood and the whole thing will come tumbling down."

When the moon rose that night, it was overshadowed by the great blaze of fire along the southern wall. Many panicked cries were heard from inside the city as the Turks watched one of their towers and a long length of the wall crumble into the void below. This breach was impossible to patch before morning's light, and it boded disaster for the besieged. The Latins had made their own gate into the city. Tomorrow the assault would begin.

The news of what Raymond had accomplished passed swiftly throughout the Crusader camp, and the other leaders informed their men to be ready to fight at daybreak. Tancred, giddy with anticipation, slept poorly. Tomorrow they would overthrow the first stronghold on the road to Jerusalem.

As soon as there was light enough to see his hand before his face, he arose from his bed and called for Ralph to bring him his arms. "Today Nicaea will fall," Tancred said to himself as he shrugged his linen tunic over his broad shoulders. He did not have time to put on his armor before he heard a great commotion outside.

"You'll be wishing to have a look at this, my lord," said Ralph, thrusting his moustaches inside the flap of the tent.

Tancred, still barefoot and naked except for his under-tunic, ran outside to find the cause of the clamor. A crowd had gathered. Every eye was directed to the top of Nicaea's keep where a symbol, the same one that had appeared to Constantine before Milvian Bridge, flamed out in the sky. It was the *Chi-Rho* stamped on the red Byzantine flag.

Nicaea had surrendered in the night, but not to the Crusader army.

# Chapter 25

Seeing the Byzantine flag flying high on the citadel of Nicaea, the Crusader lords quickly met in council to discuss the event. Many of the leaders did not fully understand the implications of what had occurred overnight.

"God be praised!" cried Godfrey. "Nicaea is taken at last!"

"Yes, but not by us," interjected Baldwin. His arms were folded across his chest in consternation as he stared up at the flag.

"This is a strange turn of events!" said gray-haired Raymond a little petulantly. To his men had gone the glory of bringing down the wall, and the Crusader lords had all acknowledged him the right to lead the first assault in the morning. Now such an assault was superfluous.

A little late to arrive, Bohemond and Tancred galloped up on their warhorses and, sliding from their saddles, joined the other leaders in conference. They had taken a circuitous route to Raymond's camp, and, coming from the lake, had found the Byzantine ships nearly deserted. "Boutoumites' men are all inside the city," reported Bohemond. "This has been planned for some time, I think."

Tancred remembered the letter carriers he had seen leaving Boutoumites' tent and surreptitiously making their way through the siege lines. "Aye, the Byzantines have been negotiating with the Turks almost from the beginning. They left us to do the hard work in the field then swooped in like a falcon once we'd flushed out the prey."

Hugh the Great, still yawning from his early morning awakening, pooh-poohed Tancred's resentful comments. "Byzantines or Latins, it's all one to me. The fact of the matter is that we have the city now, and I, for one, mean to go inside and get Boutoumites to give me a comfortable bed and a proper meal."

Bishop Adhemar, who had remained silent this whole while, now entered the discussion. "I wonder whether our Byzantine friends mean to play innkeeper. Is it not in their best interests to keep our armies *outside* Nicaea?"

"If that is the case, my men will be furious!" said Baldwin, already looking so himself. "They've waited in this filthy desert for a month aching for a sack. They must be paid with plunder. It is their due!"

"You do realize," said Adhemar calmly, "that most of the inhabitants of this place are Greeks—yes, and Christians too. Do you really want your men to ravish their daughters and rifle through their belongings? The Turks have lorded it over them for twenty years, and now they must be only too glad to be in the palm of their emperor once more. And I myself, along with the citizens, have small wish to see the city come to harm. Nicaea has a long and rich history. It was built long before Constantinople and has seen the defeat of heresies, of armies, and of empires. Surely, such a place is not deserving of pillage."

Some of the Crusader lords acknowledged the justice of Adhemar's words. Others agreed with Baldwin that it was unfair to deny the soldiers a sack. They began to murmur among themselves in rancorous tones till Robert of Flanders, that sturdy soldier, bluntly cut to the heart of the matter. "We'd best send an embassy to Boutoumites and see what he is thinking," he said. "Then we'll know how to proceed."

Applauded for his level-headedness, Robert of Flanders was chosen as the best representative. He took a score of knights and rode toward the southern gate, signaling to the guards—Byzantines now, not Turks—that he desired admittance. The knights pulled up short in front of the stationary portcullis. Several moments elapsed. Eventually, it became obvious to all those waiting outside that the gates were not going to open up in welcome.

A commotion on the battlements caught their attention. Craning their necks upward, Count Robert and his knights saw the dark visage of Manuel Boutoumites on the parapet above. Instead of his usual soldier's garb, he wore a robe of purple with a gold chain about his neck. He leaned over the crenellated wall and stared at the Crusader embassy with uncommunicative eyes.

"Greetings!" said Count Robert. "We have heard the blessed news of the surrender."

"Yes," said Boutoumites, speaking through an interpreter, "God has been for us. The Turks are in chains and will be sent captive to our emperor."

"Now that Nicaea is ours, we Latins seek entrance to the city. Is there room inside to lodge all of our armies?"

Up on the gatehouse tower, Boutoumites and his surrounding officials carried on a hasty conversation in Greek. Their swiftly spoken foreign words drifted off into the wind, and Robert waited patiently below, ignorant of what they discussed.

Finally, Boutoumites' interpreter spoke in formal phrases. "The citizens of Nicaea are uneasy to have so many armed men wander about their streets, and so it is necessary that you continue to lodge in the field. As at Constantinople, we shall open a postern gate to admit a few dozen of your men each day so that they may admire the interior of the city."

Count Robert, normally patient, placid, and imperturbable, registered some surprise at this refusal to admit the Crusaders. "You do not have the authority to deny us entrance, General Boutoumites," he said loudly. "The emperor will not be pleased."

"As newly-appointed Duke of Nicaea, that authority most fortunately is mine," replied Boutoumites through his mouthpiece. Robert's mouth dropped. So, Alexios had given control of the city to his favorite—that explained the purple robe and golden chain.

"The emperor thanks you for your service," continued Boutoumites. "The Turks most certainly would not have surrendered without the pressure applied by you Latins."

"That is a great consolation," said Count Robert baldly, with as much sarcasm as he could muster. "I bid you good day, Boutoumites!"

And with that, the Flemish count retreated with his company of knights, their horses kicking up a cloud of yellow dust as they went.

When they heard Count Robert's report, the Crusaders' annoyance rapidly became outrage. "So, this is how Alexios means to deal with us!" said Baldwin, his brows black with thunder.

"Boutoumites—Duke of Nicaea?" said Bohemond with a sneer. Tancred sensed the underlying covetousness in his uncle's tone. If the emperor had offered the dukedom of Nicaea to Bohemond, he would have taken it on the spot.

Tancred had always known that he was in the right to refuse homage to Alexios. Now, he felt doubly vindicated. In return for Alexios' military assistance on the Crusade, the other lords had promised to yield up to Alexios all cities and territories that had formerly belonged to Byzantium. And this is how Alexios repaid them, by refusing them admittance into the very city they had helped him regain!

Godfrey, who had taken much less affront than his brother Baldwin, declared his intention of applying to Boutoumites for a pass to enter the city. "Perhaps it is unkind of the emperor to keep our armies out," he said, "but I will not give up the chance to pray in Nicaea's churches."

"And I will go with you!" said Duke Robert of Normandy, not to be outdone in piety by the German. At Godfrey's urging, several of the others agreed to go as well, their seething anger softening into a mere sullen resentment.

"Tancred, will you join us?" asked Godfrey, his bright blue eyes staring appealingly at the Norman.

"Beg a pass from Boutoumites? Not I!" said Tancred with a snort. He knew how much pleasure the Byzantine general would take in refusing to give him one. But later, when the other lords had abased themselves and obtained entrance, a longing came over him to see the city he had spent over a month besieging.

"William!" he hissed softly, finding his brother resting idly back at the Norman camp.

"What is it?" asked William, a little too loudly for Tancred's tastes.

"Hush!" said Tancred putting a finger to his lips. He leaned toward his brother's ear. "How would you like to visit the streets of Nicaea with me?"

William looked over at the horizon where the sun had already sunk behind Nicaea's towers. "Is it not too late to get a pass for tonight?"

Tancred laughed softly. "Did we need a pass the time we scaled the keep at Salerno?"

A slow grin crept over William's face. That had been an adventure, when the two brothers—all at Tancred's instigation—had climbed the donjon tower at Salerno, simply to prove to their odious brother-in-law Richard that his sentries were as capable as blind old beggar women.

"Well," said William, "if we don't need a pass, I presume the daylight is also unnecessary."

"Exactly so," said Tancred, pleased that his brother had caught the drift of his plan. "We'll wait till dark and then find our way in. It should not be difficult."

The Byzantines posted around the walls and on the gate towers were as alert as an alderman after his noonday meal—which is to say, not at all. They anticipated no disturbances. The Turkish soldiers inside the city had been bound and secured—they would be sent to Alexios as soon as transport could be arranged. The scouts had brought no word of Kilij Arslan organizing any reprisals. It seemed certain that he had deserted his capital for good. The only incursions to dread then were from their Crusader allies, and the haughty Greeks had little enough fear of them. Boutoumites had given them the emperor's orders. There was no reason to suppose that the Latins would not obey.

Wearing dark cloaks that fully covered their colorful clothing, Tancred and William left their horses behind at the camp. It was a moonless night though the stars shone bright enough for them to pick out a path. The brothers had wrapped rags around their boots to mask the sound of footsteps. They opted to approach the eastern gate, certain that the south side of the city, with its breached wall, would be more heavily guarded.

"What do you mean to do?" whispered William as they approached the postern. "Bribe the gatekeeper?"

"No, I shall convince him that we are Greeks, secret messengers from Alexios. Now hush—no more of our tongue. And hunch down a little. You and I are too tall for true Byzantines."

The two Normans stepped surreptitiously toward the little gate on the left side of the tower. Tancred had raised a fist, intending to knock for admittance, when miraculously the gate opened of its own accord.

Startled, Tancred and William flung themselves backwards and pressed their bodies against the base of the wall. Was it a night patrol? Boutoumites and the Byzantines were more vigilant than they had expected. Hopefully, their dark cloaks would conceal them from whatever party sought egress.

Tancred's wide pupils, accustomed by now to seeing in the dark, picked out the forms of two large men. Like the Normans, they wore dark clothes. They seemed to be in much haste. Between them they bore a small litter, resting lightly on two carrying poles and curtained off with fabric as black as the night air. As soon as the litter-bearers had slipped through the gate with their burden, the face of the gate-keeper himself appeared. "Remember our agreement!" he grunted in Greek, his brown face illuminated by a small candle that he held.

As if in response, the curtains of the litter undulated a little. A small hand reached out and tossed a leather bag in the gatekeeper's direction. It fell at the man's feet, and the dull clink of coin upon coin was unmistakable. Satisfied, the man picked it up and placed it in the breast of his garment. The light of the candle flickered briefly then disappeared as the postern gate was shut.

The two litter-bearers began to stride quickly and quietly across the plain. Tancred waited until they reached the shallow moat then began to follow in their tracks. "But Tancred!" said William, scurrying to catch up with his older brother. "Shall we not try the gate as we purposed? We know now that the gatekeeper is corruptible."

Tancred shook his head intently. "Why see the mysteries of Nicaea when we have a better mystery right here before our faces? I must know who is in that litter and whither it is traveling. Quick! Follow, or we shall lose them!"

William sighed and fell into step behind the marquis. Here was a different adventure altogether and not one that he had anticipated.

# Chapter 26

The moonless night was a double-edged blessing to the Norman trackers. On the one hand, they could be less careful of their own outlines against the dark sky, but on the other hand, it was easy to lose sight of the litter bearers. The sturdy black figures had passed the moat and were heading east. Unwilling to alert their quarry with any telltale splashes, Tancred and William waited to cross the water until the litter bearers had passed a bowshot beyond it.

Bohemond's army, which had been responsible for cordoning off the eastern side of the city, had posted few watchmen that night. The city was taken. The sultan was in hiding. There was no reason for sentries to bite their fingernails in apprehension of an attack.

Tancred saw the litter bearers moving soundlessly through a gap in the Crusader line. In front of them rose the foothills that ringed the Nicene valley, dotted with trees and caves and other hiding places. "Hurry, William!" he hissed. "We must overtake them before they disappear into the forest." The long-legged marquis broke into a run—not even the rags wrapped around his boots could conceal his pounding footsteps—and William followed his example.

The litter bearers, feeling the vibrations of the swiftly approaching brothers, were in no position to defend themselves as long as they held the carrying poles of the litter. They set down their cargo in alarm, drew curved swords from their belts, and adopted a defensive stance in front of the litter. Whatever was behind those black curtains was worth protecting.

Seeing the faint glint of starlight on their weapons, Tancred and William pulled up sharply, threw back their cloaks, and drew their own blades. "Who are you?" demanded Tancred, first in Greek and then in Arabic. The burly litter bearers made no response.

"What is inside that litter?"

Again, there was no reply.

Tancred nodded meaningfully to William, and the two brothers lunged forward with their weapons. The bearers were ready for them, and blade caught on blade with a metallic ring that broke the stillness of the night. The Turks were adept—Tancred was certain now that these were no Byzantines—but the Normans had the longer sword reach as well as the longer arm. Each of the brothers had wounded their opponent, and it was only a matter of time before the panting litter bearers would receive their deathblow.

"Stop! I command you!" said a soft voice in delicately formed Arabic syllables. The black curtains parted like the wings of a moth revealing a dark-eyed woman in shimmery white. Her gauzy surcoat was bound tightly beneath her breasts with an embroidered sash, and her arms hung heavily with jeweled bracelets and rings. On her lap lay a dark bundle of cloth that she clung to protectively.

Reluctantly yielding to their mistress' commands, the Turkish litter bearers dropped their swords and bent their necks in surrender.

"Lady, who are you?" asked Tancred, still keeping a wary eye on his erstwhile opponents. The black bundle on her lap began to mew like a frightened kitten. In that instant, he knew the answer to his own question.

"Sultana," he said respectfully. It was the wife and newly born son that Kilij Arslan had abandoned along with his capital.

She clutched the baby to her breast and surveyed the marquis with her jet-black eyes, with one swift glance taking in the cropped yellow hair of his head, the long, keen sword in his hand, and the red cross stitched tightly to his shoulder. "Good knight," she said, "as you are a Christian, will you let us pass unharmed?"

Tancred's brow furrowed. This Turkish beauty and her royal child could be important hostages to obtain Kilij Arslan's good behavior as the Crusaders traveled south. And yet it was not in his nature to deny a lady anything she asked. "Where will you go?" he asked. "To your husband in the mountains?"

She laughed, a dark, ugly laugh that should have come from a sphinx or a gorgon. "No, indeed! Kilij Arslan has shown the world just how much he values his wife and son." She cradled the baby in her arms, the sweet tenderness of her body contrasting with the fierce anger in her voice. "I will never go back to the son of Suleiman—or should I say that son of Satanas!"

Tancred stared, bewildered by the hate in her voice, until he remembered the rumor that the Byzantine sailor had shared with him, that Kilij Arslan had murdered his own father-in-law. Later, others had confirmed the tale, adding gruesome detail to the story of betrayal and kinslaying.

The murder had happened not six months after Chaka, the emir of Smyrna, had given his daughter in marriage to Kilij Arslan. Chaka was an enterprising Turk who had built up a powerful kingdom on the islands and eastern coast of the Aegean Sea. He viewed Kilij Arslan, the sultan of Rum, as a sympathetic ally and proposed the marriage for their mutual benefit.

Kilij Arslan, having newly taken possession of his domain, was young, cunning, and ruthless. He agreed to the marriage but did not intend to let it trammel his ambitions. Asia Minor was his, and he did not want it carved up in pieces and held by petty emirs. This Chaka, with his island kingdom, was a threat to the solidarity of Rum. He must be dealt with accordingly.

Perhaps Kilij Arslan had formulated his plot even before the wedding ceremony, but in any case, it is certain that he used the close relationship to lure Chaka unarmed to a great feast. He plied him with wine till his senses were confused, and then drawing a dagger, killed his wife's father with his own hand. Some said that he had ordered all his palace women, including his wife, into the banquet room so that they could watch the horrific event.

Whatever had transpired that night, it was clear that it had snuffed out any desire in the sultana to ever see her husband again.

"Where will you go then?" asked Tancred.

"My brother is the emir of Smyrna. He will take us in and give us protection."

"Is he all that is left of your house?"

"No," she said, and her voice softened a little. "I have a sister, in Antioch, at the court of my uncle."

Tancred grunted. He knew of Antioch by reputation. It was the next significant stronghold the Crusaders would have to conquer on their route to the Holy Land.

The sultana looked at him. "You are bound for Antioch, are you not?" She did not wait for an answer. "And it will assuredly fall before you just like this city of Nicaea. I know how it will be," she said. "The sultans and the emirs cannot put aside their petty differences to stand against you. One by one, the Mussulman kingdoms will topple before your army."

She was a winsome woman, with her dark hair, almond eyes, and full breasts. The helpless infant in her lap only added to the piteous-ness of her plight. The marquis made up his mind to allow her escape. Tugging sharply on the curtains of the litter, he began to pull them shut around her. "Hurry, get you gone into the hills before the watch wakens from their wine and spots you. *Salaam*, lady! The peace of Christ go with you."

He would have called to her litter bearers and bade them take up the carrying poles, but she preempted him by placing her small hand on his forearm. "You are no common soldier," she said, having observed Tancred's bearing and dress throughout their conversation. "You are an emir? You have your own following, yes?"

Tancred shrugged in acceptance of her description. A marquis and an emir were similar enough in rank not to quibble.

"Please, listen to me," said the sultana, and she leaned her face closer to him in the stark blackness of the night. "When your people take Antioch, it will not be handed to you as peacefully as Nicaea was. I know the horrors of sack and pillage, men like animals on fire with rage and lust. I am afraid, afraid for my sister. You have dealt well with me, and I can see that you are a man of honor. When Antioch falls to your sword, will you look out for my sister there and take her under your protection?"

Tancred hesitated. She asked a boon most difficult to accomplish. "How will I recognize her? And how will she know to trust me?"

"She will be housed in the family apartments in the citadel," said the sultana confidently. "She has my countenance, but her features are even finer. There is not a more beautiful woman in all of Antioch—you will know her when you see her. Her name, in the Greek tongue, is Erminia."

She fumbled with her hands in the dark and, removing a ring with a large emerald from her finger, placed it inside Tancred's broad palm. "Take this ring," she said. "It is an heirloom of my family's. The one who wears it on his hand will have fortune on his side. You do not believe me? It is true. The ring has a power—how else would I have gotten past the Byzantine guards to escape from Nicaea? My sister will know the ring and know that it came from me." The sultana took Tancred's fingers and curled them tightly around the talisman.

Tancred considered the ring and considered the lady. He decided to dedicate himself to her desire. "Very well, I shall do as you ask." He placed the lucky ring on the littlest finger of his left hand, the only finger small enough to fit inside the slender circlet. "I will hold this ring in trust till I place it in your sister's hands."

As the marquis promised his help to the sultana, an ominous feeling descended upon him and weighed down his shoulders like a lead cloak. He had just done something momentous, although he was not sure what. The swollen rivers and the Via Egnatia were only a faint memory, and the Macedonian crone whom he had rescued was merely a day's adventure six months past.

But even though a seer's words may easily be forgotten, they will not so easily fall to the ground. *Soon you will meet a great lady who will ask your help. The choice is yours whether to render it, but if you do, you will find great love and also great sorrow.* The marquis—albeit unwittingly—had made his choice by promising the sultana his help. It remained to be seen if Erminia and the emerald ring would bring the love and sorrow that were prophesied.

# Chapter 27

"Tancred!" interrupted William abruptly. He had been dutifully guarding the disarmed litter bearers while the marquis conversed with the beautiful sultana, a younger brother's portion in life. "Look to the hills! We are not alone."

Prior to being accosted, the sultana's men had carried her all the way to the fringe of trees surrounding the valley. Now a large party of men rode out of those trees, their horses marching in tight ranks and their upper bodies fitted with chain mail.

"Do you have a tryst with this company?" Tancred asked urgently. Perhaps this was a bodyguard she had arranged to meet outside the city.

"No," she said, a shade of panic growing in her voice. "And by the look of their armor, these are no Turks. These must be Boutoumites' men." She looked at Tancred appealingly. "We cannot outrun them. What shall I do?"

Tancred cursed beneath his breath. That gatekeeper must have earned double payment tonight, once for releasing the sultana and once for reporting her whereabouts. "I will speak to them," said the young Norman. He stepped forward and interposed himself between the litter and the advancing troop. "Hold there!" he said, raising a firm hand in the air. "Who are you and whither are you bound?"

The rider in the center spoke a quick word and the armored men reined in their mounts. Tancred could not make out the man's features in the dark, but his bearing seemed familiar. "I am the Duke of Nicaea," said the man distastefully. "We are in search of fugitive prisoners. Stand aside, sentry."

Tancred stiffened. It was Boutoumites himself. Instantly, Tancred's resolve to facilitate the sultana's escape deepened. Now it was not merely a courtesy to the lady but also an ill turn that he could serve the Byzantine.

"I am no sentry, sirrah," said the marquis haughtily, and he announced his name and pedigree to Alexios' general.

"The night is late for you to be wandering outside your camp," said Boutoumites, narrowing his eyes at Tancred. He had not failed to observe the black-curtained litter deposited directly behind the marquis.

"My brother is sick," said Tancred, lying fluently. "The night air beside the city is stagnant and stifling, so I am bringing him up into the hills to cool his fever."

William listened to Tancred's subterfuge and reacted as his brother had intended. Swiftly and silently he slipped inside the curtains, hoping that the movement would not be marked in the moonless night and praying that the sultana would not cry out in distress. But Kilij Arslan's wife had enough wits to understand the situation. She pressed the little black bundle closer to her breast, pulled her gauzy white skirts tightly together, and slid over to make room for the tall Norman.

Tancred snapped his fingers at the two litter bearers and they hefted the litter—considerably heavier now with its extra occupant—onto their shoulders. Both of the Turks had been pricked by the Norman swords in the earlier imbroglio, but they stoically bore their burden without the smallest wince of pain. The sultana had chosen sturdy and faithful men to aid her escape.

Without asking leave from the Duke of Nicaea, Tancred and the carriers pressed forward to ascend the hill. Boutoumites dug his heels into his horse's belly and, catching up with them, circled the litter. "These litter-bearers are no Normans," he remarked suspiciously.

"Obviously not," said Tancred coolly. "They are Turkish slaves that I have acquired. Why would I waste good Norman sinews on fetching and carrying?" He strode on imperiously, hoping fervently that his bluff would carry the day.

Boutoumites stared after the marquis, rapidly turning over the situation in his mind. The Norman's tale was plausible enough to be true, and indeed, why would a Crusader help a fleeing Turk? Whatever the differences between the Byzantines and the Latins, at least they shared a common enemy. Perhaps it was better to let this party go and leave themselves free to continue the search for the escaped prisoner.

The litter bearers had almost submerged themselves in the forest when disaster struck. A faint cry, like the mewing of a small cat, pierced the darkness. Tancred's heart sank within him. Boutoumites, still within earshot, stiffened instantly like a bloodhound that has caught the scent. That was not the cry of a grown man coming from the litter.

Squished into one corner of the curtains to make room for William, the sultana quickly put her hand over the infant's mouth. She pressed the whimpering bundle closer to her breast, but it was already too late. Kilij Arslan's tiny offspring had betrayed his mother into the Byzantines' hands.

"Lord Tancred!" said Boutoumites, unable to conceal the triumph in his voice. "This plan of yours, to go into the hills, is not a good one. Come, we will bring this litter back to Nicaea and my own physician will attend your brother's illness." He signaled for his men to advance and they began to encircle the small party.

"No," said Tancred defiantly. "I will do as I like with my own brother. You have no reason to interfere."

"No reason?" asked the general. He lowered his spear and began to prod the curtains with the butt of the weapon.

"Leave be!" said Tancred, batting aside the spear shaft with an angry fist.

Boutoumites considered this enough provocation to put an end to all politeness. He barked an order to his men. Half a dozen of them dismounted and, despite the marquis' vigorous protests, threw back the curtains. William's pale face and the sultana's gauzy dress reflected dully in the starlight.

Boutoumites turned an accusing face to Tancred. "It is you who should have left be," he said flatly. "And now, you will suffer because of it."

There was no point to struggling—the odds forbade it. Tancred let his limbs hang loosely as they pinioned his arms behind his back.

"Since you are so determined to accompany the sultana, I will bring you with me when I deliver her to Alexios," said Boutoumites. "I daresay the emperor will want words with you over this incident."

"But the army marches within the week," objected Tancred. "There is no time for me to go to Constantinople and back."

The Greek's dark eyebrows arched. "To Constantinople? There is no need for that. The emperor is far closer than you realize. He has been monitoring the siege from just beyond the northern pass."

With a succession of short, sharp commands, Boutoumites removed William from the litter, transferred the sultana into the charge of his own men, and formed up a procession to re-enter Nicaea by way of the eastern gate. The stealth with which the troop had ridden out was abandoned now, and the Byzantine soldiers tramped through the Norman camp like a herd of high-spirited bullocks.

Bohemond, hearing the noise of hooves, was quick to rise from his bed and see the cavalcade pushing its way past his tents. The Norman count had hastily thrown on his mail shirt and snatched up his sword belt in case of trouble. By the light of the torches, he saw his nephew, or rather, both his nephews, bound and being led on foot like common criminals. He rubbed his eyes to make sure he was no longer dreaming. "How now, Boutoumites!" he demanded loudly. "What insult is this?"

The Greek general reined in his horse and acknowledged Count Bohemond with a curt salute. "Your nephews were abetting the escape of one of my hostages," he said bluntly. "I must bring them to Alexios to answer for it, or at least this one"—he pointed a thumb at Tancred—"since he is the ringleader of the plot."

Bohemond's eyes glittered like a dragon's. If *he* had caught Tancred and William at such an escapade, he would have breathed so hot a fire on them that they never would have forgotten it. But as it was, he would not stand for a stranger—and especially Boutoumites!—censuring the scions of his house. He opened his mouth to answer with words as sharp as a slap in the face.

But before they were spoken, he thought of a wiser way to handle the matter. His jaw relaxed into a nonchalant yawn. "Yes, you are quite right. Tancred must go to see the emperor and answer for his actions. How fortunate that I am planning to attend upon him this very day. Alexios has summoned all the leaders of the Crusade to receive remuneration for the successful siege, and I hear that he is nearby, just north of the pass."

Bohemond walked briskly over to his nephews and, quick as a pickpocket, slipped a dagger through the knots that bound their hands. "You can release them to me, general, and I will see that they make amends to your sovereign."

Boutoumites frowned. It had not been his intention to let the young marquis go so easily. But Bohemond was a masterful man, and the Greek general was unsure how high the Norman stood in Alexios' good graces. Unwilling to pick a quarrel with him, Boutoumites ceded the field. "Very well," he said grudgingly. "I give them into your charge." The Byzantines rode off toward the city bearing the recaptured sultana in their midst.

William stretched and yawned loudly, thankful that the evening's adventure had ended. He filed away the most interesting parts of the episode in his mind so that he could relate them to Alexandra in the morning. Usually, her buoyant presence left him tongue-tied and gawkish—but with a little bit of rehearsal, he might be able to manufacture this night's escapade into a tale to amuse her.

Tancred had no such amusements to look forward to. He stared at his hands, twirling a ring with a large, cut emerald round and round his little finger.

Bohemond gave a loud sigh like a man much put upon. "Get some sleep," he ordered his nephews, looking over to the eastern horizon where the morning had not yet risen. "We'll ride at mid-morning for the emperor's camp."

He began to walk away, then thinking better of it, turned back for one final word. "No tricks this time, Tancred."

Tancred looked up gravely, sensible that his uncle had done him a good service that night. "No tricks," he agreed. This time he would see Alexios as Bohemond required, but no man could make him feign fealty to the foreign emperor. His sword still belonged to Pope Urban.

Tancred looked back down at the emerald on his finger. The sultana had said that the ring was lucky. He snorted. It had not done any favors for its new owner tonight.

# Chapter 28

The rocky defile north of Nicaea was easier to traverse this time with the comforting knowledge that there were no ambushes waiting on either end of it. At the south end sat the Nicene valley where the Crusaders were ensconced; at the north lay Alexios with a full tithe of his court from Constantinople. The emperor had set up camp at the town of Pelecanum, near the head of the crevasse, not far from the bones of Peter the Hermit's motley army. There he had been able to easily communicate with Boutoumites and closely oversee the progress of the siege.

Bohemond, Tancred, and William left early in the morning while most of the other Crusader lords were still lying abed, but they were not long on the road before they met up with another group en route to see the emperor. It was Bernard of Valence, the chaplain to Bishop Adhemar, journeying with half a dozen knights and twice as many letters to be posted at the nearest Byzantine port.

"I'll join your company, if I may," said Bernard, giving Tancred a friendly nod. They had not spoken since Bernard had advised the young marquis against becoming beholden to Count Raymond.

"Gladly," said Tancred, reining in his horse to fall in step with the steed of the black-robed cleric. "I see you have better control of your mount today," he said with a grin. The blond Norman had ridden horses almost since he could walk, and it was a source of great amusement to see the clergyman so inept in the saddle.

"For the time being," said Bernard, his bony knuckles gripping the reins tightly with the unconfidence of an amateur. "And I see you have escaped the toils of Boutoumites," he returned with a thin-lipped smile.

"I did not know that was common knowledge," replied Tancred. His brow furrowed. Did the entire Crusader host know of the events that had transpired last night?

"It is not," said Bernard, setting the marquis' mind at rest. "But Bishop Adhemar makes a point of learning what goes on within the camp both in the daytime and under cover of darkness. He is the shepherd of this pilgrimage and must give an account for the doings of all his sheep."

"An account to Pope Urban?" asked Tancred. He wondered if his adventure with the sultana had been recorded in one of the letters Bernard held in his satchel.

"Aye, and also to God." Bernard cast a sidelong glance at Tancred. "They say you almost convinced Boutoumites that it was your brother in the litter."

"Almost," said Tancred with a wry smile, "Until I was foiled by a babe in arms. And now I must answer to the emperor for it. I think Manuel Boutoumites hopes he'll flay me alive."

"But you are not his vassal," said Bernard sagely, "and thus not answerable to him for your actions."

"Let us hope that the emperor will remember that. These Byzantines are all too ready to gouge out someone's eyes first and remember the details later."

The chaplain smiled at Tancred's dour expression. He nodded his head toward the broad shoulders of Bohemond riding several paces ahead. "Your uncle would never allow it. He is perhaps more ambitious than a pilgrim ought to be, but I do not think he will abandon you to the emperor's vengeance. And, if the matter should come to that, remember that Bishop Adhemar will stand your friend."

"I will remember it," said Tancred. "Many thanks."

It was the height of summer and because the days were long, the Normans and their traveling companions reached the emperor's court at Pelecanum before nightfall. The camp for Alexios' cortege was bigger than the town itself. The myriad tents surrounded Pelecanum like a besieging army. Amidst all the stakes, and poles, and canvas, it was easy to see which pavilion belonged to the emperor. The peak of Alexios' tent stood as tall as an oak tree, large enough to shelter all of Noah's animals beneath its branches. The sides and supports of the tent were cleverly designed to look like the turrets of a castle—the keep of a miniature Constantinople. It was as elaborate as the Jewish tabernacle, and when disassembled, it took more than a score of camels to carry the pieces.

On the outskirts of the camp, the Normans were hailed by one of the Byzantine sentries. Bohemond instructed the man to inform Alexios of their arrival. But instead of inviting them into his tents that evening, the emperor bade them wait until the other Crusader lords arrived on the morrow. He would see them all en masse.

Bohemond scowled to hear this news. He had only hurried on the road so that he might come to the emperor's attention apart from the crowd. Tancred, on the other hand, was glad of the reprieve. Perhaps he could lose himself among the other leaders, like one silver fish surrounded by a school of his fellows, and escape the emperor's notice.

Hugh the Great, Godfrey and Baldwin, Count Raymond and all the others trickled in the following day at a maddeningly slow pace. Tancred saw that Boutoumites had elected to remain in his new domain and had appointed a proxy to bring the sultana and her infant son up to Pelecanum where they could be disposed of according to the emperor's will. At the sight of the sultana's litter, the marquis instinctively glanced down at the emerald ring on his pinky finger. It caught the sunlight with a green gleam. A promise was a promise, and he must not forget to look out for her sister at Antioch.

Count Baldwin of Boulogne and many of the others still cherished some smoldering resentment over the emperor's conduct at Nicaea. He had used them to force the Turks to surrender and then refused them any part in the spoils. What is more, he had not even deigned to come in person to Nicaea to thank them, but had summoned them all like so many lackeys to wait on him at his own camp. The young marquis wondered how Alexios would mollify the malcontents—doubtless by flinging about handfuls of gold.

The emperor granted them audience in the early afternoon and the lords of the West were ceremoniously ushered into the great turreted tent. It was Tancred's first glimpse of the eastern emperor. The man was smallish, especially in comparison to the brawny Northmen. His exact height was difficult to judge since he was seated above them on a raised dais. His throne carved with lions was reminiscent of Solomon's. A jeweled crown, rounded to fit his skull, covered the top of his dark hair but the rest of it cascaded down around his shoulders. He must have been nearly fifty years old, but Tancred could see no flecks of gray in his clipped beard. His dark eyebrows curved perfectly like two crescent moons. Beneath them a pair of black eyes, hard as obsidian, covered the whole room with their stare, always observing, always apprehending, always evaluating.

Tancred felt the imperial stare rest on him and repaid it with interest. This was the man whom his grandfather Robert Guiscard—Robert the Fox—had forced into the field at Durazzo; and in the end Alexios had outfoxed him, paying three hundred sixty thousand gold pieces to the German emperor to attack the Norman's papal allies back in Italy. His grandfather had been outmaneuvered, but Tancred resolved that it would be otherwise for him. He knew that the emperor would not let him leave without demanding his allegiance, and he pledged anew to himself that he would not retreat from his position.

Some of the Crusader lords could barely wait for Alexios' words of greeting to end before they vented their spleen concerning the Byzantine behavior at Nicaea. Baldwin chose to be the spokesman for the group, but when he uttered the Crusaders' well-founded complaints, Alexios had no apologies to make. Instead, the olive-skinned monarch merely turned his head and uttered something in a low voice to the grim-faced attendant standing at his right hand. The man, presumably his vizier, snapped his fingers and a dozen or more gilded chests appeared in the arms of beardless boys. Inside the boxes lay a sampling from Kilij Arslan's treasury: gold coins, ruby-hilted daggers, engraved arm rings, amulets of lapis lazuli. The king of France would have given his right hand for the riches displayed before them.

"Behold your spoils," said Alexios with a broad sweep of his hand. The servants placed a chest before each of the lords present: Hugh, Godfrey, Baldwin, the two Roberts, Stephen of Blois, Raymond, and Bohemond. Alone among the others, Tancred noticeably received nothing.

Stephen of Blois, the brother-in-law of the Duke of Normandy, stared at his own portion openmouthed. He plunged an eager fist into the ornate chest to feel how deep the treasure was stacked. "I must write to my darling Adele and tell her of this splendor," he said, referring fondly to the wife who had browbeaten him into joining the Crusade. He looked around at the others in amazement. "Can you believe how full the sultan's coffers were?"

"Full indeed!" said a bitter voice. It was Tancred's, his white complexion flaming red with insult and frustration. "And I'm sure this is not the tithe of what Kilij Arslan possessed. It is well, my lords, that you all were kept from seeing the inside of Nicaea's treasure chambers or you would not be content with these scraps."

Alexios listened to this outburst impassively as if he had no understanding of the westerner's words. Not so his vizier. The man's stern face calcified even further, and jealous for his emperor's honor, he advanced menacingly toward Tancred.

"Ah, the young marquis," said Alexios, raising a languid hand to halt his vengeful vizier. "As you say, there is more to the treasure than you see here. There is a portion set aside for *you*—that is, once you make your oath of fealty to the Byzantine Empire. And naturally, once you make that oath, I am also willing to overlook the part you played in the sultana's attempted escape."

Tancred let out a forced laugh. "I am already bound by oaths of fealty that would leave me little room to follow your commands. First, I am sworn unto Pope Urban, to press on in this Crusade until the Mussulman rule is toppled in Jerusalem. Second, I am sworn unto my uncle, to act as his lieutenant as long as he maintains this pilgrimage."

Alexios waved aside Tancred's objections. "It is not unusual for a man to owe homage to more than one lord. I am sure that I will ask you for nothing that would conflict with your prior allegiances—merely to render up to me all formerly Byzantine lands in exchange for Byzantine military aid. You help me regain Asia Minor, and I will join your Crusade to retake Jerusalem. It is the same oath that I asked of each of your fellows, and none of them scrupled to swear it."

"That is true!" interjected Hugh the Great. His fleshy face summoned as much disdain as it could muster. "And if a Capetian prince has no qualms about it, why should a Norman sword for hire?"

The room was fraught with tension as everyone waited for Tancred to respond. Bohemond fixed a meaningful eye upon his nephew reminding him of what path he ought to take.

# Chapter 29

"What bribe will you offer me to become your man?" Tancred asked the emperor bluntly. The other lords exchanged uncomfortable glances, astonished by the young marquis' rudeness.

Alexios was caught off guard by the plain-speaking Norman. "What do you desire?" he asked, striving to look amused and failing miserably.

Tancred cocked his head and looked up at the great vaulted ceiling of the pavilion. He had already determined to ask for something so extravagant that the emperor must, perforce, refuse him. But what should it be?

"I want a cache of treasure equal to everything these other lords have received," he said.

The emperor frowned. His crescent eyebrows flattened into a taut line.

"And also," continued Tancred with barely a pause, "I want this tent for my own, but not empty. Let it be filled with gold bezants, as much as it will hold, to the very brim."

It was a laughable request, but a request that no one dared laugh at. The large throne room in the pavilion felt as though the air had been squeezed out of it. The emperor slowly rose to his feet, his dusky face suffused with anger. "I wonder that you do not also ask for the crown upon my head," he said with a stamp of his foot.

Seeing Alexios' barely contained fury, his vizier decided to escort Tancred out of the royal presence. He advanced upon the marquis and seized his upper left arm in a vise-like grip.

"Take your hands off of me!" said Tancred, adding some choice insults in the Greek tongue.

In response, the vizier's fingers closed tighter and he attempted to pull Tancred toward the door. The Greek was strong, but Tancred's youthful muscles and sinewy build gave him the advantage should he choose to exert it. He relaxed momentarily, allowing the man to think that he would let himself be led away like a spineless sheep. Then, twisting violently, he freed himself from the vizier's hold and gave him such a blow to the jaw that the man fell to the floor of the tent. He would have pummeled him further, but his uncle Bohemond interposed himself between them trying desperately to diffuse the situation.

The matter had already gone too far. Alexios barked a command and almost instantaneously the room was filled with bristling spears in the hands of the emperor's private guard. "Seize him!" said the emperor, his hand shooting out like a poison-tipped arrow straight at Tancred.

Bohemond stepped away from Tancred, uncertain whether he should interfere and place himself between his nephew and the emperor's anger. Tancred felt the desertion keenly. Bernard had prophesied that Bohemond would stand by him, but obviously the chaplain did not know how committed his uncle was to his own self-interest.

The Crusaders had been allowed to bring their weapons into the emperor's audience chamber, and Tancred now drew his sword. The imperial guards formed a circle around him, spears pointing inward, barring any possibility of escape from the tent. The western lords began to protest loudly. Few of them had any affection for Tancred, but a Latin was still a Latin when they were all foreigners in a strange land.

"Your majesty," said a calm voice from the back of the room. "I was promised an audience with you this afternoon. I have important letters to deliver."

It was a preposterous interruption from an unlikely individual. For a brief moment all attention was diverted away from Tancred to Bernard, Bishop Adhemar's emissary. Alexios waved an impatient hand at the black-robed chaplain. "Later!" he thundered, and turned his attention back to the guards and the renegade Crusader.

"Now would be much better," said Bernard firmly. Having seen how clumsy he was in the saddle, Tancred would never have suspected that he could be so audacious before an emperor. The gaunt cleric continued. "You will want to read what Bishop Adhemar has to say before you take action in this matter."

Alexios' stare demanded that he explain himself.

"I have a letter here," explained Bernard, "regarding the marquis." He held it out invitingly. Alexios gave a curt nod—the emperor's vizier, ruefully rubbing his reddened jaw, took it from Bernard and placed it in the emperor's hands. Tancred could see the impression of Adhemar's signet ring on the seal affixed to the scroll.

Whatever the contents of the letter were, they were short and to the point. It took the emperor only a brief moment to close the scroll after he had broken the seal and perused its sentences. He gave Bernard an ugly look and thrust the letter back into his vizier's hands. A quick command in Greek caused the palace guards to un-couch their spears and retreat from their threatening position around the marquis. Tancred, still wary, lowered the point of his blade but refused to sheath it entirely until he should know how events would unfold.

"Gentlemen," said Alexios to the congregation of Crusader lords, "I find that my time is too valuable to waste any more of it on this petty disturbance." He snorted disdainfully. "I will see you tomorrow to discuss your route to the south. You are dismissed."

The Latins departed from the castle-like pavilion in a drove, with Byzantine servants trailing behind them to bring their share of Kilij Arslan's treasury. Baldwin and Hugh glared furiously at Tancred while Godfrey's blue eyes shot him a look of innocent bewilderment. Stephen of Blois was too busy framing a letter to his wife Adele to pay any attention to the marquis. Bohemond set his face like stone and deliberately ignored his nephew even though they were walking a mere arm's length apart.

Count Raymond, alone among the others, attempted to strike up a pleasant conversation with the marquis. He clapped him on the back as comrades do and asked his opinion of the road ahead. "Will we see any action before we reach Antioch, do you think?" Tancred responded to his attentions thankfully. He was still raw from the treatment he had received in the emperor's tent, and Raymond's kind overtures acted like a poultice to remove some of the sting.

When they reached their own tents, on the outskirts of the Byzantine court, the band of men dispersed. Bohemond lingered beside his nephew a moment till they had all gone then fixed a cold look on Tancred. "You have ruined your chances to make something of yourself on this Crusade. God forfend that you have also ruined mine."

Tancred felt a wave of anger swelling inside himself and about to break upon his stony uncle. "You cannot forget, uncle, that when I swore to be obedient to you, there were two provisos with that promise. I will do nothing that would impair the success of this Crusade or sully my own honor. An oath to Alexios would threaten the first and the necessity of breaking it would bring about the second."

Bohemond gritted his teeth. "Then I wash my hands of you," he said and turned on his heel to leave. Tancred's clean-shaven lip curled into a faint smile. The ties of kinship were not so easily severed. His men would continue to camp beside Bohemond's, and the two Normans would continue to hold a united front before the other Crusaders. Though resentment clings like pine pitch, it would eventually rub away from the friction of constant association.

Bohemond had scarcely departed before Bernard materialized in his place. Tancred looked at the cleric with new appreciation. He was not a tall man, though his height appeared greater than average because of his thin frame. His skeletal features made it difficult to guess his age, but Tancred thought him not yet thirty, and maybe even closer to his own allotment of years. The black habit that he wore showed patches of wear and had faded from constant use. His face was gaunt and unattractive, with dark eyebrows like bushy caterpillars that nearly met in the middle. On his index finger Tancred spotted a ring that looked familiar, carved with the image of the Virgin Mary and ideal for making an impression in hot wax. Only last time he saw the ring, it had been on a much larger pair of hands.

"It seems I owe Bishop Adhemar some thanks," said Tancred, "and even more to you."

"Oh, it was nothing," said Bernard self-deprecatingly. "I am merely glad that I was able to present the epistle to the emperor in time."

"What did the letter say?" demanded Tancred.

Bernard wrinkled his nose. "I could not swear to its exact contents, but I believe it informed the emperor that you had sworn yourself to Urban as champion of the Roman Church, and bade him remember that the pope is especially concerned about your welfare."

"And Adhemar wrote that?"

"All the letters I carried in my satchel were written by Bishop Adhemar."

It was a roundabout way to answer the question, and indeed, if the letter had not been in the satchel, it did not answer the question at all. Tancred looked at the cleric curiously, and again noted the distinctive ring on his finger with the image of the Holy Mother.

"Adhemar must indeed trust you as an emissary if he provides his own signet ring for your use."

"Indeed he must," said Bernard, meeting Tancred's eye but refusing to address the obvious implication that the marquis was making. Was the letter Alexios had opened a pre-planned message from Adhemar, or was it a hastily scrawled missive by the chaplain, a ploy he had devised to protect Tancred once the situation in the emperor's pavilion began to deteriorate. Tancred was inclined to think the latter, but there could be no way of proving it without asking Adhemar himself if he had penned the letter.

"I see Boutoumites has sent your sultana to Pelecanum," said Bernard, deftly changing the subject.

"What does the emperor mean to do with her?" asked Tancred. He had undertaken the role of her protector for one night only, but even now he felt a peculiar interest in her fate.

"They say he means to release her to Kilij Arslan," said Bernard, "that is, as soon as her husband asks for her return."

Tancred shook his head disappointedly. It was the very thing the lady had most dreaded. "He will return her for ransom?"

"No, gratis—simply to show his power and magnanimity to the Turks."

"And the other captured Turks?"

"The same," replied Bernard. "Alexios must make war on the Turks to regain his empire, but he knows that no matter how far back he pushes them back, they will still be his neighbors in the east. So, even while he puts on his gauntlets for battle, he extends the right hand in friendship. That is why he asks no ransom for the prisoners."

"No ransom," repeated Tancred, shaking his head in astonishment. "The other Crusader lords will be furious. First, he forestalls our sack of Nicaea and then he lets the prisoners slip through his fingers without so much as a penny to show for it."

Bernard's thin lips turned upward in a macabre grin. "I know that Raymond took the news very ill," he said, taking a fiendish delight in the Frankish lord's displeasure.

"You are no friend to the Count of Toulouse," observed Tancred with perplexity. "I cannot think why. He has always shown me a great kindness, lending me money when my men were in the throes of hunger. None of the others—and especially not my uncle—understands my reasons for refusing fealty to the emperor. But Raymond is sympathetic. He also refused to swear the oath."

Bernard raised a thick black eyebrow but made no reply. After a moment of silence, he asked casually, "Did Count Raymond receive a chest of treasure today?"

Tancred cast his mind back to the events in the pavilion. "Why, yes, he did," he said with a little surprise in his voice. Robert, Hugh, Bohemond, Raymond—they had all received a golden box from the Byzantine servants. Tancred alone had been presented with nothing, ostensibly because he had held out against the emperor's will. And yet, had not Raymond done the same?

"Ah," said Bernard, with a knowing look. But when Tancred pressed him, he refused to say anymore on the matter.

# PART III

# Baldwin

# Chapter 30

The Latin lords rejoined their men at Nicaea laden with Turkish treasure and the emperor's promises that he would come with a great force to help them take Antioch. That city's walls were even more formidable than Nicaea's and the path there was just as daunting. The road to Antioch ran for five thousand furlongs and cut through the very heart of Turkish territory.

Since Manuel Boutoumites desired to remain in his new dukedom, Alexios dispatched another of his generals to accompany the Crusaders. Tatikios was his name. One had only to glimpse his face to discover two startling things. First, he was a Turk, not a Greek. His father had been captured by Alexios' father long ago, and Tatikios had grown up as a slave in the emperor's household. But despite the bonds of slavery that had shackled him, the boy Turk had forged other bonds—bonds of friendship with Alexios, his master's son. When Alexios rose to power, Tatikios had been elevated along with him to a position of high military command. As one of Byzantium's premier generals, Tatikios knew something of the Latins and their fighting style. The Turk had led one wing of Alexios' army against Tancred's grandfather at Durazzo, and though the Byzantines had lost that day, had commanded his cohorts with credit.

The second item to startle the observers of Tatikios' face was his nose. Like many things in Constantinople, it was made entirely of gold. Somewhere, in one of his campaigns for Alexios, the Turk's face had fallen afoul of an enemy sword. A skilled goldsmith had replaced the mutilated feature, and when the sun shone brightly, the gleam from his prosthetic proboscis could be blinding.

Tatikios was by nature far more garrulous than Boutoumites and far more good-natured to boot. The march to the southeast led the Crusaders through a mountainous region ideal for ambush from the enemy. Over and over again, Tatikios warned the Latins to lift up their eyes to the hills. "Kilij Arslan will want revenge for the taking of his capital," he said. "No doubt he stalks us even now, prowling the ridges like a mountain lion, waiting for us to let down our guard. They say that he has made peace with the Danishmends, the Turks with whom he was at odds when you surrounded Nicaea. He has proclaimed a *jihad* against you and asked all true Mussulmen to come to his aid. Only the utmost vigilance will defeat his plans, so watch, my friends, and be wary."

For three days, the Crusaders traveled on unmolested by enemies of any kind. To facilitate foraging, the host had divided itself into two sections. In the lead rode Tatikios and his Byzantine guides accompanied by Bohemond, Tancred, the Duke of Normandy, and the Count of Flanders. Following at half a day's journey behind them came Count Raymond, Hugh the Great, Godfrey, and Baldwin. On the fourth day they sighted the city of Dorylaeum. Here the road narrowed as it zigzagged through a shallow valley. The Crusaders were forced to thin their ranks and each of the separate armies straggled through the valley one at a time.

Tancred, at the outset of the march from Nicaea, had assumed the vanguard with his troop of men. He was eager to set the pace and hurry his fellows on to Antioch, but despite this impatience, he refused to forgo vigilance for the sake of speed. He kept a careful eye on the hills, and it was his lookouts that first spotted the Turks crouching in the heights. Night fell without any incident and Bohemond, who had assumed leadership over the first of the two armies, chose their campsite on a small plain with barely enough level ground to erect their tents.

Tancred, once he had made the circuit of the camp to encourage his sentries in their vigilance, returned to his tent to find William there waiting for him. "So," said William, "I suppose we shall see battle at morning's light."

"Most probably," replied Tancred, sitting down wearily and removing his boots. "Let us hope that Count Raymond and the rest of the host are not too far behind us. If my scouts are correct, the Turks are as many as a swarm of locusts, and just as eager to fly in our faces."

"Perhaps I shall make my first kill tomorrow," said William hopefully.

Tancred looked at him in surprise. "You have not killed a Mussulman before now?"

William turned a little red around the ears. "'Tis not for lack of trying! I was right behind you in the charge when Kilij Arslan's expeditionary force poured down on Nicaea. I saw you take down that large Turk, the one whose head you took for a trophy. And then I entered the thick of it myself. They were all around me, as if some foolish lad had taken a stick to a hornet nest. I could think of nothing but parrying their sword strikes and keeping my skin whole. I do not think I struck a single blow of my own once we were at too close of quarters to use the lance."

William stared at the floor while he made this startling confession, tracing in the dirt with his toe and refusing to meet his brother's eye. Tancred listened to William with surprise. He himself awaited every battle with such anticipation that he assumed all his fellow Normans—and especially those of his own kin—shared a similar excitement. He saw now that William was afraid of what tomorrow would bring, afraid and ashamed of his fear. There was too much of their father Odo's blood in him, but enough of their mother's blood to wish that it were not so.

The marquis cleared his throat uncomfortably. Every man knew that he had no patience with cowardice. What could he say to his little brother who was tainted with it?

"You were brave enough the night we fought the sultana's litter bearers," said Tancred. "I think we each would have killed our man if the lady had not leaned out to stop us."

William's face lightened a little. "That was a fine night, was it not? The lady, did she not give you a talisman of some sort?"

Tancred held out his hand with the emerald ring. "This," he said, "to give to her sister Erminia in Antioch."

"It is a lucky ring, yes?" said William with growing excitement. "Will you give it to me to wear on the morrow?"

Tancred hesitated. He did not like to loan out an item that he held in pledge. What is more, the ring, in his estimation, did not seem particularly blessed by fortune. He had no sooner placed it on his little finger than he found himself bound fast by Boutoumites and dragged ignominiously back into the Norman camp. But on the other hand, the power of such a talisman often came more from the belief of the wearer than from the thing itself. If William thought the ring lucky, then so it might prove for him.

Tancred tugged the tight ring off of his finger and deposited it in William's palm. "Do not lose it," he said dryly.

"Certainly not!" said William with a smile, and he slid the circle with the gleaming green gem onto the hand that carried his sword. "You had better try your hardest tomorrow, Tancred," he said with sparkling eyes, "for I feel it in my bones that I shall be a lion in the field, and I know how you hate to be bested in anything."

Tancred laughed. "Roar as loud as you please, little lion. I'll give you fair odds that I carve a dozen heads first."

"Done!" said William, and they gripped arms in a brotherly pact.

"Now, get some sleep," said Tancred, settling into his cot with a yawn. "The day will be long tomorrow and run red with blood before it is through."

Tancred's scouts had not been in error. Kilij Arslan was indeed lurking in the hills, waiting to take his vengeance on the foreign foe who had robbed him of his capital. At the rise of the sun, Bohemond, the two Roberts, and Tancred gave their men the order to march. They had barely left their campsite before the bloody hue of the sunrise rang with a bloodcurdling Turkish war cry. The enemy poured down from the hills like a spring torrent, sending out volleys of screams and arrows.

A reedy marsh lay to the left of the Crusaders, and Bohemond quickly directed the foot soldiers to take cover there and protect the baggage. The mounted knights formed up in lines in front of them to meet the onslaught of the Turks.

Tatikios, seeing the seemingly endless hordes that confronted them, rode over for a quick parley with Bohemond and Tancred. "We should send messengers to Count Raymond for aid before it is too late for them to get through!" His golden nose caught the rosy glow of the sunrise and lit up his swarthy face.

"Why?" asked Tancred with the boldness of youth. "We are more than man enough to take them on!"

Bohemond, with more years of experience sitting on his shoulders, agreed with the Byzantine. "Yes, send our fastest horses. Who knows how far their army stands apart from ours? It could be hours before they reach us."

Robert of Flanders, a prudent soldier, agreed with Bohemond and so the messengers were sent—three men at separate intervals so that if one fell the others might still elude the enemy and find the Franks. The Crusaders watched as the messengers galloped at a breakneck pace to flank the Turkish troops who were rapidly encircling the army. One fell riddled with arrows. The second misjudged his mount's capabilities, twisted its foreleg, and was soon dragged down by the enemy. The third ducked down low on his horse's neck to avoid the pointed missiles, and by dint of skillful riding, made it past a party of pursuing Turks and disappeared into the hill country.

"Pray to God that he makes it through," murmured Robert of Normandy as the horseman vanished from sight. The Norman duke's face was the color of ash as he looked at the howling hordes before them. Kilij Arslan had raised the whole countryside for miles around. Even Tancred, faced by this swirling stampede of adversaries, had lost a little of his bravado. The Turcopoles that had lined the banks of the Vardar were like children playing at war compared to these vengeful furies.

The Turkish strategy was simple and effective: the front line of horsemen would make a swift sally toward the penned up Normans, let loose their arrows, then circle round to the back of their own lines to notch another arrow to their bowstring. Meanwhile a second wave of horsemen would advance and mimic the maneuver. Unable to respond to these volleys, the Crusaders were pushed back farther and farther against the reed marsh.

Hours passed. The cruel July sun reached its zenith breathing out blasts of heat that made constant motion unbearable. Yet despite the sweat-drenched tunics inside their armor, the Crusaders continued to fight on, taking the brunt of the Turkish arrows on their shields and breastplates. Flight was impossible and surrender would mean captivity and slavery.

Besides pressing them backwards, the Turks were also busy carving their forces in two. They now occupied a small rise that divided Bohemond's men from the Duke of Normandy's. Tancred, desperate for some hand-to-hand combat, left his length of the line to confer with Bohemond. "I will take a quarter of my troop and secure that hill," he said, pointing to the danger spot in the center of the army. "That will give us a vantage point from which to charge the enemy."

"No!" said Bohemond sharply. "We shall wait it out until these mosquitoes come in closer. Keep to your position. Hold the line."

"Folly! Our horses are dying by the dozens. We must act now or perish!"

Bohemond remonstrated with his nephew, but it was no use. Tancred spurred his horse back to his own contingent and immediately began spitting out orders. "Richard," he barked out to his brother-in-law. "You will command the men I leave behind. William and Ralph, come with me. That hill is ours. We have only to claim it."

# Chapter 31

I t took only a word from Tancred to set his tiny band of Normans in motion. With Tancred and William at their head, they couched their lances and charged toward the ranks of opposing Turks breaking through them with the sheer momentum of their heavy warhorses. The enemy's bows were of small use to them with lance heads in their faces. Caught off guard by the charge, the lightly armored Turks pulled back from the hill. Tancred's lance skewered three of the fugitives and even William unhorsed one of the fleeing Mussulmen.

From the higher ground, Tancred's clear blue eyes could pick out the emirs ordering the Turkish assault. One young fellow, bedecked in bright colors and precious metals, gesticulated furiously at his retreating men. It was Kilij Arslan, sultan of Rum, though as of two weeks ago his sultanate had been radically reduced in power and prestige. Strutting like a gamecock, he ordered his men back to the hill they had abandoned. Obediently, they unsheathed their scimitars and initiated a countercharge to unseat the Normans.

But the Normans, following Tancred's instructions, had already formed up a close-knit line of defense. Like a wall of adamantine, they stood against the enemy, their bristling lance heads ready to impale all comers. When a few, a very few of the Turks managed to penetrate this human barricade, they found themselves outmatched again by the Latins. Their small, crescent-shaped shields were poor defense against a buffet from a longsword, and despite their superior numbers, the casualties by far were in their own ranks. Victorious, the Normans watched the Turks fall back once again, and a surge of enthusiasm began to lift the despairing spirits of the Westerners.

But Kilij Arslan was quick to learn from this rebuff. He saw immediately that the strength of the Latins lay in their lances, and as long as his men kept their distance they could not be harmed. He returned to his original stratagem, sending successive waves of archers to discharge their arrows at Tancred's men.

The Norman chain mail deflected many of the arrows, but every suit of armor has its openings, its joins, its weak spots. Tancred's men on the height became the same helpless and hapless targets as Bohemond's men in the plain. Armpits, legs, faces, necks were pierced through with flying shafts, and the horses began to look like Bellerophon's steed they had so many feathers buried in their flanks.

Tancred soon realized that there was no hope of, and no point to, holding the hill any longer. He was about to sound a retreat when some movements behind Bohemond's line caught his eye. From his elevated position, he could see that a large detachment of Turks had circled round the Crusaders and, even now, were cautiously picking their way through the reed marsh.

"Holy Mary! Look!" said Tancred, pointing out the movement that his keen eyes had captured to those around him.

"They'll fall upon the baggage and our backsides," said Ralph gruffly, for Bohemond had left only a few foot soldiers to guard the supplies, the wounded, and the women in the camp.

For half a second the face of Alexandra flashed into Tancred's mind, her brown eyes, olive skin, and dark chestnut curls. Although he had given her leave to travel in company with the Normans, he had also contrived to avoid her as much as possible in the camp. He had mostly accepted the affidavit that her quest for vengeance was over, but her southern blood was too volatile to be entirely trusted. At least, that was what he told himself. In reality, it was his own incurable sense of guilt at having slain her father that made the girl odious in his eyes. All the same, he would not wish her—or any of the women down below—to be captured and condemned to slavery in a Turkish harem, a fate only too likely if that detachment from Kilij Arslan's army succeeded in infiltrating the camp from the marsh.

William—who, in stark contrast to Tancred, had taken no pains to avoid the little Greek—cherished thoughts more tender and fears more acute. Instant action was needed to circumvent the Turks. "Quick!" he shouted. "We must warn our uncle!" Without a thought for his own safety, he plunged his spurs into his horse to descend the hill and rejoin the main force.

"No, William!" bellowed Tancred, but it was already too late.

Separated from the rest, his solitary silhouette attracted the attention of every enemy eye. More than a hundred arrows let fly at the galloping knight, and at least a dozen found their mark.

Tancred let out a roar of anguish as William slipped from his saddle transfixed by the Turkish shafts. His limp body sprawled on the ground motionless while blood pooled around him like spilt wine. He would not get up again.

Overcome with rage, Tancred's eyes darkened like one of the berserkers from the old North. He lowered his lance. Ralph, seeing his master's intention and anxious to avoid a repetition of William's fate, gave the command to charge. The whole Norman troop—or what was left of them—descended the hill on thundering hooves at the same time as the marquis. The Turks sent several volleys into the rumbling mass then withdrew from their path leaving the way clear for Tancred to rejoin his uncle.

"To the rear! To the rear!" shouted Tancred to Bohemond.

"Yes, yes, I see it!" said Bohemond, for screams had already begun to ascend from the supply wagons. The Turks had conquered the marsh and were coursing rapidly through the Norman noncombatants cutting to shreds all in their path. They could now shower arrows on the rear of the Norman and Flemish battle lines, an opportunity they took full advantage of.

"My God!" said Bohemond, with a look of panic in his eyes that Tancred had never before seen. There were enemies on every side, ringing them round like a moat of fire. "We are dead men."

He had no sooner spoken than a horn sounded from the far side of the plain, clear and piercing as mountain air with echoes that resounded off the hillsides.

"My lord," said an out of breath knight, his horse wet all over with flecks of sweat and blood. "I see a force of men coming from the north."

"What?" asked Bohemond hoarsely. His voice was as harsh as the cry of the crow. "More Turks?"

Tancred stood up tall in his saddle and strained his eyes to see the new arrivals. "Those are no Turks!" he said with excitement. "God is with us! The third rider scraped through with his message."

It was a welcome sight to see—the huge banner Pope Urban had bestowed on Hugh the Great. Its blood red cross flamed across the plain like a beacon of hope. Godfrey and Baldwin were at the fore of the relief force, and Tancred had never been so glad to see the German brothers from Boulogne. Count Raymond's men were close behind, their pennants held high on sharpened lances.

The galloping newcomers advanced across the valley like a roll of thunder. Hearing the noise, the Turks paused their barrages long enough to exchange puzzled looks. Their scouts had been remiss or lackadaisical in their duty. They thought they had wrapped the entire Crusader army in their coils and were about to crush out its life. And yet here was another battle host, as big as or bigger than the one they had trapped.

The small figure of Kilij Arslan was screaming orders like a madman riding back and forth frantically on his purebred white stallion. It was his army's turn now to fight a battle on two fronts. He split off a section of his host to halt the advance of the Frankish and German knights, but they pushed through them like an avalanche, impossible to stop.

The two Crusader forces fused together like hot metal. The small Turkish force that had come through the reed marsh was swiftly dealt with, and Tancred felt his breath come easier. Their necks had escaped from the enemy's vise.

After a swift conference among the leaders, the Latins formed a long line and began to take the offensive in the battle. None of their horses were fresh, but in a charge they could still bowl over anything in their path. As the afternoon sun waxed hotter, the resolution of the enemy waned. They were kept in the field only by the autocratic will of their sultan, and when that wore down, a retreat would be inevitable.

"Another few hours of this melee and maybe they'll take to their heels," said Bohemond with an exhausted sigh. His face was brown with blood-caked dust, and his sword arm did not swing with as much vigor as usual.

"Why wait another few hours for that?" asked Count Raymond. He had ridden over to Bohemond's section of the line to coordinate another attack. In the heat of the battle, the two men had put their mutual distaste for each other aside to fend off their common foe. Raymond directed the Norman count's attention to the hillside behind the Turkish lines. "Look there!" he said with a satisfied smile.

Up on the heights, Bohemond saw the shimmer of sunlight on armor. A band of men were quietly making their way down the rocky ridge. "More reinforcements?" asked Bohemond. "But who is leading them?" Looking to the right and to the left, he noted that all the Crusader lords were present on the battle line.

"Bishop Adhemar," said Raymond brightly, hefting his shield onto his left arm as he prepared for more action. The Frank's iron gray hair showed his age, but on the battlefield he still had the stamina of youth. "It was his idea to surprise them from the hills, so we gave him the honor of leading the ambush."

The bishop's men continued their descent in silence until they were ready to reveal themselves to the Turks. When the time was right, Adhemar gave tongue with the Crusader war cry. "Jerusalem! God wills it!" Following the lead of the courageous clergyman, his knights set spurs into their horses and charged at the unprotected backside of Kilij Arslan's battle line. The barrel-chested bishop held a huge sword in both hands, his powerful legs guiding his steed so adroitly that man and beast seemed a single creature. Right and left he struck with fury, leaving a path of cloven skulls in his wake.

198 | ROSANNE E. LORTZ

Before Adhemar's arrival, the Turks had already lost their enthusiasm for the fight. At this new and unexpected onslaught, panic overtook them. Far from holding their men together, the emirs were the first to flee. It was a complete and utter rout. A wild cry of joy went up from the Crusader line, especially from the Normans and Flemish who had fought the whole day in the searing sun. Bohemond gave the order for his men to pursue the fugitive foemen. Tancred's troop was already treading on the tails of the fliers.

The Turks lost more men in their disorderly retreat than they had through the whole of the long battle, yet even while his men were falling all around him, Kilij Arslan managed to secure his own safety. He disappeared into the hill country to wallow in the bitterness of double defeat. He would not trouble the Crusaders again on their journey.

Although the sultan eluded pursuit, he left behind a memento of the battle that was worth infinitely more than his head on a spear. The pursuers found the Turkish tents in the hills nearby, abandoned in great haste by men who held their lives dearer than their possessions. Before they had discovered the delights of dwelling in captured Byzantine cities, the Turks had been a nomadic people. It was not surprising then that the treasure in Kilij Arslan's tent far exceeded everything that Manuel Boutoumites had discovered in the citadel at Nicaea. The sultan, who had left his wife behind, had toted his treasure with him. By unanimous consent the Crusaders gave the gold into the hands of Adhemar, and later he doled it out fairly among them.

The sudden metamorphosis of despair into delight invigorated the troops like heady wine. For many, the rush of relief and the thrill of triumph blotted out the weariness, wounds, and woe of earlier hours. Tancred was no exception. As he returned from pursuing the enemy, his spirits were as high as the hills and bright as the sunlight. He spotted the brothers from Boulogne and rode up to give them greeting. "What took you so long?" he asked impishly. "Did you take a nap on the road?"

Baldwin gave a smile that showed too much of his sharp teeth. A few pieces of his long dark hair jutted out from under his helm.

"Should we have hurried? I thought that Tancred the Great could handle a few Mussulmen on his own. Apparently I was mistaken."

Before Tancred could make a retort, Godfrey intervened. "What is this? Tancred, you are wounded!" he said, his blue eyes brimming with concern.

Tancred stared at him blankly for a moment then looked down at his own body. During his furious charge down the hillside to warn Bohemond, he had become two arrowheads the richer without even noticing. One had slipped through the right armhole of his corselet, the other had embedded itself in his left thigh. His mind, too busy with the turning tide of battle and the subsequent rout of the Turks, had forgotten to feel the pain that accompanied these injuries, but at Godfrey's words, Tancred experienced the delayed agony of the arrows piercing his flesh.

The sudden awareness of his wounds brought with it a sudden remembrance of other arrows that had found their mark. "Sweet Jesus! William!" the marquis breathed aloud. Then, weak from loss of blood, he slipped ungracefully from his steed onto the sand below and lost consciousness.

# Chapter 32

Touch was the first of Tancred's senses to return to him. He awoke to feel his forehead bathed with warm water while a soft cloth rubbed the grime from his face. It was only after this that the dull sensation of pain overtook him and, reaching out an exploratory hand, he found that his tunic had been stripped off and bandages applied to his chest and leg.

For a fleeting moment his feverish mind flitted back in Italy. Emma, his mother, was bending over him, her pale gold braids swinging forward over her shoulders. Tancred knew that the moment he opened his eyes she would begin to berate him, for a careless fall from climbing a high wall, for a gash from a boar's tusk when hunting alone, for scrapes and bruises in a scrap with some bigger boys—or for however else he had incurred his injuries; his tired mind could not remember. Better to keep still, said his thoughts, and bask in his mother's sympathy instead of her censure.

Eyes still closed, Tancred felt the healing hands brush against his brow. But as the warm water trickled over his face, the suspicion trickled into his mind that perhaps they were not his mother's after all, these bony hands with calluses on the pads of their fingers. "Where am I?" he moaned. He lifted his eyelids with a great effort, like a miller hefting two sacks of grain.

The harsh, angular features of his nurse were nothing like the feminine oval of his mother's face. It was a man bathing his forehead, a man dressed all in black. For half a moment, Tancred mistook him for the black-cowled accuser from his dream. He started in terror, and propping himself up on his elbows, tried to rise. But the fellow laid two hands on his shoulders and pushed him back down on the straw pallet. "Lie still," said the man. "You will injure yourself further."

At the soothing sound of his voice, Tancred began to breathe a little easier, and when he glimpsed the unkempt tonsure, he recognized the man immediately. It was Bernard, the chaplain to Bishop Adhemar. "We are in a house at Dorylaeum," said Bernard, speaking softly like one used to the sickroom. "It has been a day since the battle, and you have lost much blood from your wounds."

The thought that had been uppermost in Tancred's mind when he lost consciousness now returned to the fore. "My brother?" he asked, remembering the tragedy on the hillside and holding out hope that William's own wounds had not proved fatal.

Bernard shook his head grimly. "Dead. God be thanked for the victory, but we lost many men in the winning of it."

A deep groan escaped from Tancred like the rending of boulders when the earth is shaken. He turned his face away from Bernard and toward the wall. His grief belonged to him alone. If he had tears to shed, they were not for another to see.

After a few minutes of silence, the marquis returned his gaze to the chaplain. "When will he be put in the ground?" he asked abruptly.

"The fallen are buried already. Bishop Adhemar will perform the funeral mass at noonday,"—Bernard paused and pursed his lips with concern—"but you are in no condition to attend."

Tancred ignored the chaplain's last statement and gritted his teeth with pain as he tried to rise. Beads of sweat formed on his brow like a chaplet of pearls. He slid his sound leg off the pallet and using his two hands for leverage tried to make the injured leg follow its fellow. The difficulty of such a movement was almost beyond him. He felt as feeble as the aged who cannot rise from their chairs. "Help me up," he demanded, fixing an imperious eye on the chaplain.

"No," said Bernard, standing up himself but refusing to lend a hand to the wounded man. "This is folly."

Angry at the other's refusal, Tancred was forced to depend on his own depleted strength. His face contorted with pain as he lurched upright and put weight on his left leg. The arrow wound in his thigh throbbed insufferably and dark blood began to seep from beneath the bandages. "Where are my clothes?" he asked, his voice as taut as a mangonel's ropes.

Bernard wrinkled his nose in opposition, but had the kindness to toss the half-naked man his tunic. It was his favorite garment, bright blue like the crest of his house and one that his mother had woven. He had worn it yesterday beneath his armor on the battlefield, and by rights, it should have been filthy and tattered. In the intervening hours, however, someone had scrubbed it clean of blood and dirt and repaired the rent from the arrowhead with tiny, even stitches. Ralph, despite his many excellent qualifications, was no needle worker, and Tancred could hardly believe that the bishop's chaplain was given to random acts of tailoring.

Bernard saw the marquis staring at the mending. "There was a girl here tending you," he said, "but I sent her away. She left the tunic."

"A girl in a green dress?" asked Tancred in surprise.

"Aye," said Bernard. "She was helping your servant change your bandages when I arrived. They were back-sore and hollow-eyed, the pair of them, doubtless from keeping vigil over you all night. The old man went to claim your brother's personal effects, and I shooed the girl away to get some sleep." He looked at Tancred curiously, displaying an all too fleshly interest in the affairs of the laity. "Are you well acquainted with her?"

"I knew her father in Bari," said Tancred shortly, having no intention of discussing Alexandra's real status with a prurient clergyman. "She travels under my protection." With William gone, Tancred reckoned that last statement was now true. He was not one to dishonor an obligation that his dead brother had undertaken.

Taking the blue tunic, the marquis gingerly attempted to shrug the garment over his shoulders, but the arrow wound in his side restricted the movement of his right arm. At first, Bernard snorted disapprovingly at the marquis' clumsy attempts to slide the tunic over his head, but after a few moments of watching this futile endeavor, the chaplain threw up his hands in exasperation and offered his grudging assistance. He tugged the garment over the tall Norman's frame, belted his sword on him, and even bent down to fasten his boots.

"If you're determined to die of your wounds, the least I can do is help," said Bernard caustically. "Lean on me, marquis."

Thankfully, Tancred cast an arm around the slight shoulders of the black-browed cleric. They proceeded out of the house and toward the church with a stride as unsteady as a child's first steps. By the time they reached the door of the church, the marquis' face had grown several shades paler, and he slipped into a seat inside the nave with as much exhaustion as a man who has marched all day in the desert sun.

It was not long before the funeral mass began. Bishop Adhemar had laid aside the chain mail and longsword of yesterday's battle to take up the robes and crosier of his office. His rumbling voice intoned the Kyrie and sent up prayers for the dead, asking the Holy Mother to intercede on behalf of their gathered armies. "Hail, holy Queen, mother of mercy, our life, our sweetness and our hope. To thee do we cry, poor banished children of Eve. To thee do we send up our sighs, mourning and weeping in this valley of tears. Turn then, most gracious advocate, thine eyes of mercy toward us, and after this our exile, show unto us the blessed fruit of thy womb, Jesus."

After the service the church speedily cleared of Crusaders. They had but one night to enjoy the town and its taverns before they were on the road again to Antioch.

"Shall I arrange a litter to carry you back to the house?" asked Bernard.

"No," said Tancred dully. "I wish to stay here a little longer to pray."

"Very well then," said the chaplain, and he left the church to attend to his other duties, promising to come back a little later to help the marquis find his way to his lodgings.

Tancred stared straight ahead in the empty building, his face set like stone. He had it in his mind to pray, but he found that every time he opened his mouth all he could utter were reproaches, mostly directed at himself. He should not have let William go into battle. He should not have brought him on this adventure.

And yet, it was not Tancred who had brought William with him from Bari. In times past his wide-eyed younger brother had parroted his every action, but the lad was no tagalong on this trip. William had already set sail when his older brother had returned from visiting the pope. He had not needed Tancred to stoke the fire of his enthusiasm.

In the midst of the marquis' ponderings, heavy footsteps sounded on the flagstones behind him. Tancred refused to turn around until a fat-fingered hand was placed on his shoulder. It was Hugh the Great, a man with whom he had never held more than ten words pleasant conference. The only speeches he had ever received from that prince were rancorous recriminations for his insolence toward Alexios. The marquis assumed that today's encounter would be in the same vein. He set his jaw defiantly, preparing himself to disregard Hugh's diatribe.

But the large Frank had accosted him for other reasons entirely. "I am sorry about your brother," he said, clearing his throat sympathetically. His long wavy hair and short brown beard covered over some of the folds of flesh around his neck. If he had been a few stone lighter, he would have been a handsome man and as agreeable to the fairer sex as his brother the king of France.

Hugh took the marquis' silence as leave to continue talking. "William was a fine companion and an honorable man."

"How would you know?" interrupted Tancred coldly.

"Why, he made the journey with me," protested Hugh, "all the way from Bari to Byzantium!"

"So he did," said Tancred in a tone calculated to cut short the conversation. He made an obvious show of returning to his prayers.

But despite this scant encouragement, Hugh sat down beside him, his ponderous weight evoking ominous creaks from the wooden bench. "It was quite the stroke of luck, you know, to have such an ardent pilgrim on the path with us." His tone waxed familiar, and he crossed his right leg over his left, looking for all the world like a man about to begin a long tale. Tancred, forgetting his injuries, attempted to abscond from the pew. A sharp pain in his thigh rewarded his hasty attempts to stand and forced him back down again. With his injured leg keeping him captive to Hugh's loquaciousness, his prayers quickly turned into a silent plea for Bernard's quick return.

The Frankish prince's arms circled round his own ponderous belly, and his hands lay in his lap while his fingers laced and unlaced themselves in a predictable rhythm. "I would have turned back, several times, I'm ashamed to admit, especially after that watery disaster on the way to Durazzo. But William gave me the will and the wish to continue on this wretched undertaking. 'Think on Jerusalem,' he would say. 'Think of her white pillars and golden gates, the Temple that Solomon built, the tomb where Jesus lay. We cannot turn back in her hour of need.'"

"He should have told you to think on the excommunication you would face if you did turn back," said Tancred with a snort. Pope Urban's punishment for those who reneged on their oath was well known, and William had been only too apt to offer this argument when he wished to keep Alexandra in their camp.

Hugh took no offense at this, and instead gave a broad laugh that made his belly bob up and down like a barrel in water. "Excommunication is hardly something unheard of in my family. My mother spent the second half of her life outside the Church's pale. By rights my brother Philip should have led our people on this adventure, but he is under the Church's ban for adultery. His wife Bertha is fertile enough but, by the rood, the lady is as fat as I am! It is no wonder that my brother seeks consolation elsewhere."

"I heard your brother repudiated his first wife and took another," interrupted Tancred, displaying a modicum of interest in the affairs of the Frankish royal family.

"He did," said Hugh, "but he had no cause, and Urban declared the divorce unlawful. And besides that, the other woman is married as well—to Fulk, the Count of Anjou. So it is a charge of double adultery against the pair of them."

"Who is the other woman?"

"Bertrade de Montfort. By God, that woman is a handsome she-devil! Although they say that no good man has ever praised her save on account of her beauty. Until my brother gives her up, he lives outside the blessing of the Church, and that is why he could not be called upon to lead this Crusade."

"What a blessing it is that you are here to lead it in his stead!" said Tancred sarcastically. Up until now Hugh had had very little voice in the Crusader councils, and of all the Latin lords, his was the opinion least respected.

Hugh nodded in agreement, the sarcasm lost upon one so convinced of his own worth. "Yes, the emperor was very happy to be able to deal with one of his own station. He admitted as much when I sent William ahead to announce my arrival. And I do think that had I not been there to smooth things over, even more of the Crusader lords would have acted as foolishly as Raymond and that young wastrel Tan—." He broke off suddenly, having enjoyed the sound of his own voice so much that he had forgotten to whom he was speaking.

Tancred stared at the fat Frank, his lip curling with disgust. "Did you come to deliver your opinion of my brother or of myself, sirrah? I have opinions of my own to share if you will stay to hear them."

Fortunately for Hugh, the marquis' growing ire was cut off at the ankles when his manservant entered the church in search of his master. Relieved at Ralph's interruption, the Capetian prince took the opportunity to excuse himself. He felt aggrieved and ill-used that his generous offer of sympathy had been treated with such scorn by the arrogant Norman. But then, what else could be expected from one of such low parentage?

Having disembarrassed Tancred of the pompous Frank, the wiry, old servant looked at his master with concern. He knew that the marquis was not well enough to leave his bed, but he also knew better than to remonstrate with him.

"So, you've seen to William's corpse?" asked Tancred abruptly.

"Aye, master," said Ralph, his eyes glimmering with suppressed tears. He fumbled in his leather pouch and brought out a small circlet. "This was on his hand."

Tancred held out his hand to take the ring. Even in the dark church, the emerald glowed with a hidden fire. At the sight of the green gleam, his rage and bitterness gave way to an unspeakable sorrow. He closed his fingers around it, crushing the ring in his fist till his palm bled.

Against all reason, he knew that this ring had conspired to work William's death. The sultana had claimed that the ring brought luck; Tancred knew otherwise. He had no sooner put it on than the Byzantines had captured and bound him. William had no sooner worn it than the Turks had filled him with arrows. A strong urge prompted him to bury it in the sand, to drop it in a well, or to hide it in a crypt—to throw it away by any means possible before it was too late. But his conscience stifled that urge as quickly as it arose. He had pledged himself to hold the ring in trust until he reached the sultana's sister at Antioch.

Tancred opened his hand to look at the emerald, now speckled with drops of his own blood. Wiping the ring clean on his tunic, he slowly slid it back onto his little finger. He had sworn to his own hurt and could not repent, but oh, how he wished that he could unsay those words.

# Chapter 33

I t was inconceivable that Tancred could keep his saddle while
saddled with such serious wounds—that was evident to all save
Tancred himself. Ralph accordingly procured a litter for his
master to ride in, but it was only after three failed attempts at mounting
his horse that the marquis allowed himself to be cajoled into such an
emasculating means of transportation.

Alexandra set herself the thankless task of keeping the marquis entertained during every step of the jolting journey. Seated on
the smallest of Tancred's three horses, she rode alongside the litter
and prattled merrily about her home in sunny Italy. At first, Tancred
groaned like a dying martyr and closed his eyes frequently in an effort
to shut her out. But soon, despite his best attempts at ignoring her,
he found that her storytelling could transport him back to happier
days in Bari—keeping his mind from dwelling on the more unpleasant
matters of William's loss and the rough road they now faced.

After burying their dead, the Crusader host continued southeast
toward Antioch. Along the way they discovered that Kilij Arslan had
enjoyed some small revenge for the debacle at Dorylaeum. The Crusaders may have taken his tents and his treasury and his prestige, but
he had taken steps to drive off every herd of livestock and trample
every field of grain between here and Cilicia. The Crusaders had to
live off of the stores they had brought from Nicaea, and there was little
enough left of those.

None of the Latins were prepared for the fiery furnace of the Anatolian plateau in the summertime. In the face of this desert, the wintry
weather the Normans had encountered in Macedonia was remembered

fondly. The only water here was the salt marshes, the only vegetation the thorn bushes. Stone wells, relics of Roman and Byzantine rule, dotted the roadside, but the vengeful Turks had broken and fouled them beyond use. Feverish from wounds and thirst, Tancred looked out from his litter and saw soldiers bloodying their hands as they tore shriveled branches off the thorn bushes, chewing ravenously on the stalks in a fruitless attempt to find moisture.

One by one the horses began to die. Turold, the red-haired Norman knight, lost his emaciated mount early to the inimical desert. Tancred could see him seated ingloriously on the thick shoulders of an ox, a ludicrous image rendered dreamlike by the hazy desert air. Other unlucky knights mimicked Turold in his choice of mount, or else warmed their feet by walking through the wasteland. The waggoners, having surrendered their beasts of burden to the riders, harnessed sheep, goats, dogs, or anything that had four legs to the traces of their carts.

Afflicted by famine, drought, and the unrelenting sun, the Crusaders began to wonder whether the weather itself was on the side of the infidels. Tatikios, the golden nosed general, had told them that the road to Antioch normally took thirty days. They would discover later that the scalding heat had more than tripled the journey as sweating knights walked beside panting horses surrounded by barren hills devoid of provender.

Somehow, in the midst of all these hardships, Tancred's youthful body knit sound and whole. A month and a half later, by the time the Crusaders reached Iconium, he had returned to his former strength, and the only visible signs of his injury were two angry, red scars beneath his blue surcoat. The death of William had left another scar, not discernible by the human eye, and noticeable only to those who knew the marquis well. His heart had grown a little harder, a little more reticent, and a little less ready to care for those around him.

When Tatikios announced that Iconium was but a day's march away, Tancred felt his healed wounds throb with the desire for revenge. An irrepressible urge provoked him to put the entire city to the sword and tear it down stone by stone. But the Turkish garrison, as it turned out, was afraid of just such treatment at the hands of the Latins. Sighting the red cross banners from afar, they deserted the citadel in a panic, and the Crusaders encountered no resistance from the inhabitants—mostly Greeks—when they marched through Iconium's gates.

The valley surrounding Iconium was a fertile one. The fleeing enemy had found no time to destroy the fountains and orchards of this enchanting oasis. By unanimous consent the Crusader lords decided to tarry here a while until the soldiers, and they themselves, were refreshed from their grueling trek through the desert.

There were others besides Tancred who had been confined to litters. A few days previous, Duke Godfrey and his men had encountered a bear—a great, grey, grizzled matriarch as big as a warhorse in size. Hunting the beast to her cave, the mild-mannered German set out to spear her and ended up being viciously mauled in the process.

Baldwin's wife Godvera had given herself the task of tending her brother-in-law. Tancred overheard his own brother-in-law, Richard of Salerno, remark that Godfrey could not help but recover with such an alluring nurse bending over his bedside. "You forget that Duke Godfrey is as close to a saint as a layman can be," said Tancred dryly. "I doubt he's ever cast so much as an unseemly glance at his brother's wife. He'd rather be mauled by the bear a second time than dream of such a thing."

Just prior to Godfrey's hunting disaster, Count Raymond had met with his own misfortune, although it did not come complete with claws and teeth. For several days he had been bedridden with a serious sickness born of the hot weather. The night before they reached Iconium his fever became so severe that Adhemar ordered a priest to offer him the rite of extreme unction.

Tancred, still indebted to the Frankish count, went to inquire about his wellbeing. At the door of the tent, however, Raymond's nephew, William-Jordan, blocked his path. An altercation, somewhat noisy, sprang up between them until a feeble voice from within inquired who the visitor was. Learning that it was Tancred, the sick man bade him come in. "Very well then," said William-Jordan, disapproval sharpening his voice like a whetstone. The stocky young man stood aside and glowered while Tancred addressed himself to the invalid.

"God's peace be upon you," said Tancred, looking at the count's ashen face with disquiet. He had never seen Raymond divested of his military garb, and now, lying prone and half-naked on his couch, the man looked ancient, weary, and worn. His iron-grey hair hung dankly about his brow and his chest heaved with labored breaths.

"His everlasting peace may soon be mine," replied Raymond with a groan. He winced, overtaken by a sudden, sharp pain.

"Not yet," said Tancred encouragingly, sitting down by the older man's bedside. "You've not seen Jerusalem yet, and we'll need the help of Toulouse when we get there."

"Toulouse," Raymond echoed dully, and Tancred could tell that his mind had travelled back to his home country. His right hand clenched the frame of the couch, holding it tightly as if he feared someone would take it from him.

"And after Jerusalem is taken," said Tancred softly, "Toulouse will want her count back. You will live to see your people again."

"My people," said Raymond, speaking with difficulty and less than his usual coherence. "Yes, mine." He licked his dry lips and tried to raise his head a little. "My brother was count of Toulouse before me. He died, and there were no sons. I was the best choice, said the knights and the merchants and the farmers. A woman cannot inherit. A woman cannot lead. The best choice was me, they said. I know that they were right."

His voice became frantic, and Tancred realized that the count had no recognition of whom he was speaking to, or perhaps even of what he was saying. His nephew, who had been hovering about like a horsefly, chose this moment to intervene. "Can't you see you are upsetting him?" he demanded churlishly, and he ordered Tancred to depart immediately.

The marquis did not care to cause a quarrel in a sickroom. He stood up to vacate the tent as bidden—but when he cast a glance behind him, he saw that William-Jordan had made no move to bathe the feverish count's brow or settle him more comfortably among his cushions. Apparently, the curly-haired young man's filial instinct only extended so far as to drive away unwelcome visitors when his uncle was raving.

A dozen yards from the tent, Tancred caught sight of a thin, black-robed cleric heading that way. It was Bernard, sent by Bishop Adhemar to ascertain whether the count had shown any signs of recovery.

Fresh from the side of Raymond's sickbed, Tancred was able to give Bernard the tidings he sought. "I fear the count has lain down before the door of death," he said with concern.

Bernard, inscrutably knowledgeable about Count Raymond's affairs, shrugged with more indifference than was polite. "I daresay he will rise again. It has happened enough times before now."

"Why, what do you mean?" asked Tancred, and the gaunt cleric gave him to understand that Count Raymond had received extreme unction more than once. Indeed, it seemed to be a frequent occurrence on his campaigns.

"Are you saying that his illness is feigned?" responded Tancred, pursing his lips with distaste. He could not imagine anyone willingly assuming the role of invalid. The weeks he had spent laid up in the litter had been as torturous to his young virility as incarceration in a cloister.

Bernard interlaced his long, knobby fingers and adopted an air of innocence. "No, no. I am saying that when the dear count recovers from his sickbed, by some divine miracle, it will doubtless be in our hour of greatest need, giving us even more reason to appreciate and praise him."

"He spoke of his brother," said Tancred, intrigued by the count's feverish ravings. The bishop's chaplain would doubtless know more of the tale.

"Ah, that would be Count William," said Bernard. "He was no paragon of virtue, that one, but he made up for it later in life—if it is indeed true that some piety at the finish can make amends for the failures of the past. He received absolution for his sins by going on pilgrimage to the Holy Land. Six years he spent there on his knees in a hair shirt. And it was only two years ago that word of his death came back to France."

"So recently?" asked Tancred in surprise. He had assumed that Raymond had held the title of count for much longer than two years— he seemed to wear it so well. "And since William was without heir, Raymond succeeded him as Count of Toulouse?"

"Is that what he said?" asked Bernard with interest.

"He said there were no sons, and the people wanted him to follow his brother as count—although he did speak somewhat of women being unable to inherit. Did Count William have a daughter?"

"Yes," said Bernard. "Her name is Philippa. She was still a child when her father departed and so he appointed Raymond as regent to rule in his place. But six years can grow a girlish bud into the flower of womanhood. By the time word came of William's death, Philippa had blossomed into a wise and well-appointed lady. She asked for the county to be given over to her as her inheritance, but Raymond claimed that there was no precedent in Toulouse for a woman to rule. Philippa disagreed, and those who take her part would argue that Raymond usurped the county from his niece."

"You being one of those," said Tancred, looking shrewdly at Bernard.

Bernard waved off the accusation. "It's no matter to me one way or the other. Le Puy is far enough away from Toulouse to make me a disinterested spectator. I only wonder that Count Raymond felt secure enough to abandon his stolen dominion so soon. But then, I suppose it was to be expected. He has spent his entire life wishing for what was his brother's. Now that he holds the land of Toulouse, he must journey east and have the reputation of piety as well.

"His son Bertrand holds the county now in his stead. Raymond begot him young, and he's nearer Bohemond's age than yours. He's a competent man, though not so cunning as his father, and a sensible surrogate for Raymond to set over the city. Still, Philippa is not some frightened pheasant hiding in the brush. She may act in Raymond's absence and deal Bertrand a backhanded turn when he least expects it."

"She is a woman," said Tancred dismissively. "What can she do?"

Bernard looked at him in surprise. "You should not need a priest to teach you what things a clever and beautiful woman is capable of. True, it is unlikely that she will lead an army to retake Toulouse herself. But she has ways of making men lead it for her. There are many lords in France who would be willing to wed her for the prospect of such a dowry. Aye, and to help her win it."

"And if Raymond should lose the county?"

"He will not care so much if he has a kingdom in the east by that time. What is the Count of Toulouse compared to the King of Jerusalem? Baldwin of Boulogne is not the only younger son looking to make something of himself here in the Levant."

These were strong statements about Raymond's character, his past actions, and his present motives for joining the Crusade. Tancred was astute enough to know that he ought not to believe them simply on the word of the chaplain. There was something rotten inside Bernard where Raymond was concerned, a heart full of bile and bitter as wormwood. Why did Bernard hate Count Raymond so?

Tancred's mind had much to mull over, and as he took his leave of the chaplain, he neglected to inquire about an offhanded comment that the man had made. Bernard had compared Raymond to Baldwin, another younger son who was deprived of a patrimony. To what lengths would Count Baldwin go to make something of himself in the East? If Tancred had been mulling over *that* question, he might have been more prepared for the road through Cilicia.

# Chapter 34

The cooling streams at Iconium revivified the entire Crusader host. Both Duke Godfrey and Count Raymond found some respite from their respective maladies, and when the Crusaders showed their backs to Iconium, the invalids were able to travel with the army. This time the Latins were well acquainted with the difficulties of the desert, and following the advice of Tatikios, they gathered in a great store of water to keep their lips wet on the way to Hereclea. Ensconced like a jewel at the base of the Taurus Mountains, that city marked the end of the Anatolian Plateau and the beginning of the descent into Cilicia. A small army of Turks was encamped outside Hereclea, but they had no stomach for fight. When Bohemond's lances charged at them, they took to their wings like a flock of sparrows leaving the city invitingly open.

The four-day sojourn in Hereclea provided another opportunity for regrouping and refreshment. The Crusader lords met in council and allowed Tatikios to present his plan for the next leg of the journey. "These mountains are too much for you," said the swarthy Turk, gesturing to the craggy rock piles that stood in their path. "The heat is too great, the passes are too narrow, your horses are too few." His gold nose glinted brightly in the September sunshine. "But if we turn northeast, we can skirt them almost entirely, and travel through pleasant plains on a good road to Antioch. Emperor Alexios himself recommended that we take this route. What do you say, my friends?"

Most of the Crusader lords were willing to trust the golden-nosed general in matters of geography. He was Turkish in ancestry and Byzantine in allegiance. This was his country, and they had no maps or advance scouts who could gainsay his description of how the land lay. It was best to trust the advice of the slave whom Alexios had elevated.

But at Tatikios' mention of the emperor, Tancred's hackles rose. "Which route is shorter?" he demanded.

"Does it matter?" asked Tatikios with a smile that could be interpreted as sly, buried as it was in his coarse black moustache.

"Perhaps not to the emperor," said Tancred. "He would have us marching in circles if that would best serve his plans. But I am determined to reach Jerusalem by the quickest road possible. Tell me, which route is shorter?"

"Why, the road through the mountains, of course," said Tatikios. "But to reach Antioch that way, you must pass through the Cilician Gates, and—ah me!—the dangers of that journey are for a Theseus or a Hercules. I'd sooner leave a child in a viper's den then lead this army through that pass. You think the path from the coast to Nicaea was narrow, and rocky, and ripe for ambush? This road is a thousand times more perilous. Better to leave the mountains well enough alone, my boy. We'll reach Antioch a few weeks later but with fewer deaths on our hands."

Peter the Hermit, whose motley army had perished near the narrow defile that led to Nicaea, urged the lords to take the Turk's advice to heart. The nut-brown fanatic was close to tears as he dredged up the tragic tale they had all heard so many times.

Hugh the Great and Robert of Normandy drowned out the hermit by voicing their own agreement loudly and clapping Tatikios on the back. Count Robert of Flanders, having calmly weighed the alternatives, also gave his assent. Adhemar put it to the vote, and the Turk's plan carried the day. Tancred merely grunted and held his peace. Beneath his close-cropped blond hair, the young Norman was devising plans of his own.

Later that night, Tancred went to his uncle Bohemond's room in Hereclea. "I've made up my mind," he said brusquely. "The rest may follow Tatikios into the plains like dumb sheep, but the mountain passes are mine when we leave in the morning."

To Tancred's surprise, Bohemond showed nothing but enthusiasm for his plan. The tall, broad-shouldered Norman gestured for Tancred to take a seat and leaned forward eagerly. "I'm glad to hear you say so—indeed, I almost sent for you tonight to suggest that very thing. We'd be fools to circle around these mountains and let the Turks shoot arrows in our backsides." Bohemond clenched his fist and pounded on the table. "Unless we establish control of Cilicia, we cannot capture and keep Antioch. And Antioch, as you know, is essential to our mission."

A wave of pleasure swept over Tancred, momentarily blinding him to his uncle's overly keen interest in Antioch. He had not expected such support from this quarter. "Shall I take my whole company?" Tancred asked, assuming the role of subaltern without any resentment.

Bohemond rubbed his clean-shaven chin thoughtfully. "No," he said after a moment's reflection. "Take only three hundred men. The smaller your force, the less attention you will draw as you travel through the pass. The Turkish troops are few and scattered in these places, and your men will be able to awe and overpower them. Once you take a town, send word, and I will send reinforcements to garrison it. The other lords will thank you when they realize you've built us a bulwark to the north of Antioch. However long it takes us to besiege the city, we'll have no fear of attack from that quarter."

Tancred snorted. He had no illusions about what the others would think. "They'll say I'm building myself a kingdom in Cilicia."

"Surely not!" said Bohemond, raising his eyebrows and his voice in mock horror. "Everyone knows that the name *Jerusalem* is inscribed on the tablet of your heart. Others may be here to acquire kingdoms in the east, but Tancred? Never!"

The door of Bohemond's room flew open with a bang and the hands of both uncle and nephew jumped to their sword hilts. A familiar raucous laugh set them at their ease.

"What's this? A family conference?" asked the intruder. It was Richard of Salerno, somewhat saturated with wine, but not enough to completely impair his senses.

"Tancred means to knock on the Cilician Gates tomorrow," said Bohemond.

"Indeed?" said Richard, his eyes lighting up with interest. As his wretched hounds and unenviable horses knew well, the lord of Salerno was happiest when inflicting pain. And when that recreation was lacking, he sought his solace in drink. The tediously safe road they had traveled since Dorylaeum had kept him opening wine cask after wine cask and plying the goblet in lieu of the sword. When he heard that Tancred had proposed a route with significantly more zest to it, his interest perked up substantially. "Would you care for some company on that road?"

"You may come if you wish," said Tancred without enthusiasm. His brother-in-law was no favorite with him, but he could not refuse him a place on this mission. He explained the gist of the plan—to storm and capture the major Turkish citadels in Cilicia and garrison them with Latins. "We leave at dawn," said Tancred decisively. He instructed Richard to go to bed and sleep off his wine if he wished to keep a steady seat on his horse in the morning.

Richard, as it turned out, was a more valuable member of the expedition than Tancred had anticipated. After leaving Bohemond's room, he promptly disobeyed the young marquis' order to head to bed. Instead, he rode over to the Germans' camp outside Hereclea and cast about for Baldwin's tent. He was hoping to catch sight of the Lady Godvera in her shift or some other state of undress, a pastime that he freely admitted to have engaged in more than once. But instead of glimpsing the lady while slipping silently behind tent flaps, the lord of Salerno overheard a singular conversation that sent him galloping back to his brother-in-law's tent—only this time he was sober as a parish priest and twice as serious.

"Baldwin's on the move!" announced Richard, bursting in upon Tancred as he was burnishing his shield to the brightness of a silver mirror. "He means to try the pass through the mountains as well, and he's bringing a damn sight more than three hundred men with him."

"How do you know?" asked Tancred sharply. He thrust his shield into Ralph's hands, bade him check the stoutness of the straps, and gave Richard his full attention.

"I heard him talking to some foreigner whom he's attached to his staff. Bagrat, the man is called. He's not a Turk, and he's not a Greek, and he claims to be the brother of some petty king from roundabout."

"I know whom you mean," interrupted Ralph. "Bagrat the Armenian. His people come from the eastern side of the Euxine Sea. They were attacked first by the Byzantines and then ejected by the Turks. A great number of them have traveled south and settled here in Cilicia. They've sworn a lip service allegiance to Alexios, but since the Turks have shortened the emperor's arm, they have been free to act independently."

Tancred and Richard were showing marked interest, so Ralph continued to share what he had learned of the Armenians. "They're a proud people and they've made few friends because of it. They despise the Greeks because they adhere to another confession and creed. They detest the Turks because they consider them an inferior race. But I do not think they know enough of us yet to hate us or hold us in contempt. This Bagrat showed up in our camp shortly after we left Nicaea looking for a Latin lord to act as champion for his people against their oppressors. Baldwin embraced him immediately. He promised to help him and began to learn all that he could of Armenian affairs."

"Doubtless not from disinterested benevolence or mere curiosity," said Tancred dryly. "Bagrat may not realize that to rid himself of the fox he has invited the wolf into the henhouse."

Richard, overcome with the importance of the news he had discovered, bade Tancred open another cask of wine to celebrate. "That will have to wait," responded his staid and responsible brother-in-law. "You say Baldwin means to make for the mountains at daybreak? Why then, we must steal a march on him. Ralph, order the men to make ready. When the moon rises, we'll rise to meet her. We'll beat Baldwin at his own game and slip into Cilicia before him."

# Chapter 35

Tancred left Hereclea under cover of darkness with only a sliver of moon to light the track to the Taurus Mountains. He had been prepared to depart without a word to Alexandra, but Ralph woke her in the night and gave her a hastily whispered summary of the marquis' plan.

"I could come with you," she offered, busying herself by stuffing Tancred's saddlebags with as much bread and dried meat as they would hold.

"Or you could stay here," he countered. He had no time to waste on cosseting a female. The Taurus Mountains threatened strenuous travel, conflict with the Turks was inevitable, and who knows how ugly Baldwin would turn when he found that Tancred had slipped his traces and sprinted ahead.

"But with whom will I stay?"

"There are women pilgrims enough in Bohemond's band who can give you lodging in their tents. Although I warn you—greedy strumpets and grumpy beldames are not as longsuffering as Ralph and I. Keep a civil and quiet tongue in your head, and you'll come out unscathed. Or if that proves impossible"—he said with a grin—"I wager you can scratch out eyes with the fiercest of them."

Tancred leaned down and, reaching into his boot, pulled out the dagger that he kept there in case of emergencies. "Take this," he said, tossing the sheathed blade to the little Greek girl. "I know you know how to use it—just try not to murder anyone who might be a friend of mine."

Ralph planted a grandfatherly kiss on Alexandra's forehead and squeezed her hand in farewell. As the soldiers mounted up, her face in the flickering torchlight looked so desolate that it evoked a slight pang of pity in even the marquis. "Such sad cheer!" He chucked her under the chin with his gloved hand. "Antioch is not so very far. We will meet again, I fear, and when we do you may vex me with long stories of your own adventures while we were in Cilicia."

Out of the three hundred men in Tancred's company, one hundred were mounted knights. The rest were infantrymen or knights who had become such through the misfortune of losing their mounts. But even though many of his men were on foot, they still moved with a speed impossible to Baldwin's ponderous army of twenty-five hundred. Tancred began the race to the Cilician Gates half a night ahead of Baldwin. By the time he reached them he had put three days distance between the two armies.

The gates were just as narrow as Tatikios had threatened, and Tancred's men could go only two abreast through the forested slopes and white cliffs. They say that the Persian Xerxes pushed his army of a million men up through this pass and that Alexander the Great filed his phalanxes through from the opposite side. The young Norman wondered how long those leaders had to halt here as they funneled their men through a passage as narrow as the neck of a perfume bottle.

It was still the height of summer in September, and the heat radiating from the rock all around them left the Normans feeling like honey cakes in a baker's oven. They pressed onward, spurred by the knowledge that the Germans were following their trail like a pack of prime hunting hounds. After a few days the oppressiveness of the air lessened as the craggy rocks gave way to the soft furrows of the Cilician plains.

The city of Tarsus lay a little over two hundred furlongs from the gates. It was thither that Tancred was bound. The birthplace of Saint Paul, Tarsus was the ancient capital of this region, and just like Nicaea, its prideful towers and powerful walls were well prepared to withstand a siege. The inhabitants were an amalgamation of Armenians and Greeks, held firmly in the grip of a tiny Turkish garrison and understandably unhappy with their overlords. Although the garrison's size was not impressive, the city's ramparts were. To take such a fortress

222 | ROSANNE E. LORTZ

with only three hundred soldiers the marquis would need either the skills of a brilliant commander or a manifestation of divine favor. Tancred was confident that he had both.

For his plan to succeed, however, there was one thing he must make sure of.

"Is my shield well polished, Ralph?"

"So well that I can see my face in it," replied the old man, twirling his moustache ends with delight. "And what a pretty face it is!"

"Ha!" said Tancred with a good-natured laugh. "So pretty that the Turkish women cover their babies' eyes when you ride by, for fear that they'll be blinded by the sight of you. But one thing you say true—the polish is perfect. I will have need of that tomorrow."

The Normans kept their distance from the city that night, and Tancred ordered no watch fires to be lit in order to disguise both their location and their numbers. When morning came, the darkness rolled back like a scroll and the townspeople of Tarsus sent their cattle out to graze. But before the sun had taken more than a few steps over the horizon, a disturbance on the north side of the city caused the garrison to sound the alarum. Frantic cowherds rushed inside the gates announcing that a band of foreigners was rounding up the cattle and looting the outlying homes. "How many?" was the garrison's immediate question.

"No more than two dozen, and lightly armed like Turcopoles."

From the tops of the towers, the lookouts could see them, a small party of rogue raiders inviting reprisals with their mischief. The Turkish governor opened the gates and deployed over two thirds of his garrison. His men shoved and jostled for the chance to slap at this cloud of gnats that was buzzing around their battlements. They leaped onto their shaggy ponies with gleeful yells and administered sharp kicks to the bellies of their steeds.

The looters, a small band of Latins who had stripped down to the bare minimum of armor, heard the Turks shrieking like the north wind on its way through a stand of pine trees. As if on cue, they dropped their stolen cargo and darted for their own horses. The number of naked scimitars coming their way was five times the number of their own party. Unless they could find some way to elude pursuit, the charging Turks would cut them to pieces.

As the Turks closed the distance, the looters seemed to scatter haphazardly—although a careful observer might have noticed that in the midst of the scramble the Latins all headed on the course set by one wizened old man with carefully groomed moustaches. The Turks let out a shout of glee when they saw the direction the foreigners were taking. Obviously unfamiliar with the terrain, the poor fools were riding themselves into a corner. A low stand of brush, almost impossible to cross with their high-stepping horses, lay straight in front of them. In a few more gallops, the garrison would have them pinned and could exact vengeance for their depredations.

To the right of the brambly brush stood a small elevation. From the top of this hill a man could easily see all the surrounding country and be seen in turn by those below. Amidst the distraction of pounding hooves and pounding hearts, the fleeing Latins each kept one eye trained on that hill, and just before they were brought to bay, their watchfulness was rewarded. A brilliant flash, the sheen of brightly polished metal reflecting the sun, split the summer air three times. It was the shield of a knight catching the light like a mirror. At that signal, the fliers pulled hard on their reins, and like one man they turned to face their pursuit.

The Turks were surprised to encounter this concerted resistance. They drew rein as well. Their surprise heightened and turned to dismay when they heard hoof beats to the rearward. Jerking round the heads of their mounts, they discovered that a hidden company of armor-clad Crusaders, awakened from hiding by the signal, had encircled them on all sides. Lowered lances blocked every route of escape. The outnumbered garrison gave shrieks of terror as they were overridden, unhorsed, and trampled underfoot.

Ralph, the mustached leader of the decoy looters, hailed Tancred as he saw the marquis descend the hill. "Joshua needed the sun to stand still to finish off his ambush, but we've cut them all to pieces much quicker."

"The sun was still on our side today," said Tancred. His plan to use the polished shield as a signal had worked wonderfully. "God willing, we disposed of the lion's share of the garrison. Hopefully, their governor will despair at this day's work and surrender the city without any delay."

That night there was no secrecy shrouding the Norman camp. The army drove in their stakes on the flat level plain that spread outside the city walls. Tancred flew his banner high above his tent and, when night fell, bid his men build all the watch fires they had wood for. "The higher the flames the better," said he. "Let them fret the night away thinking we are a great host. I wager they'll call for a parley at daybreak and hand over the keys."

The parley that Tancred prophesied did not materialize according to his timeframe. Three days passed. The Normans waited in the plain outside the city, screeching their war cry like a muster of peacocks and waiting for the remainder of the garrison to capitulate. Waiting was the only option open to them. The walls were impossible for a force of their size to storm, and besides, they had brought no siege engines with them in their hasty race through the Cilician Gates.

On the third evening, after the sun had gone down, a delegation of the chief citizens slipped surreptitiously out of their homes and made their way hesitantly to the Latin camp. The Norman sentries escorted them to Tancred's tent. There they beseeched him to take possession of the city and remove the infidel yoke from their necks. Appreciative of their confidence in him, Tancred quizzed them carefully on the Turkish numbers and defenses. He was delighted with what he learned. Nearly the whole of the garrison had been destroyed by his ambush. The city walls were still intact, but they were manned by only a handful of men. The governor, so rumor whispered, had despaired of any reinforcement and was in the mood to do something desperate. Tancred thanked the men of Tarsus for their information and promised to afford them all the relief he was able.

That night the marquis once again ordered his men to pile the wood high on their fires. The plain lit up like a Viking's funeral pyre. The city itself, in stark contrast, produced only the dimmest glow from its houses. It looked as if the governor had enforced a strict curfew on the citizens forbidding them to light any unnecessary flame. Strangely enough, however, the hills to the north of Tarsus were dotted with a thousand other small fires, little pinpricks of light in the distance twinkling like orange stars. Several of the sentries called these to Tancred's attention, stating that they had not noticed them on any of the previous nights.

"Could they be Turkish reinforcements?" asked Richard of Salerno.

"From the north? Unlikely," replied Tancred. "There are no Turkish strongholds in that direction. But perhaps it is nothing more than the lights of several outlying villages." The explanation was weak, but it satisfied Richard and the unimaginative sentries. Tancred's perspicacity had developed a more plausible explanation of whose fires those were, but he determined to keep his inklings to himself and let time unfold the mystery to the rest.

When the morning sun ascended, it came to light that the Turkish governor and his diminished detail of soldiers had disappeared during the darkest hours of the night. Once again the chief citizens came out to meet Tancred, and this time they delivered to him the keys of the city. He was not fated to hold them long.

While his men were breaking down their campsite to move their gear inside of Tarsus, Tancred looked around him for a soldier with a swift horse and a cool head. "Gervase!" he said, spotting one of his favorite knights, a seasoned soldier of Bohemond's generation. Gervase's sandy hair had flecks of gray in it, and his face had begun to fold with the wrinkles of experience. Tancred trusted him to pick his way through unknown territory and locate the main army as it circumvented the mountains. "Tell my uncle we have taken Tarsus, and we need reinforcements to hold her while we continue on through Cilicia."

The marquis had no sooner seen the messenger off than he felt a sharp tug at his sleeve. "Look, master!" said Ralph urgently. He gestured toward the shallow hills to the north of the plain. Wending their way into the valley was a large host of armored men, pennants flying high on their elevated lances. Here were the lighters of last night's distant campfires. Tancred did not even have to look at the leader's crest. He knew without question that the man at their head was Baldwin of Boulogne.

"What do we do now?" asked Richard, licking his dry lips. His usual leer had collapsed into concerned creases.

"Into the city! Move!" said Tancred, his voice snapping against the ground like the crack of a whip. Sitting tall in the saddle, the broad-shouldered marquis ensured that his men made all the haste they were able. His fair skin flushed with exertion and his short blond hair became damp with sweat as he rode to and fro shouting orders. Once they heard that the silver stream coming down from the hills was Baldwin's men, the soldiers themselves were in no mood to tarry. By the time the Germans set hoof on the plain, the Normans had embedded themselves behind the walls of Tarsus and locked the gates for good measure.

Baldwin, it soon appeared, was more apprised of their doings than they were of his. His scouts had already discovered the when and the why of Tarsus' capitulation. Armed with this knowledge, Baldwin drew his men up in front of the city and demanded entrance. The Normans politely refused.

Undeterred by this rebuff, Baldwin rode out in front of the ranks of Germans, mounted on a great destrier of the same inky color as his long hair and beard. "Come down, Tancred!" he said imperiously, lifting his visor and looking up the height of the walls. "I would have speech with you."

From the summit of the gate tower, the marquis listened to the German's insistence on a parley. He frowned in thought.

"I would not go if I were you!" said Richard of Salerno, drumming his fingers anxiously against the battlements. "Baldwin's as devious as a serpent, and hard as it may be to believe, I think he hates you more than he does me!"

"I would not have him think me afraid," replied Tancred, and shrugging off Richard's cautions, he descended the spiral staircase of the gate tower to emerge from a small postern gate.

# Chapter 36

Many men would have dismounted from their stallion to speak with a man on foot. Baldwin preferred to remain in the saddle, giving himself the opportunity to look down on the intolerable Norman.

"Have you come to offer me your felicitations on my newest conquest?" asked Tancred, starting off the conversation with an antagonistic note. His cocky grin dared Baldwin to explode in exasperation.

The German, however, had already decided how to deal with the young marquis. "When did Tarsus surrender to you?"

"This morning at sunrise. The governor and his men fled during the night."

"Ah," said Baldwin pointedly. "They fled after they saw my campfires in the hills."

"What do you mean?" asked Tancred, losing a little of his self-assured stance.

"I mean that Tarsus would not have surrendered if she had not seen my men so near. Your force would never have been sufficient to frighten her. Her capitulation redounds to my credit, not yours. If you were a man of honor, you would acknowledge this and hand over the keys to her gates."

Tancred's jaw dropped. He stood silent for a moment, dumbfounded at such audacity. "And if I am not a 'man of honor', as you put it?"

"Why, then I will be forced to claim what you have stolen from me—by force of arms if need be," said Baldwin. His smug smile revealed a mouth full of sharp, wolfish teeth.

Tancred's stomach churned with rage at this bald faced treachery on Baldwin's part. He looked at the right sleeve of Baldwin's surcoat—on it was stitched the same red cross that adorned his own. And yet the German would dare to jeopardize the solidarity and success of the Crusade for the sake of one Cilician city!

Enduring Baldwin's mocking glance for a moment longer, Tancred organized his jumbled thoughts. Mentally, he charted the wisest course to steer through the perilous waters that had suddenly beset him. He could hole up in the city and show the arrogant Germans the double fisted fig. But what would be the point of waiting out a siege? The Normans had a relief force expected, but it was doubtful that Bohemond would spare many men, even if apprised of the exact situation. Tancred's whole goal was to reach Antioch and Jerusalem quickly, and a siege could trap him here for months.

He could wind the horn of battle and give fight to the Germans. But what were the chances of victory? Tancred was as confident as Alexander in his own mettle, but even he could see that it was suicide to bring his three hundred against Baldwin's thousands. He was here to oust the Turks from Cilicia, not to fight another Thermopylae.

There was a third option as well. He could lower his dignity and surrender the city as Baldwin demanded. But the thought of this last was as unsavory as a mouthful of moldering horseflesh. Better to fight and die than endure such ignominy!

Words of defiance had already formed themselves on Tancred's tongue, when another voice, not his own, rang through the corridors of his mind. "It is right to feel guilt over the shedding of Christian blood." He saw the spare frame of Pope Urban warming his hands over the brazier on that cold summer morning in Rome. And following the pope's words, he remembered the sentiments he himself had expressed that day. *When a man asks you for your tunic, you are to give him your cloak as well. When one of your cheeks has been struck, you must offer the other too.*

What was Tarsus, anyway? Only an out-of-the-way city of little importance to the course of the Crusade. Perhaps there was nothing here to hang onto besides his long cultivated sense of pride.

Tancred swallowed it down with a herculean effort. He dug into the neck of his surcoat and pulled out the chain from which swung the iron keys to the city. Slowly, he placed them in Baldwin's gloved hand. That simple action was one of the hardest things he had ever done, harder than submitting to Bohemond on the journey to Constantinople, harder than begging Count Raymond for money to feed his men. "Here is Tarsus," said Tancred, striving to eliminate all emotion from his voice. "I wish you joy of her."

"Gramercy," replied Baldwin, his fingers hooking round Tancred's offering—the tangible sign of his humiliation—like the talons of a hawk. "Your men are free to spend the night here, though I suppose you'll be wanting to take to the road as soon as possible. If you move fast enough, you may actually succeed in stealing a march on me this time."

"Stealing is a matter more attuned to your tastes than to mine," replied Tancred brusquely, and inclining his head in farewell he returned to the city to break the news to his men.

The Greek and Armenian inhabitants of the city were confused to hear that the Normans were leaving so soon. "But *you* defeated the Turks!" said one fellow referring to Tancred's impressive ambush of three days ago. He had a beard as long as Abraham and wore the brightly colored garb of the Armenian people. "We are surrendering the city into your hands, not to this other Latin of whom we know nothing."

Tancred shrugged. "That is the way of it. The sparrow hawk must give way to the eagle when the latter demands its prey. Baldwin will garrison your city—I pray that you will not enter into worse servitude than you have suffered at the hands of the Turks—and I will continue on my way to Antioch."

The saddened citizens were forced to acquiesce to this new state of affairs. But even though Tancred no longer had any part in the history of Tarsus, they still took an interest in his further actions. "Take the road to the east," said the bearded Armenian, "and you will come upon the city of Adana. King Oshin has been besieging it long to retake it from the infidels. If you can aid him, you will earn the thanks of our people."

"Who is King Oshin?" asked Tancred. It was strange to think that there were monarchs hereabouts the names of whom he had never heard mention.

"He is the lord of our people that rules all the cities this side of the Taurus Mountains," said the Armenian "or at least, he did rule them until the Turks drove him into the hills." He pointed at a gray speck situated on a spur of land jutting out from the mountain. "Look yonder! That is Lampron, Oshin's last remaining castle. For many years he has been forced to take refuge there, but now that you have defeated Kilij Arslan and the power of the Turks is waning, he has come down from his castle to win back Adana. Go to him and give him your help. He will not disappoint you in your reward."

Having no other route already planned, the Normans took the Armenian's advice and journeyed eastward to Adana. They spent a few days in easy travel through the soft-soiled Cilician plains. The trip provided them with enough time to recover from their soreness of spirit at the unfriendly turn Baldwin had served them.

When Adana came into view, their revived spirits began to rise with anticipation and their sharpened swords hung loosely in their sheaths ready to do battle. They expected to find hostile Turks snarling like a pack of wolves at bay. Instead, they found the city gates thrown open wide. A joyful procession of people came out to meet them, laughing, dancing, and singing. The Normans had never seen anything like it. Turbaned men in red, yellow, and green silks whirled and shouted, some trying to drag the paler-skinned Latins into the dance. Their revelry was as exuberant as the bacchanals of ancient Greece, though nothing so riotous in nature.

"Are these Christian folk?" asked Tancred in astonishment. Listening to their songs, he could make out a few words comparable in sound to the Greek language, but the meanings were lost upon him. The wild garb and spontaneous celebration seemed nothing similar to the formal ceremonies of the Byzantines or the cold austerity of his own race.

"They are Armenians!" shouted Ralph, answering his master above the din. "An excitable people, no?" The procession of people overtook the Normans like a wave, and pulled them back into the city with the force of an ocean tide. As the Latins passed under the gatehouse, garlands of leaves and flowers flew through the air, looping themselves around their heads and shoulders like crowns of victory at a tournament.

On through the streets the people danced, bringing their befuddled guests in tow. At the center of the city, a large square opened up. The crowd of celebrators parted, presumably to allow some important personage entrance. Tancred, urged by the crowd to dismount from his horse, found himself face to face with a great, bearded, bear-like man, dressed in furs despite the warm autumn weather and brimming over with good cheer. He extended his right hand in fellowship to the marquis, and when Tancred took it, he surprised him by refusing to let go and clasping him close to his expansive chest.

"Welcome, friend!" said the bearded leader in fluent Greek, kindly allowing Tancred an opportunity to extricate himself from his hospitable hug. "You come on the heels of our victory, you who have done so much for our people already."

Bit by bit, Tancred began to piece together the chaotic new world that had caught him up like a whirlwind. This furry creature, embracing him with all the enthusiasm of the prodigal son's father, was Oshin, the Armenian king of whom he had heard tell. He was as little like the king of Constantinople as could be imagined. Where Alexios was eloquent, Oshin was ebullient; where Alexios was diplomatic, Oshin was artless; and where Alexios was imperious, Oshin was welcoming, a quality more precious than all the gold and jewels of Byzantium.

When Oshin had received word concerning Tancred's liberation of Tarsus, he had just that day driven the Turks from Adana. Feeling this to be an especially felicitous confluence of events, the Armenian king had waited for the marquis' arrival to celebrate his own victory and commanded his people to receive the Norman as one of their own princes. While the people stampeded with joy in the city streets, Oshin whisked Tancred away to the citadel to celebrate a lavish feast that had been laid out in his honor. Baldwin had stolen his victor's laurels at Tarsus, but the Armenian king seemed determined to replace them, and on a far grander scale.

# Chapter 37

"You come upon us in our happiest hour," said Oshin, reclining at the low feast table in the manner of eastern monarchs. His beard was so dark brown that it looked black, and in it lodged crumbs and half-chewed morsels of the food he was devouring. The Armenians all around him ate with the same zest, like men who had just been freed from imprisonment or from the rigors of a lifetime Lenten fast. Tancred, no dainty eater himself, stared visibly at their voracity. These Armenians were mighty trencher folk.

"We have been cooped up in the mountains for too long," said Oshin, with a broad smile, "surviving on old goats and birds' eggs. My men see these dates, and raisins, and honey cakes and go mad with delight." He refilled Tancred's goblet with a generous portion of spiced wine. "There was no vintage like this in the cellars of Lampron," he said, alluding to the hillside fortress they had inhabited.

"I caught a glimpse of your castle when I was at Tarsus," said Tancred. "From that distance Lampron seemed no more than an outcropping of stone, differing only from the rock around it by virtue of being man-made."

"A glimpse is the most that any foreigner has seen of it since the Byzantines ceded it to us," said Oshin. "The cliffs leading up to it are steep, and crevasses dissect every path you would think to take. Indeed, the castle is approachable only on one side, through stairs carved into the stone. Every other side boasts a drop thirty times the height of a man and so sheer it cannot be scaled. It is no wonder the Turks have left us quite alone up there, secure in our hole like a colony of rock badgers."

"But you have not left them alone," observed Tancred.

"No," said Oshin, "every time our conquerors would grow careless, we would take what advantage we could with a raid from the mountains. In this way, we have been able to gain weapons and maintain our supplies. But to take our cities back from the Turks—that was beyond the power of my small company. When I heard news of your great Crusade and the surrender of Nicaea, my heart leaped within me. I prayed to God that you would come through Cilicia to be our savior, and lo! My prayer He has heard."

"Do not give me so much credit," said Tancred, blushing at this eastern hyperbole. "Adana's surrender was none of my doing."

Oshin waved away the marquis' modesty. "It was after your victory at Dorylaeum that the Turkish garrisons dwindled. Only then did we take courage to descend from the hills and retake Adana. And when we heard what wonders you worked at our sister city of Tarsus, our rejoicing knew no bounds."

Clapping his hands, Oshin signaled the servers to bring more wine. "But I must confess," he said with a gleam in his eye, "I did expect the worker of Tarsus' good fortune to be somewhat more ancient. You are like a young David, ruddy and good-looking, and hardly old enough to leave your father's house. Indeed, I have sons who are man enough to have begotten you!"

Tancred laughed and rubbed his clean-shaven chin. "I daresay it is the lack of a beard that makes me look like such a stripling in your eyes. I have worn arms for well nigh ten years and commanded my own company for five of those."

The bear-like Armenian shook his head in amusement. "How can you expect me to believe you are a man when you have no hair on your chin to prove it?"

"How can you expect me to believe you are a king when you have no crown on your head?"

"Why, as to that—" began Oshin hastily.

"No matter," said Tancred, quickly, before his table host took offense. He sensed an undercurrent of insecurity in the jovial

Armenian. "I merely speak in jest. Your royal bearing and command of this company is every proof you need. Are you the king of all the Armenian people?"

"Not all of them," said Oshin, a little reticently. Tancred's unwitting challenge to his authority had unsettled him. But when Tancred plied him courteously with more questions, he eventually unfolded the story of the people and politics in the Taurus Mountains.

"My people began migrating to Cilicia centuries ago. But it was not until the great invasion of the Seljuk Turks, half a lifetime ago, that we came here in droves. Our line of kings in Armenia had been destroyed and we were leaderless refugees looking for a safe haven from the heathens. In the midst of the chaos, one of our generals began to gain a following among the emigrants. His name was Rupen, and he claimed to be of royal descent. It may have been true, it may have been false—but with the genealogical records lost, none could gainsay him in the matter.

"He erected a fortress in the hills to shelter us till we should become strong again. Then, forging us into an army, he built a name for us, protected us from the Turkish emirs, and finally forced the Byzantines to acknowledge us as a legitimate power. He was the first king of Armenian Cilicia, a wise and just ruler. We called him the Lord of the Mountains and were happy to submit to his sway.

"Two years ago, Rupen died, and with him went the short-lived solidarity of our people. His eldest son, Constantine, claimed the right to succeed him as Lord of the Mountains. But many of Rupen's officials, I being one of them, did not think Constantine had the capacity to rule. There are certain sacrifices a leader must be willing to make in these troubled times, and he is not willing to give up what is required."

Oshin frowned. Tancred almost interrupted to ask what sacrifices those were, but before he could say anything, the Armenian king plunged ahead with his tale. "In any event, Rupen's death caused our people to split into pieces, like a porcelain bowl thrown down from some great height, and each piece found itself a ruler who was not ashamed to take the title of king.

"On the west side of the mountains, I hold court at the castle of Lampron, and Tarsus, Adana, Mamistra—all the cities of this region—look to me for protection. Constantine himself holds the mountains north and east of here, a sizable expanse of territory, though not so great as his father's kingdom. Farther east, even beyond the springs of the Euphrates river, other chieftains have set up principalities for themselves. Thatoul, Constantine's younger brother, rules from the city of Marash. Thoros, another official in the days of Rupen, now calls himself king of Edessa."

Tancred listened attentively, determined to sort out the confusing politics of the region. He wondered which of these kings Baldwin intended to aid. Was it Oshin whose brother Bagrat had attached himself to the Germans and promised them great things in Cilicia? "There is another Latin who has followed me into Cilicia," the marquis said, his tongue treading carefully on his words, "Baldwin of Boulogne. In his retinue is an Armenian named Bagrat who claims to be the brother of an Armenian king."

Oshin growled, looking more ursine than ever. "Bagrat, that warty toad! He is the brother of Kogh Vasil, a highway robber who calls himself a king in the south. If you are on your way to Antioch, you may see him skulking behind some rocks. He is no person of esteem to true Armenians."

Tancred smiled and took a large swallow of the heady wine. His skin tingled with warmth, a combination of the strong drink and the satisfaction of knowing that Baldwin was unlikely to make many friends in Armenia on the strength of his association with Bagrat. Perhaps the German's plans for conquest in Cilicia would not come to fruition.

Richard of Salerno, lolling unceremoniously on the cushions beside Tancred, chose this moment to interrupt. Intimidated at first by the strangeness of the situation—and by Oshin's regal title—he had held his tongue over the course of the banquet. But now, learning that Oshin was little more than a local chieftain, his power virtually on par with his own, he slipped his own observations into the conversation. "I can see how this Cilician split worked out in your favor, Oshin, but it does not seem so favorable for the Armenian race as a whole. How can you withstand the forces of the Turks, small and separated as you are?"

Tancred mused inwardly on the fact that the same question might soon have to be asked of the Crusader lords—that is, if Baldwin's behavior became common among them.

"The Turks are not as unified as you might think," said Oshin, scratching his magnificent beard with both hands. "And some of us have the goodwill of Byzantium to back us."

"Some, but not all of you?" asked Tancred.

Oshin snorted. "I told you that there were sacrifices that Rupen's son was unwilling to make. In order to gain recognition from Emperor Alexios, it is necessary to become an adherent of the Greek Church. That is not so much to ask, no? You would do the same my friend, would you not? But Constantine, he kicks against the goads, and so he treads a harder road than the rest of us."

Tancred passed over the rhetorical questions without comment. It was unnecessary to share his feelings about Alexios and Alexios' demands with the Armenian. He was, however, interested in pursuing this line of inquiry about Constantine. The more he knew about the people of this land, the better. Whether the Armenians turned out to be friends or foes, intelligence of their kings, their customs, their numbers, and their religion would give him a weapon to use on behalf of the Crusade.

"So this Constantine," said the marquis, "he will not join the Greek Church because he is a pagan?"

Oshin laughed, a great, uproarious guffaw that caused everything touching him to shake. "As pagan as the Apostles!" He slapped Tancred jovially on the shoulder as if he had just made a tremendous joke. The marquis' perplexity continued to mount until Oshin enlightened him further on the state of Christianity in Armenia.

"Do you not know that the Armenian Church is the oldest Church in the world? The Franks are but babes in the faith in comparison to my people. When Our Lord walked upon this earth, the story of His miracles went out from Jerusalem. Agbar, the king of the Armenians, heard tell of Him. He wrote a letter, begging the Messiah to come eastward and teach the ways of God to his people.

"But alas! It could not be. The prophecies regarding the Christ must be fulfilled, and it was at the hands of the Jews that He must die. Our Lord wrote Agbar a letter in return, refusing his request but making him a promise: one of His disciples would come later and give him the teaching he desired.

"After the Christ's death, it was Thomas—the doubting Apostle— who remembered his Lord's promise. Thomas passed through our country on his way to the country of Hind, and he left behind him Bartholomew and Thaddeus to baptize Agbar and teach him the way in which he must walk. Agbar was the first king in all the world to welcome the Christians into his country. Following his lead, the Armenian people accepted the Apostles' teachings gladly, and thus it was that Armenia became the cradle of Christianity right after it was born into the world."

"An ancient tradition, indeed," said Tancred. "Why then does Emperor Alexios insist that you abandon it to adopt the rites of the Greek Church?"

Oshin's brow furrowed. "That is a matter for the doctors of the Church to debate. I know only that the Greeks consider the Armenians to be heretics, claiming that we do not rightly distinguish the divine and human natures of Christ. And added to that, of course, the Armenians have their own *catholicos*, while the Greeks look to the leadership of the patriarch in Constantinople."

"As we Latins look to the leadership of the pope in Rome," remarked Tancred.

"Indeed," said Oshin, "but your pope is too far away to concern himself with Armenia and to interfere with my people's doctrine and practices. Therefore, the Armenians may stay friends with the distant Latins while we quarrel with the nearby Greeks."

"But you say that you have made your peace with Alexios by joining his Church."

Oshin's sonorous voice dropped in pitch and he looked around the room cautiously. The rest of the Armenians were still at their revels, gnawing on lamb shanks, guzzling from goblets, tossing figs into their companions' mouths. "Yes, in exchange for being made his deputy, I have been baptized into the Church of the Byzantines. But there are many here"—his eyes flickered around the room—"who take offense at this necessity. 'Treachery,' they term it. It were not well to remind them of it too often lest it breed disquiet and insurrection."

Tancred nodded conspiratorially, assuring Oshin he would say nothing of the matter. The conversation returned to lighter matters and continued on in this vein until the festive gathering disintegrated with the rising of the sun. Thanks to Oshin, Tancred now understood the politics of the region much more clearly. He deposited all of his new knowledge in the treasury of memory, certain that it would accrue value in the weeks and months ahead.

"Tell me," said the marquis, pulling himself up from the cushions with the sleepy groan of a full stomach, "where should I journey next? I must wend my way eastward to meet up with the rest of the Crusaders, but I would not willingly leave the Turks a foothold in Cilicia."

Oshin yawned. "You should go on to Mamistra then," he said, gesturing southwards. "The town is not as large as Adana, but it is still overflowing with my poor, oppressed people. The Turkish garrison is small, and with your reputation, they will flee at the sight of you. But first, to your sleep, my friend. It is not wise to ride hard on the heels of such rejoicing as we have had this night."

# Chapter 38

The Normans tarried in Adana for three days. On the night before they departed, Oshin took Tancred up on the walls of Adana to see the setting of the sun and the spires of the city. The daytime hubbub had subsided, and from the church quarter of the city came the deep tolling of bells and the low chanting of hymns. The rosy glow of the setting sun reflected in Oshin's cheeks as he gazed paternally over the city. "At this time last week the air was filled with *allah akbars* and the noise of infidel prayers. God willing, those sounds will never be heard here again."

Lapsing into silence, they both stared into the distance at the setting sun. The colored sky paled from dusky rose to the cool tones of amethyst. It was a hard country, but one that mixed in delights with its difficulties. In the north and the east, the Taurus Mountains rose up from the ground imposingly like the legs of a family of giants. In the west and the south the plains unrolled like a green carpet all the way to the shores of the Mediterranean.

Tancred could see the road his Normans had walked on their way from Tarsus to Adana, a thin brown snake sliding unobtrusively through the plains. It was Oshin, however, who first saw the rider on that road. His body may have been as lumbering as a bear's, but his eyes were as keen as a hawk's. "Here comes one of your Latins," he said, pointing out a small, dark shape to Tancred.

Barely able to see the rider against the backdrop of the darkening sky, Tancred looked at Oshin in surprise. "How do you know he is one of us?"

242 | ROSANNE E. LORTZ

The Armenian laughed heartily and his beard shook up and down with the movements of his body. "It is not so hard to tell. He sits in his saddle like a Latin, solid and square and weighted down with armor."

"And an Armenian sits differently?"

"All the people of the East do. There is—how do I say it?—a fluidity between the horse and the man of the East, a fusion. When he steps into the saddle, he becomes one body with the horse itself."

At first, the rider seemed to crawl across the plain as slowly as a fly across a dish. Distance plays tricks on the eyes, however, and as the rider neared, the Norman and the Armenian perceived that his speed was so rapid as to be almost breakneck. "His errand is urgent, I think," said Oshin. "Let us go down to the gate and receive him there."

At Oshin's command, the portcullis lifted to admit the rider. The knight rode through the gate and reined in his horse sharply. The exhausted beast foundered and collapsed onto its knees. Tancred ran forward and pulled the knight clear of the ruin, saving his legs from being crushed under the horse's weight. Ripping off the knight's helmet, he knew him at once. It was Gervase, the sandy haired messenger whom he had sent to Bohemond for reinforcements when Tarsus surrendered. In the dim twilight, Tancred could see that Gervase's chain mail was torn in places and patched again with clotted blood.

"Water," said Gervase hoarsely. A full skin of it was fetched at once and poured into his panting mouth. The knight sighed and slumped over against Tancred, weary and weak from his wounds.

Afraid that Gervase would lose consciousness before he could explain his injuries, the marquis grabbed his shoulder and shook him a little roughly. "What happened to you?" he demanded. "Speak, man!"

Gervase winced perceptibly. Pausing several times for breath, he told his tale to the impatient marquis. "I found Bohemond without any trouble. He sent with me the reinforcements we needed, three hundred men to double the size of your company. But when we arrived at Tarsus, we found you had already left. I learned that Baldwin now occupied the city and begged him to allow us space to bed down inside the walls. He refused. 'Sleep in the fields with the rest of the cattle,' were his words. And so we did. We set up camp under the shadow of the walls of Tarsus.

"We posted sentries—we were not careless!—but the Turks know this country better than we do. In the middle of the night, a surprise sortie of mounted foes woke us with their yells. They hurtled through our tents with naked blades, and we, naked of our armor, put up only a futile attempt at resistance. I think it may have been the Turkish garrison that had fled, now reinforced and returned for vengeance. But whomever our attackers were, it is certain that the city saw their torches and heard our cries and sent out no one to succor us.

"My tent was one of the farthest from the point of assault, and the distance gave me time to struggle into my coat of mail. I had no time to find my horse and mount him before their war band overtook me and rode me down. The metal links of my mail turned their blades a little, and that was the saving of me. They left me for dead in a pile of slain men. When I came to my senses in the morning, the Turks had disappeared. I struggled to my feet and called out the names of my comrades, but the bodies all around me were as silent as any stone. There was still no sign of Baldwin's men exiting the city to offer us aid.

"I knew I must get word to you of this disaster, my lord. By the time I gathered my wits, several of the citizens of Tarsus had come out like a kettle of vultures to pick over the clothes of the corpses. One of them told me that you had pressed onward to Adana. The Turks had taken all of our horses that they could lay hands on, but I discovered one nag wandering on the outskirts of our camp. I found a saddle among our strewn possessions, climbed on the beast's back with some difficulty, and rode like a madman to reach you."

Gervase panted heavily from the pain of so much exertion. Tears glinted in his tired eyes. "I knew those knights of your uncle's—I diced and dined and drilled at swords with them. It would have been easy enough to give three hundred men room inside the city. Why did Baldwin refuse? Why did he hold back his help? Why, in the name of God, did such a calamity have to occur?" Unable to control his sorrow, the wounded man wept freely.

Tancred, who had listened to his account with growing horror, clenched his fists so tightly that the knuckles whitened. He blinked back the faint mist forming in his own eyes and put an arm around Gervase's waist to help him stand. "There will be a reckoning to pay for this," he said, "and not just with the Turks."

Oshin clucked sympathetically. "I do not think this Baldwin likes you, my friend. First, he takes Tarsus for himself, then he watches your soldiers die like men in a gladiator pit. What will you do?"

"Do?" repeated Tancred. "What *can* I do? I will go on to Mamistra as you have advised. But when I reunite with the main army, I will expose him for the blackguard he is—and heaven help him if he tries to deny it before the others!"

Mamistra was only a day's ride from Adana, but Tancred took the journey slowly so that he could arrive at noontime on the second day. As Oshin had predicted, the tiny Turkish garrison shook with fright at the sight of Tancred's pennants. By the time his three hundred men had advanced within arrow's distance of the gate, the Turks had saddled their ponies and shown Mamistra their tails. The Armenian citizens, now the sole occupants of the city, shouted down an invitation for the marquis to enter, and Tancred was not shy to accept their offer.

The events that followed were eerily similar to those that had occurred a week previous at Tarsus. Tancred had no sooner taken possession of the city than a lookout spotted the sheen of chainmail on the horizon. It was Baldwin and his legion of warriors, descending like a pack of hyenas on the kill just made by a solitary lion.

"That misbegotten son of the devil!" said Tancred, his face on fire with righteous fury. In his mind's eye he could see the black-haired German's gloating face as his gloved hand grasped the keys to Tarsus. "He'll not play me the same trick as last time, so help me God!" This time there were three hundred Norman deaths to chalk up to Baldwin's account, and this time the thought of turning the other cheek did not even enter Tancred's mind. With a speed of decision that surprised even himself, the marquis ordered the gates to be closed and barred.

"But it is market day!" objected one of the local merchants. "All of the outlying villagers have come down from the hills bringing their flocks and crops to sell. They will be trapped inside, unable to return to their homes."

"So much the better," said Tancred callously. The blond Norman's square jaw hardened like mortar. "There will be no one outside the city to offer aid to the Germans, and there will be plenty of food inside Mamistra if Baldwin is determined to besiege us."

"What about Antioch?" asked Ralph, prompting his master to remember past concerns. "You wished to reach it as quickly as possible so that we can continue on to Jerusalem."

But the marquis' mission had been obscured by his resentment, lost from sight like a harbor in a bank of fog. "We shall stay here till doomsday if that is what it takes," declared Tancred. "Mamistra will never be Baldwin's while there is a drop of blood left in my veins."

As expected, Baldwin requested a parley as soon as his men drew rein beneath the walls of Mamistra. This time Tancred went out on horseback to meet his rival. Only too happy to make Baldwin wait, he let his horse amble slowly out of the gate. He forced himself to breathe normally and readied his tongue to recite the speech of defiance that his mind had been rehearsing for the last two hours.

"Well met!" said Baldwin, straining to impart cordiality to his tone of voice. Tancred had expected to see Baldwin's lip curling insolently above his black beard, but instead there was a hint of worry in the German's dark eyes. Perhaps he knew he had gone too far by denying the three hundred slaughtered Normans shelter at Tarsus. Perhaps he knew how ill his actions would look in the eyes of Bishop Adhemar, his brother Godfrey, and the rest.

"Is there anything well about meeting with you or your ilk?" responded Tancred. "Forsooth, it is a foul wind that blows Baldwin of Boulogne into harbor."

"I see Mamistra has yielded to you," said Baldwin, ignoring the Norman's rancorous speech as one would a small child's petulance. "I will not attempt to tamper with your good fortune. I ask only shelter for my men and myself to break our journey on the road to Antioch."

"Shelter?" Tancred's horse felt the current of rage pulsing through his rider and began to swivel uncomfortably until the marquis reined him in. "You dare to ask me for shelter? Hear me, Baldwin. Not only do I deny you shelter, I also deny you have the right to ask it of me. You will never see the inside of Mamistra while I draw breath. Your numbers are large—much larger than the feeble company you failed to aid—but I pray that Kilij Arslan or some other infidel emir has had time to gather a heathen horde huge enough to waylay and slay you by night."

Baldwin was a man not easily abashed, but the utter detestation in the young Norman's voice singed him like the sparks from a campfire. "Very well," said Baldwin, "we shall pitch our tents in the field. I trust you do not intend to attack us yourself if the Turks are not obliging enough to appear?"

Tancred smiled sourly. "Unfortunately, I still retain some scruples. Be not afraid! You may bed down in the fields like the rest of the cattle, and sleep unmolested by any Norman. The only thing you need fear from us is inaction in your time of need."

And with that, Tancred turned his steed's head back to the gate and rode slowly into Mamistra.

# Chapter 39

The Turkish garrison that had fled Mamistra did not prove to be as bloodthirstily obliging as Tancred would have wished. No roaming bands of raiders materialized, and the Germans passed the night in the shadow of the city's walls without incident. Tancred, whose anger had dissipated a little while he slept, was relieved to discover that Baldwin had taken no action to subvert the city while the shadows of nighttime reigned.

When the Armenian villagers trapped by the unfortuitous events on market day begged Tancred to open the gates, he relented from his earlier stance and allowed them egress. One sheep farmer timidly approached him seeking permission to sell livestock to the hungry Germans. Tancred surprised everyone by granting his request, and soon the local tradesmen had set up a makeshift market on the edge of Baldwin's camp.

"By all the saints in the calendar!" stormed Richard of Salerno, uttering a few stronger blasphemies to boot. "We ought to be feeding those bastards the edges of our knives, not letting them gorge themselves on field fattened mutton. Why, in God's name, did you allow them market rights?"

Tancred shrugged at his irate brother-in-law, annoyed that he had to explain his own actions. "I should have thought you would understand why without so many questions. Baldwin is in the wrong for what he did—or did not do—at Tarsus. He is in the wrong, and he knows it. And furthermore, he knows what all our fellows will think of him when we reunite with the main army. He would doubtless welcome some treacherous action on our part to make his own scroll of sins seem shorter. But we will not give him the satisfaction of saying that we starved him or sabotaged him or set upon him in any way."

Richard's aquiline nose flared, and a loud sniff indicated that he put no stock in Tancred's reasoning. He drew his dagger and whetted the edge of it against the tip of his own finger, smiling when he saw that its keen edge had drawn a drop of blood. "You remind me of your sister Altrude—always striving to seem the righteous party in a quarrel. But I say, seeming be damned! We should act as our blood tells us, and let our reputation resolve itself however it will." He sheathed his dagger with one swift motion and turned on his heel to exit the room.

"Listen well, Richard," Tancred called out to his brother-in-law's retreating form. "There is to be no provocation offered by any of our men. If any trouble is started, it must come first from Baldwin's camp."

Richard stepped outdoors into the sunshine and sent a devilish grin back over his shoulder. "As you wish, commander. I shall make sure that all is fair and seemly." He cocked his head and squinted up into the sunlight. "But if I were you, I would keep a weather eye on those clouds. It looks like a storm is brewing, and you'll not want to be caught unprepared."

Just as Richard had warned, the storm broke outside Mamistra round about midday. A great many of the Germans were perusing the wares of the outdoor market. Rudolph, the great, bearded fellow who had provided Ralph with so much invaluable information at Constantinople, was among them, swaggering through the closely crowded aisles, making room for himself with his elbows. Merchants screeched out the kind and cost of their wares. Copper clinked as it passed from hand to hand. The hubbub was so loud that a man could hardly distinguish the sound of his neighbor's voice.

Rudolph passed by the stall of a cheese maker, and scenting a pungent piece of goat cheese, broke off a large piece and popped it greedily in his mouth. Then he continued walking, his cheeks bulging with the toothsome morsel.

The owner of the stall, witnessing this depredation, let out a howl of outrage. "Two coppers, you big lout! That's two coppers for what you've sampled!"

As the little Armenian sputtered angrily in his face, the German feigned confusion and lack of comprehension. But even though he knew no Greek, it should have been easy to make out the cause of the seller's complaints.

"What is this? What is this?" asked a solicitous voice. The lord of Salerno was lurking close by and had seen it all. The Armenian gesticulated loudly as he accused the foreign devil of pillage, making up for the smallness of his size with the loudness of his squeals. Richard heard him out and shot a look of disgust at the German. "Give the man his money, you rogue!"

"Why?" said Rudolph in a muffled voice, trying to swallow down the last of his ill-gotten gains. It was obvious that he was used to having his way with the world.

Richard smiled inwardly, pleased to have found such a willing victim. "Why?" he echoed. "Because if you don't pay for your pleasures in coin, you'll pay some other way." The crafty Norman lightly laid one finger on the hilt of his sword.

Seeing the motion, Rudolph's hand leapt to his own blade. The naked steel slid free of its sheath with its sharp point directed toward the Norman lord's breast.

"You leave me no choice," said Richard in clear tones calculated to enter the ears and memories of the surrounding crowd. He pulled his longsword from its scabbard. Instinctively, the market goers stepped back, jostling each other to form a circle a safe distance from the two men.

The big German glared, suddenly suspicious as to why a Norman knight was so assiduously championing an Armenian cheese seller. Two thoughts assailed his mind simultaneously. The first was a guilty reminder that Baldwin, only that morning, had specially forbidden a fracas with the Normans. The second was the sensible suggestion that it was too late to back out now.

A clump of Armenian tradesmen had ranged themselves in support of their defrauded countryman. From their direction, a handful of rotten figs sailed through the air to spatter Rudolph's face. Combined with Richard's smirk, it was more than a man could bear. He advanced on the Norman and struck the first blow.

By the time Tancred got wind of the incident, the summer shower had swollen into a typhoon. Blows rained down from fists and blades as blood ran freely, limbs splintered, and market stalls overturned. From inside the walls of Mamistra, the shouts of brawling men and incensed property owners could be heard. "The marketplace has turned into a melee!" reported Ralph, having gone out to reconnoiter. "It seems that one of Baldwin's knights attacked one of ours. The onlookers joined sides, and now we are at dagger points with the Germans."

"Where is my brother-in-law Richard?" demanded Tancred, already certain of the instigator of this uproar.

"I don't know his whereabouts," said Ralph hurriedly, "but I do know Baldwin's men are forming lines outside the city. Do you think he is merely making a show of his power, or do they mean to attack?"

Tancred grimaced. "He has already proved that for him anything is possible. Sound the alarum—now!"

It was a somber sight that greeted the people of Mamistra that day. They had avoided a skirmish, a siege, and a sack when the Turkish garrison fled of its own accord. Now they were threatened with all three of those by two commanders who both wore the same red cross stitched to their shoulders.

On one side of the walls, a large company of stern-faced Latins had positioned themselves in full battle panoply, with sharpened lances and stamping steeds. Behind their lines carpenters had thrown down heavy beams, and a knowing eye could tell that the pegs and ropes they held were the rigging for siege equipment. On the other side of the walls, a much smaller force of Latins prepared to utilize the defenses already constructed on the city's towers. They stockpiled a large supply of javelins beside each scorpio, so that the weapons could be fired rapidly if the Germans made a charge on Mamistra's main gate.

The heat of the day reached its peak, and sweat trickled down the noses of men standing at the ready. Still no signal was given in either camp. Neither commander wished to bear the shame of attacking first and becoming the guilty party in the eyes of the whole Crusader host. But at the same time, neither wished to risk being unprepared for a treacherous attack from the other.

The deadlock continued all throughout the night. Tancred ordered his men to sleep in short shifts so that half his force would always be awake and armed. His own weary limbs never found opportunity to rest, and he stayed on the walls all that night encouraging his soldiers to vigilance.

Ralph watched his master stifle a yawn several times without making any comment. But when his usually nimble feet tripped over a pile of loose stones on the battlements, the old servant voiced a word of protest. "Save your strength for the morning. You should shut your eyes a while and appoint a deputy to watch the walls while you sleep."

"Whom should I appoint? Richard?" asked Tancred sardonically, for ever since the brawl in the market, his brother-in-law was nowhere to be found. "When I am old like you, Ralph, I will sleep in a chair in a corner and spend my vigor in growing moustaches. But until I reach the congregation of the gray headed, I'll stay awake and increase my chances of staying alive."

When morning came, a tired Tancred was utterly confounded to discover that Baldwin's men had banked their fires, folded their tents, and were in the process of loading up their wagons. Every sign pointed to Baldwin's imminent departure. "Is this some kind of trick?" the marquis wondered aloud. He had judged the German to be as tenacious as a bulldog. What reason could he have for abandoning the siege before it had even begun?

Mounting his favorite warhorse, Tancred signaled for a score of knights to follow him out into the plain. "Ho there, Baldwin!" he shouted, sighting his nemesis and indicating his own desire to parley.

Baldwin, sitting atop his own steed, was holding his helmet underneath his left arm and gruffly shouting marching orders to his

252 | ROSANNE E. LORTZ

own men. He ignored Tancred's overtures and continued to sort out his knights into vanguard, main body, and rearguard. As the Normans advanced, they saw that his eyes were red-rimmed and his whole face hung as haggardly as Tancred's. It looked like the landless German had spent all night awake as well.

"Why this sudden departure?" asked Tancred, his youthful curiosity exceeding his desire to appear cold and aloof.

Beneath Baldwin's short black beard, his jaw clenched tightly, its edges as sharp as a stonemason's chisel. "We have wasted enough time here," he said grimly. "We will rejoin the main army as soon as we can find them. Enjoy playing at being a princeling with your one city in Cilicia."

Baldwin's sneer did nothing to discomfit Tancred. One part of him would have liked to come to blows with the Germans in hopes of taking revenge for the treachery at Tarsus. Another part of him—the wiser part—was simply glad to be seeing the last of Baldwin. Cilicia was not large enough for the both of them.

"Tancred!" shouted Baldwin, a thought coming to him before he had ridden too far. "I have something of yours I should return to you before I leave." The German barked an order to the overseer of the baggage train. One of the waggoners pushed a large, dirty bundle off the back of his cart. It fell to the ground with a yelp—there was something alive inside the wrappings.

Tancred waited to examine the gift Baldwin had bestowed upon him until the German rearguard had put the space of a furlong between themselves and Mamistra. "Turold!" he ordered. "Fetch me that bundle lying on the grass." The red-haired knight, who had happily acquired a new horse at Adana from some of Oshin's friendly people, rode up to Baldwin's leavings. With some difficulty, he hauled the ungainly cloth bag over the front of his saddle.

"What do we have here?" asked Tancred, as Turold rejoined the band of knights.

"I think it is a man."

Drawing his dagger, Tancred slashed open the brown sack and proved that Turold's surmise was indeed correct. It was a man, and by the faint moans he was making, not a dead one. Tancred seized the dirty scruff of yellow hair and pulled up the hanging head to look at the man's face. It was Richard, the Norman who had gone missing, his face a mass of cuts and bruises. He tumbled to the ground in a heap and then rose to his feet with many exaggerated groans, dusting himself off with the back of his hand.

"Ha, Richard!" said Tancred, paradoxically relieved to have his repugnant brother-in-law returned to him. "I had not thought to have seen you alive again. Whatever possessed Baldwin to put you in a grain sack?"

A grotesque smile formed on Richard's swollen lips. "He swore I talked too much." His lips pulled back, revealing a black gap where two of his teeth had been knocked out.

"He's pulled up his tent stakes in quite a hurry, like a man springing up from a pallet full of fleas. Do you know why?"

"Yes, I overheard his soldiers remarking upon it. Late last night a messenger arrived from the main army, bringing word that Godvera is on her deathbed. The main army is making for Marash in the mountains. Baldwin is going to meet them there, although it will probably be too late. The man is besotted with grief!"

"Was it a love match then?" asked Tancred, almost surprised to hear that Baldwin had the ability to shed tears.

Richard shrugged. "She was a devilishly attractive woman. I'd grieve too if I'd lost her for a bedmate." He paused to stretch out his aching limbs. "Where will we go now? Do you intend to follow Baldwin back to the main army? Who knows how many lies he will tell about us to the others if we are not there to gainsay him!"

"No, we will finish what we set out to do. We will destroy all the Turkish strongholds in Cilicia, and then take the shortest path to Jerusalem."

"But we will rejoin the main army long before Jerusalem is reached. You surely do not mean to bypass Antioch?"

In all his strivings with Baldwin, Tancred had almost forgotten the service that Kilij Arslan's wife had sworn him to. His right hand twisted the emerald ring on his pinky finger where it cut uncomfortably into the base of his knuckle. He remembered the sultana's diaphanous dress and her wide almond eyes reflecting the starlight above Nicaea. He remembered William's unlucky wish to wear the talisman and the flight of arrows that felled him at Dorylaeum.

"No, we will certainly seek out Antioch when our work here is finished. I have a pledge of honor to perform there, and I cannot afford to delay it."

# Part IV

# Adhemar

# Chapter 40

By the time Tancred had finished his tour of Cilicia, he had liberated over half a dozen Armenian towns from the Turks. He marched his men over the lower range of the Amanus Mountains, and from there it was only a short leap across the Orontes River to set himself down on Antioch's doorstep.

Of all the cities the Crusaders had encountered thus far, Antioch boasted the most formidable defenses, derived both from the elements of nature and from the hand of man. On the north side, the Orontes' swift current looped around the city. Beside it a stagnant marsh gurgled hungrily, its spongy ground ready to swallow siege engines, heavy carts, or the hooves of charging warhorses. On the west and on the east, the city's double-ringed walls climbed steeply up the sides of Mount Silpius while the whole southern side of the city had been cut into the face of the mountain itself.

An impregnable citadel, ensconced in the heights like the nest of an eagle, stared over the city a thousand feet above. The mountain springs supplied the citadel amply, and an aqueduct fed the pure, clear water to the city below. The thick walls housed palaces, markets, gardens, and even pasture land for small flocks of sheep and cattle. Of food and water there was no shortage. And once the lower city was taken—if that were even possible—a besieging army would have to begin all over again with a new siege to capture the rocky fortress up above.

Antioch may have been constructed on a slightly smaller scale than Constantinople, but its massive fortifications, built by Justinian, rivaled those of its neighbor to the north. In recent memory, the Byzantines had added improvements to the ramparts, increasing the number of towers to four hundred and topping them with ballistae and scorpios of the newest design. The crenelated battlements were arranged in such a fashion that from their summits an arrow could wing its way to every square foot of the ground below.

As at Nicaea, the fortifications the Byzantine architects had engineered had been turned into a thorn in their own side. The Turks had taken the city two decades ago and had set up a mighty military presence there. Over the past few months, Cassian, the Turkish governor, had kept himself well apprised of the Crusaders' movements. He would not make the same mistake Kilij Arslan had by underestimating the foreigners. The loudmouthed Latins had trumpeted abroad that their next objective was Antioch—Cassian was determined that his city was one objective they would never obtain.

The population of Antioch was made up almost exclusively of Greeks, Armenians, and Syrian Christians. Originally, the Turks had tolerated the residence and religions of all these indigenous factions. But with the approach of the Latins—an army purported to be in the pay of Alexios—Cassian began to fear that he had been too lenient in allowing the Greek Christians to come and go as they pleased. Antioch could hardly be taken through storm or siege, but it would only take one traitor to unbar the gates by night.

The week before Tancred crossed the Amanus Mountains, Cassian began to purge the city of all possible collaborators with the enemy. He threw the Patriarch, the head of the Greek Church in Antioch, into a foul-smelling prison and turned the Cathedral of St. Peter into a stable for his horses. All male citizens of Greek descent were ordered to report to the Gate of St. George where, without warning, the Turkish garrison forcibly ejected them from the city.

As luck would have it, Tancred's arrival from Cilicia coincided almost exactly with the arrival of the Crusader vanguard. Led by Bohemond, the advance company of the Latin host had just come from fighting its way across the Iron Bridge in the northeast. The two Turkish towers that flanked the bridge like twin dragons had halted them there for some time. Eventually, however, Bohemond was able to batter his way past the beasts and take the towers for himself. The Crusaders would find it very useful to control this crossing in the months to come.

Tancred's passage over the Orontes was less eventful. He found an unguarded ford farther down the river and without mishap joined his smaller force to Bohemond's. The two tall Normans were barely able to tear their eyes away from the unassailable stronghold long enough to exchange familial greetings. Their wide eyes wandered from the summit of Mount Silpius to the inaccessible citadel to the solid foundations of the outer wall. The compounded strength of nature and skill had conspired to make this metropolis as invulnerable as a heelless Achilles.

"Sweet Mary!" said Bohemond under his breath, breaking the spell of silence that had bound them both.

"Sweet Joseph!" echoed Tancred with a laugh. "You'll be an old man, uncle, before we finish this siege and move on to Jerusalem."

Bohemond's gray eyes gleamed covetously as he stared up at the citadel. "Perchance you are right. But if God wills it thus, I can rest my weary bones in the governor's chair at Antioch and liberate Jerusalem by proxy. You will fulfill my vow in my stead, dear nephew, will you not?"

Tancred snorted and shook his head in good-natured contempt. Strangely enough, his uncle's impious disregard for the true purpose of the Crusade no longer incensed him as it had formerly. The heart can only hold so much hatred before it eats itself up, and Tancred had found another offender far worthier of odium.

"Have you heard what Baldwin did—and did not do—at Tarsus?" he spat out vehemently.

Bohemond nodded gravely. "We received word of it at Marash from the local people. That was a fine company of knights cut down for no purpose—I knew them all by name, and we could have used their numbers here at Antioch. Rumor has it that you ceded the city to him without dispute?"

Tancred growled. "What did I have to dispute him with? My three hundred to his three thousand? He had me at a disadvantage and he knew it, like a rat trapped in a terrier's teeth. God help me, but I do not think I can spend a lengthy siege in the same camp as that blackguard without finding his face with my fist."

"You'll have nothing to worry about in that regard. Baldwin has no intention of helping us in the siege. He met up with us at Marash after we sent him word that his wife Godvera had been struck with a violent fever. It was too late, of course. Her corpse was moldering before he ever reached us.

"We had barely time to give him our condolences before he announced that he was striking out again on his own. That Armenian parasite Bagrat must still be pulling at his boot strings and promising him richer pickings than could be had in Cilicia. And so he's gone eastward, toward the Euphrates and the city of Edessa."

"What?" exclaimed Tancred in anger. "And I suppose he has taken a great part of the German forces with him?"

"No, no," said Bohemond. "His brother Godfrey would not permit it. That man is as mild as milk in many things, but when it comes to freeing the Holy Sepulcher he is as fanatical as the pope himself. Even Godfrey could see that an expedition to Edessa would serve no other purpose than the aggrandizement of his brother. The German troops are, in the main, all sworn to Godfrey, and he denied his little brother the use of them. And so Baldwin has struck out on his own into enemy territory with only a hundred lances at his back. Who knows if we'll see him again in this life?"

After Tancred realized that Baldwin had not deprived the army of too much manpower, the prospect of his absence was a positive boon from heaven. He and Bohemond quickly decided on what portion of the city they would invest and hurried to drive in tent stakes before the other Crusader lords arrived. As any man of sense would do, they seized upon the best spot—the easternmost side of the city opposite the Gate of St. Paul. The terrain was most appealing here. Bohemond reasoned that should his men need to fall back, they would be retreating into territory already annexed by the advancing Crusaders. In that direction the Orontes would be an easy obstacle to cross since the Normans had already secured the two towers flanking the Iron Bridge.

There were still places aplenty for the others to besiege. The back half of the city overflowed onto the steep precipices of Mount Silpius, but in the front, the city walls stretched out in a rough semicircle broken by five massive gates to allow admittance and egress. The gates in the middle were more difficult to secure than the one the Normans had chosen. The gates in the west were well nigh impossible to besiege without incurring heavy losses from the towers above.

As the main army filed into view, the other commanders took stock of the situation. Raymond drew up the Franks, both his men and those of Hugh the Great, on Bohemond's right hand. They were directly opposite the Gate of the Dog. Duke Godfrey was making his own decisions now without the aid of his brother Baldwin. He marched his men opposite the third gate, known to the Antiochenes as the Gate of the Duke.

"A fitting name for each man's gate!" said Bohemond scornfully, finding it ironic that the Frankish count fronted the Dog's Gate while the honorable Godfrey took the Duke's. His annoyance with Raymond had intensified during Tancred's absence in Cilicia, and he took every occasion to make a jibe at the count's expense.

After these positions had been chosen, the only remaining gates were the Bridge Gate and the Gate of St. George. By rights, these should have been barricaded by the remaining commanders. But the Count of Flanders saw that Bohemond did not have a full complement of men after sending so many to garrison Tancred's captures in Cilicia. Instead of investing one of the western gates, he nestled his force beside Bohemond's at the Gate of St. Paul. Count Robert was a plain, unassuming man and both Tancred and Bohemond were glad to have his standard next to theirs.

Of the chief commanders, that left only the Duke of Normandy and his brother-in-law, the Count of Blois, to man the westernmost side of the city. They certainly had enough soldiers to fill the gap. But the terrain there was the most difficult, exposed to the missiles of the towers above and cramped by the looping channel of the Orontes. Predictably, the lords of Normandy and Blois refused to fortify so precarious a position. They ranged their troops behind the other Crusaders who had arrived first and left the two western gates unsecured.

It was an inauspicious beginning to a long and onerous siege. The Crusaders had managed to surround a little over half of the city with their palisades. It was like trying to hang a convict with a frayed through loop of rope. As long as the Antiochenes avoided the eastern side of the city, they might come and go as they pleased.

# Chapter 41

The feast of All Saints' Day fast was fast approaching when the Crusaders reached Antioch. In these hot lands, the month of October glowed with a golden serenity. The air had lost most of its stifling heat and the heads of grain bowed down heavily in the fields. The lush valley watered by the Orontes offered up easy pasture for all their animals, and wild game abounded at the watering places. It was as near to paradise as a besieging army can come.

"At least we shall run no risk of starvation at this siege," said Tancred, striking up a conversation with Bernard. The chaplain, although misanthropic and taciturn toward the great majority of Crusaders, had taken an unexplainable liking to the young marquis. And Tancred had the singular ability to tolerate the cleric's eccentricities. It was the least he could do after Bernard had courageously pulled him out of the lion's jaws in the pavilion at Pelecanum.

"Someone said as much to Adhemar yesterday," said Bernard, "but I do not think that the bishop agrees. He told the man to remember the ants and the tree-crickets before he prophesied perpetual plenty."

"What have tree-crickets to do with it?" asked Tancred impatiently, but Bernard just wiggled his thick black eyebrows superiorly. The marquis, obviously, had not read Aesop.

Alexandra, sitting on the ground braiding garlands, found no difficulty in interpreting the chaplain's remark. "It's a story—and probably one you've heard before if you'd only taken the time to pay attention to it. The tree-crickets wasted their summer in chirping and refused to store up food for the leaner seasons. But the ants put in hard labor in the hot sun and saved up every sort of seed in their granaries.

When winter came, the ants sat cozily in their hill and survived off their stores, but the wastrel crickets suffered bitterly in the end with cold, and famine, and want."

"I see she teaches you your lessons!" said Bernard playfully. It surprised him to see this chit of a girl pontificating so confidently to the marquis.

"Aye," replied Tancred, "and forces me to play truant from my own tent if I wish to avoid her lectures!"

"Perhaps if you had heeded your boyhood tutors, you would understand the bishop's allusions and not stand in need of my lectures." Alexandra haughtily tossed her chestnut curls.

"Perhaps—though if you had endured the dullness of my father's tutoring alongside William and me, I guarantee that you would have stopped your ears too."

Alexandra had lost no time in seeking out the marquis when the main army, after meandering through Marash, reunited with Tancred's Normans at Antioch. She resumed her place beside her protector, and made herself useful as a seamstress and—under Ralph's close supervision—a cook.

Once the camp at Antioch had been established, Tancred again lodged Alexandra with some of the women pilgrims in the band. She could have stayed on at his own lodgings without any threat to modesty or virtue, but it was wise to set an unequivocal example to his followers. There was enough debauchery in the camp already. He made it known to his knights that the girl was not to be harmed in any way, and instructed Ralph to provide her food from his own stores. The only wrinkle in an otherwise smooth carpet was the lord of Salerno—but Richard, having found several other pretty faces to amuse himself with on the road, accepted Alexandra's presence with equanimity and heeded Tancred's injunctions to stay clear of the girl's path.

Unabashed by the looming shadow of Mount Silpius, Alexandra often wandered outside the siege lines to enjoy the soft grass beneath her feet. Although by night she was banished to the chaperonage of her female companions, by day she roamed wherever she willed.

Tancred's whole tent was rife with her floral creations. She had even plaited blossoms into the mane of his warhorse—which he promptly yanked out and tossed to the ground as soon as her back was turned.

Alexandra was not the only one in the Crusader camp enjoying the fertile valley, the favorable weather, and the pause from travel. So far, none of the Crusader lords, save Raymond, the Count of Toulouse, had any desire to commence the siege in earnest. "Let us strike now," said the Frank, "before the Turks have a chance to judge our numbers and spy out our strengths. God will favor us with the outcome!"

Bohemond spoke out strongly in council against Raymond's plan. "You would have us strike blindly before we have time to do the same with their numbers and their weak points. I say, wait! Alexios has promised us help, and Tatikios says that the Byzantine siege engines will be soon to come. Why waste manpower on a fruitless assault before we are ready?"

"Yes, yes," said the Byzantine general, his golden nose in high polish as usual. "Alexios will send his support quite soon. We would be like mice trying to topple those towers without it. You will not be sorry to wait, my friends."

Hearing these arguments, the other leaders threw in their lots against Raymond. Count Robert of Flanders, although he agreed with Bohemond, voiced this gruff caveat. "We can only assume that Cassian has made no movements against us because he is also waiting—waiting for reinforcements from the other Mussulmen powers hereabouts. So while it is to our advantage to wait, it is to his advantage as well."

Tancred, who had remained uncharacteristically quiet during the council, conversed with Bohemond afterward about the wisdom of delay. "The Flemish count is right, you know. Our cordon around the city has as many holes in it as a pauper's cloak, and we have seen many riders going to and fro. There are two brothers, rulers of Damascus and Aleppo, whom Cassian might persuade to assist him. And he has friends as far away as Mosul and Baghdad."

"Very true," said Bohemond, "and we shall undoubtedly have to fight off some relief forces before the siege is over. But even so, that were better than to rush bullheaded into an offensive."

Tancred nodded. "Because you are certain that the assault would fail?"

Bohemond laughed. "No, because I am afraid it would succeed!"

"What misfortune would success entail?" asked Tancred dryly. He was used to his uncle's machinations by now. He probably could have guessed Bohemond's response before he made it.

"A concerted attack and a swift victory would make us all equal sharers in the triumph. There would be no time for any of the leaders to stand out as hero of the siege. No one would be deserving of more than the common spoils. But if the siege is lengthy and arduous, impatience will prickle each soldier's skin like a coat full of burrs. They will long for the siege to be over as a port trapped pirate longs for the winter storms to cease. Then is the moment for the hero to stand forth. If he can achieve the surrender of the city by stratagems, what will he not deserve of the rest?"

"The city itself," responded Tancred, refusing to be carried away by Bohemond's rhetoric. "He cannot deserve that, for it is promised to another. There is no denying that Antioch is part of the territory that once lay under Byzantine control, and by the terms of your oaths, the place must be rendered up to Alexios once it is achieved." Tancred smiled provokingly. "Unless, of course, you have chosen me or Count Raymond to play the hero's part. We have made no promises to the emperor. If my men should seize the city, I would be well within my rights to take the title Duke of Antioch."

Bohemond snorted, a clear indication that he did not believe either Tancred or the Count of Toulouse clever enough to subvert such a formidable city. "Antioch is too big a plum for either of you to swallow without choking on the stone that lies inside. I had thought to let you share with me, Tancred, in the glory of this undertaking—but it seems you are determined, as always, to thwart my endeavors however you can. I trust, at least, that you will say nothing of this to the other commanders?"

Tancred grunted. "I will have enough to do engaging the enemy without meddling in your intrigue. Scheme on, uncle—I will tell no tales to the others."

While Tancred kept his harness bright and his sword sharp, Bohemond began looking for ways to infiltrate the city and secure friends inside Antioch's walls. The project was easier than he expected. The men whom Cassian had expelled from the city, the Greek Christians who might sympathize with the besiegers, still kept in close contact with their families by way of messengers, merchants, and mercenary guards. Using the same avenues, Bohemond began to secure intelligence about the inner workings of Antioch, learning the names of the captains of the watch, noting the men responsible for each of the guard towers.

But while Bohemond was busy planting the seed of intrigue inside the city, Cassian had formed his own network of spies. Inside Antioch dwelt many Syrian Christians who doubted whether Alexios and his Latin minions would be more appealing overlords than the Turks. Cassian had let them practice their own sect of Christianity unmolested. The Byzantines would not be so kind, and no one knew how eager the Latin pope would be to proselytize. These Syrians had no qualms about selling information to the besieged as well as the besiegers. With the help of these obliging informers, Cassian began to tabulate where the different Crusader armies were grouped, how many men were in each one, and what their itineraries were for each day.

The month of November was fading fast, and the food in the valley had begun to dwindle. Adhemar, Aesop, and the industrious ants of the fable had met little success in advising the others to store up food in the time of plenty. Now it was too late. The skinny cows of Pharaoh's dream had arisen from the Nile, and the granary bins lay empty in the face of their onslaught.

The Crusaders sent foraging parties farther afield, upstream and downstream and over the Orontes. But, whereas the foreigners had very limited knowledge of the river crossings, the Turks knew them as well as their daily prayers. Cassian's men, exiting from the unguarded western gates of the city, were able to cross the Orontes unimpeded and ambush the foraging parties where they least expected it. At the same time, the Turks were able to carry in supplies from hidden caches in the countryside or from ships that had put in to the mouth of the Orontes. "It's a strange state of affairs," said Bernard caustically, "when the besiegers have emptier stomachs than the besieged."

Losing men by the handfuls and short on rations, the Crusader lords began to argue among themselves. Clearly, the best way to stop the Turks' deadly ambushes was to blockade the western side of the city. But no one was willing to risk his knights—or even more importantly, his knights' horses—in occupying that perilous position. What did the greater good matter if one's own company was too crippled to share in it?

Now was the time when Peter the Hermit proved his worth. While the nobles exhausted themselves in wrangling, he spent his strength in preaching perseverance to the multitudes. "'Take up your cross and follow Me!' Did you think that the cross would be light? Did you think the following would be easy? It is right that we should endure much suffering for the name of Christ—misery, poverty, nakedness, persecution, want, illness, hunger, thirst. For the Lord saith of His true disciples: 'Ye must suffer much in My name.' And for those who persevere to the end, 'Great is your reward in Heaven.'

"What a disgrace it would be if these Turks—an abominable race that worships demons—should conquer us, we who have the faith of the omnipotent God and who bear the glorious name of Christ! With what reproaches will the Lord overwhelm us if you do not stand fast today, you who have committed both your bodies and your souls to this cause! *Deus vult*! God wills our faithfulness now more than ever, and woe to him who turns his back on the certain will of God!"

No matter how dismally they were circumstanced, the common soldiers never failed to greet Peter's fervor with anything other than acclamation. Tancred's men were no exceptions. Red-haired Turold heard the hermit eagerly and often and exhorted his fellows to join him at the feet of the holy man. "Truly, his words would make me content to eat even my own boot leather! As long as we are doing God's work, what does a little hunger matter?"

"What indeed!" replied Tancred staunchly. The little, barefoot man had more value than the marquis had supposed if he could keep up the soldiers' spirits in the dark times that lay ahead.

# Chapter 42

The season of Christ's Advent dawned and with it came the painful certainty that this adventure before Antioch would be lengthy, uncomfortable, and uncertain of success. Despite Tatikios' continual assurances, Alexios had sent neither men nor siege engines. Some of the lords were beginning to question whether the promised aid would ever arrive. "The emperor had only one condition to fulfill," said Bohemond in council, "to send us auxiliaries while we win him an empire. And if the liege breaks the terms of the compact, what fealty does the vassal still owe?" The answer was clear: the vassal owes nothing.

Tancred noted how cleverly Bohemond had begun to undermine the other lords' obligations to Alexios. If the emperor sent them no troops, they could fully justify themselves in refusing to deliver up Antioch once it was attained. Now Bohemond had only to ensure that he was the one who attained it.

The day of Christ's nativity came and went without any peace or goodwill in the Crusader camp. "It is our second Christmas away from Italy," remarked Ralph with a sigh, "and even more dismal than the one before. Last year we celebrated on the muddy roads of Macedonia, but at least there was still wine in the supply wagons and beef to buy at market. Perhaps your uncle Bohemond will spear us a Christmas boar!" he said, his wrinkled face waggling with sarcastic laughter. "A roast pig is the dish I like best at Yule."

"It's the Saint Basil's Day cake that I like best," said Alexandra. "We eat it hot out of the oven. And out of all my sisters, I've had the coin in my piece five times!"

"They say the coin always goes to the ugliest one," said Ralph slyly and endured a merry slap in return. They would have gone on reminiscing about frittered turnips, poached pears, imported pomegranates, and marzipan sweets, but an interruption by the marquis threw ashes on their chatter. He had less and less taste for humor of late. And besides, he had just come away from a council meeting at Bishop Adhemar's tent full of pinched cheeks and somber faces.

"There'll be no pig or cake or coins to put in it this year," Tancred said crisply. "Our stores are completely exhausted, and the rest have no more than we do."

"Lackaday!" said Ralph. "And the countryside round about is as barren as an old hen. What say the other lords? Will they throw up the siege and let us be gone from this place?"

"After only two months in the field?" replied Tancred. "Not likely. And we must achieve Antioch if we're to move forward to Jerusalem. They've decided to range farther afield in hopes of greater success. Bohemond and the Count of Flanders will follow the Orontes eastward and raid the villages along the banks. Tatikios goes with them to show the way. Godfrey is sick, I hear, and Blois and Normandy are hardly to be counted upon, so Raymond and the bishop will direct the camp in their absence."

"I daresay Cassian's spies have already brought him word of this maneuver," said Ralph cynically. It was uncanny how well the Turks had been able to anticipate the Crusaders' plans and shadow their movements over the last two months. "Your uncle had best be prepared for an attack along the way."

As Ralph had feared, Cassian had ears in the wall of every tent, and the Crusaders' new plan to go upriver was an open scroll to him. He launched a surprise attack on the fifth day of Christmas, one day after Bohemond and Robert had departed with several thousand men in their train. But, contrary to all expectation, it was not against the foragers.

The armies camped on Antioch's doorstep had been demoralized by the lack of food, the lack of progress, and the winter rains. They had been unable to surround the city, storm the city, or subdue the city; they had barely been able to survive the effects of their own siege. At this rate none of them would ever complete their vows and their journey to Jerusalem.

Cassian judged that these camped Crusaders would be easier prey than the squadrons forging through the Orontes valley. Using his unobstructed western gates, he sent out a sortie in the blackest hour of the night. The sly Turks crossed the river, circled behind their foes, and shot out like porcupine quills into the backside of Count Raymond's camp. His soldiers lay stretched out before the Gate of the Dog shivering in the rain. The unpleasant shock of an assault soon warmed the blood in their veins.

Several furlongs away, Tancred and his Normans woke to the cries of battle in Raymond's camp, but the distance between St. Paul's Gate and the Gate of the Dog was too great for them to reach their comrades before the fight was over. They came anyway, mounted and helmed, as overeager as young hounds to see some action. "Where are the Turks?" demanded Tancred, a question echoed by every Norman at his back.

"Go back to your beds!" said Raymond, breathing heavily from the battle and unable to conceal his anger. He had lost many men that night and with them an opportunity that he might never see again. None of the Franks were in the mood to describe what had happened, but Bernard, who had watched as much of the fight as the murky night would allow, gave Tancred all the details of the battle in the morning.

"The Turks came from behind us," he said, "screaming like the left hand souls on Judgment Day. At first, all was confusion. Adhemar took some time to arm and said a paternoster while his squire laced his points. I gathered up the most important of his books and letters, determined not to let them fall into the hands of the enemy if they should overset our tent.

"Count Raymond has a handful of good qualities, sprinkled here and there like wildflowers in an evil-smelling bog. I will not deny that he can keep a cool head in a hot battle. He mustered as many of the knights as had found their horses and organized a charge against the raiders. The Turks were as blithe as berry pickers, cutting and slashing their way through unarmed men. But finding a wall of lances in the way reduced some of their relish.

"When Raymond's men charged, the Turks fell over themselves in panic and retreated to the Gate of St. George which still sat open, waiting like a Spartan mother to greet her victorious sons. If she had known that her men would return in such a disgraceful, pell-mell fashion, she might have fallen shut and kept them out altogether. But as it was, their rout provided us with an opportunity to storm the city.

"I stayed behind at the camp, naturally, but Adhemar and Raymond and the count's men pressed so hard against the heels of the fliers that they found their way to the portcullis before the Turks had time to turn the winch and lower it. The door to Antioch lay as open as an inn for travelers. Adhemar cried out for our men to come on and seize the day. He and his standard bearer made for the exposed entrance at a full gallop. Raymond's men were not slow to see the advantage either. They charged at the open gate like a pack of mad dogs almost overleaping the drawbridge in their excitement.

"But suddenly, in the confusion and darkness of the press, one of our horses reared up and threw his rider. His fellows, thinking that the Turks had regathered their courage to launch a counterstrike, were whelmed with a flood of unfounded fright. It was too dark to see the truth of the matter. Lances careened wildly as colliding horses tripped over their own forelegs. Adhemar's standard-bearer was trampled in the chaos, and the bishop himself might have lost his life had he not quickly sounded the horn for retreat.

"And so it was that the rout of the enemy which had seemed a very boon from heaven metamorphosed into a rout of our own foolish forces. Our knights who had driven the Turks back to their own gate were driven back themselves over the drawbridge. They fled ingloriously to their tents, like women afraid of their own shadows.

"This morning finds us several scores shy of the muster that filled Raymond's camp yesterday. It is a good thing that the knight whose horse startled so unpropitiously had already lost his life in the fray.

The mood is so ugly here—after such a great opportunity and such a cruel disappointment—that I think they would have tied him up to the quintain and practiced tilting at him to alleviate their spleen."

Tancred shook his head in saddened amazement at Bernard's tale. His uncle Bohemond would be pleased to know that Raymond had been thwarted from storming the city in his absence. But as long as Tancred was the first to infiltrate Jerusalem, he did not much care who garnered the glory of winning Antioch. All his interest was in concluding this siege as quickly as possible and relieving himself of the emerald ring he had come to hate. It was a heartbreak of hopes to hear how Raymond's men had come so close to entering the city only to falter on the threshold through some freak mischance.

"The only good thing to come of this attack," said the marquis, "is that it leaves my uncle and the Flemings free to scour the countryside for food without worrying about the Turks on their tail. Cassian has chosen the camp as his target and the foragers may wander freely. We may not see the inside of the city for some time, but God willing, we'll see fresh supplies within a fortnight."

A fortnight was a long time to wait for men in the Crusaders' position. They had long ago eaten all the ordinary fare and were reduced to scrounging for bits of herbage, old meal, and small game that a huntsman at home would have scoffed at. In addition to the impending famine, the Crusaders' also had other worries to gnaw at their bellies. The fact that Raymond's men had not taken the city was either a sign of bad fortune or divine disfavor. When a huge earth tremor shook the camp the next day, many began to incline toward the latter view.

Celestial signs corroborated this idea that God was wroth with His people. By night, the northern sky took on a ghastly green hue, with ghostly swirls of luminescence shining brighter than the pale winter moon. By day, thick clouds poured their frigid contents over the red cross company, turning the valley floor into a mud pit and the Orontes into a torrent.

Bishop Adhemar, playing the role of *pontifex maximus*, interpreted the signs for the rest. He exhorted the people to fast from what little food they had and repent of their sins. Maybe then God would relieve their suffering from the famine and the forays of the Turks.

But the men-at-arms and the mixed multitude which followed the camp showed a marked lack of respect for the bishop's exhortations. Surrounded by idleness, fear, and discomfort, they became even more quarrelsome, mutinous, and debauched than usual. Tancred had difficulty keeping order in his own camp and threatened to expel all the loose women and hang any violators of the peace.

One morning he went to the nearby Duke of Normandy's camp to voice a minor complaint about depredations his men had committed. He found Stephen of Blois there too, shivering in a pile of blankets like a man with the ague. "Everyone I ever heard tell of Syria complained of the excessive sunshine, and now here we are in the place, up to our ears in Noah's Flood and as cold as minnows in the North Sea. I can hardly bear to take pen in hand and write to my sweet Adele of all the hardships I've suffered."

"If you paint the picture black enough, mayhap she'll pity you enough to let you slink home again," said Tancred cuttingly. He had no patience with the Count of Blois' effete whimpering. "Although it may take more than pity for her to admit you back into her bed." It was a matter of common knowledge—and common jest—that the Conqueror's daughter had barred the Count of Blois from her bedchamber when she found him too spineless to undertake the Crusade on his own initiative.

Stephen scowled at Tancred and buried his nose in the woolen bedclothes. "You are impertinent beyond belief, sirrah! I wonder that your uncle does not take a hide to you to mend your tongue."

Tancred grinned remembering all the times in childhood when Bohemond had done just that. Perhaps if Stephen's father had administered the same discipline to him, he would not be such a milksop crying to be cuckolded. His lip curled a little as he bid the Count of Blois adieu. "You may deliver your complaints to my uncle when he returns from his expedition, though I daresay you'll be too a-feared of the wet to leave your tent."

Bohemond and Count Robert, as if aware how much the disorderly camp longed for their reappearance, rode into sight a full seven days earlier than the allotted fortnight. At the sound of their horses' hooves, the whole army rose up like a single soul. They looked to the riders in expectation, like a lady pacing anxiously at the door of the hall waiting to give her long gone lord the cup of welcome and hear the news of his travels.

The sight of the wagons gave away the news before Bohemond and Count Robert were close enough to convey it themselves. When the Normans and Flemings had set out on their journey down the Orontes, they had brought many carts trailing behind them. The vehicles were intended to carry back the cornucopia of supplies that the camp needed so desperately. If the wagons had been full—their beds laden with sacks of meal and casks of pickled meats—their wheels would have bogged down in all this mud. But instead of churning madly through the rain swollen soil, the returning wagons glided over the plain with relative ease. They were empty, as empty as a broken promise.

At this sight, the words of welcome died in the myriads of hungry mouths. The returning expedition met only a field of dull, desolate stares as they neared the Gate of St. Paul.

"Did you find food?" demanded one witless man-at-arms, licking his meaty lips in misguided anticipation.

"Food?" repeated Bohemond with a frown. "Barely enough to feed ourselves on the return journey. We are lucky to have made it back alive. While you've been snoring safely in your tents,"—he did not know about the garrison's attack by night—"we've had to fight off hordes of Turkish devils. We ran afoul of a relief force on its way here and spent our strength in besting them. When you hear the story we have to tell you, there'll be more to pinch your insides than lack of food."

# Chapter 43

The report of the expedition as told by Robert of Flanders was considerably more direct than the extravagant version Bohemond would have woven, but since the greater part of the losses were his, the honor fell to him to tell the tale. "We had only gone two day's march to the south when the Turks set upon us," said the Flemish count. "Tatikios recognized their leader Duqaq—a young man, much like Kilij Arslan except considerably more cautious. He became the emir of Damascus just recently. We found out later that Cassian's own son was in his train. He had gone to summon Duqaq's help when our forces first began to arrange themselves around Antioch, but it had taken the emir two months to agree to send aid and to assemble an army.

"My men and I were a few furlongs ahead of Bohemond when the enemy warriors descended on us from the hills. They were several thousand strong and more ready for battle than we. It was like the battle at Dorylaeum all over again. They surrounded us, mistaking our company for the whole of the Latin army. Riding circles around us, they riddled us with their arrows.

"Just when we were despairing of cutting through Duqaq's cordon, the Norman knights came over a slight rise and galloped to the rescue. It is a pity for my men—especially for the fallen ones—that they did not come sooner. But perhaps Bohemond thought it wiser to hold back until the Turks became drunk with imminent victory.

"At the charge of our companions-at-arms, Duqaq's men startled like the herd of Gadarene swine. They were frantic to avoid the Norman lances. Had there been a cliff nearby, I daresay they would have plummeted off its height and plunged into the sea. And as it was,

I do not think they stopped spurring their horses till they were all the way down the Orontes.

"The victory was ours, but at a high cost of life and limb. There were many dead, both men and horses, and wounds most worrisome afflicted the survivors. We debated what course of action to follow next. Bohemond was all for continuing the foraging expedition so that we would have some sustenance to substantiate our journey. I allowed him to assuage my doubts. We continued on a little halfheartedly, sacked one or two villages, and burned a mosque. Food, however, did not come readily to hand.

"It soon became obvious that our forces were too weakened to march any farther without more loss of life. This time I swayed Bohemond to my way of thinking. We limped back to Antioch at a pace slow enough to accommodate the wounded. And here you see us—as empty-handed as when we left, and even more debilitated than when we departed a sennight ago."

This was bad news, and although the empty wagons had already hinted at some sort of tragedy, the crowd still reacted with a volley of groans. The Count of Flanders stopped his story till the exclamations of the multitude should subside, and Bohemond seized the opportunity to chime in with the remainder. "But you have not told them the worst of it!" he said. "We halted Duqaq's relief force from Damascus, but when Tatikios questioned several of the prisoners we took, they boasted there was another army soon to come our way."

"Where from?" interjected Raymond. "Aleppo?" It was a natural conclusion. To the south the city of Damascus was ruled by Duqaq, while to the northwest his brother Ridwan governed the city of Aleppo. Perhaps Cassian had also contacted Ridwan to send reinforcements.

"No, not Aleppo," said Bohemond. His gray eyes flickered over the waiting crowd. "The army comes from Mosul."

Godfrey, still pale from his recent illness, spoke up. "But that city is on the Tigris, quite far from here."

"Yes," said Bohemond. "Mosul is many miles from Antioch, and the army cannot be here till at least the spring. But the army is a great one, and—here is the worst of it—it is led by the mighty Kerbogha!"

Tancred and most of the leaders looked at each other blankly. The intricate web of Mussulmen emirs, *atabegs*, and sultans was too complex for them to keep track of all the players. A Mussulman might have said the same when faced with all the interrelated kings, and counts, and dukes of France. Kerbogha was no more than a foreign sounding name to them, despite Bohemond's attempts to make it sound menacing.

Tatikios, who had already schooled Bohemond on the caliber of the opponent who faced them, now offered the same education to the others. "You do not know of this Kerbogha, my friends? Listen, and I will tell you. He is a Turk, like the others you have faced, but he does not come from the royal lineage. Kilij Arslan, Duqaq, his brother Ridwan, the great sultan of Baghdad—they were all born into the great house of Seljuk, and it is for this reason that they are given the right to command.

"But Kerbogha, he is no prince. His right to command comes not through his lineage but through his own gift for warfare and his own skill for stratagem. He rules in Mosul as the *atabeg* because he is strong like a rod of iron and because those who held it before him were smashed to pieces as easily as clay pots. The sultan himself fears to cross the will of Kerbogha, and though as *atabeg* of Mosul he owes fealty to the house of Seljuk, he comes and goes where he wishes and no one will say him nay."

There was more murmuring among the crowd as Tatikios' words in the open plain were relayed back through the ranks of those who could not hear him. The thought of being caught between the impenetrable walls of Antioch and an immense army from Mosul was unappealing to say the least. As the tale of Kerbogha passed from mouth to mouth, the lowlier men-at-arms began to talk of giving up the siege before it was too late.

A panic might have ensued had Adhemar not stood up to calm the crowd. "Brothers," he said, "it is ill news that Bohemond, Count Robert, and our Byzantine friend bring, but let us not forget the reminder that Duke Godfrey gives us. Mosul is many miles from here. It will take months before this Kerbogha can encounter us with his host. We have all winter to subdue Antioch before these reinforcements arrive, and with the power of the Almighty God we can prevail.

"But, brothers, I warn you, we shall never enter Antioch unless we purify ourselves and cast out the evil which is among us! Why has the Lord allowed the Turks to trouble us so? Why has He afflicted us with empty mouths and pains of the belly? Have you not felt His shakings of the earth and seen His writing in the unnatural night skies?

"There was a perverse and rebellious generation in the days of the Israelites, and God did not allow them to enter the promise land. They died in the wilderness—as you also will die if you repent not. We must root out the calves of gold and the Moabite women among us and turn our hearts wholly to the cause of the Lord. Then will God be pleased to tabernacle amongst us once more and go before us as a pillar of cloud by day and a pillar of fire by night."

Prior to Bohemond's return, Bishop Adhemar's exhortations had had little effect on the lawless assembly. But the dread that Kerbogha inspired was a powerful motivator to righteousness. The bishop proclaimed a fast for three days, and the soldiers—though they had little enough to fast from—abased themselves by keeping it. The bishop ordered that all the harlots within the camp should be sent away across the Orontes. And though the women with their wiles fought to stay, the men-at-arms—for once—found the bishop's promise of God's favor more enticing than the pleasures of the flesh.

Bernard, paying a visit to Tancred's tent the next day, was disconcerted to see Alexandra still there, babbling happily to Ralph and plying her needle on the marquis' well-worn standard. "This one should have been sent over the Orontes with the rest," he said, his thin face growing stern.

His severity and ecclesiastical status would have been enough to overawe a lowlier man, but Tancred was not easily cowed. "She is no harlot," said the marquis firmly, choosing to forget her previous association with Richard of Salerno. He had taken the girl under his protection, and he would not send her off as a scapegoat into the unguarded territory across the Orontes.

Bernard snorted, looking at the girl's chestnut curls with disdain. He had no weakness where women were concerned, and he found it shameful to see the marquis so attached to his pretty paramour. "Then you had best go and plead her innocence before the bishop, for if the lots are thrown to find out why the camp is still cursed, they will fall on you! Remember the fate of Achan, my friend, and consider well if this temptress is worth a stoning at the hands of the assembly."

Annoyed at the chaplain's interference, Tancred took himself off to see Bishop Adhemar and resolve the situation. He found the bishop seated out of doors with a writing table before him, choosing the rarely seen winter sunlight over the dark confines of his tent. Tancred stared. It was incongruous to see the bishop's powerful hands forming the Carolingian miniscules with such a tiny quill pen, especially after one had seen those same hands wielding a mace on the battlefield.

"Your face is troubled, my son," said the bishop perceptively, lifting his eyes from his parchment as Tancred approached. "Or perhaps offended is nearer to the mark."

"If I am offended, it is only because your chaplain is too officious," said Tancred stiffly. He began to share, in brief, the history of his association with Alexandra. The broad-chested cleric leaned back with folded arms and nodded occasionally as Tancred spoke. He was an unobtrusive and benevolent listener. The marquis found himself confiding all the details he had been reticent to share with Bernard: her father's murder at the marquis' own hands, her attempts to assassinate him, her abuse at the hands of Salerno, and William's promise to take her under his protection as far as Jerusalem.

"Is she a whore?" asked the bishop simply.

"She is one no longer," said the marquis, his face reddening involuntarily. He cursed inwardly, hoping that the bishop would not mistake his embarrassment for something worse.

"Ah, a true Magdalene," said Adhemar approvingly. "Then there is no reason for her to be put outside of the camp. See that you lodge her with a goodwife of fair repute, and treat her, as the Apostle says, as a sister with all purity."

The bishop looked at the marquis thoughtfully. "The Scripture saith: 'For by means of a harlot a man is reduced to a crust of bread.' I fear we shall be reduced to even worse than that if our host does not repent in true humility for their pride and debauchery."

"And if we do repent?" asked Tancred bluntly. "Do you think that God will heed your intercessions and lift the famine?"

"Most assuredly," said the bishop. He gestured to the half-written letter that lay before him on the table. Several other letters, already stamped with the seal on his signet ring, lay in a pile nearby. "I would not waste the time in writing these unless I had faith in His faithfulness to those who do His will."

# Chapter 44

I t took several more weeks before the bishop's faith came to fruition and the contents of his letters became known. In the meantime, the crust of bread that Solomon spoke of so disdainfully
became a precious commodity among the famished. The bishop's prescribed fast had ended, but there was no feast to follow it.

Donkeys, dogs, camels, rats—any living creature with flesh, hide,
or bones was devoured on sight. The commanders did their best to
preserve the horses, but provisioning them with feed was even more
difficult than provisioning their men. When living animals could not
be had, the Crusaders took the hides of animals long dead, soaking
them in water to make them chewable and drinking the residue once
it had turned into a sort of glutinous broth.

Day in and day out, the hollow-eyed men-at-arms spent their
time scavenging what little could be got from the ground. They dug
to find the shoots of bean seeds and greedily grabbed any other herb
they could find. Some took thistles and ate them raw, pricking their
tongues to assuage their bellies. The poorest and most desperate folk
picked through the manure of animals to find seeds. If they had had
firewood, they could have cooked the vegetation, or if they had a
sprinkling a salt, they could have at least made it more palatable, but
most lacked even these basic accouterments.

Their tents, which had been in the field for over a year now, had
begun to wear out from the constant rain. Rotting moisture ate away at
the fabric, creating gaping holes for some, leaving others to the mercy
of the open sky. Sickness was rife. Tempers were short. The men were
far readier to curse than to pray.

One night, while the rain poured down like water from a ewer, Tancred went out into the wet to survey the line of sentries and encourage them at their posts. The cold air bit his face and exposed hands like an untamed ferret, and the marquis found his mind wistfully wandering back to the pleasant countryside of Italy and the sunburnished glories of a Sicilian summer. His frustrating father Odo would bid him stay indoors to recite, ignoring the hot air that turned the brick buildings into clay ovens and the flies that buzzed madly around his sticky skin. But Emma, most days, would find an excuse to release her sons from their father's pedantic lessons. Or if she failed to move her monkish husband, Tancred could instigate William to overcome his pangs of conscience, slip away when Odo's back was turned, and play truant.

Those were the glorious days of youth. While the sun labored like a field hand to make its way up the sky, the lads would enjoy its warmth, leaping and gamboling on the fallen columns of old Roman ruins. When the sun was at its zenith, they would find some shady glade, strip off their tunics, and wriggle like otters in the refreshing streams. Crawling out onto the sloped banks, there they would lie on the flat rocks, chewing on mint leaves and sunning themselves like lizards till some harbinger of duty—usually Altrude—would intrude on their merriment and call them back to the hall.

Tancred stamped his feet and rubbed his hands together, trying to bring some of the warmth of memory into his chilled bones. Italy and childhood were both a long way from here, and the plains before Antioch were as cold as his brother's corpse. "It looks like the Turks have chosen the wiser part and kept to their beds tonight," said Tancred, tightening his jaw to keep it from chattering.

"Maybe so, my lord," said Turold. He had drawn the unlucky lot of guard duty during this deluge. His fair skin was as white as ice tonight, and even his eyelashes were beaded with rain droplets. "Although I did think I saw some motion half a moment ago—there, to the northwest!"

Following the trajectory of Turold's arm with his eyes, Tancred picked out two dark shapes behind the sheets of rain. The first had the size and gait of a man, albeit a small one, his head bent downward in defense against the elements. Behind him came a beast of burden, most likely a donkey or mule, being towed relentlessly on a tether through the thick mud. Their steps were taking them away from Antioch and toward the Iron Bridge.

"Shall I call for him to stop and stand?" asked Turold.

"No," said Tancred peering sharply at the shapes. "There is something furtive about the way he has chosen to skirt the line of sentries. We shall be furtive as well. Come, cover your lantern and we will approach him silently."

The squelching of mud beneath their boots should have been loud enough to disclose their presence, but the drumming din of the rain suppressed even that noise until the two Normans were close enough to lay hands on their quarry from behind.

Turold pinned down the fellow's arms while Tancred addressed him sternly: "Who are you and what are you doing skulking about?"

The small man, having dropped the tether to his mule, lifted up a guilty face to meet Tancred's eye. There was no further need for him to identify himself. Tancred recognized Peter the Hermit immediately, clad in his hooded cape and long woolen tunic and still barefoot in the worst of weathers. Turold, uncomfortable with pinioning such holiness, let go of the man and stepped back.

The marquis' quick glance observed that the mule was heavily loaded, bearing a folded up piece of hide that assembled into a tent. The panniers on either side of the saddle were packed to overflowing with scraps of food the unworldly hermit had been offered by virtue of his special status.

"It looks like you are going on a long journey, father," said Tancred brusquely. Even a dullard could guess that the hermit had decided to desert the Crusaders in their darkest hour of need.

The hermit swallowed nervously. He had recognized Tancred too, and of all the Crusader leaders, he suspected that the young Norman would be the least sympathetic to his intended flight. "Only as far as the Lord leads," he said.

"And if he leads as far as Constantinople?" asked Tancred with a deceptively benevolent smile.

"Why then I must needs follow," replied the hermit plucking up his courage. "It is obvious that God no longer dwells in this camp, and a wise man does well to leave it too before His wrath is poured out." The hermit's mule gave a disagreeable snort, voicing his own opinion of the Crusaders. Had he not belonged to the holy man, this ill-tempered animal would have been seized by the hungry several weeks ago to be slaughtered, skinned, stewed, and swallowed.

"Coward!" cried out Tancred, rivulets of rainwater streaming down his sharp cheekbones. "A little famine and some talk of Turks from Mosul and you would scurry away like a cockchafer." The marquis was incensed, and he lifted his arm to strike the old man.

"My lord!" cried Turold in horror, uncertain whether to interfere with the impending sacrilege or to merely avert his gaze. Before he could make up his mind, the marquis had already smitten the holy man's face with the back of his hand.

The hermit, fully capable of inciting men to bear arms but bereft of them himself, cringed beneath the Norman's blow. "You have no reason to use me so," he said. "I am not bound to this body of men in any way."

"No," said Tancred scornfully, "and neither were you bound to those men who perished in the pass above Nicaea. Faugh! Do not deny it! They, at least, were here because of you. They heard your words and followed you to their deaths.

"Urban may have called this Crusade, but you were the fire that lit up the hearts of thousands to join it. 'We must free the Holy Land and liberate the Christians there,' you said. And with every speech, you spoke like one who knew, for you yourself had fallen into the hands of the Turks and felt their torments. You would strip your tunic bare and parade your scars to the crowds. The story spread from mouth to mouth. Other pilgrims may have recanted, but Peter the Hermit refused to curse Christ under even the most painful of tortures. You were brave then—be brave again! And lend your bravery to the thousands here who are in most painful need of it. If you flee, then all will lose hope, and the hopeless man has no armor when enemies come."

The hermit, still bitter that Tancred had dared to slap his face, had no interest in heeding the Norman's exhortation. "I do not leave because of cowardice," he said. It was a speech he had rehearsed over and over in his mind until he had convinced himself of the truth of it. "I leave because this camp is filled with men unfit to carry out God's holy purposes. The common men are brutal, dissipated, and immoral. The leaders who bear the cross have none of the humility of Him who bore it first."

He ignored Tancred's menacing gaze and continued his rant. "You are prideful, quarrelsome, greedy for gain. God will not bless this venture. Have you not suffered His chastisements already? The ax is laid at the root, and it is not long before these fruitless trees will feel the all-consuming fire of His wrath."

The marquis' face flamed hot with an anger as all-consuming as the divine wrath that Peter had prophesied. Although in quieter moments his reflection would give the hermit's criticisms their due, right now he was ready to pull the man joint from joint and limb from limb. His desertion would destroy the morale of an army already desperate from disease, disquiet, and hunger. His departure would jeopardize the entire expedition.

He would leave them all, he claimed, because he found them unworthy to associate with. But when Tancred had protested his own unworthiness to Pope Urban, what had the Holy Father said? *You will become holy through this journey. Do you think that a man who suffers the perils of the ocean, the deserts of Asia, and the swords of the Saracens will find his suit rejected in the Day of Judgment?* Was it right for a barefoot priest from Amiens to demand more from a man than the pontiff of Rome did?

"Listen to me, hermit," said Tancred, "and listen well. I am taking you back to the encampment now, and what happens then depends solely on your choice. You can come willingly and resume your place as a respected member of this Crusade—to encourage the men in good works, piety, and perseverance. If so, I will say no word of what has happened here tonight. Or you can come unwillingly, with my hands around the scruff of your neck. In that case, I will expose your perfidiousness to ten thousand starving men. And they—men who worshiped you like a saint, who scrimped and starved to offer you the last morsel from their haversacks—when they hear how you wish to abandon us to our deaths, they will pelt you with stones and curses. They will skin your evil-tempered mule and eat him before your eyes. They will take a picket from the palisade and thread it through your trunk from groin to neck. They will defecate on your corpse and watch the ravens feast on your flesh. What say you to that, hermit?"

However resolutely the hermit may have stood up to his Mussulmen captors in times past, that resolution was absent now. He submitted to the marquis' bullying and allowed himself to be led back to the encampment. Just in case this docility masked thoughts more devious, Tancred kept the bedraggled priest immured in his tent till morning so that there would be no repetition of his midnight flight. A shocked Turold was sworn to silence by the marquis. Only harm could come of bruiting this tale about.

# Chapter 45

At morning's light, Tancred pondered whether he should now let Peter loose to wander freely. He doubted he could detain the man much longer without it being remarked upon by the others. A great commotion interrupted his thoughts. It was the sound of a mighty cheering, like men who have won a great victory. Taking the hermit by the arm, Tancred led him out of the tent to find a thousand haggard faces staring hungrily in the direction of the Iron Bridge.

With the rising sun at their backs, a long procession of men was riding into sight. Bright clothes and bountiful beards suggested that they were Armenians. Their figures swayed easily on the backs of camels and donkeys. It was as King Oshin had said—when the men of the East rode, there was a fluidity, a fusion between man and beast. Riding pillion behind each man were baskets and hampers overflowing with victuals.

While the starving Crusaders stampeded closer in astonishment, Adhemar, dressed in full bishop's regalia with miter and crosier, stepped forward to welcome the caravan. Tancred left the hermit to make shift as he pleased and ran forward himself to sate his curiosity and, God willing, his appetite. He noticed that while the others jumped and jabbered like the Israelites experiencing the miracle of manna for the first time, the bishop evidenced no surprise at the appearance of the Armenians and their edibles. Adhemar, it seemed, had been expecting them all along.

The Armenians who had journeyed down to Antioch were not the Cilician plain-dwellers that Tancred had encountered in his travels. These hardy folk had come from the cliffs and the clefts of the Taurus Mountains, bringing all the victuals they could spare after a long winter. Constantine, the Lord of the Mountains was their leader there, and it was he who had brought them to Antioch at the imploration of Bishop Adhemar.

He was a tall, thin man, stately in his flowing robes and courteous in his every gesture. As Adhemar approached him, he dismounted from his camel and kissed the bishop's hands.

"God be praised for your generosity!" said Adhemar in carefully rehearsed Greek. "We will pay you what we can for this food."

The Lord of the Mountains inclined his head graciously. "There is no need, father. We bring it in gift, in token of our brotherhood–one Lord, one faith, one baptism, one God and Father of us all. You do a service to all of us to rid this place of the infidel Turks and their evil ways. We are a little people, both in numbers and in cities, and dwellers in a hard and unforgiving land, but what we have we are happy to bring to help our brothers in need."

"The ants are a people not strong," said the bishop, falling into his familiar Latin, "yet they prepare their food in the summer."

"And the rock badgers are a feeble folk," answered Constantine, continuing the quotation in Greek with barely a pause, "yet they make their homes in the crags. Our home is there as well, until such time as God sees fit to drive out our enemies. Who knows? Perhaps this army will be the instrument to effect His purposes."

Bernard, who had stepped quietly behind Tancred's elbow, began to give his commentary on the scene unfolding before them. "A learned man, this Constantine, and generous to boot."

"That last quality is characteristic of his race, I think," replied Tancred. He remembered the exuberant welcome and exotic feast that King Oshin had prepared for the Normans at Adana. The marquis gazed up and down the caravan at the bearded Armenians from the mountains. Their eyes glowed proudly as they watched their king converse on easy terms with the white-robed bishop. "This Constantine does not have half the land his father Rupen did, but his people seem to love him well."

"He holds to the old ways, unlike many of the other chieftains."

"Ah, yes," said Tancred, recalling Oshin's cutting criticisms of Constantine. "I heard that he refused—even at the expense of an alliance with Alexios—to be baptized into the Greek Church. Did Adhemar send him word of our plight?"

Bernard nodded. "Aye, he appealed to all the Armenian Christians for relief from our hunger. From the other chieftains, there came no reply. But Constantine sent back a messenger immediately. His people would give everything they had, said he. They are like the Antiochenes of olden times, only too eager to send us this gift at the urging of our apostle."

Tancred smiled. "Pope Urban chose our leader well. A man with such a silver pen is worth more than a thousand proven knights."

Just how silvery Adhemar's pen was, the Crusaders learned to their wonderment the next week when a convoy of grain ships, meant for them, came rowing up the Orontes. The nearby island of Cyprus had sent them, at the urging of one of the Greek Church's leading bishops.

While the Patriarch of Antioch had been thrown into a foul dungeon by the Turkish governor there, the Patriarch of Jerusalem had escaped a like fate by fleeing from his see. Exiled on the island of Cyprus, he awaited the day when his city would be returned to Christian rule and he would be returned to his office. The Crusaders were his best hope at achieving this. When Adhemar's letter reached him, he thought nothing of the schism and points of doctrine that separated his Church from that of the Latins. Instead, he exhorted the faithful in Cyprus to demonstrate their pure and undefiled religion by providing portions of food for the suffering soldiers at Antioch.

"How did you get the Cyprians to send us this food?" demanded Stephen of Blois in astonishment. "And the Armenians too, for that matter?" It was the question on everyone's mind.

The bishop folded his arms over his broad chest. "I asked," he said.

"Ask and you shall receive," murmured Tancred to himself. The ancient aphorism had turned out to be true after all—although a nagging suspicion overtook him, that if anyone besides Adhemar had done the asking, the results would have been markedly less impressive. His gift for promoting unity between differing branches of the Church was unique.

Thanks to the good offices of the bishop, the Crusaders now had enough food to wait out the worst of the winter months. Peter the Hermit, as well filled as a mouse living in the castle larder, made no more moves to abandon the camp. "With this bounty before us," thought Tancred cynically, "I am sure he has changed his mind about where the will of God would lead him."

The Turkish garrison inside of Antioch continued to be as well supplied as before the Crusaders had arrived. There was no reason for it to be otherwise. The Latin lords' reticence to fortify the western side of the city—due to the great peril of the position—meant that the gates there were still available for egress and ingress. The same waterway that had brought the Crusaders grain from Cyprus acted as a conduit for the Mussulmen, and the frustrated Crusaders could constantly see bales of provender and barge loads of provisions leave the Orontes and enter the city.

This frustration, more and more, began to be channeled in the direction of Constantinople. "Where is the emperor?" demanded Godfrey as the leaders met in council to discuss this problem. His brilliant blue eyes flickered with disappointment and displeasure. "We have been here four months without even completing a cordon around the city. Where are the siege engines and the naval support Alexios promised us?"

Tatikios was the only man who could answer that question knowledgeably, but the golden-nosed general had little speech of substance to offer to the Latins. "Be assured, my friends, our emperor has not forgotten you. Even now he is preparing a mighty fleet to sail to your aid. Have I not been your friend these many months? Would I not tell you if it were otherwise?"

"Of course you would not tell us," said Tancred blackly. "Alexios sent you to gull us all with your taradiddles and treacherous promises. Kerbogha will be here before Alexios lifts his little finger to help us."

Robert of Normandy, Stephen of Blois, and the others greeted Tancred's words with an unaccustomed measure of warmth. Anxiety had gotten the best of them, and they were beginning to look askance at their Byzantine guide. It was difficult to forget that he was Turkish by birth, whatever his allegiances might be at present.

Bohemond, alone among the rest, remained as composed as ever. He even allowed the trace of a smile to play over his clean-shaven face. If Alexios' aid did not materialize, then so much the better. Another savior could be found for the Crusaders, and another sovereign for Antioch.

It was not long before Bohemond found the opportunity, once again, to demonstrate just how invaluable his leadership was. Rumors rippled down the Orontes that Ridwan of Aleppo, brother to Duqaq of Damascus, was now on the march to relieve Antioch of the Crusader presence. At Christmastime, Duqaq's auxiliaries had taken Bohemond and the Flemish count entirely by surprise and frustrated all hope of success on their foraging expedition. Ridwan's relief, however, advanced with a good deal more fanfare giving the Latins ample time to prepare for their arrival.

"We should leave the infantry in the camp to ward off attacks from the city," said Bohemond, scratching out a diagram on the dirt floor of Adhemar's tent, "and mount up as many knights as we can to encounter Ridwan beyond the river."

The winter famine had left only seven hundred horses fit for service, and the Crusaders committed them all to the ambush Bohemond had devised. They came upon Ridwan just before he reached the Iron Bridge and charged into his moving mass of men before the Turkish archers could line up to fire. The river on the right and a small lake on the left prevented Ridwan's greater numbers from outflanking them, and the impetus of the Latins' lances sent the Turks into full retreat.

The second relief force had been sent home in tatters. But despite this success, the Crusaders' view of the future remained dismal. When Kerbogha's legions came into sight, it would take more than seven hundred horses to deter such a great host. Antioch must be captured, and soon, if they wanted a wall between themselves and the Turks from Mosul.

# Chapter 46

"Have you heard the tale about your friend Baldwin of Boulogne?" asked Bohemond, breaking in on Tancred's midday meal. It was the beginning of March and the weather had started to clear, but the only change in the Crusader camp was the day-by-day depletion of the supplies from Cyprus and the Taurus Mountains.

"He's no friend of mine!" Tancred spat back, his throat still filling with the blackest of bile whenever the German's name was mentioned. He reached for a cup of watered down Commandaria—the ambrosially sweet wine the Cyprians were famous for—to wash down his hatred and his last bite of bread. "Has he received his just reward?" asked Tancred bitterly, omitting to add that the reward with the most justice would be evisceration or impalement.

"Only if his just reward is to be made king of Edessa," Bohemond shot back with all the force of a ballista.

Tancred stared agog. Godfrey's little brother had split off from the Crusade with only a hundred knights in his company. How could he have captured a kingdom for himself with such limited manpower?

Bohemond poured the story into his nephew's tingling ears. "It was all due to Bagrat, I suppose, that the invitation came. You remember him? That Armenian weasel who took up with Baldwin as soon as we left Nicaea? It was he who encouraged Baldwin to take the path through Cilicia in the first place. Bagrat's prestige is predicated on the extent of Baldwin's power, and to increase his own standing before his own countrymen, he busied himself with trumpeting abroad stories of the German's prowess. You may have made friends with Oshin in Cilicia, but by the time Baldwin departed that region, those ignorant of his misdeeds were prepared to hail him as a second Hercules, one who could cut off the heads of the Turkish garrisons and ensure that they would never grow back again. Bagrat intended to inveigle Baldwin into turning south next, to lure him into the service of his brother Kogh Vasil, but the urgent message of his wife's illness sent Baldwin scrambling back through the mountains to Marash. Once there, he had other vistas open up before him, more enticing than the one Bagrat proffered.

"The Armenian kingdoms stretch for miles beyond the Taurus Mountains, and nestled in the fertile neck of the Euphrates sits the city of Edessa." Bohemond turned his head to look fondly at the city walls that jutted up before them. "It is less imposing than Antioch, perhaps, but still a great city by any standard of measurement. Edessa lies in the Syrian tract of Mesopotamia, and by the whims of fortune, the Armenians took this city from the Turks just one year before Pope Urban called our Crusade. They have been fighting desperately to maintain their hold there ever since, on the city and on the territory roundabout.

"The king there is Thoros. He was originally one of Rupen's officials, but at the death of his liege, he refused to swear fealty to Rupen's son Constantine. Instead, he struck out on his own to make himself a name—a pity that name will never be passed down to anyone of his own blood. He is old, childless, and precariously placed. Without a strong heir to protect him, he lies in danger from any Turkish *atabeg* or Armenian usurper with an eye to the throne.

"When Baldwin met up with us at Marash to grieve for his dear, departed Godvera, a messenger from Thoros was there waiting for him. The Armenian beseeched him to journey to Edessa and become the champion and heir of Thoros' kingdom. And so Baldwin put aside his grief like a worn out cloak and set off immediately, balking not a bit when Godfrey refused to let him leave with more than a hundred lances.

"Bagrat, who wanted Baldwin for his own ends, complained bitterly of the new plan. But now that Baldwin had forged his own connection with the Armenian princes, he had no need of Bagrat any longer. While the Germans were on the march to Edessa, a rumor ran round that Bagrat was now intriguing with the Turks to plot Baldwin's downfall. Baldwin put the parasite in chains and tortured him until he confessed to a plot. What happened to him next, I do not know. Perhaps he was executed. Perhaps he escaped and fled south to his brother's territory.

"In any event, it took several months for Baldwin to find his way to the Euphrates. Once he had arrived in Edessa, the aged Thoros welcomed him like the prodigal son and insisted on the adoption taking place immediately."

"So the relationship was formalized?" queried Tancred with a frown. He would have liked to hear that Baldwin had seized power through malicious means—that would give the others another reason to censure him.

"Oh, yes!" replied Bohemond with certainty. "And the Armenian ceremony of adoption is a most comical affair. The man who told me these things saw it take place, and he could hardly keep from laughing when he spoke. It happened in the great hall of the castle keep. Baldwin, it seems, stripped down to the waist, the better to simulate the appearance of a babe fresh from the womb. The Armenian, on the other hand, wore a shirt two times the proper size. Then, after Thoros had pledged to take Baldwin as his son and true heir, he took Baldwin under that tent of a shirt so their bare chests could rub against each other and seal the bond."

"Surely, you jest!"

"Nay, and the most peculiar part of the ceremony was that it then had to be repeated with the mother, in just the same way!"

The image of Thoros' aged wife taking Baldwin under her shift and pressing him to her wrinkled, old breasts was too ludicrous not to be laughed at. Tancred chortled until his sides hurt. "Well, if that is what must be done to earn an inheritance in the East, I certainly do not envy the man. You said he has been made king?"

"In all but name. He has applied a firm hand to the rule of the place, and the people respect him already as their head. It is only a matter of time before old Thoros slips into the silence of the grave."

It was not long before further news regarding the enterprising German arrived at Antioch. Tancred heard the story first this time when a messenger from Baldwin came coursing into the Crusader camp with the speed of winged Hermes.

"Thoros is dead," said the official dispatch in the rider's bag, "and I have been crowned king by the people of Edessa. I intend to remain here as long as is necessary to establish my rule and make this city a bulwark in the East against the Turks."

Tancred, supplying the messenger with a cup of the Commandaria to loosen his tongue, had a few more questions that the letter failed to cover. "How did Thoros die?"

The thirsty man was only too happy to trade an account of the lurid story for some sips of the sweet wine. It was the Armenians who killed him. Now that they had a crown prince ready to hand, they had made no delay in overthrowing the ancient Thoros and hastening his demise. The messenger's forehead wrinkled with perplexity as he told of their contempt for their former king. "I would have thought the Edessans would prefer the old man to Baldwin since he, at least, sprung from their own race—but strangely enough, he was the object of great hatred from his subjects."

"Perhaps he was a brutal and merciless monarch."

"He did not seem to be overly cruel, though an outsider cannot always discern these things. The only indictment I heard against him— aside from heavy taxation—was regarding his religion. He belonged to a different Church than the people of the place."

Tancred remembered that Oshin had compromised with the Greek Church for the sake of a Byzantine alliance, a fact that he was not eager to promulgate among his people in Cilicia. Apparently, Thoros too had sacrificed his religious traditions for expediency's sake. And the Armenians—who loved Constantine because he was with them body, soul, and baptism—judged Thoros no better than a Judas and much worse than a Baldwin.

Not three weeks after Baldwin's adoption ceremony, the Armenians had risen up like a blistering sandstorm against Thoros. An angry mob attacked the houses of the king's officials and then marched on the king's palace in the citadel. Thoros' troops deserted him. Baldwin gave him no other help than to advise him to surrender.

"Are you sure that Baldwin did not instigate this riot?" asked Tancred suspiciously.

"No, no," objected the messenger. He was Baldwin's man through and through. "Count Baldwin had nothing to do with their evil plot, and he would have saved Thoros' life if he could. But the old king attempted to escape through a window of the palace. Someone below spotted him dangling like a hooked fish. He was captured and torn to pieces by the crowd."

"And within the week Baldwin assumed his new duties as king?"

"Three days later."

"A most convenient confluence of events," said Tancred wryly. "You must offer your master my congratulations on his new kingship. Is it too much to wonder if he consolidated his power by promptly marrying Thoros' aged widow?"

The messenger was appalled. "His adopted mother? Surely you jest!"

"I merely say what a man in his position ought to have done. If he plans to make his bed in Edessa, he should take an Armenian princess to warm it. Otherwise the people will come to see that he is as detached from their traditions as Thoros was. How unfortunate it would be to have Baldwin dangling from the castle window with an angry mob below!"

Tancred refilled the messenger's wine cup with the casual indifference of a man who has a whole cellar at his disposal. There was no use bemoaning the fact that the wine from Cyprus, just like the grain, would be exhausted before the week had run its course. Better to eat, drink, and be merry while it was still possible.

The grateful man took a heady swig and leaned forward confidentially. "Perhaps I ought not to say this, but you've sounded up the situation exactly. Nothing's been formalized yet, but Baldwin's already in negotiations for an Armenian bride. Arda's her name. Her father is Thatoul of Marash. He's not the most powerful of the Armenian chieftains, but he's of the blood of Rupen and respected for his ancestry."

"Constantine's younger brother?"

"Aye, though as unlike him as night is to day."

"And the girl is pleasing?"

The messenger shrugged. "She should do well enough—if Baldwin's memory is poor enough to forget what a beauty Godvera was. Besides, her father has promised a dowry large enough to make the veriest hag a vision of happiness."

The man's cup was empty of wine. He looked to the marquis, a little expectantly, but Tancred simply reclaimed the twice drained vessel and bid the knight good day. He had learned all that he needed to know about Baldwin's new conquest. The German had the support of the populace, the keys to the palace, and a Croesus for a father-in-law. It was unlikely that he would be rejoining the Crusade to capture Jerusalem anytime soon.

But despite all these pieces of good fortune that had fallen in Baldwin's lap, Tancred reckoned there was one mishap in the mix for his German rival. The walls of Edessa stood halfway between Antioch and Mosul on the very road that Kerbogha would be taking. Whatever reinforcements came to aid the Turks at Antioch would be paying a visit first to Baldwin's new kingdom.

# Chapter 47

Easter Sunday came and with it the tightening of belts or—in some cases—the soaking, softening, and eating of those belts since other fare had become as scarce as a serpent with legs. The recurrence of the famine was a bitter surprise to some of the simpler folk. When Constantine's caravan and the Cyprian fleet had appeared, they had considered it nothing short of miraculous. The windows of heaven had opened upon them, and they expected their new supply of grain to be as long lasting as the widow of Zarephath's.

In the face of this new deprivation, the threshold of Adhemar's tent felt the pitter-patter of many hungry souls demanding that he write again to the Cyprians or to the Armenians in the Taurus Mountains. The bishop responded with patient refusal. They had given all they could spare. There was no more to be had.

And besides, the last few loads of food that had straggled into the harbor had been ambushed by the Turkish garrison before they could ever reach the Crusaders' mouths. It was small use to ask for convoys of food when they could not even convey it into their own camp. The unguarded western gates were still a thorn in their flesh, as crippling as the barb that had afflicted Androcles' lion.

It was about this time that Tatikios, and his small contingent of Byzantine scouts, disappeared without a trace. For months now the golden-nosed general had been insisting that Alexios' aid was only a few furlongs away, making as many false predictions as those prophets who foresee Christ's second coming. Now, as misery mounted once more in the Crusader camp, the man and his continual assurances were nowhere to be found.

Bohemond, alone among the Crusader lords, evinced no surprise when Tatikios' flight was made known.

"Did you see him go? Had he a good reason?" asked Godfrey, wanting to find a reason to believe the best of this betrayal.

"Aye," said Bohemond. "I saw him leaving last night and confronted him. He claimed that he was returning to Constantinople to bring back the promised aid himself." The Norman's words were neutral but his tone implied that this claim was far from the truth.

"I wager we'll not be seeing him again!" spat out pious Robert, the Duke of Normandy, manifesting some of the choler that ran through the veins of his famous family. The others agreed and denounced the absent general vociferously.

"I can see no reason," concluded the Count of Flanders, "why we should render this city up to Alexios once we have obtained it. He has promised us everything and provided us nothing—no men, no machines, no fleet, no food."

The Crusader lords concurred unanimously with this opinion. They would keep Antioch for themselves once they had overthrown its walls and fly the red cross flag from the heights of Mount Silpius.

Tancred, keeping his gaze pinned on his uncle's face, saw the fires of anticipation come alight in his eyes and the iron cast of determination curl round his chin. Alexios' claim to the city had been invalidated by his failure to send aid. Now Bohemond had only to make his own bid for the place and convince the others of his right to lordship.

Meanwhile, the indigenous Syrians began to buzz about the camp like flies over a desiccating carcass. Greedy traders had heard that there was still some blood to be sucked from the luckless Latins. They carted in provisions as musty and moldering as the bread of the Gibeonites and sold them for as dear a price as saffron.

Few of the ordinary soldiers could afford such delicacies, unless their lord possessed a strongbox as bottomless as the one in Count Raymond's tent. Tancred had no gold to spare for either himself or his men. His mother's jeweled girdle had been turned into hauberks and warhorses long ago, and the income from his estates had been eaten up before the walls of Constantinople ever came into sight.

It took great strength of will to suffer through the lengthening days on only the flesh of a field mouse and a few unnamed shoots of greenery, plucked as soon as they poked their blades through the soil. Tancred, striving to set an example to his men refused to allow the pangs of an empty stomach to lure him into lethargy, complaints, or cursing. Despite his best efforts, however, the haze of hunger still hung about him, dulling his perceptions and awareness. His normally keen eye failed to observe how many meals his closest companions partook of. He did not realize that others frequently surrendered their sustenance so that what little food there was could be put into his own bowl.

One chill evening, as the marquis prepared to go to the council tent, he bade Alexandra fetch his cloak. If she insisted on loitering around his tent with the mournful eyes of a stray hound, she might as well make herself useful.

The girl rose to her feet, a little shakily, and rubbed her arms briefly as a talisman against the crisp air. Tancred, hunched over attending to his bootstraps, glimpsed her from the corner of his eye gliding toward the tent. Then, suddenly, the motion ceased. Alexandra fell to the ground midstride. Her voice made no sound as she lost consciousness and crumpled on the dirt below.

"What is wrong with her?" asked Tancred obtusely.

Ralph stared at him. Could he really not know? "She has not eaten a bite of food in over three days," he said reproachfully.

If Tancred had ever really looked at the girl, he would have seen that for himself. The deprivation of the last several months had stripped her face and limbs of all the soft roundness of youth. The green dress, which had fit her so snugly when she came over the Strait of St. George, bagged upon her almost as grotesquely as the oversized tunic she had worn when Tancred first made her acquaintance.

Creases of concern—too late but truly felt—came over the marquis' forehead. Wearily, he walked over to where the young girl lay and scooped her up into his arms. She weighed no more than a spring calf just birthed and hung over his well-muscled arms like a garland of wilted flowers. "Why did you never speak of this?" he said, lifting a pair of remorseful eyes to the face of his old manservant. "I did not know. As God is my witness, I did not know."

While Ralph watched, Tancred laid her upon his own pallet. He bade the old man sit with her and give her something to drink if she would take it—with the Orontes and the constant cloudbursts there was at least no shortage of water. Then, pulling on his cloak, he set off into the cold twilight with a heart as heavy as his steps.

He did not go to the Syrian swindlers, although they were the only ones likely to have food. He had heard their prices just yesterday and denounced the whole pack of them as Jewish usurers. It was eight bezants for a donkey's load of week old bread and shriveled figs. Tancred could not have afforded it at a quarter of the cost.

Instead, he walked determinedly to his original destination—Adhemar's tent. As he approached the place of meeting, his sharp ears discerned that the collected lords had already begun the council without him. "It is folly to stay here any longer!" said a nasally whimper that Tancred immediately assigned to Stephen of Blois. "We should return to Constantinople and come back when we have gathered more men, more provisions, and a more definite direction on how to accomplish this siege!"

"A return journey, in our present condition, would be disastrous," stated Count Robert of Flanders. There was no reason to suppose that an army in retreat across Anatolia would find more sustenance than a stationary army on the banks of the Orontes.

Adhemar nodded to Tancred as he entered and gestured to an open seat. But instead of accepting the invitation to sit, Tancred strode into the center of the ring of men. He interrupted their deliberations with the force of a breaking dam.

"How much will you give me to shut up the western gates of Antioch?"

A moment of silence greeted his unexpected question. Bohemond's head tilted sharply. Would his impetuous nephew's throw of the dice impede the game that he himself planned to play later on?

Count Raymond was the first to recover from the shock of the marquis' offer. "I will give you twelve hundred bezants," he said enthusiastically.

"And you, my lords?" asked Tancred, turning to the rest.

They wrinkled their foreheads, pursed their lips, and cast sidelong glances at one another. "How much do you require?" asked Robert of Normandy. "We are none of us as rich as the Count of Toulouse."

"I will undertake the task for four times what he has offered," said Tancred without hesitation. If truth were told, he would have undertaken it for Count Raymond's pledge alone. He was determined, however, to squeeze every possible *denari* out of the assembly.

The price was high and the marquis was highhanded with his demands, but it was too important an offer to deride or discard, no matter how much dislike any individual leader might feel toward Tancred. Grudgingly, the lords began to inventory their resources, recalling several men of means within their own companies who might also be urged to contribute. Godfrey dug deep into his purse with promises. Adhemar nodded encouragingly at the young Norman and offered to match Raymond's sum from the coffers of the Church.

After the pledges had been made—and a small sum advanced to Tancred as a guarantee—there was little more to be said. It only remained for Tancred to fulfill what he had promised. The meeting adjourned and the participants dispersed to their quarters.

Adhemar motioned for the young Norman to stay after the others had left. After his peers had exited the tent, Tancred took a seat at last.

"So," said the bishop, brimming over like a full flagon with curiosity. "How do you propose to shut up the western gates?"

"I will build a tower between them and the Orontes, high enough to overtop the Turks' gatehouses with our arrows. They will not make any move without our knowledge, and the vigilance of our archers will make them regret any attempt at egress."

Adhemar clapped his broad hand against his thigh in approval. "A bold plan to make a tower, but it will be dangerous in the building of it. Your men will be like a leash of plovers on the open plain, with nowhere to hide when winged death descends from above. The infidels' archers are vigilant too, and their arrows will put a stop to your building if they can."

Tancred grunted. "At least a flying shaft brings a quick end. If we do not hazard all on this cast, then my men—and all the rest who look to me for food—are doomed to the much slower end that famine brings. I can think of no other way to obtain the money that the Syrian traders have stipulated for their foodstuffs. So for the sake of life we must be prepared to taste a little death."

# Chapter 48

Tancred lost no time in laying out his advance of gold to buy food for his followers and timber for the building of the tower. He did not even wait for morning's light to survey the terrain of his new command, but riding to the other side of the city, he examined the dark silhouette of each foothill and assessed its suitability for fortification.

Alexandra finally had food that night—flat cakes baked on a stone that Ralph broke into small pieces and hand fed to her until she regained the strength to sit up. Her eyes, large and luminescent above her wan cheeks, looked around longingly for the marquis—but he had already disappeared to divvy out the rest of the food evenly among his disheartened and disheveled Normans.

"Eat up!" said Ralph gently. "There'll be time enough to thank him later." It was a statement more kind than true, for Tancred's new plan had little room in it for weaklings or for women. When his company shifted quarters, Alexandra would be left behind in the relative safety of Bohemond's camp.

In the morning, when the heavy porridge in the Normans' stomachs had lightened their spirits sufficiently, Tancred broke the news that they must break their camp and relocate to the western side of the city. The whole army had so scrupulously shunned that area over the past six months that the men had built up a supernatural dread around the place. The perils posed by the Turkish towers there had been magnified far beyond reason, until a man-at-arms would as lief ascend the thundering slopes of Mount Sinai as he would go near the western side of Mount Silpius. But there could be no misunderstanding the marquis' command. His grim announcement tumbled over his men like a great boulder, flattening their usual response of immediate obedience.

"But why, my lord?" asked Turold, his voice taking on a bleat more appropriate to a sheep out at pasture.

"Because we've hired ourselves out for bread," snapped Tancred, his temper as short as the hours of sleep last night had provided. "That meal in your maw is only owing to the deal I've struck with the other commanders. And if you wish to continue to eat, you will follow me where you're bid."

Turold's shamefaced blush made the marquis regret his choler and remember his own duty to lead. "You will follow me—yes!—as you always have done, my faithful knights and true. From Bari to Constantinople, from Nicaea to the Taurus Mountains, these many leagues and more, there is not one of you who has drawn back in the day of hardship or in the hour of battle. Let today be no different, and follow me west! We'll build our tower, and earn our bread, and live to see Jerusalem."

To avoid unnecessary notice from the city, Tancred personally guided his men in small groups of twenty or thirty into the foothills on the far side of Antioch. They were on the very edge of the mountain now, past the part of the plain which the Turks still used as a corridor to access the Orontes. The rocky ground here had little use for farmers or for herdsmen, but the marquis had picked out the one spot where mankind had made his imprint.

An old monastery, uninhabited for several generations, sat on the crest of the hill Tancred had chosen. Its stone arches had begun to crumble, but its foundations were still as firm as they had been in the days of Emperor Justinian. A tower, built on these ruins, could easily overtop the lower ramparts of the city facing it. A body of passable archers, stationed in such a tower, could easily command the path and the plain below. Once he constructed his fortress, no one would exit or enter the Gate of St. George without Tancred's permission.

Ralph, seeing the place for the first time, declared it ideal for their purposes. "And the best part about it, my lord, is the rabbit's warren of stone cells we can take refuge in if the Turks turn their arrows on us while we are still building."

The old man's enthusiasm quickly spread to the rest of Tancred's troop. The marquis set an engineer in charge of them, and following his orders, even the knights stripped down to the waist in the warm spring air to cart timber and shift settled stones. They would build this tower as tall as Babel under the very noses of the black mustached Turks.

On the very day that the Normans pitched their camp behind the old monastery, the benefits of their new position became apparent. Gervase was on lookout duty at the top of the ridge. He spotted a procession of traders wending their way through the hills. Apparently the native Syrians, not content with gouging the famished Crusaders with their food prices, were also keeping up a lucrative exchange with the inhabitants of Antioch.

The Normans had no qualms about raiding comestibles intended for the enemy's consumption. "Make it quiet," were the marquis' orders as he sent a detachment of men to intercept the Syrians. The men followed his instructions to the letter. They drove off the Syrians, seized their goods, and transported them up to the new camp—all without alerting the nearby garrison of their presence.

As he counted up the captured vessels of wine, wheat, barley, and oil, Tancred shook his head in amazement. "What fools we have been! We should have fortified this place months ago. We would have saved ourselves a world of privation and pain."

But it was no use to shed tears over days long dead or over those who had died in them. Instead, the marquis made the most of the present time. Excited by the opportunity to make some progress at last on the siege, his Normans put their backs into the work and constructed the base of the tower in less time than the Crusader lords would have deemed possible.

A normal building site resounded with heckles, jibes, shouted measurements, and full-throated singing, but these makeshift masons were as silent as the ruins of the old monastery. It was not sullenness that stopped their tongues, however. The men were as happy and hopeful as they had been in months, but Tancred had given strict orders to curb their clamor. The longer they remained inconspicuous, the stronger their position would be when the Turks discovered them.

Relying on the impregnability of his city, Cassian failed to notice this silent spate of activity on the western ridge. He was awakened from his overconfidence two days later when one of his large raiding parties exited the city only to meet with unexpected and utter disaster. They had ridden out from the low-lying Gate of St. George as was their wont, a company nearly a thousand strong. They intended to use their customary crossing of the Orontes, circle round to the east, and make havoc in the rear of the Crusader camp. But what they did not reckon with were the hundreds of eyes now hidden in the western hills and watching their every movement as they stepped outside the city.

Tancred did not have many horses at his disposal, but the advantage of the high ground more than compensated for this lack. He waited until the arrogant infidels had passed too far down the plain for easy retreat. Then, ordering an organized volley from his archers on the ridge, he raked through their ranks with a hail of shafts.

Screams and neighs filled the air. Wounded horses plunged and reared. The Turks' leader, whoever he was, must have been hit by the first volley. The leaderless soldiers did not know whether to spur forward, turn backward, or peel off to the side. In the absence of a clear command, the frightened riders did all three, milling about in a melee as messy as a slaughterhouse floor.

The archers in the heights continued to loose their arrows at will. By the time Tancred gave them the signal to stop, so that he and his two dozen mounted knights could press the victory home, they had killed or wounded over half of the raiding party in the plain. When Tancred's little brigade of lances charged, the remaining Turks were terrified. As many as could still flee, galloped pell-mell back through the gate whence they had come.

The spoil from that battlefield was the first the Crusaders had seen in a long while. The Normans slid down from the heights as greedy as grave robbers and ripped the gold bracelets and jeweled finger rings off the bodies of the fallen infidels. When they had sated their search for plunder, Tancred commanded a more grisly despoilment. They had cut down seven hundred corpses; now he ordered them to cut the heads off of seventy of them.

"Shall we pile them up in front of the city," asked Turold eagerly, "to strike terror in the hearts of our enemies?"

"No, pile them up in front of Bishop Adhemar's tent," said Tancred gleefully. "This is the firstfruits of our conquest of Antioch, and it would be sin to withhold from the Church her tithe."

There are many parish priests who would have shrieked aloud to find such a donation in their tithe box. Adhemar was of a different breed altogether. He greeted the offering of seventy bloody heads with a booming laugh and bid the messengers bring his congratulations to their master Lord Tancred. "And even better than my congratulations, bring him this purse," he said, tossing an embroidered leather pouch into the hands of his chaplain Bernard. "Here are ten times as many bezants as the heads he's reaped, and may his harvest continue to yield!"

Circumambulating the scene of the ambush, Bernard followed Tancred's men-at-arms as they returned through the western foothills and climbed up to the rocky perch where they had established their eyrie. The marquis, instead of letting his men rest on their recently won laurels, had set them to work again at building the tower. They could make all the noise they wanted to now. The Turks were fully apprised of their presence.

"I see you build like the men of Nehemiah," observed Bernard, "trowel in one hand and sword in the other." He tossed the purse to the marquis with an underhand throw. "The archbishop gives you thanks for your gift, and sends his own gift in return."

Tancred untied the strings that closed the bag and whistled with delight at the sight of so many gold pieces.

"You're a rich man," said Bernard wryly, "and will be richer still once you've finished your fortress here and forced the other lords to honor their pledges." He looked up at the wall which they had already raised to the height of two men. "What will you do with so much treasure?"

"Ensure the wellbeing of my men for the rest of this siege—as they say, he who does not provide for his own is worse than an infidel." Tancred waxed pensive. "And perhaps, if there is enough left over, I can pay off my debt to Raymond." It still irked him that he had been forced to borrow from the Count of Toulouse at Nicaea. But then, if one must borrow, the count was the best sort of man to borrow from. While Baldwin was off subverting Edessa and Bohemond was scheming how to suborn Antioch, Raymond, at least, still had his heart set on Jerusalem.

"Oh, I wager he'll call up your debt soon enough," said Bernard with a sneer, "though it may not be gold that he wants in return." The chaplain's gaunt face—ugly enough when his features lay at rest—became positively grotesque when suffused with such hostility and hate.

"That's more than I know," said Tancred sharply. He did not care to indulge in such gratuitous gossip, and furthermore, the chaplain's animosity toward the Count of Toulouse was beginning to aggravate him. Sometime soon, when the rigors of the siege abated, he must sound out the reasons behind Bernard's bitterness—although whatever the story was, he would not give it credence on the word of the chaplain alone. His mind, mulling over the matter for so long a time, had become as misshapen as a hunchback dwarf. Adhemar would be the man to ask. He would know what deeds of darkness lay between his dour chaplain and his doughty comrade in arms.

# Chapter 49

Tancred's tower marked the beginning of the end for Turkish rule in Antioch. With the Gate of St. George closed to them, Cassian and his garrison were shut up like a bird in a cage. They could no longer come and go as they pleased, and they were now subject to the same scarcity of food that had afflicted the Crusaders. Beating themselves frantically against the bars of their prison, they made several sorties to overthrow the tower—but the Normans were already too entrenched and could repel all comers from behind the rapidly rising walls of their new fortress.

Although his tower had stood up staunchly to every onslaught so far, Tancred refused to relax his vigilance. His position was as precarious as it was pivotal. Stationed at such a distance from the rest of the Crusaders, the small band was isolated and unable to seek assistance when trouble threatened. Their lookouts must stay lively if they wished to stay alive.

As the constant toll of fighting by day and vigils by night began to tell on his men, Tancred tried to alleviate the strain by focusing their eyes on the prize of Jerusalem. "Antioch is as good as ours if we can only hold fast!" he proclaimed optimistically. "And by summer's end we'll walk the streets of Bethlehem, climb the Mount of Olives, and kneel before the Holy Sepulcher where Christ arose!"

Tancred's regard for his own lordship never gave way to laziness. He always took his turn at the midnight watch, and sometimes, when others were too worn out by wounds or illness, he took their turn as well. It was a gesture few soldiers would ever forget. "You have the knack of managing men just like your grandfather Guiscard did," said

Ralph, smoothing down his moustaches with a practiced hand. "He could inspire them to follow wherever he led, into the jaws and gullet of hell, if need be. And so can you—yes, and make them love you through the worst of it."

"I barely knew my grandfather. I wish he would have lived longer into my youth so that I might have gleaned more of his character and martial skill."

Ralph nodded. "Aye, he would have liked it well to see the man that you've become. But there's enough of Guiscard's blood flowing in your veins to keep the name of his house a proud one. This tower here is proof of that."

The spring rains gave way entirely to the withering heat of summer in the Levant. The month of May had almost run its course. Ceasing their abortive sorties, the Turks stayed inside the city to conserve their strength. The Crusaders, who had suffered so much, were jubilant as they imagined the pangs of hunger that must be gripping their enemies now. The threat of Kerbogha's army still loomed in the distance, but at least now there was some hope that Antioch might capitulate before the *atabeg* of Mosul arrived.

Now that Antioch's garrison had retired from its constant marauding, Tancred used the opportunity to explore. A single man, capable of climbing briskly, could go up and around the backside of Mount Silpius where the citadel lay ensconced in the heights. Until now, the Crusaders had completely ignored this means of approach. The walls there were just as unassailable as those down below, and the impossibility of bringing siege engines or mounted men up the incline precluded any assault on the rear of the citadel.

But Tancred's tower had taught him to reexamine what had once been deemed impossible. Treading carefully, in leather boots that were almost completely worn through, the marquis clambered over the crags. At first, he found little other sign of life than the mountain goats that played there. As he continued to skirt the base of the soaring citadel, however, he discovered an aperture inset in the stonework. Here one of the mountain streams was allowed to pass through the rear wall and feed the aqueduct that supplied all Antioch. At first, he assumed that the aperture was only a small culvert. There would be no space for a man to crawl through it. But as he crouched behind the sun-warmed rocks brooding on the serviceability of the spring, he heard the creaking groan of metal against metal. Something mechanical had been set into motion. He looked up. The glint of something bright, even brighter than sunlight on water, appeared from the inset stones by the culvert.

It was the sheen of a burnished helmet strapped onto the unshaven cheeks of a swarthy Turk. He wore little other armor on his body, intending to travel lightly over a hard country as he delivered whatever message had been entrusted to him. Looking to the right and then the left, he splashed through the shallows of the stream and began a brisk descent of the mountainside. His thick legs loped easily over uneven terraces and fallen boulders.

Only a few dozen paces away, Tancred pressed himself tightly against the rocks to avoid discovery. It seems there was more to the culvert than he had initially discerned. He mentally marked the place where the man had come out. The inset in the wall must conceal a secret postern—probably built by the Byzantines long ago. It was large enough to let in the little trickle of mountain water and large enough to let out a little trickle of men. With their western gates cut off, the Turks had been taking advantage of this door to send out messengers through the mountains.

Tancred watched the man's back descend the slopes of Silpius until it disappeared from sight. He pursed his lips in thought. This new discovery was certainly worth some surveillance. He must find out how frequently the postern gate was used and how attentively it was secured. It would be well nigh impossible to bring an army up into these crags, but by using the little door, a handful of daring men might be able to slip into the citadel unnoticed and find a way to admit their fellows at the gates of the city below.

And so began a week of lurking and lying in wait. Each morning— early, before the sun's stare had overlooked the horizon—Tancred slipped away from his falcon's nest at the top of the tower and crept quietly up to the pediments of the citadel. The postern, as he discovered, was employed but rarely. Only one other messenger emerged from its recesses in all the days he lay watching. He still had no idea how closely the little gate was watched, but he had dared to creep close enough to discover its more mechanical defenses: a slim iron portcullis and a heavy wooden door, probably padlocked from the inside. He speculated that an unoiled chain on the portcullis winch was the cause of the creaking groans that preceded each messenger's egress.

At the end of the week, when the afternoon heat and a worrisome pair of scorpions had almost persuaded him to retire for the day, Tancred once again heard the telltale signs that the postern portcullis was about to open. He caught his breath sharply and put his hand on his sword. This time, instead of merely observing, he had determined he would take the messenger alive. Then, through interrogation or torture, he would finally learn the workings of the door to the citadel.

Heart palpitating with anticipation, Tancred watched a figure step out of the stonework and walk into the bed of the stream. He had been expecting a thickset messenger wearing heavy moustaches, knee-length breeches, and a quilted jacket stained with travel. The Turk who emerged could not have been more opposite from his expectations.

It was a woman, and not the sort of woman who should be wandering a hazardous hillside by herself. She was obviously of high parentage, youthful, lovely, and lithe, with hair as black as polished obsidian. A thin veil hid the lower half of her face. It lent additional allure to the eyes above, which shimmered under their own veil of dark, exotic eyelashes. A gauzy tunic of blue gathered tightly at her waist. A pair of pointed red slippers dangled freely from her fingers while she walked barefoot through the rocky riverbed.

Tancred, already tensed to spring on his victim, inhaled sharply and slunk back into his hiding place. Who was this damsel and what was she doing outside the city? As she stepped away from the postern, he saw her look back at it guiltily. It was evident that she had slipped out of the citadel without the permission of her guardian or the guards. Yet once she escaped from the shadow of the wall and followed the stream out into the sunlight, her furtive manner vanished, and her small feet danced in the brook with as much delight as a child of six or seven.

The marquis, who had memorized the mechanical rounds of the sentries, knew that she had at least a quarter of an hour to herself before the lazy oafs in the nearby tower looked this way. She seemed acquainted with their routines as well. It did not take her long to find a seat in a small outcropping of rock where she could enjoy the coolness of the water, bask in the radiance of the sun, and avoid the stare of the tower above.

There was one stare, however, that she could not avoid. Tancred's blue eyes remained riveted on the Turkish girl, and his face began to burn with a heat that did not come from the sun. She was very beautiful and very vulnerable to be unescorted in such a place. A fluttering thought whispered through his mind that perhaps this was the sister—Erminia—of whom the sultana had spoken. It would have been a good enough reason to investigate further, had not a stronger reason already taken hold of him—the irresistible desire to see what lay underneath the veil she wore.

He kept quiet and crept closer, making every effort not to dislodge any of the loose stones along the way. His mind turned over and over trying to determine the best method of approach. It was impossible to come around behind her. The niche she had chosen was too tightly enclosed by the surrounding rock, and besides, he would have to cross the stream to get to her. And yet, if he advanced upon her openly, she would inevitably cry out in fear. The sentries, complacent as they were, were bound to be alarmed at the sound of a woman's scream.

Slinking behind piled boulders, Tancred maneuvered himself until he had found his own outcropping to hide behind, just a stone's throw from the damsel's streamside seat. He took a deep breath and readied his tongue to speak in Arabic. "The weather is fine today, milady." The words were as friendly and mild as he could make them, and just loud enough to travel across the brook to her.

The unknown voice, as gentle and innocuous as it was, still startled her. Gasping, she reached for her red slippers and slid them onto her dripping feet. The smallest misstep on Tancred's part would send her fleeing back to the postern gate.

"I mean you no harm. I came here only to enjoy the beauty of the sunlight and the stream—and lo!—I find another beauty to marvel at."

She absorbed his words without comment or blushes like one who is accustomed to praise. "Come out and show yourself!" she commanded, her eyes scanning the boulders across the stream to discern where the mysterious voice could be coming from.

"You will not like the look of me," he said simply. From that, he hoped she might infer that he was ill favored or rustic in appearance. He wagered that his Arabic was good enough—and rare enough for a Westerner—that she would not sound him out as one of the city's besiegers.

But as skillful as his tongue was, he did not have the knack of the accent peculiar to the Antiochenes. "Your speech is strange," she said accusingly. "You were not born in these parts."

"You have a keen ear, milady. My fate has led me far from the shores where I was born."

"Where was that?" Her tone was still tinged with distrust.

"Near Sicily." Though Guiscard's family had fought to claim it all, there were still Mussulmen in parts of that island. It was a plausible suggestion.

"What emir are you sworn to?" She seemed to know, without question, that he was a soldier.

He hesitated, then chose the obvious. "I serve Yaghi-Siyan," he said, using the Arabic name for Cassian, the governor of Antioch.

"What is your position in the garrison?"

Tancred decided to brazen it out. "I am part of his personal guard."

Her eyes glowed like fire opals. "Liar!" she said bitterly. If she were a man, she would have spat in disgust. "I know every one of those men by heart—it is easy enough to memorize the voices of my jailers. You are none of them, I know!" She jumped to her feet, poised like a gazelle that has scented danger. It would only take her half a minute to reach the postern and slip inside.

"You have seen through my artifices," said Tancred. "I bow in the dust before your wisdom." Desperately, he devised and discarded ways to keep the girl from disappearing forever. He decided to hazard all on a guess and preempt her departure with his own good-bye. "Farewell, Erminia. Peace be upon you."

She paused in disbelief. "How do you know my name?" It was a name from childhood, a name from home. Cassian's personal guards would not call her by it. She doubted whether Cassian himself had ever heard it used of her.

He kept quiet, allowing her curiosity to increase.

"Answer me, sirrah! Who told you I was Erminia?"

"The sultana of Rum, your sister. She made me her messenger to you many months ago, and it is only by the greatest good fortune that I have come upon you today."

"Come out then!" she said breathlessly. "I will stay and hear your message."

"You will not be afraid of my appearance?"

"I am no coward," she said scornfully. Reseating herself gravely on the riverside stone, she assumed the pose of a monarch upon his dais.

Tancred straightened and stepped out of his hiding place at her command, a blond giant, taller than any man she had ever seen. Glints of chainmail showed here and there beneath his brown surcoat, and though he held out his empty hands to her in an expression of good-will, she could see his longsword hanging loosely from the scabbard on his belt. His blue eyes met hers frankly, willing her not to flee.

"You are one of the *Franj*!" she said, her dark eyes opening wide with terror.

# Chapter 50

"*Franj*, yes, but also a friend."

Tancred accepted the appellation without dispute. The Turks were used to lump all the Latins together under the common name of Franks, much as the Latins themselves made no distinction between the different sects and tribes within the Turkic world.

He approached the Turkish princess slowly as if she were a skittish colt, and instead of making peace with an apple or turnip, he proffered an explanation to soothe her. "I met your sister when she fled from Nicaea. I tried—and failed—to help her in her escape. But before the Byzantines took her, she took my word in pledge that I would bring her talisman ring to give to you at Antioch." He did not tell her that the emerald circlet was only the seal of his other promise—that he would protect her from any harm when Antioch fell into the hands of the Latins.

She knew the ring he meant—he could tell that from her eyes. The sultana had said that it belonged to their murdered father. It was doubtless an heirloom from her family's history. "Where is it?" she demanded suspiciously. The sight of the ring would lend credence to his story. All Tancred had to do was reach into the small purse at his belt and pull out the sultana's talisman.

Risking the gaze of the sentries, the marquis walked to the very edge of the stream and stood opposite her. "I did not know I would find you today, and I left the ring at my camp. I can go and fetch it, but it will take time, and the sun is already beginning to go down. Will you meet me here tomorrow so I can bring it for you?"

Of all the lies he had told that day, that one was the least—and the most—necessary. He had the ring with him. He could have delivered it then. But if he did so, he shrewdly suspected that he would never see the sultana's sister again. Calculating carefully, he decided to lure her into a tryst with promise of the pledge.

At first, the girl did not seem too willing to respond to his lures. "I will be in great trouble," Erminia said slowly, "if my uncle's guards learn that I have slipped out to speak to such a one as you."

"You will be in great trouble," he said matter-of-factly, "if they learn that you have slipped out at all. But somehow"—he smiled at her conspiratorially—"I do not think that worries you too much."

"No," she said, and Tancred was certain that beneath her thin veil, two rosy lips had curled into the semblance of a smile. "I try to elude them as much as I can, and the keeper of the gate is kind to me.

"Very well, knight," she said, after some thought. "I will come to you tomorrow at the setting of the sun, and you shall give me my sister's ring as you have promised. Is it agreed?"

"It is agreed, milady," said Tancred, and he made her a courtly bow from the opposite side of the riverbank. She rose to leave then. And though her path to the postern took her, of necessity, through the riverbed, she modestly refused to remove her slippers while a man—an infidel of the *Franj!*—was watching her.

Tancred's eyes followed the back of her blue tunic until it disappeared into the concealed gate. Then, walking like a man in a dream, he made the long trek back to the tower, treading on far more sharp rocks than were comfortable with the thin soles of his worn-out boots.

Ralph, sighting the marquis as he entered the cluster of cells at the base of the tower, greeted his master with enthusiasm. "Did anything occur in my absence?" asked Tancred perfunctorily. He was certain that the only event of consequence that day had been his meeting with the most beautiful flower in the whole of the East.

Ralph handed half of a meat pie to his master. "Alexandra came over from your uncle's camp," said Ralph. He held up a basket full of similar fare. "She thanks you for your continued provision for her, and she's baked these delicacies for you to enjoy. A sweet girl—and a sweet substitute for campfire porridge!"

Tancred grunted and licked his fingers. He had forgotten how hungry he was in the excitement of seeing Erminia. Ralph lifted an eyebrow and looked at him hopefully, then continued with his panegyric on the little Greek girl. "She's regained her bloom, and is as pert and pretty as ever. I told her you would likely be gone till evening. But she waited nonetheless. Finally, it became so late I sent her back to Bohemond's camp with Turold for an escort. Perhaps you will find it in your heart to stop and greet her on your way to the council meeting tonight."

"Oh?" asked Tancred, casting his eye around the spartan quarters of the old monastery cell for something to drink. "Is there a council meeting tonight?"

"Aye," said Ralph, his voice lowering with gravity. He had saved the most important news for last. "That was the other thing that occurred in your absence—Baldwin kindly sent us a messenger from Edessa to tell us that Kerbogha will be here within the week."

"Christ preserve us!" Tancred's voice rasped with thirst and worry. "Are we sure he speaks true?"

"Sure enough for some to panic and pull up stakes, but you'll doubtless hear more of that at Adhemar's tent tonight."

Ignoring Ralph's earlier suggestion, Tancred took the shortest route to the bishop's camp without wasting any time on words with Alexandra. When he came inside the tent, he catalogued the array of stern, unsmiling faces and found one missing. "Where is Stephen of Blois?"

"Gone!" boomed Robert of Flanders. "Small surprise there!" He had traveled with the man a small part of the way to Constantinople, and he knew just how interested—or uninterested—the henpecked Count of Blois was in belonging to the Crusade.

Robert, the Duke of Normandy, posited the best possible reasons for his brother-in-law's flight. "When he heard Kerbogha was almost here, he thought it prudent to retire to Constantinople. He will undoubtedly persuade the emperor to send help."

"Or maybe he will tell him to stay at home and save himself," retorted the other Robert, "since our army is beyond any hope of preservation."

"How do we know that Kerbogha is so close?" asked Tancred, looking for confirmation of the secondhand story Ralph had relayed.

"I received a messenger from Baldwin today," said Adhemar gravely. "It seems that we have him to thank for keeping the men from Mosul from falling on us sooner. When Kerbogha reached Edessa, he decided to delay the relief of Antioch in order to humble Baldwin first. You might think that an easy task, since Baldwin branched off from our host with only a hundred lances—but now he has the goodwill of the Armenian people and the walls of Edessa to shield him.

"Kerbogha laid siege to Edessa. Baldwin was shut up in the city for over a month unable to get a messenger through to us. But even though the Turks cut off his lines of communication, they were unable to cut through his defenses. Finally, Kerbogha decided Edessa was too hard a nut for his teeth to crack and gave up the siege. Now he continues on to Antioch to deal with us! Baldwin's rider spurred ahead of the Turkish host to bring us warning. We have a week at most, he estimates, before our doom is at the door."

Gloom settled over the council like a thick fog. It seemed that no one, not even Adhemar, could devise a stratagem that would bring them safe into harbor—until Bohemond lit a beacon of tenuous hope by divulging his plans.

"It is clear what must be done if we are to save ourselves alive. We must overthrow the city immediately and take shelter within her walls."

"And how, pray tell, are we going to accomplish that?" asked Raymond.

"I shall convince one of the castellans to open up a gate for us."

It was a bold proposal, as implausible as sunny skies in winter and papered over with bald-faced presumption. Godfrey wondered aloud how Bohemond was going to find a Turkish captain willing to betray the trust of his commander and his comrades. Tancred knew that Bohemond must already have done so, or he would not have wasted their time by mentioning the possibility.

"And what reward would you require from us for this service?" asked Count Raymond cautiously. His iron gray beard bestowed the aura of wisdom on every one of his words.

Bohemond smiled at Raymond archly. The older man's habit of assuming that his greater years and weightier purse lent him additional authority annoyed the Norman to no end. "I would require the command of the city once we have obtained it."

"But Antioch is one of the cities that used to belong to Byzantium," objected Robert of Normandy. "Emperor Alexios claimed it specifically as a place that must be returned to his sovereignty."

The other lords stared at him as if he were a winebibber lost in his cups. "Alexios has forfeited the right to claim anything from us," said the Count of Flanders. "When Tatikios turned tail and fled, he took the last of our obligations with him."

"But even if we do not yield Antioch to Alexios," interjected Raymond, "let us not be overhasty in yielding it to another. Perhaps we should hold the city jointly, or perhaps there is another candidate equally as worthy as our Norman friend to take the governorship."

"Another candidate?" echoed Bohemond with a sneer. "I greatly doubt that." He turned to the others. "Listen to me, gentlemen. I am offering to procure—within the next three days—an open door into Antioch through which you can surprise the governor and take the city by storm. I am offering four walls to shelter you when Kerbogha's host arrives. In return, I ask only to be given the dukedom of Antioch. If anyone else can accomplish as much, let him speak now. Otherwise, let me perform what I have promised and receive my due reward."

"We shall put it to a vote," said Adhemar, forestalling any argument among the other commanders. "What say you, my lords? Shall we promise Bohemond the city if he can contrive us an opening?"

"I say nay," said Raymond solemnly, casting the first vote and earning a look of utter disdain from Tancred's uncle.

"I am for it," contradicted Robert of Flanders. Godfrey was for it as well, but Robert of Normandy demurred with Count Raymond.

Hugh the Great, several stone lighter after the hunger and hardships of the siege, hemmed and hawed visibly. As much as he longed for a comfortable bed and a safe haven, he was still dreadfully irked by Bohemond's presumption. Why should the Norman aspire to such honors, when a scion of the house of France sat ready to hand?

Tancred, who thoroughly despised his uncle's mercenary spirit, began to smolder with an even greater despite for those who hesitated and haggled in such a desperate circumstance. He knew that the others would think him hand in glove with his uncle, but he could no longer forbear from speaking his mind. "My lords, how can there be any dispute about the matter? If we remain as we are, we are caught between Scylla and Charybdis and certain death awaits. I am as loath as any man to concede the lordship of the city to Bohemond, but I fear we have no other choice. If he can unlock the gates for us, then give him what he asks."

Tancred's words met with a cool reception from those who had already made up their minds to dislike the Normans from southern Italy. It was up to Adhemar now to arbitrate the matter and cast the deciding vote.

Bohemond, shameless as he was, began to plead his case in front of them all by offering the bishop a bribe of the most blatant kind. "Antioch is a great city, one of the five patriarchates of olden times. Would you not like to see a Latin bishop in the place? You, or one of your appointees, could fill the see right well and bring much glory to Christendom."

Adhemar rolled up his sleeves revealing the giant forearms that his habit had concealed. "You forget that the see of Antioch is not vacant at present, Lord Bohemond. There is a Patriarch from the Greek Church who rules over the flock in Antioch. The Turkish governor Cassian has put him in chains, but he will surely return to his seat once we overthrow the Mussulmen inside the city."

"But if the city were to come into my hands," said Bohemond cunningly, "I could install the Latin mass inside the churches. A bishop of our own creed could sit in the cathedra, one who acknowledges Pope

Urban as his head." It was a powerful incentive for allowing Bohemond to administer the city of Antioch. On a lesser man than Bishop Adhemar it might have had some effect.

"I do not think you understand the desires of Pope Urban's heart, my son. We have come to heal the schism between Latin and Greek, between West and East. When we enter Antioch I will seek out the Patriarch, and far from displacing him, I will greet him as a brother and restore him to his see."

Raymond nodded appreciatively to see Adhemar reject the Norman's inducements out of hand. But the bishop had not yet finished weighing the matter in his scales, and the final balance he arrived at was much less pleasing to the Count of Toulouse.

"The rites of the Church are of little moment at a moment so perilous. The writing on the wall says Kerbogha is coming—all else is marginalia. If Lord Bohemond can perform what he has promised, we shall honor what he asks. It is the only reasonable thing to do." Walking over to the seated Norman, Adhemar placed a commissioning hand on his shoulder. "Go, my son, and find a way inside the gates. Do not fail us, and the city will be yours!"

# Chapter 51

Tancred fell into step with his uncle as they left Adhemar's tent and accompanied him back to his camp on the eastern side of the city. "I assume you have already secured your traitor for this enterprise."

"You are astute, as usual," said Bohemond. He was pleased that his principled and unpredictable nephew had supported his claim before the council. "His name is Firuz—an Armenian, but a convert to the Mohammedan religion. He commands the Tower of the Two Sisters, directly across from your watchtower on the western ridge. If all goes well, we will be infiltrating the city via the Gate of St. George."

"What incentive have you offered him to betray his trust?"

"Very little. He claims he had a dream from God—which god, I do not know—commanding him to turn over his tower to the men of the West. And besides this, my friend Firuz is desperately unhappy. He is hated by the Armenians for abjuring their faith and hated by the Turks for belonging to another race. Just recently, the governor Cassian honored him with a hefty fine for hoarding grain—another cause for unhappiness and enticement to disloyalty."

"So he has committed himself to open the gates and admit our men?"

"Not yet." Bohemond rubbed his jaw ruefully. "But he promises to give me a definite answer tonight. Come along if you will and watch the negotiations."

His skin prickling with interest, Tancred tramped along with his uncle to meet the Armenian turned Mussulman at the edge of the Crusader camp. As they passed through the squared up streets in the town of tents, Bohemond caught sight of Alexandra staring ardently after them. He was still impressed at how his nephew had inveigled Adhemar into letting him keep his doxy when all the rest of the drabs were sent over the Orontes for the sake of the camp's sanctification. "I'm surprised you don't take that little Greek chit of yours up to stay at the tower. I wager she'd welcome the attention."

Tancred looked around in confusion, and seeing his forgotten ward, greeted her with a half-hearted wave. Her eyes brightened immediately, and her pouting lips opened up like a flower into a full and radiant smile. Tancred reckoned that if Bohemond had not been there, the neglected girl would have assuredly run to his side and accosted him with a myriad of questions. She was not one to be put off by a cool reception, and Ralph *did* say that she had been waiting all day to speak to him.

Glimpsing Alexandra's distant figure at the end of the row of tents, the marquis could not help but compare her with the other lady he had admired all afternoon at the back of the mountain. Her curly chestnut hair was matted here and there with grease and dirt, not smooth and long and combed to shining splendor. The hem of her formerly green dress hung in tatters about her ankles instead of floating from her waist in a diaphanous cloud of cool blue. Her feet were grubby and bare, with no silken slippers to hide them from view. Her brown eyes had enough of a shine to them, but there was no fascination shrouding the rest of her unveiled face.

But at the same time, Tancred could not refrain from remembering what resolution and audacity Alexandra had demonstrated to bring herself thus far on the journey. Would the sultana's sister have hazarded her all and crossed a continent to avenge her father? Would the Turkish princess have bound herself with a vow to follow the Crusade till it reached Jerusalem? If Alexandra's dress was tattered and torn, it was the difficulty of the pilgrimage that had done it. If the girl was unkempt and unwashed, it was the rigors of the siege that had made her so. And all those things could be remedied by a bath, a brush, and a visit to the tailor—as long as she survived till the day when those luxuries came ready to hand.

Tancred's task, as he saw it, was to ensure the latter. He owed it to William, and perhaps a little bit to Alexandra's own merit. "The tower's no place for a woman," he told his uncle. "We're cut off from the rest of the host and in peril of our lives at every sally from the Turks. Alexandra lodges on this side of the city for good reason, and as long as Richard keeps his hands off of her, she's well enough where she is."

His uncle laughed. "And furthermore, you did build it on the site of an old monastery. The dead abbots would doubtless sit upright in their crypt at the sounds of you bedding a wench upstairs."

The two men continued on, offering no further acknowledgement to Alexandra as they passed by. It was the second time that day that she had come in search of the marquis, and the second time that she had failed to catch her quarry. Ever since his improvement of fortune, Tancred had been scrupulous to send her hampers of victuals and handfuls of coins to see to her room and board. But Alexandra's heart wanted more from the marquis than mere generosity.

Her eyes followed the two Normans till they had almost disappeared. Then, tilting her head thoughtfully, she turned her back on them as well and walked briskly to her tent. She had forced herself into the marquis' attention once before—she could do it again if she chose. He would be returning to his tower eventually. There were no shackles holding her here at Bohemond's camp, and she could make the trek up to the western ridge again when the new day came. If the third try was indeed the charmed one, tomorrow promised better things.

When Bohemond and Tancred reached the trysting place, they found the Armenian waiting for them impatiently. Firuz was a fiery little man, his conical helmet swathed in a turban so eye-catchingly bright that it defied all caution. Beside him stood an even smaller version of himself, a lad of about twelve years old, as fidgety and nervous as the patriarch Isaac must have been when he was climbing Mount Moriah with Abraham.

"So, you are here at last, Norman!" said Firuz. "Do you think it polite or politic to keep me waiting so long?"

Bohemond arched his eyebrows sardonically and apologized for his tardiness. He knew when it was necessary to let go of his dignity and humor an inferior. "Well, Firuz, have you made up your mind to admit my men?"

"At any hour, on any night, at any door of your choosing!" replied the disloyal castellan with vehemence. "And if you should see Nazar when you come through the gate—That son of a dog! May his eyes fall out and his genitals rot away!—I pray you spare him not."

Bohemond and Tancred exchanged a puzzled look. They prodded Firuz with a few careful questions and learned that his rancor arose from a startling discovery of duplicity in his domestic life. It seems that this Nazar—a strapping young member of the Turkish garrison at the Tower of the Two Sisters—had the habit of leaving his post for long lunches in the afternoons. His unsavory appetite led him down a winding street to the house of his superior, and the lunch period culminated in a bedroom tete-a-tete with the tower warden's wife.

Firuz had only just found out the truth, and the discovery had emphatically eliminated any misgivings he might have had regarding Bohemond's proposal. The profligate Nazar had rendered the entire Turkish race odious to him.

"Here is my son as a guarantee," he said, putting the anxious lad forward with a less than tender shove. "If I do not admit your men as promised, you may do with him what you will." Bohemond thanked him for his unsentimental offer of collateral, and thus the pact was made.

Now it only remained to discuss the details of the conspiracy. The plan that the two men settled on was simple, but with enough of a subtle edge that it would catch the garrison off guard. On the following day Bohemond would lead out a troop of his men eastward over the Iron Bridge—as if they were going out on a foraging expedition or abandoning the siege altogether. When night fell, they would circle back to the western side of the city where Firuz would be waiting. He would admit a few men who could then surprise the gatehouse keepers, deal them a swift death with the sword, and work the winch to raise the portcullis. Firuz would unbar the great wooden doors and the waiting army would sweep inside the sleeping city. While Bohe-

330 | ROSANNE E. LORTZ

mond's men acted like a wedge to hold the way open, the rest of the army would mobilize and enter behind them.

Once the plan had been settled, Firuz salaamed his fellow conspirators and prepared to slink back into the city. His apprehensive offspring would remain behind as hostage in the Crusader camp. "Do as these men say," he told the lad callously and left without so much as an embrace. Perhaps the recent discovery of his wife's liaison had given the Armenian doubts about the boy's own parentage—although judging from the resemblance between father and son, Tancred would be willing to swear that the boy was no bastard.

"Come with me tomorrow!" said Bohemond to his nephew. He grabbed his arm with untrammeled excitement. It was an invitation for Tancred to join his band and share in the glory of the first strike.

The marquis' eyes shone like stars. "Yes, a thousand times yes!" were the words in his throat. But before he could accept his uncle's invitation, a recent remembrance abated his enthusiasm and tied his tongue.

If he set out for the Iron Bridge with Bohemond on the morrow, he would miss his assignation with the sultana's beautiful sister. And if he missed the meeting with her, he would have no chance to warn her of the impending danger that hung over her city. He had promised the sultana he would protect Erminia from the horrors of a sack, and lo, the sack was near at hand.

And yet, at the same time, if he rejected Bohemond's offer he would reject a part in the greatest adventure that the Crusaders had yet encountered. He would forgo all share in the capture of Antioch and forfeit the glory of the whole enterprise.

The dilemma was excruciating.

"Gramercy for your offer, uncle, but I had best keep to my tower in case of any sudden sallies by the garrison."

Bohemond stared at him in disbelief. This was not the Tancred he knew. His nephew was a three-year-old stallion always champing at the bit to bound ahead of the others. "Surely you can place one of your men in command of the tower?"

Tancred kicked aside some pebbles with his toe. "There is no one I trust so much. I must stay behind myself. Perhaps I can join your company later when you make the midnight assault?"

Bohemond shook his head, offended that his generous offer had been so spurned. "I shall send for you once the city is taken, and you can crawl in on your belly through the dust of our horses. I had not thought a nephew of mine would be so lacking in spirit."

Tancred, sore at heart that he must hang back from this great endeavor, only grunted in response. He took his leave of Bohemond with a bearish good-bye and made his own trek back to the western side of the city. It tasted as bitter as gall to miss out on the mission to infiltrate the city. But at least the girl was beautiful—that sweetened the draught a little.

# Chapter 52

The next day inched by like an indolent caterpillar as Tancred waited for his tryst on Mount Silpius. Every hour he imagined what Bohemond must be doing—mounting up his men, making a feint to the eastward, doubling back north of the Orontes. In between, he watched the sun and counted up the hours till Erminia would appear at the postern gate. He half expected Alexandra to importune him with her presence sometime that afternoon, but surprisingly, the tower remained destitute of any distractions besides those swarming in his own mind.

As the sun began to toy with the idea of descending in the west, Tancred gratefully surrendered command of his men to Ralph and struck out across the ridge. This time the emerald ring was on his hand instead of tucked into his belt. As he climbed up the crags behind the citadel, he was hopeful this was the last day that the tight-fitting circlet would gnaw on the base of his knuckle.

The rugged terrain of the ridge made it easy for Tancred to conceal his silhouette as he advanced closer to the walls of the citadel. It also made it easy for any others roaming the hillside to hide themselves. A few times Tancred heard showers of falling pebbles to the rearward, in the ground he had just covered. He wheeled around sharply, trying to discern if he was being followed—but for all his caution he never caught sight of anything more fearsome than a family of rock badgers. Running a hand through his blond hair, he ordered his nerves to cease their needless worrying.

He had expected to arrive at the postern first, but Erminia was already outside, seated in the same rocky niche and waiting for him.

"Well met, messenger," she said, using Greek since it must be closer to the man's native tongue. "Do you have the ring?"

In all his thoughts Tancred had imagined her robed in gossamer blue, but she had surprised him by changing her gown to another of gold silk. It suited her, even better than the last. The bodice caught every curve of her upper body and a jeweled girdle bound it tightly to her waist. The same soft veil hid all of her face save her eyes, and the same red slippers came to a point on her little feet.

"Aye, I have it." Tancred wrenched off the ring and held it aloft as a token of good faith. Scanning the towers above for sign of the sentries, he stepped out of the concealing crags and into the streambed.

"You may toss it to me," she said preemptively. She did not want the *Franj* to come any closer.

He ignored her and continued to pick his way across the water, trying to step on stones only half submerged and keep his breeches dry. Her hands tightened on the folds of her skirt. Perhaps she had made a mistake in coming to meet the *Franj* alone. But at the same time, she could hardly have invited one of the governor's guards to accompany her. Her uncle paid them handsomely to report every one of her actions to him—a waste of good coin since her ready wit and resourceful wiles could easily elude their surveillance whenever she wished.

With the water crossed, Tancred ducked his tall, blond head under the outcropping of rock. He took a seat beside the Turkish damsel without being invited. It was a necessary precaution in case the sentries should look this way. It was a disconcerting presumption, and Erminia's nervousness continued to grow.

He was holding the ring in his hands now, playing with it much as Michael Podromos had played with his golden bauble. But still, he made no move to give it to her.

"Tell me, lady, do you ever go down from the citadel into the city below?"

"Yes, often," she said shortly, and then paused. What could he mean by asking her that? "The air is too stifling in the heights, and one grows weary of the smallness and the sameness in the gardens above."

"It were better that you should not go down into the lower city tonight or in the morning."

"Why?" she asked pointedly. She would not take orders or even suggestions from a stranger without a reason.

Tancred hesitated, unsure how much of Bohemond's plot it was safe to reveal. "There may be an assault on the city tonight. I would not wish to see you harmed."

"Ha!" she said, her dark eyes flashing with disdain. "You *Franj* have been here for seven months and more. When have you ever assaulted the place and succeeded?"

"Tonight will be different."

"Only in the amount of your losses! Now give me my ring, sirrah!" The sleeve of gold silk fluttered around her wrist as she held out her hand imperiously.

Tancred's brows contracted. Her scorn had stung him like a stand of nettles, but it had not lessened her beauty one whit. He was possessed, more than ever, with the desire to see her face. With one hand he dropped the ill-fated emerald on her open palm. With the other he reached out and pulled off her veil.

The thin piece of fabric fell to the ground and left Erminia's countenance uncovered. The soft redness of her lips shimmered softly in the twilight. The curve of her cheeks begged to be caressed. Her dark eyes, now set in the full frame of her face, became even more enchanting. The sultana had been right—there could not be two women of such surpassing beauty in the whole of Antioch.

It was a beauty, however, that Tancred would have little time to bask in. When the rough Norman pulled the veil from her face, Erminia screamed as if she had been stabbed. Any Turk who dared to touch her so would have been made a eunuch at once by the command of her uncle. Her life up until now had been shielded, but not sheltered from an understanding of the world and its evils. Everything she knew cried out for her to flee before it was too late.

And yet the stranger made no move to press his advantage further. Perhaps the *Franj* were not as wicked as the gossiping grandmothers

ROAD FROM THE WEST | 335

said. The soft breeze wafted over her face reminding her of her disha-
bille. She looked down for her veil but saw that his hand still clutched
it. Something about the man's boldness fascinated her, like the stare of
a hooded cobra. She scented danger —and the aroma drew her in until
she had no more ability to flee than had a desert flower but remained
rooted to the spot.

He was leaning closer now, his face no more than a hand's-breadth
away from her own. Erminia's breath came quicker, and she sent the
stranger a shy glance from underneath her eyelashes. With his light-
skinned face and golden hair, he was as handsome as Adonis. He must be
twice as broad in the shoulders as her cousin Shams and two head taller
than her sister's husband Kilij Arslan. She met his eyes and held his gaze
and—for the briefest of moments—neither could turn their head away.

But the scream that she had uttered still lay between them. It was
too late to retract it. The sentinels in the towers above may have been
lax but they were not utterly foolhardy. Footsteps pounded on the
walkway above the tower, and the sentries called out to each other in
delayed alarm. It was only a matter of minutes before a detachment
from the garrison would come outside to investigate.

A sense of responsibility for the safety of her sister's messenger
overwhelmed Erminia. She put her fingers to her mouth with a little
gasp. "Stay hidden here, and perhaps they will not find you,"—but the
moment that had passed between them was gone, and the *Franj* was
already busy loosening his sword in its scabbard.

Three of the guards, burly men with round shields and curved
swords, issued from the postern and stepped into the stream. They
fanned out to search for the origin of the screech that the lookouts had
heard. The princess put a quiet hand on Tancred's arm, urging him to
hang back behind the outcropping that hid them from view.

But the marquis had already made up his mind about the best
way to extricate himself from the imbroglio. Perhaps he knew that if
the Turks came forward another score of paces they would sight him
without question. Perhaps he did not want to be surrounded by stone
on three sides with the stream between him and his camp.

Whatever his thoughts were, he shook off Erminia's restraining hand with a muttered, "No, milady." He clapped some steadying fingers over his long scabbard to keep it from tripping him up, then bolted out of the niche and across the stream with the speed of a running fox.

The Turks heard the splashes, saw the runner, and gave a yell. Tancred, on his own side of the ridge now, made sure that the mountainside would screen him from arrows above. Then, drawing his sword, he swung around to face his assailants. They had already regrouped and were advancing toward him, snarling and slavering like a pack of wild dogs.

Now was the time for Erminia to slip back inside the postern and secure her own safety. Instead, she stood transfixed. They had surrounded him, three men to one, and he did not even have a shield to fend them off. A jabber from the top of the battlements revealed that the struggle was being observed. But no more of the garrison exited the postern—one *Franj* should be easy enough for three Turks to deal with.

But the marquis was adept at fighting outnumbered. His left hand had pulled a dagger from the flap of his worn-out boots. With one blade in each hand, feet planted apart, he was more than holding his own against the black-mustached Turks.

He had closed with one of them now and slashed through the man's throat with his dagger while his longsword held off the others. Erminia saw the bright splash of blood on the marquis' coat—none of his own, she was certain. She rubbed the emerald ring between her thumb and forefinger with preoccupied intensity, willing him to come through the encounter unscathed.

The fall of one Turk rendered the two remaining ones more cautious. This Western knight was the devil himself with a sword. They inched their way around to the two opposite poles of his circle of defense and made a concerted attack. Tancred's right hand, holding the longsword, easily parried the mad swings of one opponent's scimitar. His left hand, gripping only a dagger, was not so successful. The Turk caught the tip of the dagger on his shield, and with a downward cut of his own blade managed to draw blood from Tancred's thigh. It was the same thigh that had sustained the arrow wound at Dorylaeum. The marquis cried out involuntarily from the pain.

Delighted at the hit, the second Turk relaxed his vigilance—an unfortunate and fatal mistake. Tancred, without taking a moment to recover from the blow, lurched toward his attacker. Just before his leg buckled under him and sent him sinking into the ground, he swung his left hand around his assailant's shield rim. His double-edged dagger plunged full into the Turk's eye and pierced through his brainpan.

It was a mortal blow, and a bloody one at that. As Tancred wrenched out the dagger with a twist, the dying Turk stumbled forward and collapsed on top of the *Franj*. The marquis bent to the side and allowed the body to fall over his, a shield against the one remaining scimitar.

The third Turk should have finished the marquis then, before he had time to get to his feet. But the suddenness and sanguinariness of his companion's fall had unnerved him. His scimitar wobbled with hesitation.

Using his powerful shoulders, Tancred heaved the bleeding corpse off of himself and into the shins of the faltering Turk. At the same time, he rolled rapidly in the opposite direction. While the Turk stumbled over his fellow, Tancred pulled himself up against a boulder and leaned on his good leg to stand. The black-mustached man disentangled himself and charged with a fury—but now Tancred was ready for him. Longsword met scimitar, the longer blade won, and one more was added to the count of the dead.

Erminia, watching it all from across the stream, wrung her hands in dismay. The *Franj* was wounded—she could not tell how badly. The collapse of the second corpse had drenched his head and shoulders in blood, and she saw that he leaned on the boulders to give himself strength to stand. Shouts rang from the battlements. More members of the garrison were coming down to dispatch the interloper.

Erminia paled. The immediacy of the danger did not give her time to examine her own thoughts, but she did not want the *Franj* to die— that she knew. The wound must be staunched and the man helped to safety. Lifting up the hem of her silken skirt, she stepped into the stream to cross to his side.

"No!" shouted Tancred from between clenched teeth forbidding the girl to come to him. If he had to fight another bout with more Turks, he did not want Erminia in the thick of it. "Get you inside! And remember what I said—do not leave the citadel!" He turned his back on her and, limping severely, slipped out of sight behind a shelf of rock.

Instead of following him, she hesitated—a weakness for which she could not forgive herself later—and was still standing in the stream when the warriors burst out of the secret postern.

"Princess!" said Abdullah, one of her uncle's best warriors. He was astonished to see both her person and her bare face outside the citadel, but now was not the time to sift through the mystery. "Which way went the *Franj*?"

"That way!" responded Erminia, pointing to the east. Misdirection was the only means of assistance the fleeing *Franj* would let her render. Abdullah herded her protectively back into the citadel and issued his men orders to fan out over the eastern side of Mount Silpius. The top rim of the sun had just slipped below the horizon when the Turks began their search. By the time they realized that the lady had been altogether in error, the sky had darkened enough to obscure the trail of blood that would have led them to the wounded man.

Meanwhile, the marquis hobbled westward, feeling his strength ebb as his wound continued to seep blood. He scanned the rockery for a hole or cave in which he could conceal himself, but nothing suggested itself as practicable. Small slides of pebbles played tricks on his ears and he felt watched from every direction. Weary as a woman after childbirth, he leaned up against the granite cliff face. The daylight had long since departed, but the stone was still warm from the afternoon sun. Pressing his blood-crusted cheek against the rock, he closed his eyes and breathed a prayer.

"Here, lean on me," said an urgent voice. Looking down, Tancred saw the tangled mess of Alexandra's chestnut curls. With a sigh of relief, he did as she bid, and together they wended a slow and painful way back to the tower.

# Chapter 53

"Thank you," said Tancred to Alexandra, panting heavily as Ralph eased him into a chair. The old manservant untied the makeshift tourniquet that Alexandra had torn from the hem of her dress. "You tried to kill me once, but tonight you've succeeding in saving me. Now we are quits."

"Oh, no, my lord. You will not be quit of me till we reach Jerusalem," she said pertly. "And not even then, if I have *my* way," she refrained from adding.

"How is your uncle's plan succeeding?" asked Ralph, surreptitiously trying to discover whether his master had been with Bohemond when he received his injuries.

Tancred, unwilling to discuss the events at the back of Mount Silpius—or the sultana's sister—gave a vague answer. "We will know nothing till dawn. My uncle is circling around behind the Orontes even now, and if the moon shines clear we may even see his men creeping through the plain below our tower tonight."

Ralph, having cut off the marquis' breeches at the thigh and cleaned the wound, tutted anxiously. "You'll be in no condition to storm the city in the morning."

"I daresay he's in fine enough condition to pay more visits at the back of the citadel," piped up Alexandra.

Tancred looked at her sharply. Could it be that she had been spying on him all through the evening during his tryst with Erminia? It would explain how she had come upon him—ostensibly by chance—after his combat with the three Turks. "If you know what is good for you,

you will hold your tongue," he said, completely forgetting the recent service she had done for him.

"As you wish," she replied saucily, in a tone that begged him to beat her.

Ralph harrumphed grouchily and sent Alexandra away. He made up his mind to wheedle the story out of the girl later. There was some mystery here regarding the marquis and, as Tancred's faithful servant, it was his duty to discover it.

All that night Tancred lay awake. It was more from anticipation than from pain, for Ralph had procured a draught of poppy juice to ease the latter. Half the time his mind mulled over Bohemond's itinerary. Had his men already slithered through the plain like a nest of asps and stolen up to the base of Firuz's tower? The other half of the time it wandered back to the dark-eyed Erminia. Had she obeyed his pleading orders and kept herself inside the citadel?

Throughout all the days of hardship at Antioch his soul had burned to beat down the gates and sack the city. But now, as much as he longed for its overthrow, he dreaded it too. Would the sultana's fears prove true and her sister be caught up in the sack? Erminia's long-lashed eyes had bewitched him beyond what he had thought possible—and she a Mohammedan too!

The taking of Antioch was a tale that Tancred would experience secondhand. Both his refusal to accompany his uncle and the injury to his leg forbade him a part in the most long-awaited triumph of the Crusade.

When Bohemond's Normans approached the Tower of the Two Sisters, it was already the third watch of the night. As Firuz had promised, he was waiting for them in the lowest of the tower windows. He let down a ladder, made of thin but sturdy rope, and held it steady while sixty of Bohemond's best men crawled up the wall like a cluster of spiders. Following Firuz's instructions, they crept quietly through the rooms of the tower, surprising the Turkish guards one by one and silencing them with a slash to the throat. The lecherous Nazar was one of the first to fall. He had been posted specially on watch that night— Firuz had made sure of it.

Once the Tower of the Two Sisters had been fully secured, the Normans glided across the walls that branched out to right and left. More sentries were slaughtered and toppled over the openings in the crenelated ramparts. The two adjoining towers succumbed as easily as Firuz's ward.

It was time to bring up more manpower.

As the darkness began to break, the walls between the three captured towers grew rungs of rope like ivy. Hundreds of men poured over the walls and readied themselves to rush on the city. Firuz found scores of Christian Armenians happy to help in the monumental task of unbarring the Gate of St. George. On this exciting day of deliverance, they were only too willing to forget he had converted to the infidel faith and sycophantically served their overlords. Firuz was ready and willing to forget that matter too.

The redness of dawn revealed Bohemond's own crimson banner flying over the Tower of the Two Sisters, furling and unfurling in the wind. Three of the five mighty gates had swung open, and the mounted knights could enter now. The Turks in the towers not yet compromised sent out outraged horn blasts of appeal as Crusaders of every stripe poured in to attack the city. But the invaders were everywhere by now. Each cohort of the garrison was too hard pressed to come to another's aid.

Those living in the heart of the lower city woke up hearing tumult and wondering what could be the cause of such commotion. Their first guess was that Kerbogha—with his promised aid—had come at last! But when mounted Latins and looting rabble began to stream through their streets, they were swiftly disabused of this notion. Every Turk with a grain of sense snatched up his silver and ran like a rabbit up to the safety of the citadel. Not all of them found their way to the heights before the way was cut off.

The Crusaders' procession through the city was a wild and disorganized affair. The proven soldiers kept to warfare, not pillage, systematically eradicating every Turk they laid eyes on. But the mixed multitude of camp followers was not so discriminate. Firuz's own brother was killed, and many of the Christian folk lost property and pretty daughters to the ravages of the red cross raiders.

Tancred, although he had not yet entered the city, was the first to learn what had befallen the Turkish governor Cassian. Later that day, a farmer from the foothills hiked up to the marquis' outpost. In his hands he held a bloody bag and he made no apologies for its gruesome contents.

"The governor and his guards came riding through my land," he said in garbled Greek. "They were hurrying like hell itself was after them, and the ground was parlous rough. The governor's mount stumbled and fell on him—and the others would not stop to save him from the wreckage."

The farmer, with more of an eye to the horse than the man, had tromped over the field himself to see if anything might be salvaged. The horse had broken a foreleg and was not worth helping. But the rider, although bruised from the fall and wounded in several places during his escape from the city, was very much alive.

"Antioch is lost! The Franks hold it!" bemoaned Cassian as he pulled himself up from the ground. He was determined to avoid a similar fate. The stolid famer stared stupidly as the governor promised him power, influence, and the greatest of all rewards if he would only keep his presence a secret. "I will find a horse and flee at dusk," he said. "But in the name of the Prophet, tell no one that I am here."

However slow-witted the farmer may have been, he was quick enough when it came to scenting profit. If the *Franj* were in possession of Antioch, their star was assuredly rising. And how likely was it that the fleeing governor would remember his promised reward?

Anticipating greater and more reliable generosity from the new governors of Antioch, the farmer hardened his heart to Cassian's pleas. He seized up a spade and made sure the wounded man would not get up again. Inside the sack was the sawed off head of Antioch's governor—although even his closest kin would be hard put to identify him as such. The farmer had bludgeoned him so thoroughly before decapitating him that the face was hardly recognizable.

Tancred tossed the bag back to the farmer with disgust. He was still chafing at his exclusion from the assault and was in no mood to exhibit largesse. "Bring your trophy to Bohemond, the new duke of Antioch. *He* will reward you for your pains."

As noonday approached, Tancred's men approached him en masse with a petition to put before him. "Why should Bohemond's men get all the glory of the capture?" asked Turold, pushed forward by his fellows as the unwilling spokesman. "Aye, and the Franks and Germans too! If you lead us into Antioch now, we might at least see a few scraps of action before our comrades secure every sector of the city."

Tancred's natural temperament prompted him to refuse their request. As a child, when he could not beat his opponent at draughts, he would petulantly refuse to play at all. In the same way, if he could not be the first over the walls of the city, he did not wish to play the auxiliary. But even though his natural impulses incited him to sulk in the tower, other reasons—imperative and pressing—joined with the pleas of his men. "Very well, in we shall go!" said Tancred. He mounted a horse to save his injured leg, and after forming his Normans up into lines, marched them hastily through the Gate of St. George.

Inside, they found Bohemond assuming the role of grand seigneur and proudly assigning portions of the city as lodgings for the other Crusader companies. Just as Tancred had foreseen, Bohemond had been delighted by the farmer's grisly gift and had rewarded him handsomely. At the command of the new duke, the bagged head and a written demand of surrender were tossed over the walls of the citadel.

It did not take long for the Turks entrenched in the heights to send an answer back. "What is Yaghi-Siyan's head to us when we still hold the head of the city?" The reply was written by Cassian's son Shams and struck them all with its lack of filial sentiment.

"It is no more than we always expected," said Bohemond to the others. "Now that we hold the lower city, we shall have to set another siege and fight for the citadel itself."

There was still some cleaning up to do, however, before the Crusaders would even attempt a rush on the heights. While Tancred's men scattered through the streets to see if there was any plunder still to be had, Tancred single-mindedly strode to the city's refuse heap. Here they were already piling the unlucky casualties of the day.

"Is this all the dead?"

"Probably not," shrugged one of the Syrian citizens. Bohemond, in an effort to clear the streets, had pressed some of the citizens into service as pallbearers.

"Have you seen a girl among them? Turkish? Of surpassing beauty—one you could not forget if you tried?"

Every head shook in ignorance. How could one woman, however beautiful, stand out in the stench of so many dead? "I do not think you Latins left a single Turk alive," said an Armenian cobbler. His voice was devoid of sympathy. Indeed, the Armenians, Greeks, and Syrians had been only too ready to offer up their Turkish neighbors to the fury of the foreign invaders.

Abandoning the Golgotha at the edge of the city, Tancred urged his mount on through the streets and voiced his questions in every crossroads. Each uncomprehending shake of the head gave him greater confidence that Erminia had remained in the unmolested citadel. But how could he be sure?

It was Firuz, the fiery, little Armenian from the Tower of the Two Sisters, who provided the certainty he sought. "Ah, yes, the Princess Emine, Chaka Bey's daughter," he said. "She often goes about the city surrounded by her uncle's guard."

"But not last night!" said Tancred fiercely. "Surely, not last night?"

Firuz clucked impatiently. "Antioch is a great city. How could I know such a thing?" His protruding eyes sized up Tancred. "But for the right price, master, I could find the answers you seek."

Tancred reached into his purse and paid the man without a quibble. Firuz barked out a name, and within seconds his summons was answered. Out came the twelve-year-old lad who had played the hostage all last night. Once the gates were breached, Bohemond had faithfully returned the boy to Firuz, and so he was ready at hand to be of service to his father again.

Firuz and his son gabbled unintelligibly in the Armenian tongue. Then the lad obediently took to his heels. It was his lot in life, it seemed, to be imperiled for the profit of his progenitor.

"The boy has many friends, the sons of Turks," explained Firuz. "He will inquire of them at the citadel and learn what you would know."

The walls of the upper fortress were bristling with watchful and wild-eyed men, but by means of secret paths—the specialty of half-grown boys—Firuz's son gained both entrance and conference with his friends. Then it was back to his father, to spill out the information he had garnered and be rewarded with a box to the ear.

"What does he say?" demanded Tancred, who had drummed his fingers anxiously for the whole hour that it took for the lad to run his errand.

Firuz prefaced his news with the cynicism of a man recently cuckolded. "I warn you, young master, it is folly to care so much about the fate of a woman. She will do you harm and not good all the days of her life. No matter how fair of skin she seems, her heart is deceitful above all things."

A growl from the marquis cut short his rant. "Spare me your sermons and spit out your story before I grow weary of waiting and spit you with my sword."

"Very well, very well. You asked about the Princess Emine, and I have learned that she is indeed alive. She stayed in the citadel all through the night and suffered no scathe when I delivered the city into your hands. This much my son tells me with a certainty—the rest is women's talk and not fit for my lord's ears."

Tancred, desperate for any information about Erminia no matter how riddled with rumor, plied the Armenian with a few more coins. Firuz lost his reticence to tell tales.

"Why, you must already know, that the lady's uncle Cassian had promised her to Duqaq of Damascus if he could relieve Antioch from your siege. And you must also know that Duqaq failed. When your uncle drove him away at the New Year, he lost both his prestige and his promised wife. But now, if the rumors are to be believed, Emine's cousin Shams has extended the same offer to another."

Firuz's bulging eyes locked onto the clear, blue gaze of the Norman.
"They say that if Kerbogha of Mosul can retake Antioch from the
*Franj*, he will win himself a bride as well as a battle."

# Chapter 54

I t was Richard of Salerno who brought the fateful news only two days later. "Pennants in the east!" he cried, dismounting rapidly from his ragged mount. After the capture of the city, Bohemond had deputized his cousin to hold the two towers that flanked the Iron Bridge. His lookouts would be the first to sight any comers—and the first to fall before any sudden onslaught. "An army as big as the sea is advancing along the Orontes!"

With characteristic glibness, Richard had released the terrible tidings like a barrel of rats into the streets before he had even made a formal report to Bohemond or the other commanders. "Alexios?" asked a few optimistic souls, but deep in his bones every man knew it was Kerbogha.

"I'll not be keeping to my post much longer," Richard informed his cousin as he made preparations to withdraw his contingent from the Iron Bridge. "I'm as brave as any man if it comes to reasonable odds, but when there's only nine stone arches—the length of a bridge bed—between you and the devil's hordes, it's time to retreat to the ramparts and shrive your soul."

Richard had no sooner quitted his post than Kerbogha marched into the plain, his soldiers' feet drumming the sunbaked ground like the timpani of war. There was no vacillation on the Mussulmen's part when they surrounded the city to besiege it. It had taken the Crusaders six months to enclose the western gates. Kerbogha did the same in less than six days.

The Crusaders quickly learned to what dire straits they had depleted Antioch's granaries, for it was from those same granaries that their own men now must eat. "First a famine without and now a famine within," remarked Bernard blackly. He had helped Tancred limp up to the top of the St. Paul's gatehouse, and together they were surveying the thicket of Turkish tents that had sprung up around the city.

"At least we have these walls to protect us from that forest of spears!" Tancred lifted his eyes up to the citadel. "Although I grant that we will be hard pressed to withstand sallies from below at the same time as sallies from above."

He gave a sigh. Erminia must be seeing these same sights from an even higher vantage point. How did she view Kerbogha? A repulsive suitor? A gallant rescuer?

Bernard, oblivious to his companion's mood, had settled his thoughts on an entirely different subject than that which occupied Tancred. He began to chuckle softly, his gaunt frame shaking spasmodically with some unknown hilarity.

"You are a happy man, Bernard, if you can find a path to laughter through such a barren landscape."

"I have my small satisfactions," replied the chaplain. "I heard just today that your uncle has given Count Raymond the worst place of all to lodge in the city." He did not bother to mask the approval in his voice. "Crumbling brick, vermin, no access to the aqueduct…. But I daresay he will not stand the slight for long. Bohemond may have gained the dukedom, but Raymond will find some way to make himself more important in the eyes of the army."

"I am still beholden to him," said Tancred with more sympathy than his companion. "Perhaps I could intercede for him with my uncle."

"I'd sooner intercede for the devil's dam," said Bernard spitefully, strong words on the tongue of a tonsured cleric.

"Surely, a chaplain's prayers can be put to better use," replied Tancred with merriment. Then slowly, a shadow passed over his face like the cloud over the sun. His eyes grew as grave as his father Odo and twice as sad. "Use your intercessions for me, my friend. My soul could stand to have some paternosters prayed over it."

Bernard shrugged off Tancred's melancholy with the indifference of a man who has nothing to confess, or has become so comfortable in his filth that he would rather stay unwashed. The marquis went no further in confiding in the chaplain. He had poured out his fearful dreams in Urban's ears, but there was no one here who could exorcise the misgivings that continued to plague his soul.

When he lay down that night, enveloped by the threats of Kerbogha's army, another circle of horrors besieged his sleep. He saw his uncle led away in chains by the Turks, the diadem of his new dukedom fallen askew over his brow. And in the chair that should have held Bohemond, he watched himself sit down. He saw Adhemar and Urban, cold and white, two ghosts who could no longer be heard. They wandered here and there through the city, but all men were blind to their presence.

He searched everywhere for Erminia and found her not, until he had raked through the whole of the refuse heap at the edge Antioch. Her dress of gold was dull and tarnished, and when he raised her cold body in his arms it felt as light as famished Alexandra. Blood was everywhere, on her face, in her hair—but on her lifeless finger the emerald ring still gleamed.

From the heights of Mount Silpius, a roll of thunder came down, the voice of the black-cowled man with his pitiless indictment. "All this misery has come about because of thee, sinner. And thinkest thou wilt escape the judgment of thy God?"

The shuddering dreamer awoke in his bed. He was three hundred miles from Jerusalem, encompassed by myriads of foes, and encumbered as much as ever by his conscience and unfulfilled vows. The one promise he had fulfilled afforded him no more peace than the others—now the sultana's sister haunted his dreams as well.

# Author's Note

Tancred, the marquis of nobody-knows-where, is hardly the typical poster boy of the First Crusade. That honor belongs to Godfrey of Bouillon or, to a lesser degree, to Baldwin, Raymond, or Bohemond. I began my research for this book in the summer of 2009, oblivious to Tancred's existence and intending to tell the story of Adhemar, the Bishop of Le Puy. But as I pored over the primary sources, I kept running into this brash young nephew of Bohemond's, first on the line of battle, first in the fire of controversy, and first over the walls of Jerusalem. Who was this warrior that dared to beard the Emperor of the Byzantines to his face?

Bit by bit, my projected plot revised itself until I discovered that Tancred had usurped the position of protagonist in my story. His dramatic exploits refused to be bound by the covers of a single novel, and what started as an idea for one book turned into plans for two and eventually into an outline for an entire trilogy—*The Chronicles of Tancred*. As you have seen, *Road from the West* takes Tancred all the way from Italy to Antioch as he earns his place among the leaders of the Crusade. The two following books, *Flower of the Desert* and *Prince of the East*, will show Tancred's role in the conquest of Jerusalem and the establishment of the Latin kingdoms in the East.

All of the main characters in *Road from the West* are historical personages with the exceptions of Ralph, Alexandra, and Erminia. I invented Ralph, Tancred's faithful old servant, to provide a link between the marquis and his grandfather, Robert Guiscard. Through Ralph we can see snapshots of the Normans' failed expedition against Constantinople and the close ties they developed with Urban's predecessor, Pope

Gregory. Ralph also provides a voice of wisdom and experience for the young marquis—something he is not always inclined to listen to.

Alexandra is a representation of the hundreds of faceless women who journeyed alongside the more masculine members of the First Crusade. Individually, the female travelers received very little attention from the medieval chroniclers, but we do know that Pope Urban's speeches inspired the Crusading fervor in women as well as men. Alexandra—although she joins the Crusade for reasons of her own—shows the vulnerable position that many of these women pilgrims would have found themselves in and also provides a window into Tancred's guilt and his sense of responsibility for his followers.

Erminia is a composite character based on the two heroines from the sixteenth century epic *Jerusalem Delivered*. This poem by the Italian writer Torquato Tasso, showcases Erminia, the daughter of the emir of Antioch, and Clorinda, an Amazon-like warrior in the camp of the Muslims, both of which have a romantic interest in the tempestuous Tancred. I'll say no more now—lest I risk revealing too much of the story—but Erminia's character will receive much more development in *Flower of the Desert*, the second book of the trilogy.

Some of the terms used throughout this novel deserve a little further clarification than can be had in the story itself. One may be tempted to assume that the eleventh century titles of duke, count, lord, and marquis follow the same elaborate ranking system as they do in an eighteenth century English peerage. In the time of the First Crusade, however, these titles were still very fluid. It is impossible to rank the political importance of the Crusaders on the basis of their titles alone. The same could also be said for the titles in the Islamic world. Kilij Arslan, who styles himself as a sultan, is hardly more powerful than Kerbogha, the *atabeg* (governor) of Mosul, and an emir may mean anything from the commander of a troop to the ruler of a vast territory.

I have chosen to call the brothers from Boulogne and their host *Germans* in order to make an easy separation between them and the Franks. Although their lands would today fall inside the borders of France, in the eleventh century they were under the sway of the Holy

Roman Empire. Steven Runciman, the premier historian of the Crusades, refers to the three brothers as *Lorrainers*.

As in any historical endeavor, one of the joys of this project has been reconciling different—and differing—source material. The chroniclers of the First Crusade tend to disagree as much as the leaders themselves. Although these discrepancies can be time-consuming and frustrating, they are also eminently understandable since each eyewitness sees things with a unique perspective and each historian was attached to a different contingent of the Crusade. The case of the Armenian traitor Firuz is a prime example; here the historians give as many variations of the story as they do variants on his name.

The writer of the *Gesta* states that an emir named Pirus was convinced of Christianity by Bohemond and agreed to turn over his three towers to the Normans. Anna Comnena, the daughter of Emperor Alexios, avers that Bohemond persuaded the Armenian to betray his trust by means of "flagrant cajolery and a series of attractive guarantees." Fulcher of Chartres records that the traitor was a Turk, not an Armenian; he was incited to action by a dream wherein Christ commanded him to place the city in the hands of the Christians. Ralph of Caen returns to the Armenian identification and depicts the traitor as the father of a large family. When Cassian confiscated the grain that the man had stored up to feed his children, he determined to hand over the Tower of the Two Sisters to Bohemond out of desperation and revenge.

The Islamic chroniclers have their own details to add. The Muslim historian Ibn al-Athir calls the traitor an armor-maker named Ruzbih whom the Franks bribed with a fortune in money and lands. His countryman Ibn al-Qalanisi states that the betrayal was a cabal among several of the armor-makers who were unhappy about some ill-usage and confiscations at the hands of the governor. Steven Runciman's authoritative work conflates several of these versions plus another rumor circulated later, that Firouz "had been hesitating right up till the evening before, when he discovered that his wife was compromised with one of his Turkish colleagues."

My version of Firuz's betrayal strives to do justice to as many of the accounts as I can while still creating an enjoyable story for the reader—and indeed, that is the goal I have striven towards with *every* episode and chapter of this novel. The story of the First Crusade is a tale of perseverant heroes, unexaggerated peril, and quests both spiritual and temporal. It has been my privilege to unfold that story for you. I look forward to finishing the adventure in the next two books of *The Chronicles of Tancred*.

Rosanne E. Lortz

# Selected Bibliography

Anna Comnena. *The Alexiad.* Trans. E. R. A. Sewter. England: Penguin Books, 1969.

Bachrach, Bernard S. and David S. Bachrach, trans. *The Gesta Tancredi of Ralph of Caen: A History of the Normans on the First Crusade.* Great Britain: Ashgate Publishing Company, 2005.

Benjamin of Tudela. *The Itinerary of Benjamin of Tudela: Travels in the Middle Ages.* Trans. Masa'ot shel Rabi Benjamin. Cold Spring, NY: NightinGale Resources, 2010.

France, John. *Victory in the East: A Military History of the First Crusade.* England: Cambridge University Press, 1994.

Hallam, Elizabeth, ed. *Chronicles of the Crusades: Eye-Witness Accounts of the Wars between Christianity and Islam.* New York: Welcome Rain, 2000.

Krey, August C. *The First Crusade: The Accounts of Eye-Witnesses and Participants.* Eugene, OR: Wipf & Stock Publishers, 2007.

Maalouf, Amin. *The Crusades through Arab Eyes.* Trans. Jon Rothschild. New York: Schocken Books, 1984.

Nicholson, Robert L. *Tancred: A Study of His Career and Work.* AMS Press, 1978.

Peters, Edward, ed. *The First Crusade: The Chronicle of Fulcher of Chartres and Other Source Materials*, Second Edition. Philadelphia, PA: University of Pennsylvania Press, 1998.

Riley-Smith, Jonathan, ed. *The Oxford Illustrated History of the Crusades*. New York: Oxford University Press, 1995.

_____. *The First Crusaders, 1095-1131*. England: Cambridge University Press, 1997.

Runciman, Steven. *A History of the Crusades, Volume I: The First Crusade and the Foundation of the Kingdom of Jerusalem*. England: Penguin Books, 1951.

Tasso, Torquato. *Jerusalem Delivered*. Trans. Edward Fairfax. Digital version produced by Douglas B. Killings.

# Principal Characters

## THE CITIZENS OF BARI

| | |
|---|---|
| **Alexander** | A merchant fallen on hard times |
| **Nicholas** | His brother, a goldsmith |
| **Alexandra** | The merchant's intrepid daughter |

## THE MEN OF THE CHURCH

| | |
|---|---|
| **Urban** | The pope who calls for the First Crusade |
| **Guibert** | The antipope set up against Urban by the Holy Roman Emperor |
| **Adhemar** | The Bishop of Le Puy, official leader of the First Crusade |
| **Bernard** | Adhemar's devoted chaplain |
| **Peter the Hermit** | The preacher who led the first wave of unofficial Crusaders |

## THE CRUSADERS FROM GERMANY

| | |
|---|---|
| **Eustace** | The eldest brother from Boulogne, of lesser importance than his brothers |
| **Godfrey** | The second brother from Boulogne, pious and peacemaking |
| **Baldwin** | The third brother from Boulogne, overbearing and dangerous |
| **Godvera** | Baldwin's attractive wife |
| **Rudolph** | A knight of Baldwin's following |

## THE CRUSADERS FROM THE MIDDLE AND SOUTH OF FRANCE

| | |
|---|---|
| **Raymond** | The wealthy Count of Toulouse |
| **William-Jordan** | His aloof nephew |

| | |
|---|---|
| **Hugh the Great** | The ponderous Count of Vermandois, brother to King Philip of France |

## THE CRUSADERS FROM THE NORTH OF FRANCE

| | |
|---|---|
| **Robert** | Duke of Normandy and son of William the Conqueror, a pious but incompetent ruler |
| **Stephen** | Count of Blois and unwilling Crusader, hen-pecked husband of the Conqueror's daughter |
| **Robert** | Count of Flanders, a sturdy and dependable warrior |

## THE BYZANTINES

| | |
|---|---|
| **Alexios Comnenus** | Emperor of Byzantium, hoping to regain the empire's lost lands |
| **John Comnenus** | The governor of Durazzo, Alexios' oily nephew |
| **Michael Podromos** | Alexios' envoy to Bohemond |
| **Manuel Boutoumites** | Alexios' favorite general, a man of very few words |
| **Tatikios** | Alexios' other favorite general, a Turk with a golden nose |

## THE ARMENIANS

| | |
|---|---|
| **Rupen** | The late Armenian king, called the Lord of the Mountains |
| **Constantine** | Rupen's son and heir, whose idealism has harmed his inheritance |
| **Thatoul** | Rupen's second son, the ruler of Marash |
| **Oshin** | One of Rupen's former generals, now king in part of Cilicia |

| | |
|---|---|
| **Thoros** | Another of Rupen's generals, now ruler of the city of Edessa |
| **Bagrat** | An Armenian adventurer who attaches himself to Baldwin |
| **Firuz** | Keeper of the Tower of the Two Sisters in the besieged city of Antioch |

## THE TURKS

| | |
|---|---|
| **Kilij Arslan** | Sultan of Rum, the northern half of Asia Minor |
| **Chaka Bey** | The late emir of Smyrna, Kilij Arslan's father-in-law and ill-fated dinner guest |
| **The Sultana** | The daughter of Chaka Bey, Kilij Arslan's unhappy wife |
| **Erminia** | The Sultana's sister, a girl of surpassing beauty |
| **Cassian** | The governor of Antioch, uncle to Erminia |
| **Shams** | Cassian's son, but not particularly filial |
| **Ridwan** | Ruler of Aleppo and brother to Duqaq |
| **Duqaq** | Ruler of Damascus and brother to Ridwan |
| **Kerbogha** | Atabeg of Mosul, a most fearsome general |